Praise for the InCryp

"The only thing more fun than an October Daye book is an InCryptid book. Swift narrative, charm, great world-building . . . all the McGuire trademarks." —Charlaine Harris, #1 *New York Times*-bestselling author

"Seanan McGuire's *Discount Armageddon* is an urban fantasy triple threat—smart and sexy and funny. The Aeslin mice alone are worth the price of the book, so consider a cast of truly original characters, a plot where weird never overwhelms logic, and some serious kickass world-building as a bonus." —Tanya Huff, bestselling author of *The Wild Ways*

"McGuire's InCryptid series is one of the most reliably imaginative and well-told sci-fi series to be found, and she brings all her considerable talents to bear on *[Tricks for Free]*. . . . McGuire's heroine is a brave, resourceful and sarcastic delight, and her intrepid comrades are just the kind of supportive and snarky sidekicks she needs."

—*RT Book Reviews (top pick)*

"While [*Spelunking Through Hell*] veers noticeably from the urban fantasy of earlier volumes, taking place primarily in strange realms with almost no humans in sight, it still bears all the hallmarks of the InCryptid series: a clever protagonist, snarky banter, unusual creatures, and an entertaining blend of action, romance, and horror (the secret behind Alice's enduring youth and vitality is especially unsettling). At heart a love story, this entry delivers both a satisfying payoff for fans of the series and an intriguing expansion of its universe." —*Publishers Weekly*

"McGuire's characters are equal parts sass and sarcasm, set in an ever-expanding interdimensional world where Alice is on a journey highlighted by emotional chaos and roller-coaster pacing. Fans will be delighted by [*Spelunking Through Hell*]." —*Library Journal*

"*Discount Armageddon* is a quick-witted, sharp-edged look at what makes a monster monstrous, and at how closely our urban fantasy protagonists walk—or dance—that line. The pacing never lets up, and when the end comes, you're left wanting more. I can't wait for the next book!"

—C. E. Murphy, author of *Raven Calls*

DAW Books presents the finest in urban fantasy from Seanan McGuire

InCryptid Novels

DISCOUNT ARMAGEDDON
MIDNIGHT BLUE-LIGHT SPECIAL
HALF-OFF RAGNAROK
POCKET APOCALYPSE
CHAOS CHOREOGRAPHY
MAGIC FOR NOTHING
TRICKS FOR FREE
THAT AIN'T WITCHCRAFT
IMAGINARY NUMBERS
CALCULATED RISKS
SPELUNKING THROUGH HELL
BACKPACKING THROUGH BEDLAM
AFTERMARKET AFTERLIFE

SPARROW HILL ROAD
THE GIRL IN THE GREEN SILK GOWN
ANGEL OF THE OVERPASS

October Daye Novels

ROSEMARY AND RUE
A LOCAL HABITATION
AN ARTIFICIAL NIGHT
LATE ECLIPSES
ONE SALT SEA
ASHES OF HONOR
CHIMES AT MIDNIGHT
THE WINTER LONG
A RED ROSE CHAIN
ONCE BROKEN FAITH
THE BRIGHTEST FELL
NIGHT AND SILENCE
THE UNKINDEST TIDE
A KILLING FROST
WHEN SORROWS COME
BE THE SERPENT
SLEEP NO MORE
THE INNOCENT SLEEP

AFTERMARKET AFTERLIFE

An InCryptid Novel

SEANAN McGUIRE

DAW BOOKS
New York

Cover illustration by Lee Moyer

Edited by Navah Wolfe

DAW Book Collectors No. 1957

DAW Books
An imprint of Astra Publishing House
dawbooks.com
DAW Books and its logo are registered trademarks of Astra Publishing House

Printed in Canada

Library of Congress Cataloging-in-Publication Data

Names: McGuire, Seanan, author.
Title: Aftermarket afterlife / Seanan McGuire.
Description: First edition. | New York : DAW Books, 2024. | Series: An InCryptid novel ; 13
Identifiers: LCCN 2023043050 (print) | LCCN 2023043051 (ebook) |
ISBN 9780756418618 (paperback) | ISBN 9780756418625 (ebook)
Subjects: LCSH: Cryptozoology--Fiction. | Animals, Mythical--Fiction. |
LCGFT: Fantasy fiction. | Paranormal fiction. | Novels.
Classification: LCC PS3607.R36395 A69 2024 (print) |
LCC PS3607.R36395 (ebook) | DDC 813/.6--dc23/eng/20231005
LC record available at https://lccn.loc.gov/2023043050
LC ebook record available at https://lccn.loc.gov/2023043051

First edition: March 2024
10 9 8 7 6 5 4 3 2 1

For Crystal, who is bright, brilliant, beautiful,
and a better friend than I often deserve.

Price Family Tree

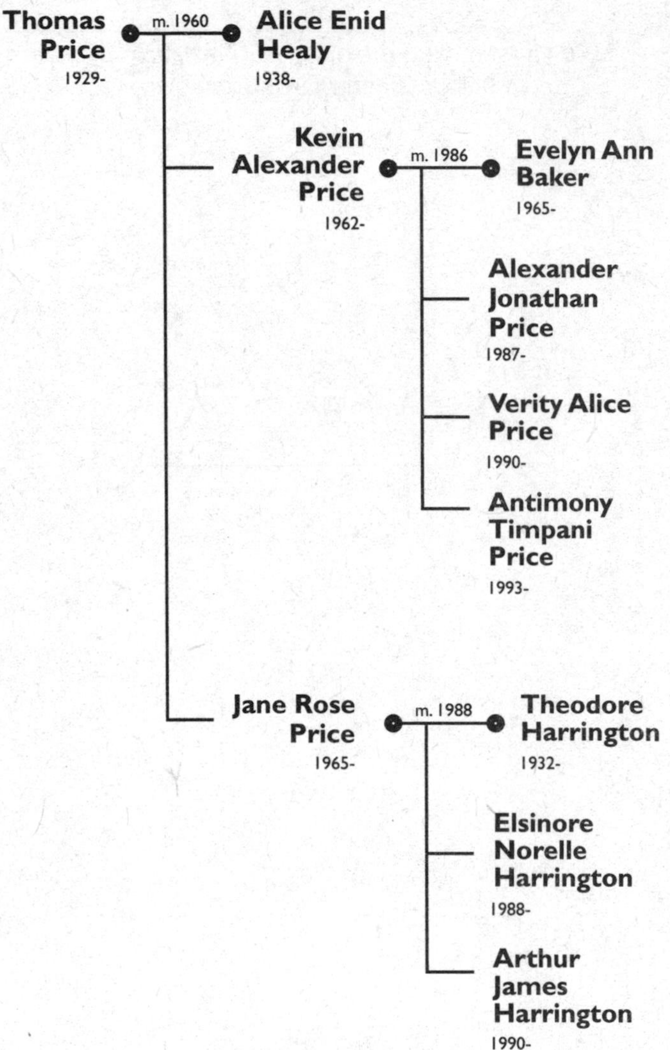

Baker Family Tree

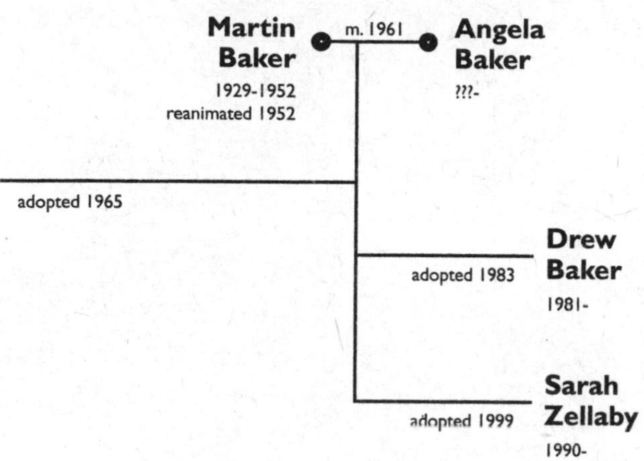

AUTHOR'S NOTE

The InCryptid series is set in a world where parallel evolution and dimensional rifts have resulted in humans sharing the planet with multiple species of cryptid capable of passing for human, among many other differences and divergences. The COVID-19 pandemic has not happened in this version of reality, a decision I struggled with but ultimately decided best suited both the narrative and the series as a whole.

I am hoping people will understand the reasons for this departure from reality. But for right now, the integrity of this fictional world is better served by not including the pandemic.

Death, noun:

1. The act of dying.

Afterlife, noun:

1. Life after death.

2. The hypothetical state of existence after dying.

3. See also “insufficient.”

Prologue

"Take a bow and leave them wanting more. That's the best thing I can teach you how to do. If your audience is tired of you, you're done."

—Frances Brown

Old Logger's Road, Buckley Township, Michigan

Eighty-four years ago

THE SUN HUNG LOW enough in the sky that Mary Dunlavy put a little extra speed into her steps, moving along the road toward town as fast as she could. She knew she shouldn't have taken Old Logger's Road after sitting for the Cherry kids—it was too close to sunset, and no one with any sense wanted to be that close to the woods *or* the old Parrish place in the dark, much less both of them at once. But taking Lakeside would have meant walking for more than twice as long, and her daddy trusted her to have dinner on the table when he got home.

Technically, she shouldn't even have agreed to sit today, but when Mrs. Cherry called and said it was an emergency and she'd pay Mary twice her double rate to come out and watch the twins for a few hours, well. Double pay was double pay, and bread and butter were increasingly dear these days. Daddy's paycheck didn't stretch as far as it used to, and wouldn't have even if he hadn't been drinking half of it downtown before he came home every Friday. She ate as little as she could, but he was a working man, and he needed his strength.

Mary had known it was a bad idea, and she'd also known she didn't have a choice. Accepting had been the only right thing to do.

Only now it was almost sunset and she was still well away from home, and it was anybody's guess whether she was going to beat her father there. He'd never say a word if he came home to a dark, empty house and no food on the table. He wouldn't chastise her or shout. But he would start drinking as soon as he realized she wasn't there to see it, and by the time she did get home, he'd be well on his way to total drunkenness, ready to greet her return with intoxicated joviality. And then the next day would be calling in sick from work while his foreman tried to pretend he didn't realize that Benjamin Dunlavy was more hung over than actually unwell, and the day after that would be the household fund dropping by the value of a new bottle of bourbon.

No. Mary needed to hurry. She needed to get home in time to prevent a sadly predictable and all-too-familiar sequence of events from playing out yet again, making everyone's life just a little harder.

She was focusing so hard on where she was going that she never bothered to look behind herself at where she'd been. She didn't notice the truck that came rolling down Old Logger's Road, bouncing with the frequent potholes that constituted half the surface of the road itself, dug deep into the gravel.

Mary was sticking close to the shoulder, only about a foot or so from the dry brown late-season corn. There should have been plenty of room for both of them to pass, and at first, it seemed like that was going to happen.

The truck was about to catch up to her when it hit a particularly nasty pothole and bounced hard, rocking to the side. The front end struck Mary in the hip and sent her flying into the corn, a sharp spike of pain driving its way all the way through her body, making what felt like every bone in her skeleton light up electric white and agonizing. The impact knocked the air out of her; she didn't have a chance to scream.

Mary hit the ground hard, and the truck kept rolling on, driving off down Old Logger's Road, never slowing down. If the driver realized that what they'd hit was a human girl and not a deer, it wasn't enough to take their foot off the gas.

They just kept going, and in her own way, Mary went, too.

Mary woke up under a hazy yellow sky, with the corn waving all around her. Somehow it had gone from brown and broken, picked clean by crows and hungry deer, to tall and green and heavy with unplucked ears. Nothing hurt as she pushed herself off the ground, staggering to her feet. The world was silent, and the air tasted like ozone, like a tornado was putting itself together somewhere just off the horizon, ready to come crashing through at any moment. The sun was a flat disk behind the layers of yellow dust clinging to the air, distant and burnished like a penny, but somehow blunted enough that she could look directly at it.

Conscious of the pain she was sure would soon be coming, Mary began picking her way through the corn, heading for where she presumed she'd find the street. And kept walking as the corn, which had been growing unattended in this semi-abandoned field since the last farmers had moved away from Old Logger's Road, stretched endlessly out in front of her. She paused, the first real inkling of something being genuinely wrong working its way through the panic over how she had clearly been unconscious in a cornfield overnight and far enough into the next day for the sun to be all the way into the sky. Her father would have gone without dinner, and then gone off to work without breakfast. She didn't know if he'd have been sober enough by that point to pack himself a lunch. If she'd been home, none of this would have happened. If she'd been home . . . if her mother hadn't died . . . if everything were different, none of this would have happened.

The corn was lush and green, each stalk so heavy with ripe ears that it looked like it should topple under its own weight, and that wasn't right either, was it? She distinctly remembered the corn being withered and dead as she walked alongside it, almost the color of that storm-warning sky overhead, and the few ears that had managed to survive the wildlife had been small and stunted, not full-sized and inviting. It was like she'd landed in someone else's cornfield.

Someone else's cornfield that went the hell on forever. Mary turned to the nearest stalk and wrenched an ear off in frustration, preparing to hurl it away into the rolling waves of corn, and paused as it squished in her hand, soft and yielding within its layers of green husk. She focused more closely on the ear, peeling back the top layers of husk, only to cry out in disgust and dismay and drop it to the ground at her feet.

The corn inside the husk was a mass of fungus, rot, and crawling parasites, attractive and enticing, but entirely inedible.

Mary glanced around. Every ear of corn was suddenly ominous, a lurking horror wrapped in placid green. Still unsure as to what was going on, she broke into a run, pushing her way toward the field, heading for the road.

After far too long, she finally broke out of the corn and onto a wide gravel road she had never seen before. Mary froze, then turned slowly, trying to get her bearings back. This wasn't possible. Unless someone had moved her while she was knocked out, this wasn't possible. She had grown up in Buckley. She knew every inch of the town and the fields around it. Put her in the woods and she'd be lost in an instant, but here, on an open road near farmland, abandoned or not, there was just no way.

As the thought formed, the land around her seemed to flicker, like she was standing in the heart of the Galway Wood, surrounded by reaching trees and unseen horrors. Then it was gone, and she was back on the side of the road, corn behind her, yellow sky overhead.

"This isn't funny," said Mary. The landscape flickered again, corn become brambles, sky becoming dark. Then the corn returned, lush and green and terrible. She balled her hands into fists, and yelled, with more strength, "I said, *this isn't funny*. Whatever you're trying to do, whoever you are, stop."

"And why should we?" asked a voice next to her ear. It was curious, almost polite, and distorted by an ominous humming noise, like the sound she'd heard an old radio tube make right before it exploded.

Mary whipped around. There was no one there.

"Because it isn't nice," she said.

"No one said we had to be," said the voice, which now sounded like it was directly in front of her.

Mary turned slowly back to the street. There was no one there, of course, but the street itself had changed. Rather than a long expanse of gravel, it was a short stretch of hard-packed earth leading to a four-way crossing, with no signposts in sight.

"Hello?" called Mary, and walked toward the impossible crossing, steps slow and cautious, but foolish all the same. She'd lived in Buckley her whole life. She knew better. But this wasn't the woods; whatever was toying with her might be willing to let her go, and the best way to make that happen was to play along. The things that took people liked it when they played along, because they enjoyed the challenge, but they didn't seem as inclined to eat the ones who played along.

She stepped into the crossing, and the sky went from yellow to bruised black in an instant, like a screen had been removed. The sound of footsteps behind her was somehow not a surprise. She didn't turn around. To turn around was to challenge whatever was moving toward her. To turn around was, very probably, to die.

"Willing to discuss your options, are you, Miss Mary?"

"How do you know my name?"

"I know a lot of things," said the voice, as its owner stepped in front of her. Mary flinched but managed not to recoil.

The figure now standing in the center of the crossroads wasn't really there, not in the sense she was used to. It was more like someone had carved the outline of a person out of the world, creating a void of absolute nothingness that shimmered at the edges with staticky distortion. It didn't look onto blankness, or whiteness, or anything else she really had the words to describe; it was a dusty, dirty, shifting absence, like a slice of television screen at the end of the broadcast day, visual static where it had no possible reason to be.

Mary stared. "What *are* you?"

"That's up to you, little girl." The voice came from the absent figure, still filled with buzzing, like a million cicadas had somehow found their voice. "We can be a figure you met on the road to your final resting place, or we can be the benevolent employer who helped you back to the life you left behind. And all you have to do is choose."

"What do you mean," demanded Mary, taking a step backward.

"Uh-uh-uh," said the voice, shaking a finger chidingly. "Don't go any further. If you leave the crossroads, we can't help you anymore."

Mary froze.

"You know you didn't survive when that truck hit you. I can see it in your eyes. Mary, Mary, quite contrary, there's so much you need to know. Like how you died, and how you tried, and where the crossroads go. I have a proposal for you."

"What's that?" she asked, barely above a squeak.

"You're dead. You know that, if you really think about it. You were still conscious when your neck snapped, and you just don't want to remember. We can understand that. You're in-between right now. You don't belong to anyone, which is a stroke of good luck for you."

"I don't understand."

"Humans are the dominant intelligent lifeform on this planet, and that means we need human spirits to speak for one another when the time comes to strike our bargains. We need negotiators, as it were."

"I *still* don't understand."

"Look, child. We are in the business of granting wishes, glorious miracles raining down on those who want them enough to come and find us. But for the sake of some 'universal balance,' we need someone who will speak for the people we bargain with, to keep things fair. Someone who will tell them we're offering them a balanced trade, and that the payment we request is justified. Someone who died with reason to remain, but no claims on their spirit strong enough to make them any kind of defined ghost. If you agree to come and work for us, we can define you. You'll be a crossroads ghost, and you'll be able to stay. With your father. Isn't that what worries you the most about dying? That you'd be leaving him alone?"

Mary frowned, worrying her bottom lip between her teeth. "I don't *feel* dead."

"We can escort you back to your body, if you'd like."

"What if I say no?"

"You have reason to *want* to remain, but nothing to tie you tightly to the twilight and keep you here," said the voice, implacably. "You would pass into whatever waits for human spirits beyond this realm."

"Would I be able to come back?"

"No."

Mary glared at the figure. "This isn't a very fair proposal, when I can't say no without being sent away forever!"

"We never promised fairness. We're offering more than is required."

Mary took a deep breath, trying not to think about the foolishness of breathing when she was no longer alive. "If I say yes, I can go home to my father? And he won't notice anything's wrong?"

"You'll be able to pass among the living as one of their own. You won't age or need to eat as they do, but you're a clever girl. You can work around that."

Mary nodded slowly. "My family comes first. You have to agree to that."

"We do?" The voice sounded almost amused. "We were not aware we *had* to do anything."

"You need me or you wouldn't be putting on this little performance. Agree that my family comes first, or I won't do it."

The figure sighed, looking as put-upon as a shape without a face could look. "Fine, then. You will keep our secrets, and when we call you, you will negotiate on the behalf of the petitioners who come before us. You will keep things 'fair.' And in exchange, we will return you to your father, and you will be able to go to him when he needs you, to interact with him as the living do, and not be bound to come to us immediately."

"My family," said Mary staunchly. "Not my father, my family."

"We weren't aware—"

"They're not in Buckley."

"Fine. Your family." The figure extended one void-filled hand. "Do we have a bargain?"

Mary hesitated for a moment, then reached out to grasp the offered hand and shook. "We do," she said.

"Excellent," replied the crossroads, and pulled her closer. "Oh, we're going to have such fun together."

As alien thoughts and ideas began pouring into her mind, Mary learned two things at once: even the dead could suffer, and some pain was too great to allow the person who experienced it to scream.

Eventually, she blacked out again.

So far, being dead was no more pleasant than being alive had been, and a hell of a lot more confusing.

Mary opened her eyes in the scraggly, untended corn field to the side of Old Logger's Road. Nothing hurt, and the sky above was still late afternoon trending toward evening. She sat up with a gasp, feeling her torso with both hands. She felt as solid as she had ever been. She scrambled to her feet and ran for the road, once again not looking back.

She already knew what she would see.

Upon reaching Old Logger's Road, Mary stopped for a moment, turning to look toward town. Alien knowledge still cluttered her mind; she knew exactly what she had agreed to do, and that when the time came, she wouldn't have a choice. But for the moment, she was here, and even if she wasn't alive, her daddy needed her.

Mary broke into a run, heading for home as fast as her legs could carry her. The sky continued to darken overhead, but she ran all the way home.

She got there before her father, and had dinner hot and ready for him when he came in the door. "You're a good girl, Mary," he rumbled, and kissed her forehead before he sat down to eat. She didn't join him. She wasn't hungry. She hadn't been winded by the run home.

After the leftovers were packed away and the dishes were done, she went to bed, and lay there in the dark and quiet, staring at the ceiling. She wasn't tired. She didn't sleep.

Mary Dunlavy was dead.

One

"Dead people who hang around after they die are people too, and that means they're not a monolith. Some of them are awful. Some of them are pretty good neighbors. None of them like a shotgun full of rock salt to the face."

—Enid Healy

A small survivalist compound about an hour's drive east of Portland, Oregon

Now

THE HOUSE WAS QUIET. That was pretty normal before eight in the morning, thanks to layers of religious prohibition keeping the mice from starting their daily exaltations before everyone was out of bed. Things wouldn't stay quiet for long. They never did. Each person who woke up would each add their specific flavor of chaos to the environment, until we were operating at standard levels. It could have been worse. We were currently operating well below a full house, with only Kevin, Evelyn, Annie, James, and Sam in residence—well, them, and several hundred talking mice who were frustratingly prone to religious mania, which could break out at literally any moment.

At this point, there's no one in the family who's been around the mice longer than I have, and even I can't always predict when a massive, ongoing, and worst of all, loud celebration is going to start up somewhere in the house. Kevin had started trying to put together a fully comprehensive calendar of their observances when he was just a kid, and Evelyn took over maintaining it after they were married, after she noticed he was missing several of the rituals specifically centered around childbirth, menstruation (human family members only, as the mice don't menstruate, and let's all pause to be grateful for that, shall we?), and, oddly enough, dusting. There are apparently things the Aeslin aren't comfortable sharing with their gods, but will happily divulge to a priestess.

Their ideas of gender roles are a little outdated, and it can color a lot of things you might think would be safe from sexism. Life—or death—with the mice is nothing if not endlessly surprising.

But anyway, Evelyn maintained the master calendar, and even she sometimes got surprised by festivals that only happened when the circumstances were right, and thus hadn't been observed in two or three or four generations. The rest of us were basically playing guess-the-ritual all the time, and inevitably getting things wrong.

If I hadn't known for sixty years and counting that Aeslin mice couldn't lie, I would have started to suspect them of inventing new traditions just to keep the rest of us on our toes.

But I digress. It was about half past seven, and the sun was up, but nobody else seemed to be. One of the wild roosters in the woods behind the compound had been crowing its head off for almost half an hour, which was a good illustration of why wild roosters never lasted long in the woods. If the coyotes didn't get it, one of the house residents would go out and shut it up sooner or later. Silence before coffee was pretty well enforced most of the time.

There were days when I missed the kids' school years. From the time Alex turned five until Annie turned eighteen, the house had started waking up at six, kids tumbling everywhere as they looked for books, backpacks, and breakfast—not necessarily in that order. We were far enough from Portland proper that it had never been possible for them to take the bus to school, and so until they'd started hitting their teens and getting their licenses one by one (and stopping there, since Annie had never seen the point of learning how to drive), Kevin had also been up by six, bleary-eyed and slouching as he bundled them into the family minivan and drove them off to learn the things the state wanted them to know.

Maybe it's cocky of me to admit it, but I was proud of the fact that none of my charges ever skipped school. I'd officially been Annie's babysitter by the time the older children started hitting the age where skipping school was actually something that could happen, and not just something the big kids did in the movies, but that wasn't enough to keep me from keeping an eye on the rest of them. Elsie was the only one who'd ever complained.

"It's not fair that we have a phantom babysitter following us around and keeping us from getting into perfectly age-appropriate trouble," she'd complained one day, after I "happened" to wander into the bathroom where she was trying to bum a cigarette from an upperclassman. Even as a sophomore, she'd been eager to get in good with the seniors, and utterly shameless in her flirting. "No one else has to deal with that."

"That's true," I'd agreed, easy as anything. I've looked sixteen since the day I died, and I'll stay sixteen until the day I decide it's time to move on and see what's on the other side of eternity, but there's one big difference between me and an actual teenager, or me and a lot of ghosts, who tend to freeze emotionally and intellectually at the moment of their death. The crossroads needed me to be capable of growing and adapting, adjusting to the world as it changed, and so I had retained the flexibility I'd had as a living girl. In short, I have slightly more emotional intelligence than a brick.

Elsie had promptly started to stand up straighter and puff out her chest in triumph.

"I'll just tell your mother you've asked me to leave you alone during the school day," I'd continued. "I'm sure that won't lead to any additional scrutiny of your activities or homework."

She'd sagged immediately, glaring at me. "Dirty pool, Mary."

"I'm the babysitter," I'd replied sweetly, and vanished, off to check on Antimony before her school day ended—the high school and middle school had been on staggered timing back then, to let the buses get between them. I didn't know if that was the case anymore. It had been several years since I'd needed to worry about the social lives of publicschoolers, and it would be several more before I needed to start worrying again. Charlotte and Isaac were just reaching kindergarten age, but they were likely to be homeschooled by the Bakers, since both of them were fairly profoundly speech-delayed, and dropping a telepathic child in a normal classroom was only going to end in tears.

We'd have to work on that eventually. Isaac was a cuckoo, one of the last in this dimension, and while he'd had the ancestral memories that inevitably caused cuckoos to murder everyone around them removed, it was still unclear how he would interact with a large group of humans. The closest thing we had to a test group for him were Morag, Ava, and Lupe, all of whom lived in Ireland with Morag's grandmother, and none of whom had ever set foot inside a public school.

There was still some discussion among the rest of the family as to whether the trio of cuckoo girls could be considered our responsibility after what Sarah had done to them, but as none of them had started to appear on the weird sort of "ghost radar" that told me when a member of our family needed me, I was counting them on the "not my problem" side of the scale. Isaac had been on the radar, so to speak, since the day Angela announced her intention to adopt him.

Olivia was four, gleefully rampaging her way through a makeshift preschool full of dragon children her own age, and what happened with her was going to depend largely on where Dominic and Verity eventually decided to settle down. I'd be there for her no matter where they were, but I had to admit it would be easier if they chose either Oregon or Ohio.

No pressure.

When I first made my deal with the crossroads, I'd been insistent that my family would come before anything they needed from me, and they'd agreed to those exact words. My father had been the only living member of my family in Buckley at the time of the incident, but I'd had the feeling, even then, that I was being railroaded; the crossroads had been in such a hurry to get me to agree to their terms that pushing back had been the only real form of resistance I had left. It had been a last flash of teenage stubbornness.

It was the exact wording that had saved my afterlife. Because Frances Healy had called me to come and babysit for her only a few months later, unaware that I was dead—no one had been aware back then, not even my father, and he'd been living with me. As a living woman she'd called, and the money had been something we could really use, which meant answering her call was a service to my family, and as a living woman she'd put Alice in my arms and asked me to be responsible for her. As a spirit, I'd agreed. Neither of us had known what that moment meant. I'd started to figure it out, just a little, about a year later, when Alice had fallen and skinned her fleshy toddler's knee on the gravel driveway. The blaze of her distress had flashed across my thoughts, and even though I'd been nowhere near the Healy house when it happened, I had been there an instant later, helping her up and dusting her off.

She was my family. Accepting that seemed to make it all the more true, and in short order, the same could be said of all the Healys: I knew when they needed me, I could hear them call my name, and while it was only Alice who could pull me away from the crossroads if I was working when she called for me, I always understood where they were. The crossroads had given me the power to go to my family when they needed me, and oh, I did.

And then, a few years later, my father's tired old heart, broken by my mother's death and further weakened by his drinking, had finally given out in the middle of the night. He died without ever knowing I had died long before him, and when he stopped showing up for work, people got concerned. Eventually someone called the Healys, since everyone knew I was Alice's babysitter, and Fran had come to the house to check on him.

What she'd found was a corpse, and a terrified, traumatized ghost girl absolutely convinced she was about to be exorcised, or that the loss of her father would mean the bargain she had with the crossroads was no longer in effect. He was her only family after all, right?

I'd still been a teenager in every sense of the word back then, sixteen years alive and three years dead adding up to leave me young enough to scare easy. Fran had seen that, the same way she'd seen I was no threat to Alice, that being dead didn't make me a bad person. She'd arranged to have my body recovered from the cornfield where I'd left it, and buried it behind the house in Buckley, laying my bones down easy in a grave she'd dug with her own hands, giving me a chance to rest. Solidifying my place with the family.

I became an honorary Healy because I was Alice's babysitter. To keep the position, I've been babysitter to every Healy who followed, and every Price, and every Harrington. Even a couple of stragglers from other families who got absorbed into ours. It's a chaotic position to hold, family babysitter for a group of cryptozoologists with minimal common sense and no capacity for self-preservation.

I wouldn't give it up for anything.

At the moment, it was ten o'clock in New York and Ohio. Olivia was having snack time with the dragon children of the Nest where she lived with her parents, and Charlotte was at the park with Isaac and their mutual grandmother. I didn't know exactly what they were doing there, but there were no signs of distress coming from that direction, and so I figured Angela had it all under control.

In the beginning, there was only Alice. As long as I could keep her alive, I was doing my job, and doing it well enough to call myself a good babysitter. But I'd done my job too well, and she grew up and got married and had two kids of her own, both of whom I needed to keep alive. Then both of those kids had grown up and had kids—five total—and then the adoptions had begun. Sarah Zellaby was Evelyn's baby sister, adopted by the same people and then adopted by my family as a cousin. So that was one more for me to look out for. Then the new generation of kids had started growing up and going out into the world, and coming home with significant others—three so far—children of their own—two, three if we counted Isaac, who was

Sarah's little brother—and adopted siblings they refused to put back where they'd come from. The count on those, by the way, currently stood at three, although we didn't know yet whether Mark was going to register as a member of the family to my weird ghost radar when he finally woke up. If he ever woke up. There was every possibility he wasn't going to.

But with the actual children taken care of for the moment, I was free to come to Portland and make breakfast. Cooking is fun. I enjoy it. Best of all, I'm dead, and unlike some ghosts, I'm not particularly hungry—oh, I like chocolate as much as the next girl, but I'm not constantly haunting diners and hoping someone will buy me a burger, to give a suspiciously specific example. Not being hungry means I never rush, never get distracted by the smell of what I'm making, and never find myself running out of something because I've been snacking without noticing it. Even better, when the bacon starts to sizzle and throw little drops of grease into the air, they go right through me.

If I hadn't been a babysitter, I could have had a very happy career as a line cook, is what I'm saying.

I had shown up in the kitchen at seven on the dot, and now that eight was looming and all my ingredients were prepared, I was ready to put my evil plan into action. Dropping four slices of bacon into a skillet, I poured a serving of batter into the wafflemaker at almost the same time, then leaned over to flip the coffeemaker's "on" switch into position.

A variety of enticing scents began to fill the kitchen, even before I opened the pre-heated oven and popped in the tray of cinnamon rolls I had ready to bake. When trying to attract the herd, it's a good idea to bring out the serious bait. Bacon, coffee, and baked goods are about as serious as it gets.

Indeed, I didn't have to wait long before Annie came wandering into the kitchen in her Pokémon pajama pants and an old Slasher Chicks shirt she had repurposed for sleeping in after it got too tattered to wear out of the house, her hair snarled and sticking up in all directions. She made an incoherent grumbling noise. I blew her a kiss.

"Good morning, fireball," I said blithely. "Coffee's ready if you want some." She was already opening the cupboard to take down a mug, which she filled halfway with miniature marshmallows before pouring coffee over them, resulting in a sticky, half-melted mess that bobbed to the top of the liquid almost immediately. She didn't bother to stir before she flopped into one of the seats at the kitchen table, taking a noisy slurp.

Annie takes after her paternal grandfather, Thomas Price. She's an elemental sorcerer, with the ability to both create and control fire. I'm not sure who was more surprised when she started striking sparks in her sleep, her, me, or the mice. Her because she was the one whose hands were actually on fire. Me because I'd still been working for the crossroads back then, and I was well acquainted with their generalized hatred of sorcerers, which could sometimes extend to trying to influence the people around them to make deals just so they'd have an excuse to get the sorcerer out of the way. The mice because they had always assumed, in the absence of other evidence, that if Thomas passed his genes for sorcery on to any of the kids, they'd know. They'd expected signs during childhood, or a tearful confession to the clergy. Instead, Annie had waited until her late teens to start with the pyromancy, and had managed to hide it well enough to get herself sent undercover with the Covenant, a decision I disagreed with at the time, and one that we were still paying for today.

The trouble with living in the present is that we're always acting on the information we have available, and we never have the whole picture. In hindsight, it should have been obvious that when you're dealing with something that passes through family lines and have five living candidates for inheritance running around, at least one of them is going to come up a winner. It should also have been easy to figure out that maybe infiltrating the headquarters of a paranoid organization of monster hunters that already has your whole family on the "kill on sight" list was not as good an idea as people thought it was. But we'd needed information and we'd been desperate, and Annie had agreed to go.

I couldn't even say it had been all bad. Going undercover with the Covenant had forced Annie into hiding for a while, which naturally meant she'd gone and taken out a cabal of evil magic-users operating out of a major amusement park, whose actions had probably been hurting if not killing hundreds of people on an annual basis. She had ended up in Maine, eventually, and came home with a boyfriend, an adopted brother, and the blood of the crossroads on her hands. Yeah. My old employers? Annie killed them, which should have been impossible, since they were an ageless, timeless, staggeringly powerful cosmic force outside true human comprehension. Killing them had involved some time-travel shenanigans that I *still* didn't understand, and had restored the Earth's anima mundi, the true spirit of the living world, which is what should have been there all along.

We hadn't known I'd be able to survive past the destruction of the crossroads when Annie effectively challenged them to single combat, but they'd been mad enough at me by that point for not somehow keeping her under control that they'd been well on the way to erasing me from existence. I'm a ghost. "Killing" me won't exactly work. But something that's big and nasty enough could absolutely unmake me, and the crossroads qualified as both big and nasty. By the time Annie had gone off to beat the crossroads into the ground, no one could blame her for thinking I was well and truly done for.

But I wasn't, and I was glad for that. I pulled the first waffle out of the wafflemaker and plopped it onto a plate, carrying it over to drop on the table in front of her. She made a grumpy, agreeable noise—a neat trick—and managed to smile at me through the tangle of her hair.

"What do you want on your waffle?" I asked. "I have all the usual toppings."

"Not banana," she mumbled.

"Three-syllable word before you finished your coffee," I said. "Not bad."

She glared, momentarily focusing on drinking.

Annie's live-in boyfriend, Sam—who I expected to come along any second now, since he could be kind of on the "clingy" side, and would notice soon that she'd been gone too long to just be using the bathroom—is a fūri, a kind of yōkai, which is the catchall term for the Asian cryptids. His natural state is a lot more simian than human, prehensile tail and all. He's not a big fan of monkey jokes, and the fastest way to piss him off, culinarily speaking, is to offer him a banana.

This doesn't stop the mice from referring to him as the "Large Monkey Man," having not yet reached the conclusion the rest of us have, that he's never voluntarily leaving, and thus not given him his godly title. I can't wait to see what that's going to be. Surprisingly, Sam accepts it from the mice, saying it's different when it's one cryptid talking to another.

Somehow the fact that science considers ghosts a form of cryptid—by the strict definition of the term, which is "a creature whose existence has not been proven to science"—is not enough to give me monkey privileges. I'd sulk, but mostly I'm too busy snickering.

Annie slurped more coffee. I looked at her expectantly.

"*All* the toppings?" she asked.

"It's a special occasion, so yes, all the toppings," I said.

She hesitated for a moment, then said, "Bacon, vanilla ice cream, strawberries, and chocolate sauce?"

"Pushing your luck, huh?" I retrieved her plate and moved to fix up her waffle while I popped the next one out of the machine and poured in a fresh batch of batter. The trick to a successful breakfast for this many people is all about the assembly line. The more continuous you can make it, the more you're likely to accomplish.

Annie smiled sleepily as I set the waffle back down in front of her. "Always," she replied. "What's luck for if not pushing?"

I laughed, turning back to my bacon, which was sizzling and spitting and ready for transfer—minus the two slices I'd already put atop Annie's waffle—to the paper towels to drain. There was a small *clink* as she picked up her fork, followed by mice popping out of holes all over the kitchen, their whiskers pushed forward and their noses quivering.

Putting the second waffle onto a plate, I slid it down the counter. "In exchange for staying out of the cooking area," I said.

The mice cheered and descended, and everything was peaceful and normal and chaotic, just like it was supposed to be. Just like it could never be for very long.

As you have almost certainly gathered by now, my name is Mary Grace Dunlavy, and I am really quite sincerely dead. Have been for coming up on a hundred years, which is longer than most ghosts choose to hang out and haunt the living. Before Annie killed the crossroads, it wasn't like I had a choice—serving as a crossroads ghost isn't one of those afterlife assignments that come with an exit strategy—but after she killed them, I could have chosen to move on. I didn't, because my family needed me. My family will always need me.

The Price-Healys may be terrifyingly effective killers to the cryptid world and traitors to the Covenant of St. George, and I won't argue that they're not good at their jobs, but to me, they're sort of like a nest of adorable coyote pups or bobcat kittens. They hiss and fuss and show their claws, but at the end of the day, they're effectively defenseless. Only unlike puppies or kittens, they keep making more babies, even more defenseless ones. They can't be trusted to take care of themselves.

I've spent a lot of time in the starlight, the level of the afterlife just below the one most commonly frequented by human ghosts, and talked to a lot of people, both dead and never living, about my situation. After all, I was a crossroads ghost, and then I wasn't anymore, but I still existed, which should have been impossible. Well, it turns out ghosts are like anything else. Old forms die out, and new ones are born. It would be perfectly reasonable to assume that made me something new.

But it didn't. It made me something very, very old. See, once, people had lived more isolated lives, and once, it had been common for a caretaker—sometimes a grandparent, sometimes an unmarried woman, sometimes a nanny—to have virtually full responsibility for raising a child. And sometimes those caretakers had been so wrapped up in their feelings of duty and obligation that when they died, they'd kept right on doing their jobs. From there, things could go one of two ways, one very good for the ghost, one very bad.

If the nanny ghost was allowed to keep taking care of "their" child, the kid would grow up safe and loved, unusually lucky, and then, when they got old enough to have kids of their own, either their nanny would move on or would keep taking care of the family children. Some families could get three or four generations of care out of the same nanny, and in some communities, a phantom nanny was seen as a good thing, a sign that the family was special or blessed in some way.

But if, on the other hand, the nanny was denied access to the child they'd been taking care of before they died, they would begin to twist and turn vicious. A lot of them turned hostile, and some even started attacking their children, trying to keep them from growing up. A thwarted nanny could be viciously possessive, to the point of homicide. Maybe that's part of why they fell out of favor, as well as a growing social pressure to raise your own children, not hand them off to someone else. Living nannies got less common, and nanny ghosts all but disappeared.

"Nanny ghost" sounds a bit too much like "nanny goat" for my comfort. I prefer to be called a caretaker, which is a lot more general, and encompasses both the beginning and end of a person's life. The kids I care for are my responsibility forever, no matter how adult they may become, and when they need me, I'm there. I've nursed Alice back to health before. Now that she and Thomas have finally agreed to get old together, I fully expect to sit with them both on their deathbeds. So "caretaker" it is. A new name for a very old thing.

As a caretaker, I have an option I didn't have as a crossroads ghost: I can quit. Any time, I can quit. I can walk into the starlight and let go of the tether that keeps me here, and find out what's on the other side of the afterlife, which isn't the same thing as eternity. Back when I was alive and needed to sleep, I used to love the period between getting into bed and drifting all the way into dreams. It was warm and safe and my thoughts would quiet, worries fading into silence for the only time in my waking life. Being a ghost is sort of like taking a long pause in that moment, an in-between state that isn't awake and isn't asleep, just existing.

You can't stay in that pause forever. *I* can't stay in that pause forever. But I figure I've got a nice long time before it's going to feel like it's time to go, and I have a lot of waffles to make.

I liked babysitting when I was alive. It was a good way to make a little extra money, and I was good at it. The kids liked me. And it was a job a girl could do without damaging her reputation, which was important when I was alive. My daddy worked at the factory, and he didn't make much money. What he did make, he had a tendency to drink. He wasn't a bad man. He was just a broken one, trapped in a dead-end job in a little town where everyone remembered the face of his dead wife, and where he couldn't escape feeling judged for not being able to save her.

I don't know what I was thinking when I insisted on "family" rather than "father" during my negotiation with the crossroads, beyond "I don't like being told what to do," but I suspect part of me was thinking of my mother. She died two years before I did, of an untreatable cancer that ate her alive one bite at a time, until she was little more than a shadow tucked into a hospital bed, and as soon as I understood what it meant to be dead, I went looking for her. I combed the twilight and the starlight both, I searched the graveyard and every corner of our house, but she was nowhere to be found. Like my father, Mama died and moved on the way people are supposed to.

Not me. I didn't get to have much of a life, so I've been busying myself with having as awesome a death as I can when constantly responsible for a family of passively suicidal cryptozoologists who get into trouble the way ducks get into water. I've seen a lot of movies, read a lot of books, attended a lot of concerts, and ridden a lot of roller coasters. You know. Normal stuff.

And I make a killer waffle.

The mice were racing away with the last fragments of their waffle when Sam shambled into the kitchen, still in his natural form, which was what he normally wore around the house, and always wore to sleep—unlike most therianthropes, who default to "human" when not making an active effort otherwise, his default form is the one with the tail.

Kevin has some theories about that. Mostly, he believes the fūri were better positioned to avoid the Covenant of St. George's periodic pushes into Asia, and thus didn't undergo the unnatural selection process so many therianthropes were subjected to. For a lot of species, once the Covenant came to town, the ones who couldn't hold human form effortlessly and for extended periods wound up as statistics. I have another theory. I think an adult fūri is roughly five times stronger than an adult human, and any Covenant operatives who made contact stopped being a threat immediately thereafter.

Not that Sam was a threat, especially not early in the morning, when he was just sort of wandering around the house with his eyes half-closed, hoping to stumble into food. Or Annie, who was frequently near the food, and thus a good target for his bleary questing.

He collapsed into the chair next to hers, wrapping his tail around her lower leg before his head hit the table.

"Good morning to you, too," said Annie, sounding amused.

Sam made an incoherent grumbling noise.

"How you people ever survive field work is entirely beyond me," I said, walking over to put a coffee mug in front of him, already doctored to suit his preferences, which were at least less ridiculous than Annie's. Sam reached for the mug, making the grumbling noise again, but this time with a lilt that sounded thankful. Unlike Annie, he blew on the contents before he started drinking. Then again, unlike Annie, he was still sensitive enough to heat to scald himself.

"Why are you making so much breakfast?" asked Annie. "Did I forget a birthday?"

Sam lifted his head to stare at her in patent disbelief. I dropped a new batch of bacon into my frying pan and swallowed the urge to burst out laughing. It wasn't easy. There was something charming about Annie's confusion. But a fireball wasn't going to do my breakfast prep any favors, and so I managed to resist.

"Not quite," I said. "Either of you want some eggs?"

"Sunny-side up, please," said Sam.

"Are you just doing eggs, or is this an omelet day?" asked Annie.

"Omelets," I said.

"Trash omelet for me, please, with extra cheese."

"Got it." Eggs aren't like waffles and bacon. It's better to cook those to order than to pile them up to get cold and rubbery. I turned back to the stove, the better to not see Annie's face when realization sank in. There was no possible way I could see that happen and not start laughing at her.

"Oh," she said, with dawning understanding and horror. "Oh, *fuck*."

"Yes," Sam gravely agreed. "Oh fuck."

I did laugh at that, breaking an egg into my frying pan. At least everyone was on the same page now. I was in the kitchen cooking before most of the house was awake because three members of our family were already in motion, tucked safe in an airplane as they flew over from Las Vegas, where they'd been for the last week while Uncle Al—not a real uncle, and not a family member in the sense of my weird ghost powers—set up impeccable new fake IDs for the two of them who hadn't been maintaining a presence on Earth for the last few years. Or, in Thomas's case, decades.

Today, after so many years that it felt like forever, Alice and Thomas Price were coming home. I gave it fifteen minutes between the front porch and the first fistfight, which was why I was doing everything in my power to calm the mood of the house before things could get ugly.

Kevin staggered into the kitchen, glasses slightly askew where they perched on his nose.

"Do I smell cinnamon rolls?" he asked.

I smiled.

Two

> "Some of my best friends are dead. Not 'some of my best friends have died,' although I guess that's true too. More 'some of my best friends were dead when I met them, and we became friends anyway.' Life's too short to be picky."
>
> —Juniper Campbell

Still in the kitchen of a small survivalist compound about an hour's drive east of Portland, Oregon

THE CINNAMON ROLLS WERE done, out of the oven, and had been solidly decimated as member after member of the family came drifting in, lured by the scent of bacon, coffee, and carbs. Even James had eventually woken up and come down from his room, although he had refused my fresh homemade waffles in favor of blueberry Eggos from the freezer. I would have been offended, but given that he was wound so tight with anticipation that I wouldn't have been surprised if he spontaneously froze himself into a block of ice, I figured he could be allowed a little comfort food.

He didn't bother with the toaster, instead passing them to Annie to heat before he smeared them with a layer of whipped butter and began dipping them in his coffee. No one reacted. Every family has their weird food habits, and ours sometimes seems to have more than most. It's better not to comment.

Kevin glanced at his watch. He still wore an old-fashioned one, gears and glass on a leather strap. It was a gift from Aunt Laura on his fifteenth birthday, and I was pretty sure he was never going to replace it. Laura. The thought was enough to make me grimace. She was Kevin and Jane's honorary mother figure when they were growing up; losing her was the root of the infection that rotted the ground between Jane and Alice. Any day now, one of them was going to realize the crossroads no longer had the ability to stop my tongue; they could ask me what happened to her, and I could tell them.

I just didn't know what I was going to say when that happened. As there was no sense in borrowing trouble, I was doing my best not to think about it, and not to let it show when I *did* think about it and realized the implications.

Some information needs to be shared. Some information wants to be shared. And some information should go unshared for as long as humanly possible, because no one sensible chucks a fox into the middle of the henhouse when they have any choice in the matter.

"Jane and Ted should be getting here any time now with the kids," he said. "Mom's plane is supposed to have just touched down in Portland, which means, with time for deplaning, picking up their luggage, and getting the rental car, they're probably about two hours out."

"I still say we could have picked them up," said Evelyn.

"Mom insisted we not put ourselves out," said Kevin. "I think she wants to just rip the band-aid off in one go, and not be meeting up with us one by one all day long."

"Yeah, but if we'd picked her up, we could have had the whole drive to get to know Grandpa before Aunt Jane got here," said Annie wryly.

"Your aunt promised me she'd be on her best behavior," said Kevin.

"Uh-huh. And you believed her?" Annie took a long drink of marshmallow-topped coffee. She was on her third cup, and had moved on from the mini marshmallows to the freeze-dried Lucky Charms marshmallows she ordered off the internet in bulk. Sometimes I wondered how she could breathe, since her lungs were probably solid marshmallow fluff by this point.

Kevin opened his mouth, then paused and sagged in his seat. "Not entirely," he admitted. "She's *going* to lose her temper, and she's *going* to start yelling. But being on her best behavior means she's going to at least try to delay that for as long as she can."

"Be nice to your aunt," said Evelyn mildly, picking up a piece of bacon and giving it an experimental nibble. As a human raised by a cuckoo and a revenant, her food preferences can be odd even by family standards. Fortunately, it's hard to make bacon *too* weird without eating it raw, and her human physiology means she can't do that without risks, something her brother has always been happy to mock her for. (Her brother, Andrew, is a bogeyman. Also adopted, obviously, and immune to most human parasites, which simply can't find a foothold in his slightly out-of-synch biology. Bogeymen aren't obligate carnivores, but they eat a lot of rare and even raw meat, probably due to the fact that many of them have been driven underground, where "safe cooking" is a misnomer.)

"Not if she fucks up our chance to talk to an actual sorcerer," replied Annie.

Evelyn sighed, but didn't argue.

Annie and James were both sorcerers. Annie, as I've already mentioned, was a pyromancer, capable of creating and controlling fire. James was the same in reverse, a cryomancer who could create ice and snow and cause frostbite with a touch. He didn't appreciate Elsa jokes very much, while she was perfectly fine with *Firestarter* references, which I suppose shows the difference in perceived coolness between a Disney princess and a Stephen King protagonist.

And neither of them had ever been given what I would call "proper training." Sorcery, again, as previously mentioned, is genetic. Most types of magic use aren't. Routewitches just happen. Ditto for umbramancers and the like. But sorcerers require at least one sorcerer ancestor, which is why the crossroads were able to do such a good job of eliminating them. I'm ashamed to admit that I played a part in that; through the bargains I brokered, the crossroads were able to eliminate more than a dozen sorcerous bloodlines from the world, and those were gone forever. Thomas didn't have proper training either. He was self-taught, like most sorcerers. It was just that he was also decades older than Annie and James, and had been successful at both controlling his powers and figuring out their non-elemental applications. They were hoping they could convince him to train them.

Jane screaming in his face as soon as he came through the door wasn't going to help with that. But then, Jane's issues were and have always been mostly with her mother.

Kevin's phone beeped. He pulled it out of his pocket, looking at the screen before he nodded. "Jane and Ted are at the gate," he said. "Evie?"

"Yes, dear." Evelyn, who was closer to the end of the table, stood and walked over to the intercom box on the wall, where she pressed the button to release the locks. A moment later, the intercom buzzed to signal that the gates were sliding open.

The level of security around the family compound can sometimes seem a bit excessive, but when you've spent several generations getting ready for an inevitable clash with the paramilitary organization your ancestors ran away from, it becomes a lot more reasonable. Every lock and every failsafe was installed to protect against a specific problem or suite of problems, even down to the ultrasonic pest-repelling units that Kevin had recently installed on the fence, intended to ward off cuckoo incursions.

Not that there were enough cuckoos left on Earth to mount a proper incursion. Sarah had seen to that. Still, there were other things that could be driven off with the right ultrasonic frequencies, and after James and Alex had both made modifications to the units, I was willing to bet they'd keep us safe from *something*.

The front door slammed just before Jane called, "Hello? Anybody home?"

The mice cheered.

"We're in the kitchen," Kevin called back. "You know someone's home, or the gate would never have opened to let you in."

"You could have all hurried out to hide in the barn, I don't know, maybe you had a vital dissection project in process," said Jane, bustling into the kitchen. True to expectations, she looked to be in a foul mood already, as if she'd been pre-gaming her incipient anger since she woke up. She brightened a little when she saw the platter of waffles.

I waved my spatula at her. "Breakfast?" I asked.

"I already ate," she said, which I hoped was true. Jane was the least physically active member of the family, having chosen to live inside the city of Portland proper, where her associations with the cryptid world were normally of the domesticated kind. She belonged to at least three cryptid book clubs that I knew of, and a support group for the parents of part-cryptid children, and several other organizations that kept her busy but didn't keep her moving. That would have been fine, had she not come from a family of obsessive athletes who spent most of their time jumping off of buildings or skating around roller derby tracks.

And that still might have been fine, had we not come from a society where women's value was frequently defined by their waistlines. Jane had flirted off and on with disordered eating for her entire life, no matter how much all the rest of us told her that her weight didn't matter, we'd love her no matter what. Even coming from Ted, that hadn't helped as much as we would have wanted it to, and Jane's diets remained a frustrating, occasionally frightening constant. Add that to a tendency to skip meals whenever she got stressed, and I had to seriously question whether she had eaten that day.

Jane read the doubt in my expression, because she reached over and touched my arm. "Really, Mary, it's fine," she said. "Everything looks fabulous, but I didn't know you were going to be making breakfast, so I had some oatmeal before we hit the road."

"She did," verified Ted, coming in behind her. Unlike his short blonde wife, Theodore Harrington was tall and dark-haired, with a leading man's bone structure and twinkling eyes. Before Annie came home with Sam, he'd been the tallest member of the family, and had only managed to lose the title by about half an inch, which he didn't seem to resent in the slightest. As always, he was dressed to disappear in a crowd, grays and browns without a single pop of real color. For an incubus, he was committed to the idea of not attracting attention.

Everything Verity knows about the "making yourself look like someone else with the addition of a pair of glasses and a cheap blazer" routine she so excels at—calling it "Clark Kenting," which is accurate enough, in its way—she learned from her Uncle Ted. That man could make himself look harmless with a shift of his posture, and he normally chose to stand that way.

Being big and slow-aging and supernaturally attractive would have been easy things for a less gentle man to take advantage of. Thankfully for everyone involved, Ted has never been that sort of guy. He and Jane met while in college, and only started dating because she wore him down with her constant requests for dinner and a movie. Even then, it might not have worked, except that all the currently living Price-Healys by blood are descended from a woman named Frances Brown, Alice's mother.

Fran was an amazing woman. Kind, ridiculous, foul-mouthed, an incredibly practiced horseback rider, and an even better shot. And a devoted mother, although she didn't get to hold that title nearly as long as all of us would have liked. What she never knew while she was alive, and none of us knew until long after she was dead, was that she wasn't entirely human. One of her recent ancestors—probably one of her parents, given the circumstances under which Fran had been found and taken into the carnival that raised her—was a type of humanoid cryptid called a Kairos. Kairos manipulate coincidence more than pure luck, although the two things can look very similar from the outside.

Kairos are also resistant, if not immune, to most known forms of psychic manipulation, including both cuckoo telepathy and Lilu pheromones. Meaning Jane may have been the first woman Ted ever met who liked men but wasn't impacted by his preternatural attractiveness. She'd been flirting like a sledgehammer because she was interested in *Ted*, not because he was an incubus.

Not love at first sight, maybe, but definitely a solid, healthy relationship, and one I had been delighted to see Jane find for herself. Ted was good for her. Always had been.

Motherhood was also good for her, inevitable fussing about her weight in the aftermath of both births aside, and Jane had been there for both her children the way she had wanted Alice to be there for her. Elsie didn't have a lot of what I might call "ambition" or "motivation" or desire to move out of her childhood bedroom, but she made up for it in sweetness and loyalty. There was no one better to have in your corner when things got rough, something that had always benefitted her younger brother, Artie, who was much more introverted and inclined to hide in his room with his computer and his comic books.

Or he had been, anyway. Before he took a trip to another dimension with a bunch of his cousins and wound up getting his entire personality deleted. It was an accident, and the cousin who did it—Sarah Zellaby, cuckoo, childhood best friend, and longtime unconfessed love—probably felt worse about it than anybody else, even Artie. He couldn't understand why she was avoiding him so assiduously. Sure, she broke his brain, but she'd put him back together afterward, and everything was fine now, right?

Right?

Wrong. Everything was very, very wrong. What Sarah had done had pieced together a reasonable facsimile of the man we knew, but the cracks had started showing almost immediately. This current Artie was built from the memories other people had of him, not the memories he had of himself: his internality was gone, replaced by an amalgam of other people's ideas.

As he stepped into the kitchen and moved to get himself a waffle, I couldn't help but feel like I wasn't the only dead person in the room. Although at least I knew my life was over. Artie—Arthur, as he had started asking us to call him—was still operating under the assumption that he was alive.

"There's vanilla ice cream for the waffles," I informed him, and he shot me a grateful smile, heading over to open the freezer and get out the carton.

"So when are they getting here?" he asked. "Mom's been wound tighter than a jumping jack all morning long."

"I have not," said Jane.

"Have so," he replied, sounding almost disinterested. "You yelled at Elsie for having a Diet Coke instead of coffee. And you yelled at Dad for not knowing where you left your house keys."

Jane made a huffing sound.

Artie scooped ice cream onto his waffle, returned the container to the freezer, and moved to sit down next to Sam. The kitchen table, which was generally used for breakfast and small groups, was reaching capacity. I frowned, removing what would hopefully be the last waffle from the wafflemaker.

"We should probably move to the dining room, now that we're all here," I said. "There's no room for anyone else to sit."

"God forbid we inconvenience the incredible Alice Healy," said Jane, tone bitter.

Kevin sighed. "You said you were going to behave today."

"I said I would *try*."

"Well, you're certainly trying." He stood, taking his plate and mug with him. "Mary, you need help with anything?"

"I'm fine, Kevin, thank you," I said.

The next ten or so minutes were a chaotic blur of motion, as we relocated all the people and their breakfast to the much more spacious dining room. We had just finished when I paused, cocking my head.

Someone was calling me.

"I'll be right back," I said, as reassuringly as I could, and disappeared.

As a caretaker, I can take myself to any member of my family in an instant, if they think to call for me. After as long as I've been doing this job, I've figured out some of the loopholes in that statement: for example, they don't have to be *calling* me, just saying my name in conversation with someone else. Having a name like "Mary" means that even when they're trying to be careful, almost everyone I'm supposed to keep an eye on invokes me on a pretty regular basis. It's convenient.

I vanished from the dining room and reappeared in the Portland airport a moment later, thankfully on the "you're allowed to be here" side of security. There wasn't much chance of me being caught on the security cameras either way—ghosts tend to glitch out electrical surveillance systems, which is nice, since otherwise my range of motion would be getting narrower year after year. It's not like there's some grand conspiracy to hide the existence of ghosts from the living. It's more just that . . . well . . . most of us don't care, and those of us who do can give you whole lists of why knowing about us would absolutely wreck a lot of lives.

Life is short and death is long, so ghosts who aren't terrible people do what we can to preserve the sanctity of the former, even if it means being a little cagey about the afterlife.

I was standing in a short alcove that had probably been intended to hold a vending machine at one point, looking out on a wide expanse of cream tile and beige carpeting. I stepped out of the alcove, glad my "cooking breakfast for the family" clothes were also suitable for going out in public. I tend to dress like a refugee from the nineteen seventies, making me wildly old-fashioned in today's world, while still daringly modern by my own standards; at the moment, I was in my normal combination of blue jeans and white peasant blouse, although I had thrown a brown fringed vest over the top in a fit of outdated accessorizing.

Really, my clothes weren't as much of a concern as my hair. It was pale blonde when I died, and over the first year of my death, it bleached itself to pure bone-white. It's still that color now. Even with the crossroads gone, the changes I always assumed came from them endured.

Fortunately, with modern hair-care techniques and dyes, a girl my apparent age with white hair doesn't stand out the way it used to. I continued cautiously forward, trying to find the people that called me to the airport.

I was near the rental-car desks, and as I scanned the area, I caught sight of my party standing by the farthest of them. It was shabby compared to the others around it, more likely to be a local than a national chain, just based on the condition of the desk and its surroundings.

Alice was at the front of their little cluster, having apparently been declared spokesperson due to her more recent experience with this sort of thing. Thomas was right behind her, drooping a little with exhaustion, for all that he was trying to stand up straight. Sally wasn't even trying. She was sitting on the floor, which was part of why I had initially missed them—I was looking for three people, not two people and the very top of someone's head in the middle of a nest of suitcases.

It was sort of impressive, how quickly they had gone from no to minimal earthly possessions to each of them needing a full-sized suitcase for the trip from Vegas. Or maybe not that impressive: people who travel with at least some luggage are easier to overlook than those traveling without, and they were trying to project the appearance of a normal family group on their way to visit relatives.

I walked closer, until I could hear Alice speaking to the clerk in a low, measured tone. "We have a reservation," she said. "Please check again."

"I'm sorry, ma'am, but I have nothing under the name Price," said the woman behind the desk, with a supercilious smile that nicely reflected the fact that she wasn't even looking at her computer screen.

Alice swore under her breath and reached into her back pocket, pulling out a crumpled piece of printer paper, which she dropped between them. "Our number. Which your system confirmed. Please, look again."

"It's cool, Mom," drawled Sally from her place on the floor, hitting her Mainer accent a little harder than she normally would. I stopped where I was, curious to see how this was going to play out. "She's just a classist. Or possibly a racist, or maybe she's managed to hit a bingo and she's both. It'll make for a nice online review after we call a cab."

"What?" asked Alice.

"I beg your pardon?" said the clerk.

Sally shrugged, pushing herself to her feet. She was even shorter than Alice, who was not what I would call a tall woman, with glossy black hair that hung to her mid-back, currently tied back in a rough ponytail. Like Alice and Thomas, she looked exhausted. Unlike them, she had no visible tattoos, while almost every inch of their skins below the neck was covered in ink—and in Thomas's case, his throat was covered as well, by a large cameo tattoo that must have hurt like nobody's business when he gave it to himself.

"You learn to hear the tone of it," said Sally. "There's just this smug little twist that means 'I'm doing this because you don't look right to me.' And whether you're doing it because I'm Asian or because my folks used to be bikers doesn't matter. It's done either way."

The clerk sputtered. Sally shrugged.

"Oregon was founded by white separatists who made it literally illegal for people of color to own homes or work certain jobs or marry white people," she said. "They mostly had a hate-on for Black folk in the beginning, but they expanded it quick enough once they remembered that other colors of people they could hate existed. If I wander away, will you miraculously find my parents' reservation?"

"It's not— I'm not—"

"Yeah, but see, you're not the right kind of mad. This isn't 'how dare you accuse me' mad; this is 'how did I get caught' mad. So you are."

The woman paled, then reached under her desk and grabbed a piece of paper from the printer she had hidden there, thrusting it at Alice. "Your contract," she said, through gritted teeth.

"Funny, I didn't hear the printer just now," said Sally.

The clerk gave her a strained look, even as Alice signed the paper and handed it back.

"This is where you check her license," said Sally.

Alice shot her a sharp look. "Now you're just torturing the woman," she said.

"Torturing racists is a moral obligation," said Sally primly.

Alice laughed, and held out her license for the clerk to inspect. The woman gave it the most cursory of looks, barely long enough to verify that the information matched the contract she had clearly printed out before deciding to flex her minimal power, then nodded and handed Alice a set of keys.

"Cars are that way," she said, indicating the door.

"Great," said Alice. "Thanks for all your help."

"I'm still leaving that review," said Sally, as the group began to turn away, grabbing her suitcase.

The woman blanched. Neither Thomas nor Alice said anything, only collected their own bags and turned with her. Thomas paused, looking briefly pleased.

"Mary," he said. "I was wondering when you were going to join us."

"I'm assuming you're the one who called for me, then?" I asked, strolling closer. "Hey, Alice. Sally."

"That's my name," said Sally blithely. "Sally Price. I'm still debating middle names. I want one—the one I used to have was Korean, and it feels appropriate to continue having *some* sort of name that doesn't scream 'generic white girl,' but I haven't decided what it's going to be yet."

"Sounds reasonable to me," I said. "Congrats on the surname."

"Seemed fitting," said Thomas. "Given that she already shows up on your internal iteration of the family tree."

We were moving toward the doors. Sally gave him, then me, a curious look. "Doesn't everyone in the extended family?"

"Only the ones who've been well and truly adopted," I said. "Uncle Al, who you just met, doesn't, and neither does Uncle Mike, in Chicago. The caretaker bond seems to distinguish between 'ally turned honorary family member' and 'actual member of the family.' You crossed that line a while ago."

"Oh," said Sally, looking quietly pleased.

I looked to Alice and Thomas. "In case the two of you were wondering, the rest of the family, or at least the portion in this half of the country, has gathered to await your pleasure."

Alice looked briefly uneasy. "All of them?"

"Everyone in this time zone."

"Oh."

"You were going to have to face her sooner or later, you know."

"I know, I know. I was just sort of hoping for a little bit later." She managed to muster a smile, which was impressive, given how clearly unsettled she was to know that Jane was already at the house.

"You don't need to worry about sharing a bathroom with her, at least?" I offered. "She's planning to sleep at home, so you'll have your pick of the guest rooms."

"Ah," said Thomas. Unlike Alice, who looked relieved, he sounded more than faintly disappointed by this news. "Thank you, Mary. I called because I wanted to let you know we had landed safely, collected our luggage, but were having issues with the rental car."

"Which I resolved," said Sally, with an element of smugness. "James is there, right? Where we're going? He didn't chicken out and run off to hide in a cave somewhere?"

"He's there," I confirmed. "I worry about his blood pressure, but he's been waiting for you all week, and I'm pretty sure nothing's getting him out of that house today short of an actual act of god."

"Good," said Sally.

"Gang's all here," said Alice, pressing a button on the key fob she'd been given. One of the cars in the lot beeped, headlights flashing as the doors unlocked. "That'll be us. Mary, you going to ride back to the house with us?"

"No, thanks," I said. "I'm not a road ghost, and I don't like to be crammed in. Besides, it looks like there's already somebody in your back seat."

All three of them turned to see what I was looking at. There was a figure sitting in the back seat of the car that had reacted to Alice's key fob, head bowed and attention apparently focused on whatever they had in their hands.

Sally stopped dead. "I'm going to kill her," she said, almost philosophically. "We call her on her bullshit, so she gives us a car that she's already given to someone else? Nope. Not okay. I'm going to kill her."

"You spent a little too long in the closed-off murder dimension," said Alice. "We can't just go around killing people because they're assholes."

"Wanna watch me?" grumbled Sally mutinously.

Alice laughed and turned back toward the car. "Maybe they just got into the wrong one," she said. "A lot of these have to be keyed to the same fobs. I'm sure whoever it is will move when we explain the situation."

She started walking again, faster this time, and for all her feigned certainty, I could tell by the way she was moving that she was on high alert. If that car *was* the one they were supposed to be taking, this person could be an innocent who'd made a mistake—or they could be a Covenant operative looking to spring a trap. I didn't like it, but there was really no degree of paranoia that wasn't justified, especially not when there was any chance a Covenant operative might have escaped New York with the news that Thomas Price was somehow mysteriously back from the dead.

Alice reached the car, paused, and bent to look in the rear window. Then she straightened, suddenly at ease as she turned back to the rest of us.

"It's just Sarah," she said. "Come on, let's get this puppy loaded."

"Just . . . But we left her in New York!" objected Sally. She scowled. "I do not appreciate how much of this family is cavalier about linear distance."

"It's only three of us," I said, as reassuring as I could. "And Rose and I have limitations."

"What about Sarah?"

I hesitated. "Sarah . . . means well. I'm a little surprised she's here. She's been doing her best to avoid Artie ever since the incident."

"The . . ." Sally threw her hands up. "I get it, I get it, I'm the newcomer and you all have all this history that I don't know yet, but can we try not shorthanding things in ways that are comic-book-level ominous, maybe?"

"It's a long story," I said. "Still, I didn't think Sarah was going to come anywhere near here if she didn't have to."

"How is she already in our car?"

Again, I hesitated. Then I shrugged. "No idea. Try asking her."

As previously mentioned, Sarah is one of the inhuman members of the family: she's a cuckoo, a psychic species originally from another dimension, and while she looks like the sort of girl who winds up playing the lead in a forgettable romantic comedy that goes on to air weekly on the Hallmark Channel until the heat death of the universe, she biologically has more in common with a wasp than she does with those leading ladies. The event that led to wiping out Artie's memories and original personality also involved exposing Sarah to so much psychic energy that she underwent a sort of metamorphosis, like a grasshopper becoming a locust, and became a new form of her species, a cuckoo queen. There had been cuckoo queens before, of course, but none of them survived for long after their change. Sarah was still figuring out what she was capable of, while the rest of us watched anxiously to be sure she wasn't going to accidentally crack the planet or something. You know. Normal growing pains.

These days, she was a little less skilled at seeming to appear human, a little more likely to let her alien nature shine through. Not because she wanted to—near as any of us could tell, she'd lost touch with a certain essential degree of humanity. She was something else now.

Among her expanded capabilities came a tendency to treat space as malleable. It was just math you could walk through, after all, and all she needed to do was bend it when she wanted to get somewhere in a hurry. I followed Sally to the car, where Alice had crouched down to talk to Sarah through the open window.

"You going to the house with us, honey?" she asked, as we approached.

Sarah looked up from the thing in her hand—some sort of portable gaming device, by the shape of it—and blinked guilelessly as she met Alice's eyes. As was often the case these days, there was a faint white film over Sarah's pupils, like the early formation of cataracts. "That's why I'm in the car," she said, politely.

"Why are you riding with us, and not just going directly there?"

Sarah blinked again. "The car doesn't have any real security systems in place to keep me out of it. The house is much less suited for dropping in. I can, but it would upset Kevin and Evelyn if I put myself inside without an invitation. So it seemed best to ride in with you, when you had already been invited."

"Her logic's pretty solid," I said. "Sounds like you're about ready to head for the house, so are you going to need me right now? There's no room for me in the car."

"No, honey, you can go," said Alice, while Thomas flashed me a quick smile.

"It's always good to see you," he said. "I missed you very much while I was away."

"Same to you, Tommy," I said, and vanished.

It was going to be a long day.

Three

"The future isn't set in stone. It's set in the layer of grease at the bottom of a casserole dish. Sure, you can get it off if you soak and scrub right away, but if you let it sit for too long, that's it. That's what you get to live with."

—Laura Campbell

The dining room of a small survivalist compound about an hour's drive east of Portland, Oregon

BREAKFAST WAS MOSTLY FINISHED when I popped back in. Evie had dragged Jane off to the kitchen, and I could hear the two of them doing dishes. It wasn't a gender thing—Evie was just better at calming Jane down than Kevin was, and dishes were one of those soothingly monotonous tasks that knocked the grumbling right out of her sails. By the time they finished scrubbing the frying pans, Jane would be calm enough to deal with her mother, or at least that was the hope.

Kevin was Jane's big brother. He loved her fiercely, and would happily hurt anyone who hurt her, but he had spent their mutual childhood as her tormentor as much as her companion, and more, he didn't share her uncomplicated opinion of their mother. To Kevin, Alice was the woman he remembered from his earliest childhood, the one who would never have left him if she hadn't had an excellent reason to do so. She had reappeared periodically as he was growing up, and his memories of Thomas, while fuzzy and distant, had still been clear enough that when she told him she was looking for his daddy, he'd been able to understand what she was talking about. Jane, though . . .

To Jane, Alice was only and forever the woman who had run away before the ink was dry on her birth certificate, the one who had looked at her newborn daughter and said "Nope, not a good enough reason to stay." The mice had told both of them stories about their parents, but where Kevin heard a fairy tale, Jane heard a horror story, the tale of a woman who loved her husband so much that she'd been willing to abandon her children in pursuit of something that was never going to happen. Not to say that Kevin and Alice had an easy relationship, because they didn't, but it was nothing compared to the animosity that existed between Alice and Jane.

There had been a time, when I'd first realized how bad things were getting, where I'd tried to intervene, to help Jane understand that Alice had good reasons to believe Thomas was alive somewhere for her to find, and more, that Alice had been given a perfect model of an overprotective parent by her own father, and was a little more willing to leave her children with people she trusted because she was trying so desperately hard not to turn into him. Jane hadn't been ready to listen, not then, and not as she got older. To her, Alice was a deadbeat who had brought her children into the world knowing they would never be able to live normal lives, and then run before she had to deal with the consequences of her actions.

And now we were going to put them in the same house in the name of a family reunion that only about half the people involved actually wanted. Wasn't this going to be fun?

Annie looked over as I appeared. "All good?" she asked.

"Yeah," I said. "They were just having some issues with the rental-car desk. They got everything sorted, and they're on their way. With an extra bonus passenger."

"Really?" asked Annie. "Aunt Rose coming in?"

Rose used to be a hitchhiking ghost, before she got a little too involved with the dead gods and received a promotion to "Fury." It's a long story, and not mine to tell. But assuming she'd be a passenger with our travelers wasn't too far out of line. Still, I shook my head.

"Sally's with them, right?" asked James.

"Sally's not really optional," I told him. "She has the last name Price on her ID, same as you do. Our adoptions may not be strictly legal, but they're definitely binding."

"She was always family to me," said James.

"Well, now she's just family on paper, too," I said. "No. They've got Sarah riding with them."

Artie perked up a bit. Elsie frowned.

"Sarah?" she asked. "What the hell is Sarah doing here?"

Elsie could seem a lot more easygoing than her mother, and in most ways, she was; she didn't get as hung up on appearances as Jane did, and when she wanted a cookie, she ate a cookie without berating herself about it. She took after her father in a lot of ways, and was all the better for it. But when it came to holding a grudge, justified or not, she was all Jane, and she blamed Sarah for what happened to Artie.

Everyone else who'd been there at the time had tried to explain to her that what happened wasn't Sarah's fault; she'd been deep in the throes of world-changing mathematical wizardry when Artie touched her bare skin, something he should absolutely have known better than to do, and got his mind blasted before anyone could pull him away. Sarah didn't know what she was doing. She couldn't have prevented herself if she'd been trying. The only way to protect Artie would have been for him not to touch her, and we would never know for sure why he'd decided he had to do that.

Artie wasn't the only one who'd come back from that little trip changed in some fundamental way. Annie and James had both had their memories of Sarah wiped up to the moment the chaos began. Annie no longer remembered growing up with Sarah, and apparently the missing memories made their multi-year Dungeons and Dragons campaign utterly incomprehensible. Sarah had been able to convince her that they knew each other, mostly because she hadn't deleted the memories of the mice who were with them, and like all Price children, Annie had been raised to believe the mice above all else.

James hadn't been quite as inclined to rodent-based credulity, but he also hadn't had nearly as much memory to lose; his adjustment had been faster and easier. Of the three, while they'd all been changed, it was only Artie I could really say had been *damaged*, and it was increasingly unclear if the damage was ever going to go away.

I turned to focus on Elsie. "I don't know why Sarah's here; I didn't ask. But I do know she's family, and that means she's allowed to be here any time she wants to be. It's good that she's here. We want to get this out of the way if we can. A proper family reunion isn't really in the cards for us currently, since calling Verity and Alex home would leave their territories undefended."

"Yeah, and tactically speaking, putting all your high-value targets in one place is never a good idea," said James. "If the Covenant has discovered the concept of the air strike, it could be the last thing we ever do."

"Thank you for that cheerful thought, James," I said. "She did say she felt uncomfortable coming through the wards and upsetting everyone, so she wanted to hitch a ride with people who were already coming from out of town. Maybe that was her motivation. And maybe she just missed Portland."

"Maybe," said Elsie dubiously. "I'm going to keep my eye on her. if she so much as twitches toward my little brother, I'll—"

"Do nothing and be happy for me," said Arthur firmly. "If she's ready to stop avoiding me, I'm ready to not be avoided."

"Artie—"

"Arthur," he said.

"And see, that's the problem. You always hated being called Arthur, until she broke your brain and stuck it back together with craft glue and pipe cleaners. You're still not entirely well. I don't want her to hurt you worse than she already has."

"If it looks like she's going to rip another hole in the fabric of space and time, I promise I won't go with her this time, all right?" he said snidely, pushing his chair back from the table. "My broken brain and I are going to go to the library now. I think I want to be by myself for a little while."

"Arthur . . ." she said, pleadingly.

He didn't respond, just rose and stalked away. Kevin sighed, putting down his coffee cup.

"Thank you for breakfast, Mary. I know you were trying to make today go a little smoother, and I'm sorry it's all fallen apart so quickly."

"Hey," I said, keeping my voice light. "No one's been stabbed, shot, or set on fire yet, and we have how many Prices in this house? I think this may be some sort of record for nonviolence."

A cheer rose from under the table as the mice who had been listening in to the whole conversation seized upon something that could potentially form the basis of a new celebration. I shrugged. As far as things the mice could celebrate went, this one was fairly harmless, and at least somewhat entertaining. Let them party.

"I know." He sighed, glancing at Annie and James. "I was just hoping we could be a little less . . . us, for the homecoming."

"Hey, kiddo. Alice knows you, and she loves you the way you are. And Thomas, well, he married Alice. On purpose. He's going to think you're fantastic, all of you."

"I hope you're right." Kevin paused then, glancing around. "Where's Ted?"

"Is he in the kitchen with Jane and Evie?"

"I don't think so . . ."

"He went to the library a while ago," said James. "Can Lilu see the future?"

"No," said Elsie. "But he seems to have an easier time understanding Arthur than the rest of us. Dad probably guessed Arthur was going to wind up in there at some point, and didn't want it to look like he was following him."

"We have, what, half an hour before they get here?" asked Annie. She popped to her feet, grabbing James by the wrist and hauling him after her. Sam rose on his own, not to be left out. "Come on. We'll get all anxious and weird if we just sit here until then. Let's go get some skating practice in."

"I don't want to play roller derby," said James.

"Tough. You're a Price now, and until you find a combat form you enjoy, you're going to practice the ones I'm good at. We could bounce on trampolines and throw knives, if you'd prefer?"

"I'll get my skates."

The three of them hurried off, leaving me alone with Kevin and Elsie. I took one of the now-open seats at the table, pausing to cock my head and check on the actual children I was supposed to be sitting for. Olivia was asleep, the warm contentment of her preschool dreams coloring my impression of her. Charlotte was awake, and watching a colorful bird outside her window. Isaac was likewise awake, and reaching out telepathically to Shelby, Charlotte's mother, for comfort and a cuddle. He'd have them soon enough: Shelby was on her way to his room. Everything was normal; everything was quiet and content.

That probably meant something was about to catch fire, since "quiet" is usually the pause between the ignition and the explosion, but for the moment, I was willing to accept it.

"You doing okay with all this?" I asked, focusing on Elsie.

She scowled for a moment before she seemed to realize that I wasn't the one she was supposed to be mad at and took a deep breath, visibly forcing herself to calm down. "Yeah," she admitted, with a sigh. "Mom's pretty spun up about *her* mom coming to visit, but I'm excited to meet Grandpa, and I love my grandmother. She's always been pretty cool to me."

"Some people make better grandparents than they do parents," I agreed. "And some people do best with other people's children."

"You were a pretty great babysitter," she said.

"I always thought so."

"Do you ever wish you'd been a parent?"

"Not really. Wanting to have been a parent would mean wishing I hadn't died, and I got over that a long, long time ago. I didn't get to grow up, but I got to watch you all grow up, and that's been pretty amazing, really. Instead of one or two kids, I got eleven and counting. And I get to do it all without getting sick or sleep-deprived or anything silly like that. *And* without me, you people would probably have sold your souls to the crossroads a few dozen times over, instead of just the two you've managed so far."

Elsie snorted. "I guess that's true."

I grinned at her. "I'm a pretty awesome babysitter."

"This is also true."

"You're lucky to have had me."

"Now that, I cannot question in the least." She stood. "I'm going to get a cup of coffee. Either of you want anything?"

Kevin shook his head. "I'm good, thanks. I hope your mother's feeling better."

"Mom's tough; she's fine by now," said Elsie.

I wasn't so sure about that. I didn't say anything, just watched her walk away before I turned and focused on Kevin.

He met my eyes, mustering a watery smile. "Hi, Mary," he said.

"Hi, Kev," I replied.

All the Prices are my kids, whether they joined the family as adults or not, but Kevin is special. He was my first true charge after Alice herself, and there had been a period, when Laura was still adjusting to the unexpected shape her life had taken in Alice's absence, where I had been his near-constant companion. It hadn't been the way it is now, not back then; these days, none of my kids gets my undivided attention for long, because even if I discount the ones who are grown up and technically don't need me the same way, I'm still bouncing between three under ten, and will be for a while. But once . . .

Once, it was just Kevin and me. His memories of Alice included memories of me being the one who brought him his bottle or wiped his tears away, and even as Jane had been clinging tightly to Laura as a surrogate mother figure, he'd been wailing in the night for his babysitter. She'd been my responsibility as much as he was, but she'd never *wanted* me in the same way, and so for years, I'd been his constant companion, the only thing he really felt he could count on in a world that had already demonstrated an unsettling tendency to change without his consent.

I wasn't sure when the job description for "babysitter" had been expanded to include "stable point," but whatever. I wasn't complaining.

"You okay?" I asked.

"Yes," he said, automatically. Then he sighed. "No. I don't know."

"You want to talk about it?"

"Honestly, I don't know where to start."

I smiled a little, thinking of Sally and her frustration at the easy shorthand with which we tended to describe family history. "Start wherever you like."

"My sister hates my mother, and I can't say for sure that she's wrong to hate her, but I don't think she's all the way right, and I know she's armed, and they're both about to be in the same house with three of my children."

"That's a good place to start, and a reasonable thing to be conflicted about, really."

He sighed again, dragging one hand backward through his hair, making it stick up in the front like he was some sort of frustrated inventor out of a science fiction movie. "It was easier when we were kids. The worst Jane usually had was a slingshot and some knives, and I'm fast enough that even if she lost her temper, nobody got hurt. And Mom was . . . Mom was Mom. She showed up, wished us a happy birthday even if it was nowhere near our birthdays, dropped off a bunch of presents and promised *this* trip was the one where she would find Dad and bring him home, *this* trip was the last one, for honest and for true." He paused, looking at me mournfully. "But it never was. There was always just one more, and Jane got older, and they got farther and farther apart, and now it finally *was* the last trip, and it feels like there's so much distance between them that it doesn't even matter. She did the impossible. She found our father. That wasn't supposed to happen."

"Are you unhappy that she did?"

"Yes! No. I don't know." He sagged. "Part of me is ecstatic. I've been waiting my whole life for him to come home. And part of me feels like we did our grieving a long, long time ago, and he should do us the courtesy of staying dead instead of coming in here and messing everything up."

"I can understand that," I said. "It's okay to be conflicted. This is a big, confusing thing that changes way too many things about the overall family dynamic for it to rest particularly easily. Thomas is back now, and this is going to be confusing for him, too. He disappeared before you were out of diapers, and now you're a grown man with children of your own. You pay taxes. How's he supposed to adjust to that?"

"True . . ." said Kevin, with a hint of a smile.

"And Jane! I would *not* know what to do with Jane if I hadn't watched her grow up. She's brilliant, beautiful, and stubborn as a damn mule." I shook my head. "And again, adult, children, taxes. He's going to be so confused, and he's going to be trying his best to hide it, but there's disorientation and adjustment to be done on both sides of the equation. Just remember that. He's someone who was trained all his life to cover up any weaknesses, but he's just as out of his depth as you are."

Kevin shot me an amused look. "Are you really trying to pull a 'they're more scared of you than you are of them' on me right now?"

"Maybe. Is it working?"

"Maybe." He laughed. "You always know how to calm me down."

"If I can hit the buttons, it's just because I installed a whole bunch of them," I said. Then I paused, frowning. "Huh. That's funny."

"What is?"

"Olivia just woke up. But she should be asleep for another hour. It's naptime." I pushed my chair back and stood rather than vanishing from a seated position. It's always awkward to transition while I'm sitting down. Unless there's something for me to sit on where I appear, I can pop back into existence and fall down.

Oh, yeah. Learning how to be a ghost was a barrel of laughs the whole time.

"Babies wake up," said Kevin, smiling fondly at the thought of his granddaughter. "I wish you could transport living people the way you do yourself. I'd love to see her."

"Sorry," I said. "Ghost rules say no carrying the living through the lands of the dead."

"I know, I know. It would just be nice if you could."

"I bet her parents would agree." Verity hadn't returned to New York intending to stay there in the long term, but now it looked like she was going to be on the other side of the continent until the situation with the Covenant was resolved, which could take years. I winced as Olivia began to cry. Crying is one of the ways babies and small children announce their need for their babysitter, in the days before the phrase "Mary I need you" is their first response to waking up alone. It had been a while since Olivia cried to get my attention. "Look, I have to go. Olivia's really upset, and that means it's babysitter time."

"I remember how this works," he said, with an easy smile. "Go ahead and take care of your charge, and tell Verity to call me."

"You could always text your kid," I said, and vanished to the sound of his laughter.

I reappeared into chaos.

Verity and Dominic had been living with the dragons of Manhattan in their aboveground Nest since the Covenant began seriously poking around the city. It was a way for them to keep an eye on one of the largest stable cryptid communities left in the area, and to remain flexible in case they needed to respond quickly to an attack. While the dragon community had faced some challenges, there had been no signs that the Nest itself was compromised, and the last time I'd checked, they had been discussing the possibility of opening themselves up to even more refugees. They had the space, and about a dozen non-dragon cryptids were already living there. It was a stronghold. It was a bolt-hole.

It was on fire.

Or at least the second floor was on fire, which was more than sufficient to qualify as a problem, since that was where I'd appeared. The Nest was built inside a repurposed slaughterhouse dating back to Manhattan's past as a city trying to be completely self-sufficient: the walls were solid stone, the floors designed for easy drainage and cleaning. The second floor was more like a series of hotel rooms surrounding an interior courtyard than an actual residential space, in part because it had originally been offices and break rooms, not living space. There wasn't much here that could burn. But it was doing its best.

Sometimes, being dead means I don't react as strongly to life-threatening peril as I probably should. I was standing on a burning walkway, shouts coming from below me as the occupants of the Nest reacted to the situation, and all I could think about was how difficult it really was to get a building like this to go up in flames. Sure, it could be done, but it wasn't the most efficient way to destroy the place. It was, however, likely to be the most terror-inducing. I looked up. A large chunk of the ceiling was missing, meaning someone had probably launched an antiaircraft missile at the place, blasting and igniting the masonry. The sound would have been enough to wake Olivia, and explained why she'd started crying instead of calling for me nicely, like a big girl. She was so proud of being able to use her words to get my attention that crying had become less common of late.

Part of how I could be so calm was that I knew beyond the shadow of a doubt that she wasn't dead. I could still feel her fussing, unhappy and overtired, but not actually physically harmed. As long as that remained the case, I could afford to be calm.

I'd appeared on the burning walkway because I learned a long time ago that popping right into the bedroom of a fussy child is a great way to escalate mild discontent into an active tantrum. It doesn't matter how used to me they are. They don't like to be startled, and I can respect that.

The flames were licking at the door to the room Verity and Dominic had converted into Olivia's nursery. That didn't mean the room itself was on fire, and I wasn't feeling any pain from her, but did mean that opening the door probably wasn't a great idea. I took a deep, unnecessary breath and walked forward, through flames and door at the same time, stepping into the nursery.

Olivia was sitting up in her bed and clutching her blankets against her chest, dark blue eyes huge in the dim glow of her moon-and-stars mobile. The room had no window, a consequence of its construction, and there was no interior sign of what was going on outside the nursery. That was a good thing. I didn't want to freak her out any more than we absolutely couldn't avoid.

She released her death grip on the blankets when she saw me, reaching out with tiny hands, fingers spread wide. "Mary, *up*," she said, almost imperiously, fear having knocked her sentence structure back by over a year. All preschoolers are demanding. Preschoolers who recognize me as their dedicated babysitter are a special sort of demanding. They have no reason to expect that I would ever tell them no.

"Not yet, bug," I said, bustling to the room's small closet, where I pulled out her suitcase. Like all Prices and Healys, she had her own go bag, packed for her by her parents before she'd even been born. It contained several changes of clothing, all her essential documentation, a full set of fake documentation, copies of her favorite bedtime books, and a teddy bear identical to the one currently in her bed, to hopefully make the trauma of running less severe.

Aging that teddy to match the one she slept with had been an undertaking in and of itself, and not one that any of us had particularly enjoyed.

Olivia watched me with eyes still open as wide as they could go, mouth beginning to screw up in frustration. "Mary, *up*," she repeated, with more force.

"In a second, sweetheart. Right now, you need to stay where you are, and not get out of your bed." I hesitated, then said the one thing that would all but guarantee obedience: "If you can do that for me, we can go to the playground soon, all right?"

Olivia stayed where she was, shoving her thumb into her mouth as she nodded vigorously.

I like them at this age. They're malleable. Holding her go bag in one hand, I let my sense of the family drift, looking for the two who should be geographically closest, and probably losing their shit right about now.

Verity was easy to spot, an incandescent mixture of rage and fear about six blocks away. Dominic was more reined-in, mostly anger mixed with a sort of murderous resignation. He was even closer, three blocks over at the absolute most. If he wasn't already on his way to the Nest, he would be soon. I blew Olivia a kiss and disappeared. Small children are much more sanguine about people vanishing in front of them than they are about people popping out of nothing. I've never been sure entirely why.

I reappeared on the rooftop of one of the area's uncounted retail structures, Olivia's bag still in my hand. I can transport things that aren't alive with me when I travel, as long as I can lift them, although it's a strain if I try to move things that are too large for me to lift easily. Living things are a different matter. Oh, I can take them. They're just not alive when I reach my destination.

I've never been particularly worried about being spotted by the living. People, by and large, aren't as observant as they think they are, and they don't *really* want to believe in life after death that looks as messy and inconvenient as life before death. When I appear out of nowhere, unless I'm right up in somebody's face, they'll generally ignore me or justify it away, writing off my sudden apparition as a trick of the light or them just not noticing me before.

Dominic probably wouldn't have noticed if I'd been there for the last ten minutes. When I popped in, he was standing over the bodies of three downed men in charcoal and camo, all of them unconscious at the absolute minimum. I'm not a psychopomp. The only way I know if someone's dead is if I check their pulse—or if they're family.

When family dies, I know right away.

"Hey," I called, trying to keep my voice easy, so as not to startle him. I needed to stay solid if I didn't want to drop Olivia's go bag, and even if wounds can't kill me, they can still hurt like hell.

Dominic whirled around, eyes wide. There was a trickle of blood running from his left temple, and a smear on his bottom lip. He might have come out on top, but the fight had been far from effortless. He blinked, falling out of his combat-ready stance and into something more relaxed—at least until he saw what I was holding, and tensed.

"Mary," he said. "Why are you here?"

"Nest's on fire," I said. "If you have an SOS phrase you can text Very, you should, because I need to get back to Oregon and tell Sarah

I need her help getting Olivia out of here. Can I take her back to the compound?"

Dominic hesitated. I would have expected nothing less. I was asking if I could take his daughter to the other side of the continent via the unstable-telepath express, *and* telling him his primary safehouse was in the process of burning down. Not comforting stuff, when you really stopped and thought about it.

"Yes," he said, finally and decisively. "Can we—will we be able to say goodbye?"

"I don't think it's safe," I said. "The fire has her trapped in her room right now, but she's not in pain or any real distress, and with Sarah's help, I can get her out. I'll call as soon as we reach Portland."

"Swear."

"I swear."

"These bastards . . ." He kicked the nearest body, and from the boneless way its head lolled, I knew it *was* a body now, not an operative. "They ambushed me on the way home. They had some sort of rocket-launching device."

"I think they have another one, because whatever hit the Nest hit the roof first," I said, and vanished. It would have been easy to stay and gather information, but that ignored the urgency of the situation. Fire moves fast when it gets going. Olivia was safe for now. She might not stay that way.

Once again, I emerged into chaos.

Thomas was standing with his hands on Kevin's arms, the two men staring at each other and crying silently, apparently communicating through some silent father-son telepathy that skipped over even the normal psychic channels. Elsie was standing behind them, watching hungrily, her empathy clearly leaving her eager for her turn. Alice was on the other side of the room, being shouted at by Jane, while Evie tried to push her way between the two women and Sally lurked near the far wall, clearly uncomfortable. There was no sign of anyone else.

"Hey!" I shouted, dropping Olivia's go bag so I could clap my hands briskly. Everyone stopped what they were doing except for Jane, who continued shouting at her mother. I couldn't even make out the words, she was so incensed. I clapped my hands again, and this time I yelled louder, "*Hey*! One two three, eyes on me!"

Sometimes it's good to be the babysitter. Jane stopped yelling and swiveled to face me, the same half-petulant, half-guilty look on her face that she used to get when she'd been sneaking cookies before dinner.

Nice to know that berating her mother ranked up there with purloined dessert. I lowered my hands. "Where's Sarah? Does anyone know?"

"Artie—sorry, Arthur, met us at the gate," said Alice. "He said they needed to have a conversation, and he took her for a walk around the property."

"Great," I said. "I'm going to go find them. Elsie, if you could take this bag upstairs to one of the childproof guest rooms? I'll explain when I get back."

I vanished, leaving them all gaping.

Taking myself directly to a family member who hasn't called me and isn't actively in need of my attention is difficult at best, and sort of like trying to use one of those overhead photos of an overly elaborate corn maze to navigate while actually inside the damn thing. I can, and usually do, wind up in the wrong place, but still in the vicinity. An active call is like a beacon, something I can follow.

Still, "a walk on the grounds" was enough of a narrowing-down of their possible locations that it would at least help. I reappeared near the front gate, looked around, and then vanished again, repeating the process from the field behind the barn. It only took three hops before I found Sarah and Arthur sitting at the firepit we used for barbecues during the summer. The bonfire was extinguished, wood blackened with charcoal and grayed with ash, but the oiled logs used as seats for the younger members of the family were still in place. Each of them had their own log, leaving plenty of distance between them. Sarah's body language was closed-off, her shoulders hunched and her hands between her knees, while Arthur looked more like he was trying to argue his case before an unfriendly courtroom.

They both stopped talking when I appeared, focusing their attention on me.

"Sorry to intrude," I said. "Sarah, the Nest has been attacked. It's on fire now."

"Yes," she said.

"I—I don't even want to know how you know that," I said. "The fire has Olivia trapped in the nursery. I need you to come with me. I can't bring her back here alive."

"You know the math gets complicated when you want me to transport someone."

"Yes, and I wouldn't ask if it weren't an emergency."

"As long as you're willing to risk the consequences," said Sarah, tone mild and almost dreamy. She looked off into space like she was studying something I couldn't see, eyes darting back and forth. "Carry the two, and I'll see you there," she said, and vanished.

When I disappear, there's no inrush of air or sound. I'm a ghost: I'm basically made of air that's just figured out how to turn itself solid for a little while. Sarah is more solid. Her disappearance was marked by a shattering sound, like someone twisting a stick of chalk between their fingers. Arthur shot me a despairing look.

"Do you know how *hard* it was to get her alone?" he asked.

"Your baby cousin is in danger of burning to death," I snapped, and followed after Sarah into the ether, letting the beacon of Olivia's increasing distress guide me. She still wasn't in pain or broadcasting the sort of panic that would imply active danger, or I would have been a lot less calm about the situation, and I wasn't calm at all, not really. I just had years of experience dealing with a family whose survival instincts were underdeveloped at best, and who sometimes came home holding venomous reptiles or loaded weapons long before they knew how to handle them safely. I had a doctorate in not panicking.

The fire had spread when I reappeared in the Nest. Sarah was nowhere to be seen, but the flames now surrounded Olivia's door. The shouting from below had all but died out, the relatively fireproof dragons no doubt evacuating their guests. Or at least I hoped they had. I wouldn't put it past them to have declared that no one was getting rescued without paying a salvation fee, and be standing there watching as their companions burnt to death.

You never can tell with dragons. I took a breath and walked into the fire, through it, and through the door, back into the nursery, where Olivia was no longer in her bed.

Instead, Sarah was holding her propped against her hip. She blinked at me, eyes even more clouded over white than they normally were, as if the cataracts she sometimes seemed to have had spread. "What took you so long?" she asked.

"Livvy's too scared to call for me on purpose," I said, retrieving her blanket and her stuffed elephant from the bed. "Dominic already knows we're taking her back to Portland. Let's go."

Sarah turned to look sadly at the wall. "There's going to be a lot of burning here," she said. "We should have brought Annie with us. She could have called the fire back to heel."

"Can't you just go get her?"

Sarah shook her head. "This will make three times across the country in a very short period, twice with a passenger. The math is getting too large to be safe. It gets more dangerous with each passage. Reality is a crystalline matrix, and I'm convincing it to connect in ways it doesn't necessarily approve of. I can get Olivia home to the compound. If I tried to come back here with Annie, one of us might get lost in the crossing."

"Okay, that sounds . . . bad. That would be bad, right?" Whatever form of subspace or unreality Sarah was traveling through when she did her terrifying cuckoo math, it didn't seem like it would be a nice place to leave someone.

"Yes," said Sarah gravely. "That would be bad."

"All right. Let's get Olivia—" I stopped, wincing, as Verity was suddenly yelling about how much she needed me.

Sarah's expression turned sympathetic. "I'll see you in Portland," she said. Her eyes flashed white, and she was gone, taking Olivia with her. Verity was still shouting for my attention, and while she was no longer strictly my responsibility, no one else was yelling at the moment.

Time to face the music. Even as a babysitter, abducting people's children is generally frowned upon. I closed my eyes and reached for Verity's distress, and the air changed around me. When I opened them, I was on another rooftop, this one close enough to the burning Nest that I could see the smoke rising into the sky, and the flashing lights of the fire trucks that had inevitably been called. The locals thought the Nest was a woefully underdeveloped eyesore in a desirable part of town; they were probably thrilled to see it go, as long as the damage didn't extend to their own properties.

Verity grabbed my shoulder and whirled me around, and I let her, not allowing the shock to turn me insubstantial. I had just stolen her child. She was within her rights to be furious.

Instead, she jerked me into a hard embrace, hugging me close and resting her chin on my shoulder for several minutes before she let me go and stepped away. I blinked at her.

"Dominic told me where you'd gone," she said. "I got back to the Nest, and the hall outside Livvy's room was in flames. I couldn't get through. I couldn't get to her. I couldn't even yell for her, because she wasn't crying, and if she heard me, she'd start crying. The only thing I could do was cause her more distress when she was already in danger. Did you . . . Is she . . . ?"

I nodded, and Verity exhaled, sagging.

"You are the best babysitter in the entire world, and I am so sorry for everything I ever did to make your job harder than it absolutely needed to be," she said. "I will never contradict you again."

"There's a promise I could have used when you were thirteen," I said. "Olivia's fine. Sarah took her back to Portland, and we already have her go bag." I retrieved the blanket and stuffed elephant from where they had fallen when she embraced me. "Do we know what happened yet? And have you been able to get the flammable people out of the Nest?"

"The dragons are taking their time clearing out all the valuables, and they're not planning to leave until the firefighters start coming into the building," said Verity. "Officially, no one lives there, so the fire department's letting the structure collapse while they control the blaze, rather than putting firefighters in danger for a piece of real estate."

"I wish that didn't make sense," I said. Even if the building was officially uninhabited, there could have been squatters, people who just needed a warm place to sleep, and who didn't deserve to be left to burn to death because they didn't have the money for something better. But in this case, the policy was working in our favor: it was better the firefighters not break into the Nest, with its clear signs of habitation and dragons still gutting the place. "Was anyone hurt?"

Verity nodded, expression genuinely miserable. "The Madhura have been building a hive in one of the old storage rooms at the very top of the Nest. Big windows, lots of sunlight, all the things they need for healthy larvae. The first hit took out half their roof, and the whole thing was on fire before anyone realized. We lost three of the adults and all but two of the larvae. I don't know how they bounce back from this. One of the bogeymen was on the upstairs walkway when the bombs hit, and he didn't make it. And Cara . . ." She paused, swallowing. "Dragons are pretty much immune to fire, but that's the only thing they're immune to. She was trying to get into the room where the dragon kids nap. Olivia would normally have been in there with them, but she's at the age where she bites sometimes, and if she bites one of the boys he'll bite her back, and boy dragons have much more dangerous teeth, so it's better to separate them when she's in one of her moods, you know?"

"You're babbling, sweetie," I said. "Focus."

"Right, right." Verity took in a sharp breath through her nose as Dominic approached across the roof to our right. "Cara was trying to get into the room where the dragon children were sleeping, to get them out. The hallway ceiling collapsed on her. She was crushed. The children were all fine; they've been evacuated now. Cara, though . . ."

"I'm so sorry."

"So am I. How did those bastards even find us?" She looked at me, eyes wide and pleading. "We've been so careful since we eliminated their last set of strike teams. There's been no whispering about us being followed, no signs that they had any idea where we were, and now they're using some kind of missiles to take out our roof? What the hell? There were *children* in there!"

"Not if you ask them, there weren't," said Dominic, stepping off the edge of the roof next to ours as he approached. There was only about a three-foot difference between the two, and it was a sign of how long he had been involved with Verity and her cavalier approach to gravity's whims that he didn't even blink, just dropped and carried on walking. His hips were going to regret that in a few years, but then, approaching things head-on was currently how he was giving himself the chance to get old and regret his youthful choices.

Verity shot him a quick frown. He continued toward us, stepping up behind her and sliding his arms around her waist.

"Cryptid young are not 'children,' and if they seem to resemble children, it's only so they can more easily lure their prey," he said, the weary disgust in his voice robbing his words of their sting. "And better for a child of traitors to die young and innocent, to have a chance of getting into the Kingdom of Heaven, than to grow old and irredeemable, working against the interests of their own species."

"Did those three you took out have anything useful to say?" I asked.

"There were five of them," he said. "I hunted down the other two after you left. The first three died too quickly to tell me anything. The last two were a little more communicative. They didn't know for sure that the Nest was our headquarters, but their surveillance had flagged it as an anomaly, both in terms of power draw and traffic, and one of their teams had the brilliant idea of seeding the surrounding sewers with tracking devices. They followed a bunch of municipal workers home. They also got one of our bogeymen, or someone else who was using the sewer for transport. Whoever it was probably stepped on a tracker and didn't even realize it. That, along with the anomalies they'd charted, was enough to make us a target."

"I had four," said Verity. "They set off their launcher just as I hit the roof. If I'd been a few minutes faster—"

"This wasn't your fault," I said, firmly.

"Wasn't it? We've had plenty of chances to take the fight to the Covenant, and we haven't done it. So they brought the fight to us. I'm going to have to stand up in front of Priscilla and William and try to convince them that we didn't put the dragons in danger by turning their nest into a safehouse. Olivia could have been *killed* . . ."

"And she wasn't," I said. "She's safe with her grandparents. Very, you have to breathe. This is terrible, and it's not over, but it's not your fault. Dominic, keep her from freaking out, and call me if either of you needs me. I need to get back to Portland."

"Can Sarah bring her back here?" Dominic asked, abruptly.

I shook my head. "Sarah says it's not safe for her to make the trip that many times in quick succession, and since we don't have a rule book for how she works, I'm taking her word for it. We'll get Livvy back to you just as soon as we can." That didn't feel like enough, under the circumstances, so I added, "Promise," and disappeared.

Why does everything have to be complicated? Just once, can't things be easy?

Four

> "Eternal youth isn't everything it's cracked up to be. Sometimes it's a burden that doesn't have a name, and there's no way to explain it to the people who think you're a lucky child who needs to stop complaining."
>
> —Apple Tanaka

The upstairs hall of a small survivalist compound about an hour's drive east of Portland, Oregon

IN A FLASH OF déjà vu, I appeared in another hallway, outside another closed bedroom door. This hall wasn't on fire, which was a very nice change. Evelyn had apparently just come out of the room; her hand was still on the knob, and she jumped when she saw me.

"What the fu— Oh, Mary. You shouldn't sneak up on people like that."

"Sorry, Evie," I said, with less repentance than I was aiming for. "Any trouble getting her down?"

"She's not going to stay down for long, if that's what you're asking; she was just about done napping when she got woken up. But she needs a little quiet time to adjust, and being downstairs wasn't going to help settle her nerves any."

"No, I can see where it wouldn't," I sighed. "They still going down there?"

"Jane agreed to stop yelling at her mother after you blasted through. She's in the library with Ted, or was when Sarah popped in, dropped a small child on me, and disappeared again." Evelyn smiled, but I could see the tension around her eyes, drawn tight and glaring.

"Verity's fine," I said, telling her what she no doubt really wanted to know. "There's been a Covenant attack in New York, and they took out the Nest where our people have been holing up. Some casualties,

Dominic and Verity caused at least half of them, and neither one of them has been injured. I just needed to get Livvy out of there before she got hurt."

Evelyn visibly relaxed. "Oh, those poor kids," she said. "And the dragons . . . ?"

"The Nest looks like it's going to be a total write-off. But they're dragons, so I have no doubt they have the best insurance on the market, and they'll walk away better off than they started." Well, not Cara. And not any others who might have been crushed or cornered during the devastation. But as a whole, the Nest would make it through this.

The dragons who have managed to survive into the modern, human-dominated era are masters of staying alive, no matter what. They'd be able to turn this situation to their advantage, assuming they could survive whatever the Covenant was getting ready to attempt.

"Did Sarah say anything before she"—I waved a hand, trying to articulate a complicated concept without words—"blipped out on you?"

"Oh, she didn't blip this time. She just thrust Olivia at me, muttered something about breaking down crystalline matrices, and ran out the back door. I'm a little concerned about her, but I needed to get Liv down for her nap before I could go after her." Evelyn sighed. "Have things always been this complicated, or have we just reached some sort of complication critical mass, where everything happens all at once forever?"

"Every person you add to a situation adds a whole new set of possible problems," I said. "We've been acquiring new people at a record pace, even before people decided to start making babies again. The trouble with you and Jane deciding to get your babies out of the way when they'd be able to grow up together is that it means they all reached the stage of wanting their own within a few years of each other."

And it *had* been a tactical decision. Jane had never shared Evelyn's love of field work, but she and Evie had both thought it would be good for the cousins to grow up together, giving them a built-in social group that was equipped to actually understand them. By the time Annie had been born and Evie was ready to go back to the field, Jane and I had been accustomed to wrangling all five of the little hellions, and no one had really been considering the population explosion that was waiting twenty-five years or so down the line.

Well, it was here, or the start of it was here, anyway; of the five cousins, only two had actually gotten around to having children of their own. Annie had stated her intention to never have children, and honestly, I wasn't sure it would have been biologically possible with her current partner, or that Elsie or Artie would be able to reproduce if they decided to try, Lilu genes notwithstanding. Lilu can breed with almost anything, but no one had realized when Ted and Jane got married that Fran had been part Kairos. We'd always thought Elsie and Arthur were half-human. Human being a lower percentage of their DNA meant that it was possible even Ted's Lilu genetics wouldn't be enough to let them have babies of their own, assuming they ever wanted to. Sam and Annie were probably a genetic bridge too far.

Although if James and Sam were any indication, Annie was going to deal with her inability to extend the family tree in a traditional manner by going out and press-ganging people into becoming part of the extended clan. One thing was for sure: our numbers weren't trending *downward*.

"Come on," I said, and started for the stairs. "We should let everybody else know what's going on out there, since I'm sure we're going to get sucked into it sooner or later."

"I don't like that Verity's out there without any backup," said Evelyn, following me.

"Olivia's here, which means Very can fight without worrying about her kid, and she has connections in the bogeyman and dragon communities that most people would kill for," I said. "If the Covenant has reached the stage of mass daylight attacks, everyone's going to start calling in allies."

"Meaning Drew might already be on his way to New York," said Evelyn, sounding relieved.

"Probably," I agreed.

Andrew Baker—Drew—was Evie's brother. Adopted, just like she was, and nonhuman, like Sarah and their parents. Unlike them, he was a bogeyman, and had been living with the bogey community in Toronto for the past several years, getting in touch with his roots while keeping an eye out for the Covenant. Drew would make sure the New York bogeymen didn't put too much of the blame for their current situation on Verity's shoulders.

Oh, a substantial amount of it was hers to carry. The Covenant wouldn't have been here *now*, looking for signs of cryptid activity, if Verity hadn't gone on network television as part of a dance competition.

She'd been unmasked when a giant snake burst through the floor, courtesy of a very poorly timed summoning by the local snake cult, and the Covenant's interest in North America had been renewed.

Of course, the family had promptly made things worse by sending Antimony undercover at the Covenant's English headquarters, Penton Hall. While there, she'd managed to attract the attention of Leonard Cunningham, heir apparent to the whole damn thing, and make an enemy of his sister, Chloe. So not only did the Covenant know Verity was alive, they knew she was part of a community. Not great if the goal was disappearing back into peaceful obscurity.

The living room was quiet as we approached, which meant Jane probably hadn't come back yet. We came down the stairs to a much less crowded room than we'd been in before: Kevin was there, still standing next to Thomas, both men with tearstains on their cheeks, and Alice was sitting on the couch, Sarah next to her, the cuckoo having slumped all the way over, so that her head was resting in Alice's lap. Alice was running her fingers through Sarah's hair, slowly, a communal sort of comfort contact that looked like it was helping them both feel better.

I paused, frowning. "Where's Sally?" I asked.

Thomas looked around, focusing on me. "She thought it would be better if she could have her reunion with James free from the prying eyes of honorary parents and authority figures, and went out to locate him on the grounds. I believe he'd gone off with Antimony and some of the others for 'skating practice'?"

"Ah." That made sense. I switched my attention over to Sarah. "Decided not to go back outside?"

"I can only stand the dissonance for so long, and I'm tired after crossing the continent twice in quick succession, especially after modifying the equations the second time so I could bring a second person with me. His mind is . . . not soothing." Sarah sighed heavily, and closed her eyes for a moment. When she opened them again, the white glaze that was so frequently in front of her pupils was gone, and her eyes were unfiltered blue. "It used to be soothing, and now it's not, and feeling like it should be only makes it worse. So I can't be around A-Arthur for too long, even if I should want to be."

"It's not your fault, Sars," said Evelyn firmly. Sarah's age made it easy to forget that she was actually Evelyn's sister, but Evie never forgot. She was staunchly protective of Sarah, when she got the chance to be. "Everyone knows it."

"Elsie hates me for hurting her baby brother," countered Sarah, closing her eyes again, so she wouldn't have to look at the rest of us.

"She tries to say she doesn't, but she does. She's not good enough at hiding her thoughts from me to make it so I won't know that. I can't change her mind as easily as I could someone who's not family, but I can read it. I don't want to."

"Sweetie . . ." We'd all been assuming she was mostly staying in New York and Ohio, with the members of the family who hadn't been impacted by her devastating cross-dimensional journey, because she was trying to avoid Arthur. Maybe she'd been trying to avoid a lot more than just him. "She's mad at you. She doesn't hate you."

"She hates me because she understands something no one else wants to admit."

"What's that?" I asked.

"I killed her brother." The statement was calm, almost placid, and on the surface, it seemed to be virtually serene. It was only if someone really knew her—like I did—that they'd be able to pick up the layers of self-loathing and recrimination under the words. No one would ever be able to blame that girl as much as she was already blaming herself. She would go to her grave blaming herself for something she'd had no control over and couldn't have stopped if she tried.

"Sarah . . ." said Alice.

A sobbing cry from the baby monitor on the coffee table brought Evelyn snapping back to attention. "Looks like Livvy's awake," she said. "I'll be right back down." She bustled away up the stairs.

Thomas focused on me. "Mary, did you have any idea the Covenant was getting this active again?"

"No. As far as I knew, the strike teams you helped clear out were most of the local agents. They must have brought in a whole new detachment—one that's working with deeply modern methods, and not all that concerned about possible collateral damage. They bombed the Nest in broad daylight, and it's in the middle of a pretty popular part of the city. If the fire spreads, a lot of people could die."

"That's a good sign, at least," said Thomas.

Kevin turned to look at him, disbelieving. "Dad?" he asked.

Thomas shook his head. "I know how that sounds. I'm not saying it's better if more people die, or that I want collateral damages. But if the Covenant struck the Nest this boldly, they may have assumed the dragons were keeping *all* their treasures there. Including the irreplaceable one."

"William," said Kevin, understanding.

"Precisely. There is no living member of the Covenant of St. George who has seen a grown male dragon with their own eyes; his true size may have been difficult for them to estimate, depending on the reports they've managed to get. How did they find out he existed?"

"People talk, darling," said Alice, tilting her head back to rest against the cushions as she looked at him, fingers still working through Sarah's hair. "They always have and they always will. The dragons in Southern California knew the Manhattan Nest had a male when I was there with Verity, and if the information crossed a continent, who knows where else it went? It's entirely possible the Covenant had already heard before the televised snake incident, but were dismissing it as wishful thinking and bragging. But then there's a real-live Price making threatening statements on the air, and maybe they start to question how many of the things they've heard out of North America might not have been true after all."

"We know Sarah wiped the memories of the team who grabbed the children; are we sure they didn't document it in some way, or send a report back before they were stopped?" asked Thomas, with dawning horror. "They must have had some sort of mission plan. They must have found the children somehow."

"Dragons aren't the only things living underground in Manhattan," said Alice. "There's a fairly healthy bogeyman community, and you know they view information as a form of currency. I can't even blame whoever told. If they'd been caught by a field team and thought it might get them out of it alive?"

"It wouldn't," said Thomas, with grim finality.

"But people always hope," said Kevin. "That's what lets them keep being people. That's how you're even here. If Mom had given up on hoping and come home when it seemed like the easier thing to do, or if Annie had shrugged and poisoned James's coffee, or if Sarah had stopped trying to find a way to survive the equation that eats worlds, you wouldn't be here. *We* might not be here. So somebody spilled something they shouldn't have, in the hopes that it would keep them alive, and I can't be angry about it. I want to be. But I can't."

Evelyn came padding down the stairs, Olivia holding onto her right hand and walking along beside her, silent and droopy. She perked up when she saw Sarah, releasing Evelyn's hand to race toward her more-familiar cousin.

"Sarah!" she shrieked. "I woke up and it was all fire and now I'm here and where are we?"

Sarah opened her eyes and sat up, repositioning herself to receive a preschooler to the midsection with surprising grace for someone who had never been much for children.

Olivia still ran a little awkwardly, with the funny half-conscious locomotion of someone who was still getting really good at this whole "walking" thing. Human children and toddlers are miraculous. They have so few instincts that watching them figure out the primal motivations they *do* have can be enthralling.

I could spend eternity doing it. Luckily for me, that seems to be precisely what I've committed myself to doing.

Sarah's catch was beautifully timed and spoke not only of telepathic foreknowledge but of experience.

"Your mind *is* soothing," Sarah informed Olivia, who leaned forward to tuck her head into the crook of Sarah's neck, snarling both hands in her cousin's hair. Sarah barely winced.

"It's all right, Mary," said Sarah, glancing from Olivia to me. "Verity trusts me with her, and I'm not going anywhere for at least another hour, unless the dissonance comes into the house badly enough that I have to run away. Even then, I'll probably run upstairs to my bedroom and lock myself in before I go elsewhere."

"We need to call everyone together, and it would be best if you could stay, Sarah," said Kevin. "I think this is important enough to warrant a full family meeting."

Sarah looked momentarily alarmed. "The math doesn't support going to Ohio to get the others," she said. "I would collapse something if I tried."

Since there was a decent chance "something" was local space-time, I was happy to accept that answer, as was Kevin, judging by his brief recoil.

"No one needs to go fetch anyone," he said firmly. "We have a paid videoconferencing service for a reason. We'll just dial them in, so Alex and Shelby can be here. But if the Covenant has stepped it up to daylight assaults, we need to inform everybody."

"My parents, my brother, the carnival . . ." said Evelyn, looking faintly distracted by the scope of the list.

"I can call Rose, but there's no guarantee she'll make it here in time, and I don't think they have good internet on the Ocean Lady," I said.

"It's fine," said Kevin. "If this gets bad enough, the road will inform her soon enough."

Alice stood. "All right. I'm going to go out and find the kids, then. Mary, dear, can you fetch Jane and Theodore?"

"I'm on it," I said. Because what I love doing most of all is trying to convince Jane, when she's in a justified bad mood, to come and play nicely with the rest of her family. It's fun for me. No, really.

Since she wasn't actively calling for my presence *and* she wasn't one of my current charges, being in the same house was about as close as I was going to get. Faster to walk than to try appearing and disappearing and count on hitting my target. I started deeper into the house, heading for the library.

Kevin and Jane were both born in the family home in Buckley Township, Michigan, and raised by the Campbell Family Carnival, which moved around constantly—as carnivals are wont to do—but wintered in Florida, resulting in both of them developing a strong desire to settle somewhere and not live in a house on wheels anymore. But Michigan had been out of the question. The house was too haunted by the things that had happened there, the losses that had already been suffered, and the occasional flitting form of Alice as she passed through on her endless journey. Living there wasn't an option.

Kevin had been the one to hit on the idea of making a place where the whole family could live, forever, and never need to worry. He'd chosen Portland because while the family had no specific allies there or ties to the area, they didn't have enemies, either, and there was a healthy-enough resident cryptid population that fitting in wouldn't be as much of an issue as it would be in some other places. It was outside the Campbell Family's normal circuit, which meant they'd be safe if the Covenant ever came sniffing around; less to tie them to the family was better, as far as Kevin was concerned. The carnival was friendly to the cryptid community, and several of their members were representatives, but they were also relatively defenseless. The kind of cryptids who choose to travel with human carnivals aren't normally your heavy hitters.

So Kevin had pooled his resources, borrowed money from various people who'd been interested in seeing the Prices settled and reasonably stationary, and purchased a large piece of land outside of Portland, one that had been previously developed for logging and farming interests, then abandoned as the economy of the state began to shift. Clearing the old structures off the land and designing a compound that could work with the natural features of the land had been the work of several years, and had been aided by the local cryptid population, many of whom had been deeply curious about their new neighbors. And bit by bit, Kevin's dream had taken shape.

One main house, with enough bedrooms that even now the entire family could come together, extras and recent adoptees included, without being stacked on top of each other. The guest house was only half as large, which still made it large enough to be a permanent residence for two separate families of five, with guests and room to spread out. The barn was reserved for doing horrible things to horrible things, and the training facility had won two family votes—by a landslide—as "structure most likely to get us flagged as a militia by the local government." It was a large, boxy building that contained a full basketball court and flat roller derby track, suitable for most forms of physical conditioning that didn't require a swimming pool or a horse.

We didn't have either of those things. Kevin had been building his childhood dreams, not his childhood unreasonable wish-fulfillments, and while the compound couldn't be called "reasonable" by any normal standards, it was small enough to manage. Mostly.

The main library was close enough to the living room that it was a fairly short walk, and I slowed as I approached the door. It was open. While people might use the library for semi-private meetings, closing the doors simply wasn't done unless it was a matter of life or death. The library was where we kept all the publicly accessible field guides and biology texts, and without them, people could find themselves getting seriously hurt.

I could hear low voices coming from inside, not loud enough for me to make out words or individual speakers, but enough to give me tone. The conversation was relatively calm, no shouting or raised voices. I still gathered a fistful of my own hair, holding it up and shaking it as I stepped into the room.

"White flag," I explained, before letting it fall back down around my shoulders. As expected, Ted and Jane were settled in two of the library's overstuffed reading chairs, Jane perched on the very edge of hers, resting her knees against his. They were holding hands. Somewhat more surprisingly, Elsie was also there, leaning against the nearby wall, arms crossed and expression mulish. None of them looked particularly surprised to see me. I've always been the family peacekeeper.

I suppose it's a natural extension of my position as babysitter. When you're babysitting, keeping the kids in your charge from killing each other is a large part of the job. If you can't do it, you're not going to have a job for long. Or kids to take care of, for that matter.

Jane had been more temperamental than her brother basically from the start, and knowing Alice as well as I did, I sometimes thought their antagonistic relationship had always been inevitable; even if Alice had somehow been able to stick around, she was hard-headed enough that she and Jane would have been clashing from basically day one. Instead, they'd clashed in absentia, and the mother Jane railed against was a more idealized, less human version of the woman who actually existed. Jane knew that. She just couldn't seem to stop. She looked at me with weary resignation.

"I guess you're here to tell me I'm not being fair, because she came back and really, that's what I always used to say I wanted," she said. "For Mom to admit that we were more important than running around chasing a ghost." She paused before adding, "No offense."

"None taken," I reassured her, and moved to one of the open chairs. "And no, that's not why I'm here. You're a grownup. If you want to keep hating your mother, that's up to you. I wouldn't, if I were you, but I'm not you, and so I don't really think I get a say. Now, if you were still my responsibility, I'd send you to your room to think about how we talk to people in this house and not come out until you could be civil, but you took yourself to another room when you needed to, and that shows solid emotional regulation. I'm proud of you for that."

Jane perked up a bit but didn't change positions. Elsie scowled at me. I tilted my head back, meeting her eyes.

"Something you wanted to say?" I asked.

"I don't understand why no one else is mad at Sarah for what she did," she said, choosing her words with slow precision. "I get why they weren't mad in the beginning, when we didn't understand how much damage she'd actually done—we were all just so relieved to have him home again that we couldn't see past it. But whatever she slammed together isn't my brother."

"Elsie," said Jane, disapprovingly.

"What? You see it too. He doesn't like the things he used to like, he doesn't sound the way he used to sound—he's not the *same*, Mom, and that's not even going into his weird 'call me Arthur' routine. That's not Artie."

"Maybe it's not," I agreed. "Maybe he's somebody new now, because you can't experience death of the psyche and come back unchanged. But that's not Sarah's fault, and based on what everyone says about what happened—including Arthur, and including the mice—she didn't do anything on purpose. He touched her when he should have known better, and she wasn't in control of herself at the time. It's like when your mother was eight and shot Kevin with her slingshot. The ball bearing went clean through his arm. He still has the scar. But he wasn't in her field when she lined up the shot, and it's not her fault that he decided it would be funny to run into the way when she was already pulled back and in the process of releasing. Sometimes we hurt each other, and it's always our responsibility, but it's not always our *fault*. You can be mad at Sarah if you want to. I won't blame you. But I wish you could stop blaming *her* for something she didn't do on purpose."

Elsie's scowl deepened. "She's dangerous."

"We're all dangerous, El. She's not special just because she's dangerous."

"Why does no one want to see what I'm saying?"

"Maybe because she's family, and we love her."

Elsie screwed her eyes shut in frustration. "That isn't *fair*."

"Maybe not, but it's what we've got."

Ted sighed. "Why are you here, Mary?"

"Family meeting," I said. "We're going to set up videoconferencing for everyone who can't be here physically. There's been a Covenant attack on the dragons in New York, and yes, there were casualties, although our people are fine. It looks like they're moving into the next stage of this war."

It had been a cold war for long enough that it had become easy to pretend open hostilities would always be a problem for the future, something we would never have to deal with in the living "now." We didn't have that luxury anymore. The Covenant was moving, and that meant they were changing the game. We needed to be prepared for whatever they were going to do next. And we didn't know what information they had.

Dance or Die had been filmed in Southern California, which meant they knew that Verity, at the very least, was sometimes on the West Coast. How did they get their information about the dragons? Observation, blackmail, or taking people apart? The family had done their best to stay below the radar for a long time, but that sort of stealth only worked so long as the Covenant was on a different continent, not plugged in to the North American rumor mill.

Here, everyone who was connected with the cryptid world, even tangentially, knew about the Prices. To the hunters and poachers, they were nightmare figures that would sweep out of nowhere to disrupt carefully laid plans. To the cryptids, they were either the monsters in their individual closets, bloodthirsty killers who would never be truly separate from their Covenant roots, or undependable saviors who could solve any problem if they were in the area when it happened. Start asking questions in North America, and you'd very quickly find proof that the Price family never truly died out, only managed to become slightly less visible from space.

From the looks on their faces, Jane and Ted both knew this. Ted grimaced and stood, tugging Jane along with him. He put an arm around her shoulders, holding her protectively close.

"Can they find us here?" he asked.

"I don't know," I replied, honestly. "It depends on how many teams they have in the country right now, since we know they just took some losses in Manhattan. They could be covering this coast, but it's a matter of manpower and how long they've been moving into position. They have the advantage on us here."

"Doesn't someone always?" asked Elsie. She pushed away from the wall as she started for the door, passing my seat. I turned to watch her go.

"Elsie—"

"'Family meeting' means the whole family," she said. "I don't get to skip it just because I'm mad. And I *am* mad. I'm not going to stop being mad because you tell me I'm not being fair. Maybe I won't ever stop being mad. No one gets to make me."

She left then, before anyone could say anything. Ted sighed. He looked at Jane. I looked at her in turn, waiting for her to speak.

Jane frowned, just a little, glancing down at the floor. "I guess I've taught her a lot about holding a grudge, huh?"

"Just a little," I said. "You might want to work on that."

"Might be too late."

"Sadly true."

"Sarah really didn't mean to hurt Arti—Arthur. I know that. Everyone knows that, except for Elsie. And Sarah, I guess. That girl's already beating herself up enough. If he hadn't come back, would Elsinore be half this angry at her cousin?"

"If your mom had never bothered coming to check on you when you were a kid, would you be so mad at her now? Or are you mad because she kept coming back and reminding you of how she wasn't going to stay?"

Jane was quiet for a moment. Then, finally, she said, "I think . . . if she had just vanished when I was a baby, and I was meeting her for the first time right now, I think I would probably be a lot more inclined to forgive her for what she wasn't able to give me then."

"Oh?"

"If she wasn't going to stick around, I didn't want her to come at all. And I didn't know how to say that, and it always made Kevin so *happy* to see her, so I didn't want to say it, but it feels true." She looked at me mournfully. "The damage has been done at this point. Saying 'I might hurt less if things had been different' is like saying 'We wouldn't have as much trouble with the Covenant if all their weapons were made of cottage cheese.' But I still think it's right."

"That's a start," I said, and offered her my hand.

After a pause, she took it.

When I came back into the living room with Jane and Ted, Sam was on his back under the television stand, tinkering with the wires connecting various black boxes and transmitters to the screen, while James focused his attention on the laptop he had balanced open on his knees. Antimony had a large bowl of popcorn kernels, popping them with the hand she held spread above them. Sarah and Sally were seated on the couch to either side of Alice, both looking deeply uncomfortable. Olivia was still on Sarah's lap. Thomas remained next to Kevin at the end of the room, while Elsie had stopped next to Evelyn, the two of them sharing a loveseat.

It was possibly the most tension I'd seen at a family gathering since the decision was made to allow Verity to compete on reality television, and that meeting had come with flowcharts and PowerPoint arguments explaining why she wouldn't be putting the rest of us at risk. Well, that had been incorrect. Hopefully, whatever decisions we reached today would be better ones.

It wasn't like they could be all that much worse, no matter how badly this went.

Sarah waved me over. I walked toward her, and she whispered something to Olivia, gesturing toward me. Livvy looked disappointed but climbed off of her lap, moving to stand next to me, taking my hand while she popped her other thumb into her mouth like she was still two, and not four, heading toward five. Sarah shot me a grateful look and then winked out, vanishing like she had never been there at all.

"Where—" began Sally.

"She'll be right back," said Alice. "She's just making sure her mother is all set up on their end, and she's done the math to be sure she can pick up something called Greg. He's an emotional support animal? What the hell is an emotional support animal?"

Antimony snorted clear amusement. "You might be better off asking what the hell is a Greg, but I wouldn't want to spoil the surprise."

"She didn't say any of that. I don't like this thing where you have telepaths who can just drop information into your heads without informing the rest of the class," said Sally sourly.

"Sorry, hon," said Alice. "She's being careful with you, because you're new."

"Don't worry," said Arthur, coming in from the kitchen with a tide of mice at his heels. "That won't last."

He sounded bitter, and so sad that I wanted to go to him and tell him things were going to be all right. I didn't, because there was a very good chance they weren't going to be. He moved to take one of the remaining open seats, and the mice spread out through the room like a drop of food coloring swirling into a glass of milk, until they were everywhere, the floor, the furniture, the people. They just kept on coming, dozens of them becoming hundreds, finally tapering off as what must have been the entire resident colony joined us in the living room.

I can hear you, said Sarah's voice in my head, as clear as if she were standing next to me. From the way everyone but Arthur and Elsie twitched, or tensed, or angled their heads, I wasn't the only one; she was close enough to be broadcasting to us all. Of course, with her recent increases to her range, that didn't really tell me much.

Greg and I are out by the firepit; I'll listen to the meeting from here, she continued. *I don't think I should bring him into the living room with new people, but I need him or I'm going to panic, and that would be . . . very not good.*

I was willing to believe her on that one.

"Okay, honey," I said under my breath. "You just let us know if you have anything you want to contribute."

Sarah didn't answer, but I felt her approval.

Sam pushed himself out from under the television. "Okay, that should get it," he said. "Jimmy, you wanna?"

James tapped the keyboard, and a loading screen sprung up on the television, quickly subdividing into multiple small black boxes, each with its own spiraling hold symbol.

"We're ready," he said. "Opening the meeting now."

There was nothing to do after that but wait.

Five

"Yeah, no. Forgiveness isn't an obligation. It doesn't get to be. You forgive someone when you want to, or when the anger gets too heavy to carry around anymore. No one gets to tell you it's time. Time may never come."

—Rose Marshall

The living room of a small survivalist compound about an hour's drive east of Portland, Oregon, surrounded by more people (and mice) than is necessarily comfortable

One by one, the little loading spirals vanished and were replaced by familiar faces, some more anxious than others. Verity and Dominic were the first to come online, their backdrop a stony gray wall and the glitter of carelessly mounded-up gold. That wasn't the real attention-grabber of the scene, though, and neither was the blood on Dominic's lip or the massive shiner covering Verity's left eye.

No, that honor went to the reptilian head the size of a Volkswagen Beetle that peered curiously out from between and well behind them, far enough back to be contained within the small frame. The dragon—because that couldn't be anything other than an adult male dragon, even if it had been trying to be something else—had pearly green scales and pumpkin-orange eyes, and an expression of deep concern.

The mice cheered as the absent family members appeared, rejoicing in the image of their gods, and then fell eerily silent, so they could make note of every word and intonation. They had already decided, in their strange Aeslin way, that this was one of those moments that was going to be recreated beat for beat at some seemingly random point in the future.

"Hey, Livvy," said Verity, exhaling in her relief as she waved to her daughter through the screen. Dominic waved as well, although he didn't smile as widely as his wife, probably out of a desire not to split his lip even further.

Olivia pulled her thumb out of her mouth. "Can I come home now, Mom?"

"Sorry, baby, but it's not safe right now," said Verity.

"But I don't want to be here!" Livvy waved her free hand wildly, still holding on to me with the other. "I want *home*."

"Soon, pumpkin," said Dominic.

"I want my daddy," said Livvy. She sounded totally miserable. "I want home."

I winced. She was too young to really understand what was about to happen, and too old for us to assume she wouldn't pick up enough to be terrified. "Do you want to go see Greg?" I asked her.

"Greg?"

"He's outside, with Sarah," I said. "I can take you there."

Olivia adored Greg, as only a small child with no preconceptions or preexisting phobias could. She brightened and nodded.

"Let's go."

"Thank you, Mary," said Verity.

"It's my job," I said, and led Livvy out of the room, with Evie calling, "We'll wait for you," after me.

I walked Olivia to the front door and out, circling the house to the firepit. It was a short-enough distance, but walking it was tedious compared to my normal forms of travel. Since pulling Livvy through the land of the dead wasn't an option, I was constrained to her speed.

Then we were approaching the firepit, and she spotted Sarah, seated with the vast, hairy lump of Greg leaning up against her leg. Olivia squealed, pulling her hand out of mine as she took off running for the giant spider, flinging herself at him without hesitation.

Mary? Sarah's mental voice was confused.

Can you just watch her for me for now?

Sure. Greg likes her.

Great. Get someone to call me back to the living room?

I heard Evie's mental call a split second later, and waved at Sarah and Livvy as I blipped out, returning to the rest of the family.

They had clearly waited for me. Thomas was sitting bolt upright, eyes as wide as saucers behind his glasses, which he reached up and deliberately removed, wiping them on his shirt before putting them back on, and asking, in a delicate tone, "Now that we're ready to resume . . . Pardon me if this is inappropriate, but Verity and Dominic, who is that behind you?"

"Oh, this is William," said Verity, gesturing to the dragon like the presence of an entire male dragon was no big deal. "We're using his account, since our computers went up in the fire."

"My wireless is extremely stable, and my monitor is very large," said William. His tone was dry, his accent as British as Thomas's, although clearly much, much older; he was from an earlier era, a time when things were said a little differently. "Some of you are familiar. Others are not. As this matter has already impacted me and mine, I requested to attend this meeting."

"We're sorry about Cara," I said. So far as I knew, she was the only dragon to have died in the attack on the Nest. Being essentially fireproof is sometimes a useful adaptation.

William briefly closed his eyes. "She was among the most recent of my wives," he said. "She should have had many years to spend with her sisters and her children, and with me. She will be properly grieved."

From the looks on the faces of more than half the people in the room, they had just realized we had no information on draconic funeral rites, and were going to wind up asking some vaguely inappropriate questions later. So long as they didn't do it right now, I didn't mind that much.

"We're just waiting on the others now," said Kevin. "Very, you're sure you're all right? You don't need reinforcements?"

"Honestly, I want to call an all-hands and scramble every gun we've got out here, but I don't think it would help," she said. "Olivia's safe in Portland, and I need her kept as far as possible away from this whole mess. As long as I know she's okay, I think I can get through this."

"Istas was fairly badly burned, but she's at St. Giles's for treatment, and Dr. Morrow expects her to make a full recovery," said Dominic. "Ryan turned himself to stone as soon as he realized what was happening, and he's fine, although angry with himself for allowing her to be put at risk."

That sounds about right, said Sarah.

"Sarah says that sounds about right," I said. No one looked particularly surprised that I was relaying messages from her when she wasn't in the room, but no one else looked like they had been about to speak, either. She was listening to us all, but apparently, I'd been chosen to serve as her intercom. Fascinating.

Another square blinked on, and the mice cheered again as Uncle Mike in Chicago appeared, his wife Lea visible behind him, along with several lesser gorgons, the snakes atop their heads exposed and twining together anxiously. Their surroundings were palatial, polished wood and hanging velvet, and clearly the lobby of an expensive hotel. They were at the Carmichael, then, a gorgon-owned establishment that had been the heart of Chicago's cryptid community for decades.

"Miss Evelyn," said Mike, respectfully, with a nod for the lady of the house. Then he looked around the room, clearly taking note of the new faces, and raising his eyebrows at the sight of Thomas, being smart enough to know what a heavily tattooed man who looked that much like Kevin was likely to mean. "Ma'am, is that your father-in-law?"

"Yes, it is, and you know you don't have to stand on protocol with me," said Evie. "Thank you so much for joining us on such short notice."

"And thank you for including us in a family meeting," said Lea. "I know you must be taking a very generous view of the word 'family' for us to receive an invitation, but we still appreciate it. We heard a rumor that there had been an attack in New York? Is everyone okay?"

"Yes, there was, and no, we took some losses, but we can't recap the whole thing every time someone logs on," said Verity. "Let's let the others get here, okay?"

Lea nodded.

She and Evelyn chatted quietly as one by one, the other windows came on. Alex and Shelby in the kitchen in Ohio, Martin visible behind them; a dimly lit tent wherever the Campbell Family Carnival was currently staked, the carnival's current leadership clustered around a splintery wooden picnic table; a motel room in Toronto, the curtains drawn and Drew barely visible in the shadows; even a chrome-and-vinyl diner that looked like something straight out of the 1950s, Rose and Apple sitting side by side in a narrow booth. I blinked at that one.

Apple almost never leaves the Ocean Lady, which is both a literal goddess and a level of the lands of the dead. She was calling in from a whole separate layer of reality. Talk about long distance.

"I think that's everyone," said Kevin. "Can everybody hear me?"

General assent from the group confirmed that yes, they could hear him. There were some discontented mutters from the carnival, as not everyone seemed to have appreciated being summoned to a meeting.

"We're getting to it," said Kevin. "Verity? Would you care to make your report?"

Verity took a deep breath as she shifted positions to put herself at the center of the screen. "Approximately an hour and a half ago, the Covenant of St. George launched an attack on the aboveground Nest of the dragons of Manhattan. One dragon, two bogeymen, and eleven Madhura were killed in the strike, and far more were injured. Seven Covenant field agents were killed in our response. We don't know how many of them escaped. They were using missiles fired from nearby rooftops, to hit our roof, and they took out half of it, setting the rest on fire. The structure has been effectively demolished. The dragons are fireproof, and were able to clear out their hoard before the upper floor collapsed completely."

Meaning the authorities would find signs that the place had been being used for illegal habitation, but not the ridiculous amount of gold that had been stored there for the health and comfort of the dragons.

"Let me be clear," said Verity. "We have no idea how the Covenant was able to locate us. The last known field teams in the city were eliminated four months ago. We've seen no signs that they'd been replaced, and we've been watching. Our best guess is that they managed to smuggle another team in somehow, and they combined the intelligence they had from the first team with their own more subtle information-gathering efforts to pinpoint the location of the Nest."

"What else do they know?" asked Mike. "How many of them are left?"

"We don't know," said Dominic. "We didn't even know they were here until they attacked us."

"Did Kitty make it out?" asked Drew.

Verity nodded. "She's fine. Some minor lacerations from trying to dig the bogeymen we lost out of the rubble, but nothing that can't be taken care of quickly. Why?"

"Let her know I'm going to be calling in a few favors and activating the Toronto gossip tree," said Drew, gravely. "If they got this information from the bogeyman community, even tangentially, someone will know about it. If they didn't, there's still a good chance one of us will know about it."

"I'll do the same here on the West Coast," said Jane. Drew nodded his approval. Everyone in the family knows that when you want gossip, you go to Jane. She's plugged into more whisper networks than anyone else, even most bogeymen, and she has the credit to burn—and the secrets to trade—to learn virtually anything she wants to know.

"If you start picking up activity traces all the way out there, we have a problem," said Drew.

"I think we already have a problem, Uncle Drew," said Verity sourly.

"I mean a bigger one," he said. "An attack in Manhattan is awful, but it mirrors what we've been seeing. The Covenant is mostly European, so they're assigning target priority based on what they believe about the United States. And if you listen to media, the only important cities we have are New York and San Francisco."

"On behalf of Chicago, I would like to invite them to screw off," said Mike.

"Yes, we—" Drew stopped as another window blinked onto the screen.

This one showed a redheaded woman in some sort of underground chamber, various blondes clustered behind her, all of them looking absolutely terrified. Kevin and Evelyn both sat up straighter.

"Hello," said Evelyn. "You are?"

"Osana," said Alice, sounding delighted. "Hello, dear! How's the new husband working out?"

"Oh, he's keeping the ladies quite distracted with his care needs," said Osana, politely. "He'll never be a husband for my daughters—wrong species—but he'll make a fine mate for theirs."

Verity interjected then. "I sent an invite to the Burbank Nest, because I was near there when the snake incident happened. They're not family, but they may be at risk because of my actions."

Antimony rolled her eyes and muttered something. Verity, for once, ignored her.

"We're here to observe, if that's all right," said Osana.

William lifted his head and said, solemnly, "I vote they stay. They have one of my sons, and an attack on them is an attack on me, at least until he reaches his adulthood."

We're still learning the social rituals of dragons, which seems silly, given how long we've been existing alongside them, but is a natural consequence of having cut the species in half and driven them to the border of extinction rather than sitting down and asking them how they liked to do things. William's statement was firmly enough made that it became inarguable, and might well cause serious problems if we tried to contest it.

"That's fine," said Kevin. "Honestly, it's probably a good thing that you're here. Do you have any contacts with your local bogeyman community?"

"This is Hollywood," said Osana. "We're some of the most in-demand extras and audience-fillers in this city. We have contacts everywhere. What do you need to know?"

"Has there been any muttering about the Covenant of St. George recently? Anything at all? It doesn't matter how small, or how silly, it seemed when you heard it; we're looking for signs that they're outside New York, or that they're planning more attacks like the one they just pulled off."

"Not that I've heard, but I'm not the one to talk to," said Osana. "I'll ask Brenna as soon as she gets back, and if she doesn't know, she'll be able to find out. I know the atmosphere around town's been tense the past few months, but the atmosphere around town is always tense, if you're talking to the right people."

"Thank you," said Kevin. "All right: you all know what we know now. The Covenant got a new strike team into Manhattan and destroyed the aboveground Nest. New safehouses will need to be established, and until we find out where they got their information, we'll have to be very, very careful. For the moment, assume anyone not on this call may have been compromised unless you have strong reasons to believe otherwise."

General nods and murmurs greeted this declaration. No one looked happy about it. Everyone had a friend or relative who couldn't be present, and the desire to trust them was as strong as it had ever been. It was, sadly, still understandable.

"Does anyone have any questions? If not, thank you all for your time, and please, be careful out there."

Before anyone could sign off, someone screamed. I searched the monitor, trying to determine which of the smaller screens the sound had come from. Everyone was yelling, leaning closer to their cameras, trying to see what was going on. Someone else screamed, and the square for the Campbell Family Circus was briefly outlined in white, marking them as the dominant speakers.

The carnival elders were scrambling to their feet, the only ones not looking at their screen. Instead, they had turned to look toward the tent wall as more screams erupted in the distance.

Jane leaned closer.

"Where are you right now?" she asked.

The elders, yelling and pointing, didn't reply to her question.

"Dammit, *where are you*?" she demanded. "We can't send help if we don't know where you are!"

Another scream from outside, and one of the carnival elders

whipped around, apparently grabbing the laptop they had been using to connect to us. "Boise!" he yelled, desperately.

Something hit the top of their tent. We saw it bulge inward. Then there was a flash of light, and their window was gone, replaced by nothingness for a bare second before the other windows expanded to fill the space it had occupied.

Alice was already on her feet. So was Antimony.

So was Jane.

"What are you doing?" asked Kevin.

"Boise's about six hours away by car," said Jane. "I'm going to get our people."

Sam rose. "Looks like we're having a road trip."

"Apple?" Antimony looked to the screen. "Any chance of an assist?"

"My routewitches are not a rideshare service," said Apple. She looked as distressed and off-balance as the rest of us. Looking away from the camera, she addressed someone we couldn't see. "Do we have anyone?"

There must have been an answer, because she nodded as she looked back to the camera. "Bon can be in your area in twenty minutes. She's out gathering distance on one of the new passenger vans, so she's making loops around the country. Her vehicle seats five, if you don't mind being a little cozy."

"We don't," said Alice, before Jane could object. "Thank you, Your Majesty."

"You did us a solid in New York," said Apple. "Just don't get too used to it."

"I think we can now safely say that there's more than one Covenant team operative," said Mike. "Everyone stay alert and mind your twenty. We're going to stay put for right now, help the Carmichael shore up against possible attack, and see if we can make contact with our local Nest."

"I'll be reaching out to the Nests who have been in contact with us since my awakening, to see if any are prepared to take custody of my sons," said William. "Negotiations are still ongoing, but our survival counts for more than a fair contract. Any of them who are safe and ready will find themselves approved."

For a human to speak so casually of selling his children—some younger than Olivia—to strangers would have been a horrifying violation of social norms. For William, the last known adult male dragon, it was a necessary concession to the situation his species was in.

Female dragons could reproduce parthenogenically, for centuries if needed, but couldn't have male offspring without a male getting involved. When the Covenant had hunted the great male dragons to their supposed extinction, they had rendered the species all-female and frozen.

Finding William asleep under Manhattan changed everything, where the dragons were concerned. He took half the dragons in the Manhattan Nest as his wives, and they began bearing male children. The other Nests were understandably interested in those boys, and as dragons only got larger as they aged, it was in their best interests to transport them early so they could grow up in what would become their territories. The adult females would raise the infant males to eventually become husbands to their daughters, and the species would endure.

There are a lot of human social rules that don't translate well to intelligent but nonhuman people. This was one of them.

Since dragons biologically need gold for good health and strong children, it made sense that part of the negotiation for the boys was based around payment. Money could be turned into gold, and gold would mean more baby boys were born. Everyone benefitted. The species would have some nasty genetic bottlenecking to deal with if we didn't find another adult male, but for the moment, they had a degree of hope they hadn't possessed in a very long time.

"I'm on the bogeymen," said Drew. "I'll call when I have something."

"We're going to be handling cleanup here," said Verity. "Mary, tell Livvy we love her and we'll see her soon."

"I will," I said.

"Bon's en route," said Apple. "If you're catching a ride with her, get moving."

One by one, the windows winked out, until the screen was dark.

While it was natural for almost everyone to want to check on the carnival where Kevin and Jane grew up, the people who'd been the first to stand made the most sense. Jane was still in close, regular contact with the carnival; Antimony had trained there, and so had Alice, although her training had been years previous. Sam, meanwhile, was the grandson of another carnival's owner, as well as being ridiculously strong and fast. As a group, they were the best equipped to go.

Even if it did mean putting Jane in a car with her mother for six hours, which seemed like a good way for somebody to wind up dead. Neither of them looked happy about it. Really, everyone looked distressed. Even the mice weren't cheering. Seeing the proof that we and our allies were being hunted down wasn't precisely comforting.

"I'll be right back, I'm riding to Boise with you all," I said. Jane looked relieved. Antimony just nodded.

I disappeared.

Sarah was still out by the firepit with Greg and Olivia. Me knowing where that was, plus multiple family members being there, meant that when I aimed for it, I hit my destination, blipping from the living room to the edge of the dirt-and-gravel ground. The grass had been cleared back from around the central bonfire, and from the logs, creating a decent firebreak. Not that they needed it much these days, not with Annie standing by and ready to shut any runaway sparks down with a wave of her hand.

Sarah was sitting on one of the logs and Olivia was on the ground near her feet, both of which were normal. The shape Olivia was snuggling up to was a lot less normal, by Earth standards. Oh, it was a standard-enough design, fuzzy, with eight legs and too many eyes, but the size was daunting. Not that many jumping spiders the size of bears locally.

None of us has ever been able to figure out how he stays alive. It's not just that he's more than pushing the upper limits of how long we know jumping spiders can live; it's that the laws of physics should be looking to have a word with him. Annie swears he must have lungs in there somewhere, to explain how he doesn't suffocate, but his legs are normal spider legs, and the square-cube law says they should shatter in Earth's combination of gravity and atmosphere. Apparently, extradimensional spiders get their own laws of physics.

That, or even the universe is afraid of what would happen if they killed a cuckoo queen's emotional support animal. Even if it is a fuck-off enormous spider. Sarah was stroking his head with one hand, her head bowed so that her hair fell all around her face and masked it from view.

I walked cautiously closer. Greg caught sight of me and turned his body slightly in my direction. Spiders don't have necks, so this was a more involved motion than it would have been coming from a mammal. His pedipalps waved, a gesture that looked more like a friendly greeting than a threat. He knew me, after all. Not that it would have mattered if he'd been threatening me. I don't particularly *want* to be mauled by a giant spider, but being dead means I don't have to worry about that kind of thing very much. He had one arm tucked around Olivia, which was far more of a concern. I'd be fine, and she would be dead.

"Sarah? Honey?"

"They're going, aren't they?" She didn't lift her head. "Running off to join the carnival."

"Are you all right?"

"I can't read minds as far away as the people everyone was talking to," she said. "Not unless I'm really trying, and I don't like to really try. It makes my brain feel buzzy, like it's been carbonated, and sometimes I'm scared there's still more changing to come. I don't want to change more than I already have."

"Only way to stop changing is to die," I said, walking over to settle next to her. "And honestly, even dying doesn't stop it completely. When I died, I would never have worn *pants* in front of *boys*. I didn't know what a mobile phone was, or how many episodes of *Criminal Minds* I could watch in one sitting. And I didn't know you. Knowing you is a change I would hate to have missed."

"It's not the same for you," she said, still petting Greg. "You were human when you died. Technically, you're still human now, just human and dead. I'm not human. I'm an insect, and insects metamorphize under the right conditions. I've already done it once. I don't want to do it again. What if next time my skin splits open and a big bug comes out, like happened in that one *Resident Evil* game? I don't want to be a giant wasp."

"Okay, you're right; biologically, you have some concerns that I don't share. But I don't understand how they apply right now. Can you explain it to me?"

Sarah sighed heavily and raised her head, looking at me. That white film was covering her pupils again. It struck me, and not for the first time, that none of us was really equipped to help her. The best we could do was listen, and try.

"I can't read minds as far away as Boise or New York," she said. "I'm not like you. I don't hear my family calling even if they're on the other side of the world."

"Until we broke my tie to the crossroads, I wasn't like me, either," I said.

"I know." She ducked her head. "I'm worried because a bunch of you are going to go away and I won't be able to get to you if something goes wrong."

"Okay. So let's try to find a way around that." I shrugged. "Every hour, call for me in your heart, just as loudly as you can. You're family. I'll hear you, and I'll be able to come. If I can't come for some reason, like if we're still in the car, I'll ask Annie to text you. And then once I come, I can tell you what's been going on, and if we need more help, I can ask you to do your space-bending trick and join us." I waggled a hand like I was trying to illustrate her mechanism of teleportation. "Although, about that . . . if you're worried about stretching to read minds that are too far away from you, isn't hopping around like distance is irrelevant just as bad?"

"Distance is a sort of math," said Sarah. "Nothing is any farther away from where we are right now than anything else. It's . . . it's hard to explain? It's like I'm a fixed point, and all I'm doing is moving myself. It doesn't feel any more like stretching than taking a step does. It's all moving. I can't make the same trip too many times in quick succession without twisting the numbers, and that's bad for reality, and I can't transport people unless I have the time to line up the equations, but I can come to you if you need me."

I nodded, no more sure what she was talking about, but substantially less worried about hurting her by mistake. "Okay, sweetie. You're going to be okay staying here with Art—with Arthur?"

"I have to be." She sighed deeply. "He's not Artie anymore, and I know it's not my fault, but it is, and Elsie's right to be so angry with me. I still love him. Isn't that silly? He thinks he loves me too, and that's the worst part of all, because I love a dead man and he loves a patchwork girl made up of other people's memories. Some of them were mine. I don't think I left him any choice. Once I broke him down and put him back together again, I became inevitable, whether or not that was fair."

"It's not fair, to either one of you." I stood. "I love you, you know. And not because you made me."

"I know, Mary," she said, and smiled at me, sweet and sad. "Apple said she'd send a routewitch. Well, the routewitch is here. You should go."

A bare second later, I heard Antimony's silent call. I nodded to Sarah and popped out, outside at the top of the driveway, where a black minivan that looked like it belonged in the hands of a suburban soccer mom was stopped, engine idling. Roughly half the family was outside, Jane and Antimony each equipped with backpacks, while the others were empty-handed. Jane was talking quietly with Ted, and Alice with Thomas, the two women forming a doubtless unintentional mirror of one another. Annie and Sam were a few feet away, being addressed by Kevin and Evelyn.

This wasn't necessarily the group of people I would have chosen for a field operation, mostly because I had some valid concerns about Jane, her mother, and so-called "friendly fire," but I had to admit it was reasonably balanced. Alice was ridiculously lucky and an excellent shot; Jane was familiar with the modern makeup of the carnival and reasonably skilled in hand-to-hand combat; Antimony could start fires with her mind, and Sam was Sam. They might kill each other, but they would do a lot of damage to the Covenant first.

The routewitch behind the wheel leaned out the driver's-side window, frowning at the group. She was a Caucasian woman in her mid-forties, hair dyed black and streaked with bands of lilac, making her look like a particularly over-dramatic orchid. "Hoy," she called, Irish accent thickly coating her voice. "You lot coming, or nah? I need to get back on the road if I want to make Chicago by nightfall."

"We're coming," called Antimony. She hugged her mother quickly, kissed her father on the cheek, and then jogged toward the van, Sam close on her heels.

"Shotgun," said Alice, turning to stroll more languidly toward the van.

I was tempted to claim seniority, but doing so would have meant putting Alice and Jane in the backseat together, as both the van's rows of seats had space for two, and Annie and Sam were already settling in the far back. Better to give Alice the front and give Jane a little distance.

I slid into the middle seat, smiling at Jane as she buckled in beside me. She scowled back.

"Thanks, Bon," said Alice, as she got into the front and turned her attention to the routewitch. "You hear I finally found Thomas?"

"I see him, and the whole damn network knows you went and found him," said the routewitch, cranking her engine back to full. It came to life, smooth and easy, a rumble like a purring tiger. It sounded like more power than belonged in a minivan. "We're pretty well impressed. Pretty well horrified, too, but the impressed takes priority. Your lot does like to break the laws of nature, no?"

"Says the woman who's about to break the laws of time and space getting us to Boise," said Alice.

Bon laughed and hit the gas.

Six

"Mothers and daughters . . . oh, they always fight, and they don't always make up. People will tell you they do, but those are always the people who had easy relationships with their mothers. Sometimes the schisms go too deep. Sometimes nothing heals."

—Eloise Dunlavy

Packed into a minivan being driven unreasonably fast by an Irish routewitch, heading for Boise, Idaho

SOMEHOW, BON'S RADIO PICKED up local stations from Dublin, Ireland, something which sent Alice into gales of laughter when she realized what was happening, and which caused Jane to roll her eyes and sink deeper into the sulk she'd been cultivating since we left the compound. I frowned, leaning over to pat her knee in what I hoped would be a reassuring manner.

"You didn't have to come, you know," I said.

"They're my family more than anyone's," she replied. "And *she*"—she jerked her head toward Alice to illustrate who she was referring to—"is never going to respect me if I don't do more fieldwork."

"Honey . . ." Alice twisted around in her seat, frowning as she peered into the back seat. "You don't need me to respect you. I *love* you. Isn't that enough?"

"I see the way you look at me, and the way you look at Kevin," snapped Jane. "Or the way you treat Arthur as compared to Alex. You only respect us if we live our lives the way *you* would want us to live them. If you're actually planning to stick around this time, which I frankly doubt, you're *going* to respect me, and that means I'm going to show you that I stay out of the field because I *choose* to, not because I *have* to."

"Jane . . ." Alice visibly wilted, shooting me a pleading look before she sank back into her seat, facing forward once more.

Bon patted her reassuringly on the shoulder and kept on driving. The minivan was chewing up road faster than would have been possible with anyone else behind the wheel. Routewitches are sort of the base form of whatever it was Sarah was becoming, although from what I could tell, they had a slightly better understanding of what it was they were doing when they traveled. For them, distance translated directly into power, and they could somehow borrow potential power from their planned routes to bend the map, shortening the distance they actually had to travel.

Think of it as someone saying they could hand you twenty dollars to use in buying lunch, or they could just hand you lunch. The end result is the same—you get fed either way—but one way takes longer. By bending the map willy-nilly, Bon was sacrificing the power she *would* have acquired for covering that distance, but her reward was the distance already covered, with no need for the boring travel parts.

It should have taken more than six hours to get to Boise, without accounting for bathroom breaks and snack stops. At our current rate, we were going to be there within the hour, which was great, since it meant Jane wouldn't have a chance to murder her mother. I loved them both, but at the end of the day, Alice was the one I'd actually been hired to care for. If it came to blows, I knew where I would have to intercede.

"See?" hissed Jane, leaning closer to me. "She doesn't respect me. She's never going to respect me. She couldn't stick around to raise me, and now she blames me for not growing up to be a tiny clone of herself."

It was my turn to sigh. "Jane, you know that's not true."

"And *you* know she thinks the only real work happens in the field." Jane folded her arms and flopped backward, sulking like the teenager she hadn't been in years.

I looked farther back, into the rear bank of seats. Sam and Antimony were both asleep, two non-drivers with plenty of experience at getting their rest where they could find it. She had slumped over until her cheek was resting against his forearm, looking half-melted as she lolled there. Sam, who had the hood of his sweatshirt pulled up to keep passing motorists from seeing his nonhuman features, had his tail wrapped around her leg and one of his hands folded over hers. At least they weren't witnessing this latest iteration of an old, familiar fight.

"That's not so," I said firmly, looking back to Jane. "Everyone contributes to this family. Thomas didn't do any fieldwork for years, and she still married him."

"He was trapped in his house because of a careless bargain he'd made *in the field*," said Jane.

Alice twisted around in her seat again, unable to let that one slide. "That 'careless bargain' is the reason you exist, Jane," she said. "We weren't together yet when he bartered with the crossroads for my life. If he'd decided not to be 'careless,' you would never have been born."

"Maybe that would have been better," retorted Jane.

Alice's face fell. "You don't mean that."

"You're right, I don't," said Jane, with a pained sigh. She rubbed her face with one hand. "I need to exist for my kids to have been born, and my kids are pretty great."

"Mine, too," said Alice.

Jane scowled. "You don't get to say that. You never earned saying that."

"Oh look, Idaho," said Bon, in a bright, artificially cheerful tone. "How did we get here so fast hmm I don't know maybe the driver thought it was a good idea to dip into her reserves and speed things up before you two decided to kill each other on her nice new upholstery." She shot a glare at the rearview mirror, directing it at all the car's occupants, even the sleeping ones. "Yes, thank you, Bon, it was very kind of you to go out of your way and put yourself in danger by risking being spotted by a Covenant field team in order to get us to our destination that much faster. We absolutely will not kill each other in your vehicle."

We weren't in the city proper, although we must have been close, as she started slowing down. "This is where you all get the hell out of my van."

"Thank you, Bon. I won't forget this," I said, politely.

I'm not a road ghost, no matter what some people have assumed when they saw me playing at being alive, something which is normally the preserve of hitchers and the like. I am, however, still a reasonably polite person, and more, I respect the Ocean Lady. She has no power over me. That doesn't mean I'm going to go thumbing my nose at a god, however young and still solidifying her powerbase she might be.

For one thing, Rose would kill me, and she's a Fury. If there's anyone who *could* kill me, Rose is probably on the list.

"None of you ought," she said, tone grumpy, as she steered to a stop by the side of the road. "This is the second time we've been called on to play taxi for you lot in just the past few months, and it can't go on."

"I hardly think the first one counts," objected Alice. "That happened because Apple insisted we go to New York to deal with the Covenant field teams that were harrying her routewitches. We shouldn't be penalized for doing your Queen a favor."

Bon thawed slightly. "That's fair enough, given what our lady asked of you, but still. This isn't a habit you ought to be getting into. Out with you, now, we're here."

I unbuckled my belt and leaned into the backseat, giving Annie's shoulder a shake. "Wake up, sleepyheads. We're here."

She sat upright, and Sam opened his eyes, clearly jostled by her motion. "I'm up," she said.

Sam made a grumbling noise.

"For two people who hate to get out of bed in the mornings, you sure do wake up fast when there's a chance you might get to hit something," I said. "Come on."

One by one, we slid out of the minivan, Alice waiting until the rest of us were gone before she leaned over and said something quietly to Bon. I could see them speaking through the window, but I couldn't hear them. That was probably intentional. Finally, looking pleased, Alice nodded and opened her door, following the rest of us to the side of the road.

As soon as the door was closed, Bon went screeching off down the highway, as if she were afraid we might change our minds and pile back in. The horizon seemed to reach out to meet her, and faster than should have been possible, she was gone.

I turned to look at our surroundings. We were standing by the side of the road—not the highway, but a frontage road of some sort, the city of Boise visible on the other side and past a series of fields to our left, while to our right, what looked like a small fairground was occupied by the shattered wreckage of a large carnival. Grudgingly, I had to admit the Covenant had been right to choose this as their second target.

The Campbells gave shelter to a sufficient number of cryptids that they were inclined to choose isolated fairgrounds over centralized ones; it might cut into their profits, but it also meant their nonhuman members were safe, or safer, at least. Cryptid kids could roam freely in the mornings rather than being confined to the boneyard out back, hemmed in by the tents and trailers where they spent most of their time. And cryptid adults could help with setup and teardown, meaning they made back in efficiency what they might have lost in walk-through traffic.

The carnival was set up close enough to the city to have made the attack easy enough to mount, but far enough away that the chaos had apparently not attracted any attention. If there had been fires, the carnival put them out on their own. If there had been casualties, they weren't going to be inclined to hand the bodies over. It was a closed ecosystem.

And the carnival had clearly taken several vicious hits. We fell into a formation of sorts, Alice and Sam at the lead, Jane and Antimony close behind, and me at the rear. I wouldn't normally have placed Annie at the middle of any group, but this time, it made sense; no one knew a carnival like Sam did, and Alice was the most likely to hit with her first shot. If Jane and Antimony were engaged, we were in serious trouble.

Not that we weren't already.

The difference between a carnival and a circus is down to animal acts—circus—and motorized attractions—carnival. Either can have sideshows and tent-based attractions, and there's a lot of gray area between them. But the Campbells don't travel with live animals, and they prefer to focus most of their budget and attention on mechanical attractions, hiring their sideshows from local communities. Local bands, comedians, whatever they can find. It means the show is always different, and brings in more local foot traffic, since everyone has friends or family who might want to come and see them perform.

Sometime they'd book an act with an actual platform, up-and-coming folk groups or fire-spinners, and those nights were always high box-office takes, offset by the stress and cost of additional security. They did the best they could. That was all any of us could do.

The Covenant had, it seemed, also done their best, but what they'd been trying for was destruction. The Ferris wheel, crown jewel of any midway, was leaning at an angle as unsafe as it was unstable, and looked like it might finish the process of toppling over at any second. Only the tethering cables used to brace the frame against high winds were still keeping it as upright as it was, and at least two of them had already snapped.

The carnival normally had three main tents. One, always put up nearest to the gates, held the food and beverage stalls most likely to be shut down by a light rain; there would also be picnic tables inside, for use by townies eating in the evening, and carnies eating during the morning. It would be empty for most of the day, and whoever chose the targets had clearly known that, because that tent appeared to be untouched.

The second tent was used for local acts and stunt shows—things like Annie's knife-throwing act or Sam's trapeze. That tent was scorched on one side, but the source of the fire appeared to have been a nearby corndog stand, which was now a smoking shell. Again, there was no sign that it had been hit directly.

The third tent was another matter. It was the one that was erected for appearances as much as anything else, which the carnival used as a social area and casual gathering place. And from the looks of it, it had been the target of a direct hit with something that looked a lot like the missiles Verity described as having been used in New York. A massive hole had blown away half the roof and most of one wall, leaving the canvas flapping in the breeze. What remained was charred black and ripped in multiple places, more like a rag than a functional tent.

The tent and the Ferris wheel hadn't been the only targets. Half the midway appeared to have burned, and only the Scrambler was still moving, albeit slowly, the rotating arms swinging around in a jerky, jarring dance that seemed to be winding down even as we watched. Worst yet, the damage to the third tent had also torn down much of the canvas wall separating the carnival from the boneyard, and many of the trailers appeared to have burnt.

Antimony made a small sound of dismay and started walking faster, clearly fighting the urge to break into a jog. She bumped against Sam.

He grabbed her wrist. "No," he said, voice low.

She shot him a vicious look. "No?" she asked.

"Annie, look." He let her go. "I don't see anyone moving. That doesn't mean the Covenant's actually gone. This could be a matter of everyone hiding while they try not to get shot with a rocket launcher. No one runs off alone."

Annie twisted her arm free of Sam's grasp, glaring at him, but slowed back down to pace the rest of the group. He sighed in clear relief, and we kept moving.

"Mary?" asked Alice. "Can you tell if anyone's still alive?"

I eyed her. "I'm not a Geiger counter for the living," I said. "No, I can't just look around and tell you if anyone's still alive. Shouldn't you know that by now?"

"The rules changed so much after the crossroads went away—"

"You mean after I retconned their cosmic asses right out of our universe," said Annie.

"—it seemed worth checking." Alice shrugged. "We're pretty exposed right now."

"If anyone's in hiding, they'd be in the food tent," said Jane, gesturing toward the first tent. "It has space, its own generator, and supplies. Plus it's not as tempting a target as the other two."

"All right, we look there first," said Alice. "Good call."

Jane blinked, looking taken aback by her mother's easy acceptance of her suggestion. Alice didn't seem to notice. She was already moving toward the tent, Sam pacing her, and the rest of us followed along behind.

Walking down a carnival midway in the middle of the day can have a certain haunted-house feel to it, like you're trespassing somewhere you're really not meant to be, somewhere that's not meant to *exist*—carnivals are things for twilight and darkness, not the blazing light of the Idaho afternoon. That feeling swept over me now, worse than it normally was, because we really *weren't* supposed to be here: no one was.

The authorities would eventually show up, after receiving a call from a motorist who saw the damage, or when darkness fell without the carnival lights coming on. If we were here when that happened, we were going to have a lot of deeply awkward questions to answer.

Alice was the first to reach the tent. She stopped at the closed flap, looking to Sam and nodding. He nodded back, and when she pulled the flap open, he surged into the tent, moving faster than a human would be capable of. Shouts and gasps from inside met his appearance, but no gunfire. That was a nice surprise.

More cautiously, the rest of us followed him in, blinking in the dim light. The long picnic tables were mostly full, carnies huddling together, children sitting on the floor or in the laps of their parents, all looking shell-shocked and a little shattered. Someone had turned the condiment stations along one tent wall into a sort of buffet, breakfast foods and an unusually large assortment of things they would normally have been holding back to sell after opening that night.

Not that they were going to be opening. Alice stopped near the entrance, drawing her pistols and standing at uneasy attention, while Jane and Antimony moved toward the tables.

A tall, dark-haired woman rose as they approached, and Annie embraced her, the two hanging off each other as if for dear life. Jane took a seat near an older woman, her hair streaked with white and one arm in a sling. They began to talk quietly, their voices pitched too low for me to hear. I drifted toward Alice.

"Aren't you going to go and say hello?" I asked her.

She shook her head. "Not my place."

"But you grew up—"

"None of these people were here when I was doing that," she said. "Maybe the very oldest of them, but I don't recognize them, and what am I supposed to say? 'Sorry you had to raise my kids and get old while I ran around doing whatever the hell I wanted for fifty years'?"

"That's not what happened."

"Might as well have been."

Annie and the woman let go of each other, Annie stepping back and nodding as she listened to whatever the woman was saying. Jane, meanwhile, rose, patting her conversational partner on her uninjured shoulder, and looked around the tent before heading over toward us.

Alice tensed at her daughter's approach. I frowned.

"Yes?" she asked, once Jane was close enough.

"Clarissa says they didn't know the people who'd been lurking around all week were Covenant," she said. "They've been seeing the same trucks for days. Some of the people came to the carnival. More than once, even. The man who seemed to be in charge, he came by during setup, asked some pretty standard questions about how long they'd be staying, where they were going from here, what the best nights would be to bring a date, but he never made any threats. None of them did."

"Is she sure this was the same group of people?"

"They didn't see the ones who attacked the tent," said Jane. "Everyone was inside when that happened. Looks like another missile. But when they evacuated to try to get out before they got burnt to death, they ran into more of that group. And they had guns. Six people got shot before they managed to scatter, and then the person with the missile launcher hit the Ferris wheel. That seemed more like a warning."

Annie squeaked, sounding dismayed, and broke away from the woman she'd been talking to. She hurried toward us, Sam bounding over to join us, so that they reached our little cluster at the same time. "Robin says—never mind what Robin says. We need to get out of here, *now.* Mary, can you get to Rose? Maybe the routewitches will send another car, or hell, maybe we can steal a plane or something. I don't care. We just can't stay here."

"What?" demanded Alice and Jane, in a unison that would

probably make them both unhappy when they stopped to realize what they'd done.

"Why?" continued Alice.

"Because according to Robin, after the attacks stopped, the Covenant team that launched them came to talk to her," she said.

"Why her, and not Clarissa?" asked Jane.

"Clarissa stepped down two years ago," said Antimony, impatiently. "She's old enough not to want to deal with the day-to-day logistics of keeping the carnival going. If I can continue?"

"Sorry," said Jane, who didn't sound sorry. If anything, she sounded offended, like nothing should have been allowed to happen without the queen of gossip's approval. She also looked oddly shaken—if she'd missed this, what else had she missed?

"They wanted to tell the survivors to stay where they were," said Antimony. "They allowed them to gather their fallen and move them to the big tent, but they weren't allowed to leave the carnival, not even to go into the boneyard. They had to stay here."

"Why?" asked Sam.

"Bait," said Alice, utterly horrified. "They were bait, for us."

Antimony nodded. "Unnecessary bait, since we would have come anyway, but yeah. Bait. This was an attempt to flush us out."

The dark, muttering atmosphere of the tent suddenly felt much more oppressive. I tensed, looking around. They weren't likely to have ghost traps, but it wasn't impossible, and even if they didn't, I don't like seeing my family in danger.

"But after that initial strike, no one called us or tried to contact us in any way . . ." said Sam, slowly. "How did it help to order them to stay here? What did that change?"

"The hit knocked out the carnival's local internet, and the cell signal in this field is crap," said Annie. "It's part of why they made getting their own Wi-Fi a priority. The box they used to supply the carnival was also a cell booster. So they couldn't get a call out if they wanted to. If they'd been allowed to leave . . ."

"They could have called us from the city, told us not to come," concluded Jane. "Keeping them all penned in here meant we'd have to come in person if we wanted to find out whether they were alive or dead. It's a clumsy plan, but it's not a bad one."

"And now here we are," said Alice. "Do your friends know how many bodies the Covenant has?"

"Sounds like about a dozen," said Antimony, voice tight. "Enough that I don't really want to go picking a fight with them."

"No," said a new voice, from the tent opening. "That probably wouldn't be a very pleasant activity. For any of us, really."

As one, silent, we turned.

The man standing in the tent's entry was tall and slim, with sandy brown hair and a pointed chin. His accent was pure upper-class English, the vowels polished until they shone, and he was dressed far too formally for a field by the side of the road in Idaho. He looked like the kind of man my father used to point at when we'd see them in line at the bank, the kind who had never picked up a hoe or worked a factory line.

"*You're going to marry a fancy boy like that, Mary, you wait and see*," he'd say, and if there was a mercy to him having died when he did, it was that I'd never been forced to sit down and explain that I wasn't going to be getting married, to anyone. The dead, as a rule, do not marry.

Not that this man looked like he was in the market for a wedding. Incongruous white shirt and tan trousers aside, he was carrying a large pistol, and his expression as he looked at us was that of someone who had smelled something particularly unpleasant.

Sam glowered at him, lips drawing back from his teeth in a simian snarl. Apes have much larger teeth than humans. It normally wasn't that noticeable when Sam spoke, good-natured as he was, but looking at him now, I couldn't help but think about how much damage those teeth could do to someone's throat.

"Really, Annie," said the man, sounding disgusted. "If you must continue to dally with monsters, can't you learn how to keep them under control? I've studied fūri biology since we last met, young Samuel. If I shoot you, I assure you, it won't end as well for you as it did the first time."

Annie put a hand on Sam's arm, narrowing her eyes. "What the hell do you want, Leonard?"

"You," he said, as simply as if it were obvious. "The same as I always have. Eventually, you'll have to tire of playing traitor. You'll come to your senses and come home to Penton Hall, where we'll welcome you with open arms. There is no hero so adored as the redeemed."

She took her hand off Sam's arm, balling it into a fist a bare second before both her hands burst into flame. It was red-orange, the color of a cozy bonfire. That was probably a good sign. If she was burning, she was upset, but if she was burning at a low temperature, we weren't in *that* much danger.

"I don't need to be *redeemed*," she spat. "I'm already the good guy here."

"It's all a matter of perspective, I assure you."

"Why did you attack the carnival?"

"Oh, we didn't only attack this one," he said, calmly.

All of us blinked. Jane spoke first, demanding, "What?"

"Her little background was too meticulous for her not to have spent time with a carnival," he said, eyes still on Annie. The rest of us were apparently so much background noise to him. I couldn't entirely blame him—the girl with the fists on fire was definitely a more immediate concern than anyone else—but I also couldn't see the wisdom of dismissing Alice, ever. It seemed like a good way to take a bullet to the head. "So we just tracked down the North American carnivals that fit the profile closely enough to be a possibility, and staked them all out. It's a dying game, you know, this carnival life. We only found five shows that could have sheltered you. You led us straight to them."

Annie snarled, the fire around her hands getting brighter as it shifted from red into yellow. Sam actually took a half-step away, repelled by the heat that was rising from his girlfriend.

"So when we judged you'd had enough time to have been informed about the events in New York, I ordered my teams to hit the carnivals."

"Oh, and I'm supposed to believe you just happened to be at the one we came running toward?"

"Give my research more credit," said Leonard, voice cool. "Of the five possibilities, this one was the most likely. It fit all the geographic markers for places where we knew your family had been seen, and it had the resources to have given you the training you demonstrated in your time with us. I have teams at the other four locations, taking care of the wreckage."

It was Sam's turn to snarl, lips drawing back to show strong, square teeth.

Leonard gave him a disdainful look before he focused on Antimony again. "*This* is what you'd choose over me? This . . . mockery of the human form?"

Jane had had enough. She stepped forward, bumping Annie out of the way and narrowly avoiding her fists as she stalked toward Leonard, shoulders tight and lips thinned. She looked like every mother who's ever raged, and he pulled back, clearly confused by what this soft-featured, apparently unarmed woman could be thinking.

Jane stopped right in front of him, reached out, and poked him in the chest with one finger, rocking him backward.

"I— What?"

"You, sir, are an arrogant *asshole*," Jane spat. "You attacked people because, what? You thought it would attract my niece's attention? You think she's going to leave a boy who spent *years* waiting patiently for her to come home because you flex your boarding-school biceps and say 'Oh I organized a terror campaign to make you like me'? Does the Covenant not teach logic anymore, or did they figure out that teaching your baby terrorists how to think for themselves just leads to more of them leaving the fold? Prejudice very rarely survives long in the face of actual reality."

"Madame," said Leonard, with every scrap of pride he could gather in the face of her furious onslaught, "who are you?"

"Jane Price," said Jane, leaving off her husband's last name as a means of keeping him out of this. If necessary, Theodore would still be able to run. It was never going to happen, but at least the possibility was there.

"How many of you people *are* there?"

"More than enough," said Alice. "Drop the gun."

He gave her a dismissive look. "I think I know which one you are. As you were clearly clever enough not to come alone, what makes you think I did?" He returned his attention to Antimony. "The offer's still on the table, my dear, but it won't be for much longer."

The fire around her hands paled again, staying yellow but shifting from deep to very, very light, verging on white.

Leonard took a step backward, looking toward Alice, who was the only person with a drawn weapon. "You can fire," he said. "You can shoot me now. It won't end the Covenant. It will just enrage my father, and stoke their rage against your traitorous family to even greater heights. But you can kill me. And as soon as you pull the trigger, my people will cut this tent to ribbons."

The carnival survivors who had been sitting in frozen silence through all of this gasped, and some of the children started to cry. Leonard shrugged, apparently unmoved.

"The choice is yours," he said, and took another step back.

As soon as he had exited the tent and could no longer see me, I blinked out. I reappeared at the edge of the field, where Bon had dropped us to begin with, and looked toward the carnival.

Leonard had been telling the truth. I could see at least twenty people arrayed around the intact tent, all armed, all of them clearly prepared to fire. He'd never said they *wouldn't* shoot if he was allowed to leave unharmed; he'd just made it clear that the timeline on them opening fire would be severely reduced if he went down. What the hell was their game, anyway?

Attacking the carnivals to draw the Prices out of hiding wasn't the worst plan I'd ever heard. Sam's grandmother wasn't currently on the road; her show had been severely damaged during a previous encounter with the Covenant, and was still in the process of rebuilding. We didn't need to worry about her. The fact that only five shows had been identified as possible targets made a depressing amount of sense. For a show to be a match to the background Antimony had given the Covenant, it would need to be of a certain size and age, independently owned, with enough in the way of performance acts—rather than just rides—for her to have been trained there.

When I was an actual teenager, there might have been dozens of shows like that operating around the country. But time had whittled them away, and it was almost surprising to know that as many as five had managed to survive this long.

No telling how many would still exist tomorrow. Carnivals that fit the profile would be as likely to attract cryptids as the Campbells were, and that would make them prime targets for a purge. And it's relatively easy to purge a carnival, when compared to actual locals. There will always be people who say "think of the children" like it's a commandment, right up until it's applied to a bunch of carnie kids.

We couldn't save the other four carnivals. We needed to save this one.

I concentrated and blinked out again, reappearing inside the tent. Alice turned to look at me.

"What did you see?"

"There's somewhere between twenty and twenty-five people out there, all visibly armed, surrounding the tent," I said. One of the children started to audibly cry. "I'm betting they're waiting for the order to fire."

"They won't wait long," said Alice.

"Annie, I know the Wi-Fi's down, but I need you to figure out how you're going to get a message to Sarah."

Annie blinked at me, startled enough that the fire around her hands went out, and they were just hands again. "What? Why?"

"I told her we'd keep her updated on what was going on, and we may need her."

"I'm not following *that girl* into a dimensional rift," said Jane. "I refuse to vanish on my family for a year."

"Her control's gotten better, but I'm not asking her to do that," I said. "Just to be aware of the situation, in case we need backup."

"Is there any break in their line?" asked Alice.

"They have the tent fairly well surrounded," I said. "But they're thinking like humans. I didn't see any of them trusting the rides they broke to be stable."

"Meaning they've left the high ground open. Sam?"

"Yes, ma'am?"

"The Ferris wheel looks like it's about to fall over, but I think it's still in good enough shape to handle a little jostling. What do you think?"

Sam thought for a moment. Finally, ponderously, he nodded. "Those are the cables we used to use when we were worried about bad weather, but not bad enough to shut down preemptively. They're graded to stand up to a tornado. I can get to the Ferris wheel without knocking it over."

"Wonderful." She pointed upward, to where one of the tent seams gapped just enough to let the daylight in. "Can you split that and get out?"

"I think so."

"Even better. I want you to start taking the children to the Ferris wheel. Get them out of the line of fire."

Sam blinked, and then nodded quickly. "I can do that," he said. "What if the Covenant sees me?"

That was a possibility. Even with the forces surrounding the tent and on the ground, all it would take was one person looking up at the wrong time and they'd be trying to shoot a fūri out of the sky instead of focusing on the traitors they'd come to apprehend.

"We hope they don't see you," said Alice. "But we need to get those kids out of here more than we need to worry about that."

Sam nodded again, accepting the logic of her instructions, and moved to start talking to the children and their parents while Annie produced a knife and quickly shimmied up the central support pole. Once at the top, she started cutting stitches.

Alice moved over closer to Jane. "We could evacuate you, too," she offered.

Jane shot her a withering glare. "I'm not a *child*, Mother. I don't turn back into one just because you're feeling bad and want a second shot at not fucking me up."

"I didn't mean . . ." Alice looked abashed. "It's just that I know you prefer to avoid the field. Twenty Covenant operatives with guns is very field-shaped to me."

"I'm almost done waiting, Annie," called Leonard from outside.

"They really want her, don't they?" asked Alice.

"A sorcerer? Even one who's only half-trained? That's a weapon you want with you, not against you," said Jane. "All the better if they can get her by taking her away from us."

"She's not a weapon," said Alice. "She's a Price."

"That's not how they think, and you know it."

"I suppose I do." Alice sighed heavily. "It's all just means to an end to them."

"I have no idea what that's like," said Jane, not looking at her.

"Jane—Janey." Alice reached over and wrapped her hand around Jane's wrist, gently, holding her fast. "You know you're not just a means to an end. I was a terrible mother, but you're still my daughter, and I love you. I will always love you. You can be as nasty to me as you like, it won't change my loving you."

"Then why did you leave?"

"My father—your grandfather—loved my mother more than anything in the world. He loved her so much it pulled all the oxygen out of the room, until there wasn't room for anything but loving her. And when she died, it was like she took all that pulled-away oxygen with her, like she left him suffocating in an empty room. He got so scared that I'd vanish just like she did that he nearly smothered me to death. I loved him and I hated him and I didn't feel like I could live my own life until he was dead. I never wanted to be him, ever, and then, when Thomas disappeared . . . it was like he took all the air with him. I couldn't breathe."

Jane looked at her silently, eyes wide and grave.

"If I'd stayed, if I'd done the smart thing and turned my back on the possibility of finding him again, I would have done to you and your brother what my father did to me. Love is a weapon, and when you turn it against yourself, you can love someone to death. Running was the only way I protected you from the worst monster in the room. Me." Alice paused to swallow, hard. "I knew there would be consequences. I guess I just thought . . . I don't know how much I was capable of thinking."

Above us, Annie had opened the seam and Sam was passing children to her on the pole, one by one, letting her nudge them out into the sunlight. Their parents were watching anxiously, but none of them had asked to go with their kids. They understood the fragility of this possible escape.

Alice nodded toward them. "Look. See how willing they are to let their kids go if it might save them? Maybe they're right and maybe they're wrong, maybe sending the kids away just leaves them more defenseless, but they have to try." She sighed. "I had to try."

One little boy started crying, grabbing for his mother's hands as Sam hoisted him and passed him up to Annie. She was clinging to the pole through the sheer strength of her legs, and I thought Verity would have been impressed if she could see her baby sister. Not that Annie would have believed that. Sometimes I'm glad that I was an only child whose family life only got complicated when people died. It seems a lot more straightforward than the politics of belonging to a large family.

"Are you armed?" Alice asked, looking at Jane again.

Jane swallowed as she nodded, producing a small handgun from under her shirt. Alice frowned, and passed Jane one of her pistols.

"This was your grandmother's," she said. "My mama never missed a shot she meant to take, and today, neither will you. There's only twenty of them. That's five each. That's almost unfair."

"Spoken like a woman whose luck has always been on her side," I said, wryly, as Sam boosted the last child up to Annie. She started to climb down the pole. He leapt up to grab it just above her, and used his tail to pull her close as he kissed her. She kissed him back, neither of them seeming to care how many people might be watching. When he finally let go, she slid the rest of the way to the floor, and he vanished through the hole in the tent roof, not a word having passed between them.

"Is Sarah coming?" I asked, as Annie approached our little cluster.

"My phone can't get through, so I've been shouting in my head, and I don't know whether I heard her or my own imagination, but for right now, let's assume she's on her way. We just don't know how long she'll be." Her hands lit up again, blazing bright. "We ready to do this?"

"No," said Jane, with an uncomfortable laugh. "But I'm not seeing where we have a lot of choice. If that boy out there didn't want to take you home like a midway prize, they'd already be shooting us until we stopped twitching."

"Good thing for us I'm irresistible," she said. She turned to the nearest carnie and hissed, "Get everyone into the middle of the tent and lay down flat on the ground. We want to minimize target area."

The carnies began to do as she said. The rustling sounds this created were loud enough that someone outside must have heard it; an unfamiliar voice shouted something.

Sounding almost bored, Leonard said, "Very well, then. Fire."

The guns began going off, and everyone else hit the ground in a ragged series of thumps, Jane hissing as she fell. I stayed where I was, bullets whizzing harmlessly through my intangible torso, and scowled at the tent entrance. "Is this always how you handle rejection?" I shouted. "You could be a little less bang bang and a little more sweet talk and chocolates."

The gunfire continued. I looked down at Annie, flat on the ground. "I don't think Leo's feeling chatty," I said.

"Can you go check outside?"

"On it." I blinked out, reappearing once again by the side of the highway. Apparently that was just my default here. But this time, I didn't reappear alone.

Sarah turned to look at me, expression serene. I jumped.

"Whoa! Fuck! Sarah, we're going to *bell* you."

"I like bells, and I'm too far away for you to have heard a bell anyway," she said. "Annie called, I came. Was I not supposed to?"

I didn't really have an argument for that—or an answer. I looked back toward the tent.

It was still surrounded, the Covenant agents closing in as they fired, slowly tightening their ring around the structure. Soon enough, they'd be right on top of it and could do whatever they were planning next. To be honest, I was sort of hoping they were planning to go with arson. Annie could stop the fire if they did that. Burning your enemies to death is a lot harder when one of them can politely ask the flames to go away and stop being a problem.

Their proximity did matter, however. The closer they got, the easier it was for them to reliably aim downward, and they had to know we had people on the ground.

Motion from the Ferris wheel caught my eye. I glanced that way. Sam had the kids at the very top, huddled down in the swinging cars, holding as still as they possibly could. The motion was Sam, who looked like he was about to launch himself at the Covenant below. It would be a gloriously effective suicide run, and Annie would never forgive him.

Honestly, neither would I. He was family at this point, keyed into the weird network I used to track familial relations, and strange as it may seem, I've never actually experienced the death of someone I considered my responsibility. Fran, Enid, Alexander, and Jonathan all died when I was still a fresh ghost, more tied to the crossroads than I was to the Price-Healy family. Only Alice onward had been filed under "take care of this one" for me.

I didn't know what kind of trauma would accompany feeling one of my people die, and I didn't want to learn.

I started toward the carnival. Sarah paced me, giving me a curious look. "Aren't you concerned about attracting their attention?" she asked.

"What are they going to do, shoot me?" I countered. "I'm already *dead*, Sarah. Bullets can't bother me."

"Ah."

"If you're worried, you can go—"

"I'm not worried," she said. "Bullets require a certain adherence to mathematical constants to find their mark. I've had plenty of time to prepare. They won't hit me, if their guns fire at all."

"If you say so."

We made an odd pair, two women, one with black hair and one with white, walking casually toward an ongoing gunfight.

"How close do you need to be to make them stop?"

"Not much closer."

"Great."

We were close enough now that a few of the agents had noticed us. They stopped firing as they reoriented their guns on our chests, preparing to take us out. "Stop where you are!" shouted one of them. "You can't be here!"

"But we are," said Sarah dreamily, her eyes starting to cloud over from the inside, like her vitreous humor was turning to ice. "We're right here, and you're right there, and you're the ones who ought to stop what you're doing." With that, her eyes flashed white from side to side, and the gunfire abruptly stopped. The Covenant agents turned toward us, faces blank and muzzles now tilted downward.

"What do you want me to do with them?" asked Sarah, voice not fluctuating at all. She sounded like she was asking me what flavor of ice cream I wanted. "Oh, don't be scared, Mary, I couldn't do this to you if I wanted to. The dead are difficult to grab hold of. You'd slip through my thoughts like fog through a sieve. But I can't hold them here forever, and I'll have to put them somewhere eventually."

"Can you . . . can you make them not be Covenant anymore?"

"Not without doing to them what I did to Artie, and I don't want to do that," she said, beginning to sound agitated. "I can't change who they are that fundamentally, or I'll break them. Breaking people is bad and wrong. I won't break them. You can't make me break them."

"Can you . . . make them shoot each other?"

"You prove continuity of personality after death. Killing them is less mortally suspect than erasing them. Yes, I can make them shoot each other."

Sarah cocked her head. Before she could do anything, Leonard strode the last several feet to the tent mouth and fired into the darkness, once, shouting, "*Death to all monsters!*"

Someone from inside answered fire, and he went down, dropping where he stood without another sound. His gun was knocked from his hand by the impact.

Someone inside the tent screamed, and then Alice was bursting into the sunlight, pistol in her hand, shooting at the frozen Covenant agents like she was at a shooting range and someone was grading her on time. She didn't pause once to take aim, and she didn't seem to notice that they weren't moving. They dropped, one after the other, until the pistol was exhausted and she swapped for a smaller, more modern gun—the one she'd taken away from Jane, which apparently still worked well enough to use when shooting fish in a barrel.

As it clicked empty, she seemed to realize the Covenant agents weren't moving, just standing there placidly letting her kill them. With a shriek of rage, she ran forward and jerked the gun away from the nearest one, slamming the butt of it into his nose. It crunched horrifically, and he went down, only for her to stomp, repeatedly, on his face.

"Alice is very angry," said Sarah, sounding perplexed. "All she thinks is anger."

I opened my mouth to answer her, and stopped as a horrible silence filled my thoughts, all-consuming, so loud that it drowned out absolutely everything else.

"Oh, God, no," I said, and vanished.

Seven

"... oh."

—Jane Harrington-Price

Inside a somewhat damaged carnival tent surrounded by a bloodbath, just outside of Boise, Idaho

I COULD HEAR ALICE rampaging around the outside of the tent as I reappeared inside, and a horrifying, inhuman screech as Sam leapt down from the Ferris wheel to join her. With Sarah holding the remaining Covenant members stationary, it seemed almost unfair to pit them against two of our nastiest physical fighters, but only almost.

I didn't know how Leonard had been able to break free of her control for as long as he had, and I honestly wasn't sure it mattered anymore. I manifested in the tent to find Annie on her knees and wreathed in flame, so bright it hurt my eyes. She was kneeling over Jane, who wasn't shying away from the heat, not even as Annie pressed burning hands against her chest, trying to stem the blood. Jane wasn't moving.

Jane wasn't in my head anymore, either. She had dropped out of the shining mental map that I normally had of the entire family, leaving a blank space behind, with nothing to fill it but the sound of silence, like the wind blowing through a graveyard. Silence has a sound. That may seem like folk-music lyrical bullshit, but it's truer than it sounds. Normal silence is shallow. You can break it with a hit. This was deep and thick, as sticky as molasses and twice as likely to drag me down. Eternity was on the other side of this silence, and if I didn't break out of it soon, I was going to get a closer look than I had ever wanted.

What is a babysitter when her charges are dead and gone? A parent who loses a child is expected to grieve. Was I?

I walked toward Annie, grief causing me to lose my hold on my carefully modernized image. My clothes moved back in time by a decade with every step, until I was wearing the skirt and jacket I'd had on when I died, out of date and out of place and very, very young. Only my hair didn't change back to what it used to be. Ghosts like Rose, who consciously chose to change their hair, can shift it around; people like me can't. I was a blonde when I was alive, and I have white hair now, because I got it from the crossroads. There's no changing back when I didn't change for myself.

"Annie," I said. The fire on her hands went out, but she still kept pressing down on Jane's chest, the blood now visible around her splayed fingers, clearly trying to perform some form of CPR. Jane didn't move. "*Annie*."

"He shot her." She raised her face toward me, burning tears rolling down her cheeks. She was crying fire. Actual tears would have evaporated from the heat before they could fall. It was as terrifying as it was terrible. "He just . . . We were . . . The gunfire had stopped, and we were starting to get off the ground so we could go and see what was . . . what was happening, and then Leonard was in the doorway again and he . . . he *shot* her!"

That was the shot we'd seen him fire. Either his aim was very good or he had managed to get very lucky; from the blood on Jane's shirt and the placement of the scorch marks left by Annie's hand, he had managed to catch her to the left of her sternum, a single shot that would have nicked her heart at the very least, if it hadn't pierced it outright. Fran's pistol was on the ground by Jane's outstretched hand, having fallen with her, and I could only hope that she had been the one to fire the shot that knocked that bastard down.

Jane's eyes were open, and she hadn't blinked once since I came back into the tent. The sound of gunshots and flesh being struck had faded from outside, replaced by Alice howling, the primal, shattered misery of an animal that had just seen its child die.

"Annie, can you put out the fire?"

Annie blinked like she didn't understand what I was saying. I reached my hand toward her, and she took it, flames flickering out as she got back to her feet. Only the burning tears remained, rivulets of lava trickling down her face to drop, sizzling, to the ground. The hard-packed earth wasn't giving them any purchase, and she had thus far failed to set the tent ablaze. Hopefully, she would keep it that way.

"I'll be right back," I told her, urgently. "If Alice, or Sam and Sarah, come looking for me, tell them I'll be *right back*."

I waited until she nodded slowly, eyes dull and confused, then dropped down into the twilight.

Earth's reality is sort of like an onion. There are layers to it. Virtually everyone who's alive shares one layer, commonly referred to as the daylight—much like the layers of the ocean, which are named for how much light gets through, the layers of reality are named for how much sun gets through. Using names connected to the sun means there's no cultural value attached to them, no misunderstandings that attach themselves to words like "heaven" or "hell." Those places exist, but they're neighborhoods, not levels.

When humans die, if they're going to stick around and haunt the living, they appear first on a level called the twilight. Immediately below the daylight, it's as close to the world of the living as you can get without actually becoming manifest. Most new ghosts don't have the strength for the daylight, not yet, which is why you don't hear a lot of stories about murder victims whose ghosts stay standing after their bodies fall down, or phantoms testifying at their killer's trials.

Seen in the twilight, the area around me was a confused mess, half field at its most verdant and ideal, half Campbell Family Carnival in its heyday. This wasn't the carnival as I had ever known it—this was Fran's carnival, the show as it existed before I was born. Everything was bright and new and perfect, and if it was also patched and well loved, there was no contradiction here. What's loved endures in the twilight.

But not everything leaves an actual ghost. People, especially, can choose whether or not they want to linger unless they die in one of the ways that casts them in a preset role the universe has an interest in seeing filled. Why does the world want white ladies and phantom hitchhikers so much? No idea. Above my paygrade.

I looked frantically around the ghost of the tent. There were carnies there, but no one I recognized; these were people who had died with the show, somewhere on the road, and just chosen to never leave. They traveled with the carnival still, even if they never once stepped into the daylight, and their homely haunting helped to give the show its soul. The Campbell Family Carnival was a living thing, in part because its bones were full of ghosts.

It was still alive, even after the blow it had been dealt by the Covenant. Looking around, I had the sense of something deeply wounded but perhaps not fatally so, something that was doing its best to keep breathing. If they were willing to rebuild, the Carnival would be there to help them.

But I didn't see Jane. No matter how hard I looked, I didn't see her. I paused, catching my breath and trying to steady myself. Human ghosts only linger when they have something they need to finish. Maybe she—

I stopped. Human ghosts. Fran was half-Kairos, and even though the bloodline had been diluted, her descendants were never going to be entirely human. I looked down, although directions really didn't matter here, breathed slowly in through my nose and out through my mouth, and *dropped*, out of the twilight, into the layer below.

Into the starlight.

If the daylight is the land of the living and the twilight is the land of the human dead, the starlight is where the nonhuman intelligences go. They may have shared the twilight once, before things like the Covenant of St. George made it impossible for most of the Earth's occupants to feel safe sharing an afterlife with humanity, but these days, if you're dead and not human, the twilight's not where you hang out.

If the twilight seemed like a somewhat oversaturated and nostalgic version of the living world, stepping into the starlight was like shifting into the fantasy-novel iteration of the same setting. The carnival tent was gone, replaced by the nacreous shell of a great snail, drilled through with holes to support the poles that had been used to string the trapeze. Trapeze artists swung overhead, their bodies angled to form the proper shapes, their gauzy wings trailing behind them like banners.

Whatever species they had belonged to must have been extinct in the daylight, because I'd never seen anything like them before, and it was difficult not to gawk in the brief instant when wonder knocked the grieving out of me.

But grief is a strong opponent, and I had barely managed to catch my breath before it came surging back, wrapping its arms around me and squeezing tightly enough that if I had still actually *needed* to breathe, the air would have been knocked out of me. The habits of seeming to be alive come with appearing alive, and were easier to disregard here, two layers below the lands of the living. I looked around.

Like the tent above it, the shell was occupied by carnies. Not as many, and all of them in some way visibly inhuman, allowing themselves to walk freely as they could never have done in the daylight. The ground was covered in a film of tiny white flowers with lavender stems and leaves, and the sunlight through the shell gleamed like it had come shining through stained glass. If I went outside the snail, I knew I would see wonders such as I had never imagined, the sort of idealized carnival that could only exist in an afterlife designed by minds that weren't human and had never wanted to be.

I couldn't focus on the magic of the starlight. I had to find Jane. I looked around again, searching for anything that seemed out of place, and there, under one of the tables, I spotted a child. She was tiny and blonde, wearing a pleated plaid skirt over black tights, with a white blouse under a brown vest. She had her knees hugged to her chest and her face pressed up against them, and I blinked out, reappearing next to her under the table.

"I knew you loved that skirt, but I didn't know you remembered it," I said.

Jane lifted her face. She was every bit the angelic little girl she'd been when she was actually seven years old, daughter of the early seventies, with her hair cut in a severe bowl cut that her children would later mock, looking at her childhood pictures. But her eyes were older than they had ever been during her actual childhood, old and wise and stolen from her adult face.

"I'm dead, aren't I?" she asked.

"I'm afraid so."

"Isn't there anything you can do?"

"I . . ." I stopped. "The crossroads are gone, Jane, and the anima mundi isn't a resurrectionist. If we knew where the man who built Martin was, but . . . we don't. I'm sorry. I don't think anything *can* be done."

"Figures." She plucked one of the little flowers, looking at it critically before crushing it between her fingers, letting out a sweet scent somewhere between cinnamon and honeysuckle. Then she looked back to me. "Did I get him?"

"What?"

"The bastard who shot me. I fired as I was falling. Did I get him?"

"I think so. Someone did, and it was the first gunshot I heard, so I think it was you."

She nodded, looking pleased. "Good. Glad I got at least one of the bastards."

"I can't . . ." I paused, swallowing. "I can't bring you back to life, but you're my responsibility."

"Is you being my babysitter the reason I'm a kid right now? Because you've always seen me like this? I guess I should just feel grateful you didn't like me better as a toddler. At least I had some autonomy by the time I was seven. I could run around the carnival without Laura chasing after me, as long as she knew where Kevin was and that you could go right to me if I got into trouble."

"Don't be silly," I said. "You never stopped being my responsibility."

Jane laughed, and she was a gawky twelve, hair grown out and braided to either side of her head, skirt replaced by bellbottoms and a loose blouse in paisley swirls. There was no transition or transformation: she was one thing, and then she was something else, and there was no contradiction there. The starlight worked the way it liked.

"Guess that's true," she said, looking at her larger hand with approval. "I'll always be your problem."

"Janey, I can't . . . I can't help you be alive again, but if you were planning to go back, I can help you get there faster than you'd be able to manage on your own."

"Nah," she said, calmly.

I frowned. "What do you mean, 'nah'?"

"I mean, nah, no thanks, I don't need the help." She shrugged. "I'm dead. Let me be dead."

"You don't have *any* unfinished business?"

"Are you kidding? I have loads. This is going to mess Ted up forever. Kevin's not going to take it too well either. I want to see Elsie figure out what she wants to do with her life, and find a nice girl, and be happy. I think there's something seriously wrong with Artie. I want to see him get to the other side of it all, whatever that means, and become the man he was always meant to be. I want to be there for my family, and I want to see us win this damn war. I have so much unfinished business. None of it's special. None of it means I should get to stick around when most people don't have the option. I think I'm done."

I hesitated. "You didn't mention your parents."

"Ah, Mom. That's what you meant, right? I don't feel like I have any unfinished business with Dad—I don't know him, it wasn't his fault, getting to know him now wouldn't change that, and getting to know him as a ghost seems a little mean. 'Sorry, guy, you took too long, and now your kid—who looked older than you already—is dead, hope you enjoy chatting about creaking hinges in doorless chambers.'" She snorted. "Mom, though . . . I know her. And I feel like I know her even better after today. But I also feel like I've heard her whole apology. She doesn't have a better reason for what she did, and she's not going to find one, because she told me the truth."

Jane shrugged again as she looked at me. "Saying 'sorry' isn't like casting a magic spell. Even if you do it with all the sincerity in the world, it doesn't fix the things you broke. It doesn't undo what you did. Did she do the right thing when she left us? She knows herself better than we ever got to know her, and I believe she believes she did the right thing. No way to know for sure now. Maybe there never was. She's said her sorrys, and I've accepted them as much as I can, and I spent my whole life mad at her. I don't feel like spending my death the same way."

"Don't you want to say goodbye?" I asked, almost desperately.

"Most people don't get the chance. Why should I be any different?" She climbed out from under the table, and when she straightened, she was twenty-five, young and brash and beautiful, the way she'd been when she came home and told us she was getting married. I followed her, awkwardly getting to my feet. Our eyes were almost level with each other.

"I have all the unfinished business in the world, but none of it's unique enough to justify staying here when no one else is allowed to. I'm not a special kind of ghost. I don't have a job I feel compelled to do, and I don't want to stick around long enough to get one. If I hadn't managed to shoot the guy, that might be a compelling reason to try. Good thing I was such a good shot, huh?" She quirked a little smile, and reached over to smooth my hair away from my face, tucking it back behind my ear. We were both ghosts. I felt her fingers just as if she were alive. They were even warm.

"Tell them you found me, and tell them I'm okay; tell them I loved them so much it hurt sometimes," she said. "But tell them I'm not coming back. Dead is dead and done is done, and I'm dead and I'm done, and I'm going to go now."

She began to turn away. Almost desperately, I blurted, "Wait!"

Jane stopped, glancing back over her shoulder at me. "Yes?"

"I don't know what happens if you decide not to go back up to the daylight *and* don't keep a firm grasp on the starlight," I said. "I have no idea what comes after this."

"So it's a mystery to both of us," she said, and smiled, bright as anything. "Isn't that fantastic? You were a great babysitter, Mary Dunlavy, and I think you're probably one of my favorite people in the whole world. I'm glad I got to be part of your unfinished business. Whatever comes after this, I'll try to hang out there long enough for you to catch up, all right?"

This time, when she turned away, I didn't call her back. She started walking toward the exit, and every step she took seemed to carry her infinitely farther away from me. The entrance stayed where it was, and she just . . . dwindled into the distance, like she was walking down a road I couldn't see. As she was reaching the horizon, so small she was almost a mirage, she turned and looked back at me. Then she walked onward, and was gone.

I put my hands over my face and cried.

Eight

"Dead's dead for everybody else. I don't know when we got to be so sure that we were somehow the exception."

—Frances Brown

Inside a somewhat damaged carnival tent surrounded by a bloodbath, just outside of Boise, Idaho

I REAPPEARED INTO SILENCE.

Alice had rejoined the others inside the tent, and someone—probably Alice, judging by the blood on her hands—had lifted Jane's body onto one of the picnic tables, covering her with a dusty tablecloth. Jane would have appreciated the symbolism, I was sure. The carnies were gone, probably off to reunite with their children and start preparing to tear down as much of the show as could be rapidly salvaged. There were so many bodies outside. They might have survived the day, but it was going to cost them everything.

Annie turned toward me as soon as I was there, her cheeks now streaked with actual tears, her eyes wet and wounded. She rushed toward me, grabbing for my hands. "Did you find her?" she demanded, grabbing for my hands. "Did you?"

"I did," I said, and looked down for a moment. "She doesn't feel like she has any unfinished business she needs to be here to handle. She's already moved on."

"What?" Antimony stared at me. "No, that can't be right. Go back and tell her that isn't right."

"Annie—"

"Aunt Jane can't just move on, she's supposed to be here. You have to go and get her."

"Baby, I can't."

Annie started crying again, hard, doubling over as she did. The sounds she was making were nearly enough to break my heart, or would have been, if I hadn't been so numb with the weight of my own grieving. It had been so long since we had to deal with a funeral. We were going to need to find a way home now, another routewitch or . . . or something. Maybe one of the carnies could loan us a car.

But if we borrowed a car, we'd be driving the traditional way, and we'd be spending seven hours on the road with a human corpse. Even in good air conditioning, that was going to be miserable. Nothing fun about road-tripping with a dead woman. Not that 'fun' was the descriptor for literally anything that had happened today.

New York, and then the carnivals. Had the Covenant been prepared to hit anywhere else? What was their goal here? They wanted a war, that was true, and that had always been true, all the way back to the beginning. Oh, maybe not the absolute beginning. Maybe when the first group of brave knights rode out to slay a dragon, they'd just wanted to survive. But then they slew the dragon, and they became heroes.

It's a nice gig if you can get it, heroism. Worship, adulation, and all the maidens and mead you can handle. Somewhere along the line, the Covenant got addicted to being heroes, and they lost the ability to understand what it was that enabled them to be the good guys. Kill monsters, get glory. That was what they remembered. Only they'd done too good a job, and the modern world no longer recognized the need for monster hunters. Would wiping out one family really change that?

Killing the Prices might let them get a foothold in North America, but it wouldn't change the fact that their time was over, had *been* over for a long time. They were relics, just as much as William . . .

I stopped. William. This had been about William the entire time.

What good are monster hunters without a big, impressive monster to hunt? They'd wiped out all the really iconic monsters centuries ago, but it all started with the dragons. If they could produce a dragon in a major metropolitan area, that would reestablish them as necessary for humanity's safety. Kill the Prices—or recruit, I guess, in Annie's case—and take out our network of allies, and then there'd be no one to interfere when the Covenant "heroically" unearthed William.

He wasn't normally a threat. But oh, he'd become one if the Covenant threatened his wives and children. Given how willing they were to kill humans, I had no doubt they'd be willing to butcher any number of dragons to get William angry enough to become the monster they needed him to be.

"We have to get back to New York," I said, voice small.

Annie glanced at me, still crying. Alice didn't take her eyes off of Jane. She was standing next to her fallen daughter, hands resting on Jane's arm, shrouded as it was by the tablecloth. She had recovered her mother's gun at some point; they were both in their holsters, snug against her hips. Unlike Annie, she wasn't crying. I didn't feel like that said anything about the depth of her grief. She was clearly shattered. She just wasn't someone who cried that much when she was grieving.

I cleared my throat and forced my voice a little louder as I looked at them. "Where are Sam and Sarah? We have to go to New York."

"Sam's getting the children back to their parents," said Annie. "The Ferris wheel didn't fall, but we don't want to leave them up there any longer than we absolutely had to." She dragged the back of her hand across her nose, snuffling hard at the same time. "Fuck, I wish I had a tissue."

"Sarah . . . I don't know where Sarah is," said Alice, glancing up again. "I don't hear the hum."

"It's not constant anymore," said Annie. "She's been learning to control it."

That was sort of terrifying. I've never picked up on what the rest of the family calls "the hum"—a sort of low-grade psychic static that tells them a telepath is nearby. Something about being dead makes it difficult for me.

"I thought that was impossible," I said.

"That word means something different when it's applied to Sarah these days," said Annie, and glanced over to where Alice stood next to Jane. "Is there really nothing you can do?"

"I'm sorry," I said. "Maybe before the crossroads went away, it would have been possible, but—"

"But it would have been expensive as hell, and we would have all been sorry," said Annie. "Yeah. I get it. I— Fuck, Elsie is not going to handle this well."

"None of us are," I said. "How far away do you think Bon is by now?"

"A routewitch without anyone else in the car? She could be in Australia."

"Any chance we can get her back here?"

"I can hike toward the highway until I get cell signal and try calling her," said Annie. "But Mary, we are *not* going straight to New York. We have to go home. We have to take . . ." Her voice broke, and she faltered. "We have to take Aunt Jane home before we can go anywhere else."

"We should probably find out where else they've hit," I said. "It won't just have been New York and the carnivals, no matter how much Leonard wanted you."

"I . . ." She stopped. "I can call Uncle Drew. He won't tell anyone that Aunt Jane's dead, even if I slip and he figures it out. But he may know if anyone else has been attacked."

No one gets the gossip like a bogeyman. It was a little odd to realize that with Jane gone, Drew was going to be the main source of family information. I sighed and turned toward the tent entrance.

"Where are you going?"

"You try to phone Bon. I'm going to try to summon Rose." Rose was a lot easier to summon when she was a hitchhiking ghost whose death was, technically, my fault. These days, what with her being in direct service to the gods of the twilight, she can be a little difficult to rouse. Hopefully, the fact that she was still a psychopomp—more of one than I'll ever be—and a member of a family she's always been associated with had just died would mean that her attention was already slanted in this direction. Hopefully, she'd come when I called.

Rose and I aren't close, but we aren't enemies, and that's about as good as it gets, given that she's dead because of me. Sometimes you take what you can get.

I stepped outside. It was late afternoon by this point, and the sky was starting to shift tones, color becoming deeper and richer without actually getting any darker. The world is saturated in the late afternoon. Blood stained the scrubby grass and the outside of the tent, and bodies were scattered around the perimeter, grisly reminders of Alice and Sam's assault, which would never have been possible it not for Sarah holding them in place.

I still wasn't sure about the ethical ramifications of her just holding them there while they were torn apart. But then, I'd been on the verge of asking her to have them shoot each other—would that have been any better? Any better at all? The ethics of battle are complicated things, and sometimes self-contradictory.

There was no sign of Sarah. I could see Sam over by the Ferris wheel, scaling the rickety structure with more care than he'd shown when we were in an emergency situation, then descending with the children he'd stowed there, bringing them down one and two at a time. It was a slow process, but every child he brought down was immediately grabbed and whisked away by their parents, who hurried them toward the boneyard without looking back.

A lot of municipalities put up with carnivals and carnie folk on sufferance. They know their citizens could use an entertainment, something to break them out of their daily grind, and carnivals are good for the economy; plenty of people, having decided that carnival food is too expensive, will buy coolers full of snacks and drinks from local shops and load them into their cars, where half of them will go uneaten as the smell of a fresh funnel cake proves impossible for mortal men to resist. Carnies make money, and then they spend money before they move on, and that's all well and good, but far too many people think it would be better if the carnies spent twice that in bail and then never returned.

When the police inevitably showed up here, it was going to get ugly, fast. These folks were just getting out ahead of the tragedy. I wanted to blame them. I didn't have the heart. Instead, I took one last look at the devastation around the tent and froze.

Sarah was missing. So was Leonard. Out of all the fallen, his body wasn't where it had dropped. Had anyone checked to make sure that he was dead? And how had he been able to break Sarah's control to begin with? It was a question I didn't want to spend too much time dwelling on, but which would have to be answered eventually.

Shuddering, I walked off along the midway, putting the tent behind me and focusing on the most devastated slice of the carnival. They were going to be years rebuilding, assuming they could rebuild at all. It was possible that this would be the end of the Campbell Family Carnival, and the thought was a knife to the heart, almost unendurable.

It had already been the end of Jane.

Sweet, shy, silly Jane, who never met a wet earthworm she didn't want to rescue from the pavement, who used to gather snails when she was little, building popsicle stick and cardboard "circuses" for them and making them the stars of their own snail big tops. Jane, who had inherited her mother's hair and sharp eye for target shooting and inability to let go of a grudge. How were we supposed to go on existing in a world that didn't have Jane in it anymore? It seemed impossible, but the other option was just as bad, and so it seemed we were going to have no real choice in the matter.

Once I was a reasonable distance away from the tent, I stopped, and let go of solidity, if not the daylight. I stayed exactly where I was, standing on the skin of the land of the living, the wind whistling through my insubstantial bones, a ghost where no ghost belonged. "Rose Marshall," I said, aloud. "I was responsible for the bargain that eventually killed you. I raised the woman who brought you to a family that could keep you human, even as the afterlife tried to wear your humanity away. I know the town where they buried your bones, for mine are buried there as well, and I have need of you, if you can hear me. You were a hitchhiker once. Hitchhike your way to me."

I closed my eyes and bowed my head, aware of the moment when my chin touched my chest without actually feeling it. Being insubstantial is more difficult than it sounds. Ghosts in the daylight have three states—solid, not solid, and invisible. Both solid and not solid require focus and effort, because you have to convince the light there's something to refract off of, while not convincing the air that it can't go through you. It's a complicated in-between state, and there are ghosts who never figure it out.

I remained that way long enough that the sounds from the Ferris wheel died down and I started to hear vehicles pulling out of the boneyard, while people moved past me to begin scavenging what had survived from the stalls and games on the midway. The insurance would probably write this off as arson and refuse to pay out; if this wasn't the end of the show, it would only be because the Campbells had advantages other carnivals didn't: allies with deep pockets who were willing to pay to keep them on the road and keep the cryptids of North America just a little bit safer. But it wouldn't be the same. They'd lost rides that had been running for fifty years or more, and they'd lost people, and they'd lost a sliver of the trust that had kept them going for so long.

Everything changes, and not always for the better. I breathed in, smelling only dust; I breathed out, and thought of roses. One rose, in specific, the Graveyard Rose, the Girl in the Green Silk Gown. I was never a haunting, not like Rose was. While she was hitchhiking the backroads of America and spreading her story from one coast to another, I was changing diapers and wiping noses and trying to navigate the changing trends of entertainment for toddlers. So she got a few dozen names, depending on the ways her story spread, while I remained a true phantom. I was just the Babysitter. And that was good enough for me.

"Rose, we need you," I said, and scowled. "Please don't make me sing."

"I would never be so cruel," said Rose, from behind me.

I opened my eyes and turned, and there she was, blue jeans and short brown hair and a French-sleeved blouse the exact shade of green that she had once worn to her ill-fated prom. I lifted an eyebrow. Ghosts can control their wardrobes, to one degree or another. Lucky ghosts like Rose can also control everything else. If she was wearing that shade of green, it was because she was trying to make a point.

"Thanks for coming," I said.

"I was already nearby," she replied, and glanced over her shoulder at the tent. "She said to tell you she wasn't sorry. I got her as far as I'm allowed to go, and she still wasn't sorry, and she didn't change her mind."

That was actually reassuring, in a way I would have had trouble explaining if someone else had asked me. Jane had chosen to leave me, to go deeper, and Rose had been waiting there to meet her and lead her into the true afterlife, the place I couldn't go until I was ready to stay.

"Annie's trying to call Bon, and I know the routewitches aren't a taxi service, but we need another one," I said. "We need to get back to Portland. We can switch to commercial air from there, but this is too important to screw around with."

"That, and you probably wouldn't be able to take her home if you hired a normal car service," said Rose. She bowed her head, and for a moment—just a moment—her face was a skull grinning at me from the shadows.

I hate that "oooo I'm a scary ghost" bullshit. There's almost never any call for it. "And we have to take her home," I said.

"She knew this was a risk."

"They all know, all the time. That doesn't mean it isn't a tragedy when it happens." I shrugged. "Can you help us or not? We need to get home. We need to find out where else the Covenant is attacking. Their resources can't be endless, but we don't know who they've been getting their information from, or how they're tracking us down. They could go for the compound, or for Alex and his family out in Ohio."

"They've already taken a swing at Chicago," said Rose, almost placidly. "Real clever Charlies, going into a gorgon-owned hotel with guns and no eye protection. Uncle Mike's a happy man."

That almost certainly wasn't true. In my experience, Uncle Mike was a viciously angry man who mostly managed to keep it contained through thick chains of loyalty, duty, and keeping his people safe. The Covenant represented an existential threat to his people greater than any he'd ever gone up against. But adding Chicago to the list of attacks we knew about meant we were up to seven separate Covenant attacks, all coordinated, all targeting locations the family had been known to frequent. We *needed* to find the source of their intelligence, or this was going to keep getting worse.

Sadly, Jane had been our best shot at getting that information, and now she was—

Even thinking it was difficult. For someone who's been with a family that takes this many risks for this long, you'd think I'd have more experience at dealing with death, but I came in during a surprisingly peaceful period. It's been chaotic, but we've survived. That's been enough.

"The routewitches were already going to send people to help the carnival with salvage and triage; I'll talk to them, and I'll get you a driver," said Rose. "But this *has* to be it, you understand? Anything more risks attracting the attention of the Ocean Lady, and that's a risk you don't really want to take, especially not when people are already dying. She collects souls as surely as any other god, and she might start asking for payment."

"I understand," I said. "Thank you, Rose."

"Don't thank me yet," she said, and disappeared.

I turned to walk back toward the tent. Sam was inside now, his arms wrapped around Antimony as she leaned against him, her eyes closed, shuddering. Alice hadn't moved from Jane's side. It was like she thought she could make up for a lifetime's absence by being present now, by refusing to be moved now.

It was almost admirable, even if it was entirely wrong. Nothing was going to make up for the years she'd missed. All we could do now was keep trying to move forward, and hope that we could survive this.

I had turned solid again during my walk along the midway, and Annie opened her eyes at the sound of my footsteps, turning to look at me. "I'm sorry," she said. "I tried calling the truck stop where Aunt Rose says the routewitches like to go during their distance runs, but the man who picked up didn't know what I was talking about, and the connection was bad enough that I'm not sure he could understand me either. I didn't know who else to try."

"It's okay," I said. "I talked to Rose. She's going to send us another routewitch to get us home. But she says we shouldn't ask again, because we're on the verge of attracting the attention of the Ocean Lady, and we don't want that."

"The anima mundi wouldn't let the Ocean Lady take me," said Annie, with quiet certainty.

"Have you gone and pledged yourself to the anima mundi while I wasn't looking?" I asked. She shook her head. I snorted. "Then don't be so sure. The Ocean Lady's a highway. She's also a goddess, and she takes what she wants. That's the benefit of being a goddess."

"I liked it better when we weren't all wrapped up in gods and weird divinities," said Sam.

I looked at him flatly. "When was that, exactly?"

He didn't have an answer. I walked over to Alice, laying a hand on her arm.

"Ally."

She didn't look at me.

"Ally."

She still didn't look at me.

"One two three, eyes on me," I said, keeping my voice soft and gentle. She finally turned to look, eyes wet and bloodshot from crying, tears still dripping down her cheeks. She looked wrecked. I was sure Jane would have been surprised to see her mother looking so gutted over her, and just had to wish she'd been here for this moment. I had to wish this whole damn day hadn't happened.

"Rose is going back to the Ocean Lady to get Apple to send us another routewitch," I said—a sentence that had quite possibly never existed before on Earth, and might never exist again.

"We're not leaving her here," said Alice, with sudden fierceness.

I shook my head, trying to look soothing. "No, we're not. That's why we need a routewitch. So we can get her home, and not have to deal with any of the mess of transporting a body across state lines. Ally, are you with us? Can you come back from wherever it is you are right now, and be with us? Please? We need you."

"I found Thomas," she said, voice very small. "I found him, and I brought him home, and we were going to be a family again. Finally, after everything, we were going to be a family again. How can we be a family if she's dead?"

"Honey, they were a family the whole time you were gone, and they would have been a family if you'd been there. No single person gets to make the decision of whether or not something is a family. They would have been a family if you'd never come back at all, and they're going to be a family with you and without her. Families change. There isn't a single static definition that says 'You must have this exact assortment of people to be a family,' and we wouldn't want there to be. We're all going to be grieving for a while. But we don't honor her by giving up, and we don't respect her death by leaving this fight unfinished."

Alice took a shuddering breath and nodded, standing up a little straighter as she wiped her eyes with both hands. "I was hoping she'd come back."

"Don't wish hauntings on the people you love," I said. "It's almost never as pleasant to be a ghost as you hope it's going to be."

To my delight, Alice actually laughed at that, and followed me back over to Sam and Annie. "I climbed up to the top of the Ferris wheel to get better reception and called my grandma," said Sam. "Our show wasn't attacked. She's fine, and she says any of the Campbells who need a safe place to go for a little while can come and join them at the winter yard. Maybe they can combine the two shows for a season or three, while the Campbells get their feet back underneath themselves and everything steadies out."

"It would be better than losing the Campbells entirely," I agreed. "Rose said the routewitches were on their way. They'll help preserve what can be preserved before it's too late."

"What about the other shows that were attacked?" asked Sam.

"Do you have any idea how to find them?" I asked him, baldly. "Because I don't. I wish I did. We can't take care of everything."

"They were attacked—"

"Because the Covenant is a bunch of prejudiced zealots who attack what might be different. It took this long because we've been keeping them out of North America. We didn't cause this attack, Sam. We delayed it."

He grumbled but looked away, backing down.

"What do we do about the dead Covenant members outside?" asked Annie.

"If we weren't trying to keep the carnival from getting in trouble, I'd tell you to torch them," I said. "This was pretty clearly some sort of an attack, and given that we have multiple dead carnies and the Covenant agents were all shooting at each other, I think law enforcement is going to come up with a pretty straightforward explanation for what happened here. It won't be correct, but since when has that stopped anyone? With the attacks on the other carnivals making it look like some sort of organized hate movement, they should be able to get out from under this pretty easily."

I was downplaying the potential legal difficulty, but only because I knew there was no way we were hanging around to help. We couldn't. No matter how much we wanted to, I was dead, Sam wasn't human, and Alice's legal status could get extremely precarious if someone ran her fingerprints and realized how old she actually was. Did the government have her fingerprints on file somewhere? I didn't know, and I didn't want to find out by becoming an unsolved mystery.

The tent opening darkened as a brown-skinned, broad-shouldered man in a red flannel shirt stepped into it, blocking the light. His short-cropped hair was dusted with gray, and the knees of his denim jeans were dark with grease. He looked around at the little group of us, nodding to Alice, before he focused on me.

"Mary Dunlavy?" His voice was a pleasant baritone, and entirely unfamiliar.

"I'm sorry, do I know you?" I asked.

"We haven't met," he said. "I've met that one," he nodded toward Alice again, "but that's about all. I'm Darius."

"Nice to meet you, Darius. How did you . . . ?"

"Rose called, said to look for the teenager with the white hair, told me that'd be my contact." He paused, quirking a very slight smile. "Her description was pretty on the money, have to say. She said you needed a ride home for four people and one . . ." He faltered. "Former person."

That could have described either me or Jane, under the circumstances. I nodded. "That would be ideal, yes. We're heading to Portland. Well. Outside Portland. Are you good to get us there?"

"As long as you don't mind riding in my girl, and if you do, we might have a bit of an issue, since I was the only person available to do the run," he said, and beckoned for us to follow him as he turned to leave the tent.

Alice gathered Jane's body in her arms before she joined the group, carrying her daughter as she'd never done when the other woman was still alive. The tablecloth slipped away. Jane's head lolled limply against Alice's chest, eyes closed. I turned away. I'm intimately familiar with death—in some ways, more familiar than I am with life. I still didn't want to look at that.

It still hurt.

Sam and Annie fell in step, Annie leaning up against Sam, Sam keeping his tail wrapped around her waist like he was afraid she'd float away and disappear if he let go for an instant. We followed Darius away from the carnival, away from the carnies who were picking through the wreckage of their lives for whatever they could find, and back out to the side of the road. There was still no sign of Sarah. I wasn't sure yet whether I needed to be worried about her or not. Probably not, but I was going to worry about her anyway.

What we did find by the side of the road was a big green sedan, engine idling, chassis radiating heat like some great, camouflaged predator. Alice smiled, just a little, and glanced to Darius.

"Still sailing on steak and platelets?" she asked, and the car made sense, and I managed not to recoil. Barely, but still.

Modern routewitches are what happens when human magic adapts to the changing environment. Road witches have always existed. It's only in the last few hundred years that they've been moving as quickly and consistently as they do in this modern reality. People aren't the only things that have managed to adapt.

No one really knows for sure where the sanguivorous cars came from. Some people think they're a form of giant leech. Other people think they escaped from some other layer of reality, down deep in the midnight or from the other side of the crossroads. They look like cars. They drive like cars . . . assuming they like their drivers, that is. Because if they like you, you can go forever on a couple of pints of blood once every six weeks or so. And if they don't like you, you'll get to experience exsanguination the hard way.

Darius saw the way I was looking at his car and smiled almost apologetically, walking over and unlocking its trunk to reveal a cavernous black space that he had already lined with plastic. "She's not hungry right now," he said. "And she knows we don't eat passengers. Cars who eat passengers don't get treats."

I didn't want to know what a vampire car considered a treat. Alice walked around to where Darius stood and carefully, almost reverently, lowered Jane into the trunk. She paused before straightening again, brushing Jane's hair out of her face and making sure her arms were straight, not bent at odd angles. The trunk was almost large enough to let her stretch the body out fully, and in the end, only Jane's knees were bent slightly to the side.

Darius frowned as he watched this. When Alice did straighten, he asked her, in a sympathetic tone, "Relative of yours?"

"Daughter."

"I'm sorry for your loss."

Alice's eyes welled up with tears, and she was silent for a moment before she nodded and said, "I don't think it was my loss as much as it was everyone else in the family's, but I appreciate the sentiment. Is there room for Mary to ride with us?"

"Actually, I think I'm going to try figuring out where Sarah went," I said. "You all have a good drive. Annie, call me when you get back to Portland. I want to be there to grieve with the rest of the family."

"Of course, Mary," she said, and pulled away from Sam long

enough to lean over and give me a firm hug. "This isn't how we wanted things to go, but I'm glad you could be with her when she went."

"I am, too," I said, and pulled away, vanishing.

Sarah wasn't actively calling me. If anything, Sarah was actively hoping not to be found. But my connection to the family isn't on the same signal as her telepathy, and she wasn't able to block me out entirely. I could find her general vicinity, if not her precise location. I focused, and the carnival was gone, and I was standing in a hospital waiting room.

There were no windows. Instead, vintage-style informational posters covered the walls, situated between large potted plants, reminding anyone who read them in large, cheerful letters to "MAINTAIN SECRECY" and to remember the "SIGNS THE COVENANT MAY BE WATCHING YOU." None of the colorful cartoon figures who presented this information were visibly human; they closest they came was a blonde who could have been a dragon, whose shadow confirmed it, forming the shape of a large predatory reptile behind her.

The chairs were the thinly padded plastic sort endemic to hospital waiting rooms everywhere, and were currently unoccupied. I turned a slow circle, trying to get my bearings back, finding no signs of Sarah. If she was here, I'd managed not to arrive on top of her.

The reception desk was currently unoccupied, but seemed like my best bet for finding out what was going on. I walked over, leaning across it to look for an on-duty nurse, and when I found no one, dropped back to the flats of my feet and hit the little bell labeled *ring for service*. The chiming sound almost seemed to fill the room.

And no one came.

I stepped back, hugging myself, refusing to extend my sense of where the family was. It wouldn't get me any closer to Sarah, but if it picked up on one of the smaller children experiencing some momentary discomfort, I might feel myself seized with the need to do my duty. Family members don't always have to summon me, precisely. It's just hard to resist the young ones, especially when the things they're crying for should be easy to fix.

And no one came.

Depending on how fast Darius could coax that car of his to go, Alice and the others were probably somewhere in Oregon by now. Bending space is child's play for a good routewitch, and anyone who could control a vampire car was definitely going to qualify as a good one. Using routewitches to shortcut distance is one of those things you can't do forever; it will inevitably come back to bite you if you cheat too much, like the universe itself recognizes the inherent unfairness of bending the real world like folding a map. The more you do it, the more the Ocean Lady will come to see you as an investment, and I don't mess with gods. Too many years in service to the crossroads to be able to trust them in the slightest. The best way to live a peaceful life—or enjoy a peaceful death—is to keep them from noticing you for as long as possible.

And no one came.

I debated ringing the bell again, but decided against it. I knew Sarah was nearby, or I wouldn't have ended up here; I didn't know that she was the reason the hospital staff seemed to be missing, and forcing them to come pay attention to me while they were doing actual hospital things would be the height of bad manners. I abandoned solidity instead, walking through the desk and turning toward the swinging doors that would lead me into the hospital proper.

Time to go hunting.

St. Giles's Hospital is the only cryptid-inclusive hospital in New York state, and covers many of the surrounding states as well, providing healthcare, surgical services, and even pharmaceuticals to the cryptid community. I say "inclusive" rather than "*ex*clusive" because the staff at St. Giles's has provided care to several members of the Price family when necessary. They *can* help humans; they just prefer not to, since their resources are already thinly stretched, thanks to their somewhat unique position.

I'm not a hospital administrator. I don't know how a hospital is supposed to work. I never spent much time in them when I was alive—a few terrifying visits while Mom was dying, some checkups with my pediatrician—and I've spent about the same amount in them since I died, usually when a member of the family was having a bone set or giving birth to my next responsibility. So maybe this was all perfectly normal. I looked back at the desk, giving the things on top of it a cursory glance.

The computer was much newer and sleeker than I would have expected if this place had been publicly funded, the sort of cutting-edge nonsense that could do everything in the world but demanded an active internet connection if you wanted to play solitaire. There was an open appointment book next to the keyboard, and from the pencil scratches and cross-outs, it was used more extensively than the computer.

Ah, well. Everyone gets comfortable with modern technology at their own pace, and it wasn't like I was some sort of dead computer wizard. I paused to look at the calendar box for today. There was nothing written there.

Emergencies don't normally do you the favor of calling ahead. Remaining intangible, I turned and walked through the double doors that would lead me deeper into the facility.

On the other side was a long white hallway that could have been stolen from the backstage of any medical drama in the world. It looked perfectly generic, probably in part because it had been built by people whose only model was those dramas. Real hospitals were complicated and variable, but this one, while it was real, had been constrained by the space in which it was being constructed more than by budget. A place where an oviparous biped could get proper prenatal care was worth a lot: even the dragons had willingly invested in the construction of St. Giles's, and continued to pay more of its operating costs than most people would have believed.

I wouldn't have believed it, if it hadn't been explained to me in detail by Dr. Morrow himself while he was looking over Isaac, after Sarah and the others had returned from their cross-dimensional excursion. But he'd been surprisingly forthcoming about the challenges of running an underground hospital, keeping it staffed and funded, even in the face of threats like the lurking Covenant strike teams, who had been less of a danger then but had always been on the mind of every sensible cryptid living anywhere near humanity.

Some of the doors to individual rooms were closed, little green lights lit above them to signal their occupation. I considered sticking my head inside, and decided against it. I wanted to find Sarah. It wasn't a need, not yet, and until it became more pressing, I wasn't going to invade the privacy of perfectly innocent cryptids who probably didn't expect a ghostly guest in their hospital beds.

Halfway down the hall, I finally heard voices. I moved toward them, turning down a smaller hall and into an antechamber occupied by half a dozen people in hospital scrubs. Dr. Morrow was easy to spot, his broad white wings standing out even among a cluster of nonhumans. He was holding a clipboard, as he so often was, and looked unsettled in a way I wasn't accustomed to, the small white feathers that topped his head in place of hair beginning to rise up like a cockatiel's crest.

"We can't remove her," he said, to the others. "It would be unsafe to approach her physically in her current condition."

"What do you want us to do, then?" asked a dark-skinned woman in nursing scrubs. There was a faint, almost indiscernible pattern of scales on the skin of her arms, marking her as a female wadjet. They make fabulous medical professionals, being immune to most mammalian diseases and the majority of known toxins.

"Hope she leaves when she realizes visiting hours are over?" he suggested, wearily.

The other Caladrius in the room, a smaller woman whose wingspan was nonetheless greater than she was tall, straightened as she spotted me. "Excuse me," she called. "This is a staff meeting. You can't be in here."

All of them turned to look at me, and Dr. Morrow's expression softened when he realized who I was. "Mary Dunlavy, as I live and breathe," he said.

"Dr. Felix Morrow, as I do neither," I replied. "Can I safely assume that all this fuss is about Sarah?"

He blinked. "That's a fairly specific guess."

"I'm here because I was trying to find her, and I generally can't pop in precisely on family members who aren't actively looking for me," I said. "So when a search for Sarah drops me in your hospital, and I find half the staff muttering in a private area about a visitor you can't safely approach, well. I don't think it's much of a leap to go from there to 'I found her.'"

"She showed up a little while ago, and went straight to her friend. When one of our head nurses tried to inform her that visiting hours were over, she—the nurse—went to sleep and hasn't woken since."

"We poured water on her," said the wadjet. "Nothing."

"Tell me where she is," I said, with a shrug. "I'll get her to stop knocking out your staff."

"Down that hall, third door on the left," said the female Caladrius, pointing. Dr. Morrow shot her a sharp look. She lifted her wings in what looked like the avian equivalent of a shrug. "What? We can't have an out-of-control cuckoo rampaging around the facility, even if she *is* a friend of the Price family, and even if her rampage is extraordinarily subdued. We need to be able to move through our workplace with confidence."

"She's with a patient," said Dr. Morrow—a fragile protest, and one which she ignored.

"If you can get her to talk to you, please ask her to let Nurse Michelle wake up before she leaves? She's supposed to be taking the evening shift, and I don't have the staff to cover for her if she's unavailable."

"Got it," I said, with a quick salute, before I took off down the indicated hall.

The third door on the left was labeled LONG-TERM CARE, which didn't bode terribly well, and there was a gray-skinned bogeyman woman in scrubs asleep on the floor outside. I stepped over the woman and through the door, into the room on the other side.

It was small and square, windowless, dominated by the large ergonomic hospital bed in the middle of the floor. A figure was stretched out there, unconscious under white sheets, connected to multiple machines and monitors. They beeped and measured away, charting everything but a heartbeat.

Because Mark didn't have one. No cuckoo does. They're highly evolved insects, more closely related to wasps than they are to any sort of mammal, and the antifreeze-like hydrolymph they have in place of blood moves through decentralized vascular pulses. I don't know how they keep it oxygenated, but they apparently do a pretty good job of it, since his displayed blood oxygen level was in the high nineties. His eyes were closed, making his shaggy black hair the closest thing he had to a splash of color. Like all cuckoos, he was pale; unlike most cuckoos, he was pale enough to have faded all the way to the shade of bleached bone, barely distinguishable from the dead.

Sarah was sitting next to the bed on a rolling stool she had pulled over for that purpose, her head down on her folded arms. I took a step toward her.

"You should stop," she said, voice dull, without lifting her head. "I wouldn't come any closer."

"I'm dead, Sarah," I said. "You said it yourself: ghost thoughts are hard to grab hold of. I don't think you can hurt me, whether on purpose or by accident."

"Do you really believe that?"

I stopped where I was. "I don't know. But I know you're one of my kids, and you're hurting, so I'm going to take the risk either way. You don't scare me. I love you too much for that."

She finally lifted her head. There were tear tracks on her cheeks, but her eyes were clear, not bloodshot in the least. Without blood, her capillaries might burst, but it would never show when they did. "Jane's dead," she said, voice almost devoid of inflection.

I nodded, risking another step forward. "I know."

"Jane's dead, and they're going to take her body back to Portland, and Elsie's going to grieve because she's lost her mother, and *I don't know what Artie's going to do.*" Her voice was low and urgent, pitched like she was trying to tell me something terribly important but didn't know precisely how.

I frowned. "He's going to grieve."

"Is he? *Can* he? I built him from memories and experiences that happened outside him, and rewrote them so they would feel like they were his own. But they didn't include grief. They didn't include him learning to understand what death was. I took him away from his family, from his mother, and now she's gone, and I don't even know if he'll be able to mourn for her."

"Why did you come here?"

"Mark's family doesn't even have a stranger in his body to turn to," said Sarah. "I visit them, sometimes. They don't know who I am, but Cici—his little sister—she suspects I'm the same sort of thing he is, and she always looks at me like she wants to tear my throat out, like she knows what I did. She can't possibly know. She still . . ." She sighed heavily. "It's hard."

"Life is hard, honey. That's what makes it worth living." I took another few steps toward her, angling to go around the bed. I can pass through living people, and most of them don't even notice. Passing through a comatose cuckoo seemed like a gamble I didn't need to be taking right now. "None of this is your fault. You know that, right?"

"Why couldn't I hold on to Leonard?" She looked up at me, eyes perfectly clear. Her pupils were a fully normal shade of black, not clouded by the traceries of telepathy. Whatever she was doing here, it wasn't communicating with Mark in any way. In fact, if I'd been asked to guess, I would have said she'd pulled herself back as hard as she could, keeping even her passive psychic effects to a minimum.

If not for the sleeping nurse outside, I would have thought she'd shut them off completely. It was . . . jarring. "I don't know, honey. He's had encounters with Annie before, and with the rest of us. Maybe he was wearing a telepathy-blocking charm of some sort. Not strong enough to keep you from grabbing him in the first place, but enough to give him that little extra edge to break free when he thought he needed to. He could see into the tent from where he was frozen. He wasn't shooting at random when he *did* break free. He was shooting to do as much damage as he could, and he succeeded, but that isn't your fault."

"Aunt Jane dropped her guard because she thought I'd neutralized the threats," wailed Sarah, sounding genuinely distraught.

Time to find out whether my false bravado over how much damage a cuckoo could do to a ghost was justified. I finished walking up to her and set my now-solid hand upon her shoulder, gripping tight to ground her in the moment. And nothing happened. My mind didn't fragment and shatter, or sweep away into nothingness; my borrowed molecules didn't scatter.

"She knew better than to assume any enemy still standing was fully neutralized," I said. "She didn't drop her guard. She just got unlucky. It happens. Even to people with Kairos blood. Eventually, everyone gets unlucky. You didn't do anything wrong."

"I did something wrong to Mark, and to Artie," she said miserably. "I *hurt* them."

So she was conflating Jane's death with the telepathic damage she'd unwittingly done to her friends. Of course she was. "You put Arthur back together as best you could, and he should have known not to touch you during a working as large as the one you've described to me," I said. "I think *Artie* did know. He may not have realized how bad it would be, but he knew there would be consequences, and I believe he accepted them. It's not your fault they were more than he could carry. It's not."

Sarah sniffled. "Mark asked me to take the ghost memories out of him. The ones we inherited from our mothers, the ones that taught us how to be cuckoos. They're like eggs in our minds, and when they hatch, they leak all over everything. They change every bit of who we are and how we understand the world. My egg never hatched, because Angela stole it from me, and because Angela is the way she is, she didn't have an egg. Mark's egg, though, it hatched, and it had a long, long time to soak into every bit of who he was. And he asked me to rip it out, so I could have more processing power. I did, because he called me a coward. He made me so angry that I didn't feel like I had a choice anymore." Her eyes were starting to fill with tears.

I squeezed her shoulder but didn't say anything. This was something she needed to get out, and until she did, she wasn't going to be a reliable ally. We needed her reliable. We needed her steady and dependable and coming when we needed her.

"I pulled it out, and I filled that whole space with an equation that was supposed to crack a world in two, and when I solved for zero, when I finished the problem, I pulled it back out again, because it's too dangerous. I couldn't let him keep it. And now he won't wake up."

"Is he still there, when you look into his thoughts? Can you find Mark?"

She nodded, hesitantly. "He's not like it was with Artie. With Artie, there was just . . . nothing. It was like I'd reformatted his hard disk. Mark is just all fragmented and broken up inside, everything in pieces. It's more like I ran a magnet across him again and again, until everything was pulled out of true."

"And is he getting any better?"

Again, she nodded. "It's hard to tell, because he's so deep down that I can't interact with him at all, but he seems to be pulling the pieces of himself back together. He's more Mark every time I look at him."

"Sounds like what happened to you."

Sarah looked at me again, sharply this time, alarmed. "You mean I might have triggered his next instar?"

"I suppose so."

"Can that even *happen* to male cuckoos?"

"Honey, I know as much about cuckoos as you do, if not less. They're not my field of study. But I'd say you're a relatively low-sexual-dimorphism species, and there's no reason to think that if cuckoo queens are possible, cuckoo kings might not be under the right circumstances. He's sleeping because he's healing. He's safe here in this hospital. You didn't hurt him—or if you did, it was because he asked you to, in order to save everyone else. To save Annie and Artie and James, and yourself, and Isaac."

Sarah bit her lip. "I guess. I just . . . I just want him to wake *up*. His sister needs him."

Of all the people Sarah felt guilty for hurting, Mark was the safe one: he was still unconscious, and he couldn't blame her for what she'd done. So she used him as a stick to hit herself with, because it was safer than hitting herself with any of the others. It was unhealthy, almost brutally so. I kept my hand on her shoulder.

"Honey, we need to get back to Portland. We need to be there for the family meeting. I know you feel bad, but running isn't the answer, and knowing what it felt like when Leonard slipped out of your control is probably going to help us understand what happens next." I grimaced as a wail rang through the network of familial need. "And you need to go ahead without me, because Charlotte is yelling for me now. I think she's—"

Isaac started crying as well.

"—okay, now she's woken Isaac. Sarah, I have to go. Can you wake up the nurse in the hall outside and head back to Portland for me? Please, can you promise me that much?"

Sarah nodded, very slowly. "I have to go back there anyway. Greg's there," she said.

"Yeah. Go get your giant spider." I leaned in and kissed her forehead before winking out, back into the no-space space between the world of the living and the world of the dead.

Nine

"This is not how I expected my life was going to go. Isn't it wonderful?"

—Enid Healy

In transit to a comfortable if creepy family home in Columbus, Ohio

WHEN NOT DROPPING MYSELF onto a specific level of the afterlife, I move too quickly to truly say that I was occupying the twilight, or the starlight, or anywhere at all. I still existed, but I existed in a void, of sorts. I sometimes thought I might be crossing through the space that used to belong to the crossroads, when they were still something I needed to be concerned about. Which might mean I was taking shortcuts through the backyard of the anima mundi, and would eventually need to rethink that whole "don't mess with gods" idea.

Then I was standing in the room at Angela and Martin's that had been turned into a bedroom for the two children. Charlotte and Isaac were close enough in age that they could share space without keeping each other awake all the time, and young enough that the fact that they were basically brother and sister wasn't an issue yet. They wouldn't want privacy for a few more years, and if they told the various adults they interacted with about sharing a room, it wouldn't trigger unfortunate questions. Alex and Shelby had been sharing the only open room in the house for ages, and creating a nursery had required finally gutting Andrew's childhood bedroom. Sarah still stayed at the house enough that converting her room was out of the question. Alex was making inquiries around the neighborhood for homes that might be going on sale soon. If he found one, the family would help with the purchase cost, adding it officially to their collective holdings, and he and Shelby would be able to move out with Lottie, leaving Isaac to have his own room.

But that was a matter for the future. The children were huddled together in one of the beds, clinging to each other. Charlotte stopped crying in order to sniffle and look at me appealingly, tears still leaking from her eyes as she freed one arm and reached for me. She had gotten the full family package, where looks were concerned; Alex marrying Shelby had only reinforced the family's tendency toward cherubic-looking blue-eyed blondes. Isaac, on the other hand, had the black hair and eerily blue eyes universal to cuckoos. He looked almost exactly like a younger version of Sarah, down to the white glow in his pupils, which guttered out and died as I looked at him.

He'd learned pretty quickly that telepathic compulsions didn't work well on me. They could sometimes be used to snare Shelby, who didn't always remember to put on her anti-telepathy charms, but everyone else in the house was resistant, for one reason or another. Instead, he held up his arms in a silent, pleading gesture.

"What do we say when we want to be picked up, Isaac?" I asked.

His face screwed up in momentary frustration before he said, "Up, please, Mary."

"That works," I said, and hoisted him onto my hip as I moved to check on the sniffling Charlotte. She looked at me pleadingly, then sat up in the bed and reached for me with both arms.

"Me, too, please, Mary," she said.

"It's a good thing there's only two of you; I'm already out of hands," I said, scooping her up and resting her on my other hip. "Can I put either of you down? I won't be able to open the door if I'm carrying you both."

Both children wailed in what sounded like genuine fright and latched on to me, clinging tight as limpets. They weren't as verbal as they should have been at their age, and the language skills they did have seemed to have mostly deserted them in the face of their fear. I squeezed them close, trying to bounce them enough to calm them down. They were getting too big for this sort of thing, a natural transition between the stages of childhood that never failed to break my heart a little. It was wonderful to watch my charges turn bit by bit into people with opinions and ideas that they could actually articulate, rather than tiny people whose idea of a good time was trying to flush a banana down the toilet, but I always missed the days when they were small and I felt like I could keep them safe.

I didn't feel that way right now. They were both still crying, and Charlotte had wrapped her arms around my neck, squeezing tightly. If I'd needed to breathe, it would have been a problem.

"Honey, Mary needs you to stop trying to strangle her," I said, voice a little strained. Mimicking a human form means mimicking things like vocal cords, and when they get squeezed, they don't work as well. "It won't hurt me, but your mommy won't appreciate it."

Something fell over in the hall outside with a resounding crash. My head whipped around, staring at the door, and both children stopped crying like a switch had been flipped. It was eerie, the way they cut off, voices going silent in unison. I looked at Isaac. His eyes were white from side to side. I'd seen them cloud before, but I'd never seen them go all the way white.

Cuckoos too young to have unlocked their ancestral memories aren't really in control of their powers. Everything they do is instinctual and can generally be written off as normal baby behavior. Sure, their parents tend to be more conscientious about serving dinner on time and laxer about making them do chores, but not to such a degree that it really becomes noticeable. If Isaac was exerting himself to—I presumed—tell Charlotte to stop crying, it was because he was frightened to the point of seeing the need.

I moved back to the closer bed and lowered them both to the mattress, making shushing noises when they whimpered and clutched at me. As soon as I pulled my hands away, the two children grabbed hold of each other, clinging so tightly that their grips looked painful. I straightened and turned toward the door.

The crash hadn't been repeated. It might have been my imagination. But Isaac's eyes were still white, and both children were still silent.

It wasn't my imagination.

Carefully, I stuck my head through the door and looked toward the sound of the crash. It would be an odd sight, I knew, a white-haired woman's head emerging out of solid wood. In the moment, I didn't particularly care.

Angela had a comfortably old-fashioned sense of home décor, and was fond of little decorative tables with pretty things on top of them—vases of flowers, or small ceramics. Nothing too expensive; it was all the sort of thing you could find at any thrift store or estate sale, the detritus of a thousand grandmothers' collections that had been liquidated when their minimalist grandchildren didn't want their dust-catching treasures. Despite her youthful appearance, Angela was closer to the grandparents' generation than the grandchildren, and she was happy to give their ceramic clowns and porcelain dancers a home.

She'd been saying lately that she'd need to pack up her treasures soon, to keep the children from hurting themselves as they grew older. Looked like she should have started sooner, because there was a garish blue and yellow vase in shards on the floor, next to the broken remains of a teak accent table. There were no people. I stepped fully through the door into the hall, looking in both directions.

There weren't really any footprints. Sadly, the vase had been empty when it broke, so I didn't have the convenient guide of water on the floor. There were, however, more shards of vase kicked to one side than made sense from impact alone, and so I took a guess and started walking in that direction, dialing down my solidity just enough to be sure my own footsteps would make no sound.

I turned the corner to find two unfamiliar figures in black tactical armor, their faces covered by mirrored helmets, walking in a shooter's crouch, automatic rifles in their hands. If I'd been an actual member of the Price family, instead of an adjunct, I could probably follow that up with make and model number, but I'm not, and I've never been a big fan of firearms. They were big and looked lethal and that was enough for me to not like these two strangers having them.

I folded my arms and cleared my throat, remaining insubstantial. "Excuse me," I said. "This is a private home. Were you invited?"

Both of them spun around, and one fired a burst of bullets which passed straight through my torso to impact with the wall behind me. It was an exterior wall; the repairs would be expensive, but no one was likely to have been hurt. That was the only thing that kept me from losing my temper more than I already had. I narrowed my eyes.

"Gonna take that as a no," I said. "You can leave now."

"Ghost," said the one who'd fired with disgust, straightening up. "No threat."

"Excuse me?" I asked. "No threat? What?"

"If it were a poltergeist, it would already be throwing things at us," said the figure. "It's just a lingering spirit. Probably some local kid they tortured to death for a dark ritual or something. We'll send a purifier team in when we're done sweeping the house."

I narrowed my eyes. "You will do no such thing. You will leave, right now."

"Ma'am, I don't know why you're so determined to haunt this place, but from the looks of you, you were human when you were alive. The people who own this house aren't human. They're monsters."

"Do tell," I said, lifting an eyebrow.

The other figure tugged on the first's arm, muttering something low and urgent. The one who'd been speaking to me sighed. "We're not here to explain ourselves to a dead woman," they said. "We need to sweep this place. We've heard sounds, and we know someone's here. We're not giving them a chance to get the drop on us."

Meaning the children had stopped crying because Isaac heard the thoughts of people who had ill intentions as they looked for him, and had shushed Charlotte in a way she couldn't ignore. Good boy. I'd have to give him extra tomato slices the next time we did snacks.

"I'm guessing neither of you has a spirit jar on you, or you'd already be trying to get rid of me," I said, starting to walk toward them. I don't have the malleability of a ghost like Rose, but I do have some control over how alive I look. I mentally grasped the slider and yanked it down, hard. My skin began to take on a leprous, rotting look, my eyes sinking deeper into my skull as my hair began to rise in wispy strands around my head, until I looked like I was walking in a cloud of luminescent cobwebs. My clothing melted into a winding shroud, and I knew from past experience that I now looked like death walking, some horrible specter summoned from the pits of hell to ruin their afternoon.

I kept moving forward, speeding up, and watched them flinch with some satisfaction. Sadly, they were right about one thing: there wasn't much else I could do. If I turned solid enough to start throwing things, they could shoot me, and while you can't kill the dead with bullets, you *can* hurt us—enough bullets and I'd lose cohesion for a while, which wasn't something I really wanted to deal with right now. I could be eerie as hell at them. I could make them uncomfortable. That was all.

I would never have expected to miss the crossroads, but in that moment, I did. They'd been a larger power source that I could plug myself in to, a bigger predator that would have my back, as long as I stayed too useful to be worth eating. Now, I was just one ghost, alone.

The two Covenant operatives—because what else could they be?—fell back, clearly unnerved. "You will leave this house," I boomed, in the most sepulchral voice I could manage, deep and hollow and filled with the echoes of the grave. "You will go, or my curse shall be upon ye!"

Something about talking like you're in the middle of a really cliché Dungeons and Dragons session tends to get under people's skins, and fast. They fell back again, and one of them grabbed a radio from their belt, raising it to the vicinity of their mouth. It crackled as they pressed the button down.

"I have a confirmed spirit encounter here," they said. "Apparently female, late teens, white hair, very, very dead. Can you run that through our known list of local hauntings, over?"

"We only know three of the local haunts," said a weary voice. "None matching that description. You're probably looking at a white lady or a homecomer of some sort. Mostly harmless, as long as you don't incite it to attack, over."

"It, uh, looks pretty incited, over," said the operative.

"So walk *away* from it." Whoever was on the other end of the radio was probably the senior agent for this team, judging by their obvious frustration. "You're not hunting ghosts, you're hunting monsters. If anything, the presence of a ghost confirms that you're very likely in the right location. Keep going, over."

"Right location for what?" asked a bright, female voice, each syllable slathered so broadly with an Australian accent that anyone who had ever met Shelby Tanner for more than a minute would have known she was playing it up for an audience. The two operatives whirled to look around the corner they were pinned against, their faces concealed by their masks but reflecting the distorted image of a blonde woman in a white blouse and khaki shorts.

"G'day, mates," she said, still as bright and cheerful as she'd be when meeting visitors at the zoo. It was as artificial as her clichéd Australian phrasing. She was *pissed*. If they'd been smarter, they'd have picked up on it, not just stood there with their guns pointing toward the floor, presumably gaping at her.

"Was having a kip when I heard you lot shooting up my mum-in-law's hall; she's likely to be a bit put out when she gets home from the store," said Shelby. "Gunshots aren't usually the way you wake a lady, must say. Can I help you with something?"

"You are a traitor to your species," said one of the operatives, finally bringing their gun up to take aim—not that aim was that important with an automatic. All they'd need to do was rake their shots across the hall and they'd hit her, possibly several times. And unlike me, Shelby wasn't dead yet.

I dove into the wall and through the closet on the other side, emerging around the hallway corner in front of Shelby. I snarled at the operatives, trying to seem as terrifying as possible.

"My curse shall be upon ye even unto the third generation if you touch her," I snarled.

"I thought it was seventh," said Shelby.

"Seventh is unfair," I countered. "By the time the curse runs out, no one even knows why you're haunting them. Three means everyone is still spitting on your grave by the time it's lifted."

"Ah," she said.

Her hair was mussed; that was the only sign that she'd been in bed when these home intruders started shooting up her hall. Shelby's approach to combat was most often what I considered a sort of weaponized distraction. It was similar to Verity's, in that both of them banked on their opponents being too off-balance to react quickly, but unlike Verity's, which was built on sex appeal and sequins, hers was based on seeming like she'd just escaped from a *Crocodile Hunter* rerun. No one under the age of forty wants to shoot someone who makes them think of Steve Irwin.

Especially not a hot femme Steve Irwin whose breasts had been known to stun whole rooms into silence when she wore shirts with the right neckline. Oh, she was deadly, no matter how you looked at her, but when she was making an effort, she was a reasonable counter to a small army.

"May I ask what you're doing in my house?" she asked, focusing on the intruders again.

"We don't answer traitors," said the one who had gotten their wits back a little faster.

"How am I a traitor?" she asked. "I'm not quite clear on that one. I'm a human being. I'm engaged to another human being. When we bred, we produced a third human being. That seems about like my duty to the species, quite well accomplished. Did I miss something?"

"Our records say there's a cuckoo living at this residence," said the second operative. "Ma'am, whatever you think you're doing here, your mind has been altered without your knowledge or consent. You are a victim. We would prefer not to harm you." The "but we will" was a silent coda, hanging unspoken in the air like a warning—or a threat.

"Ah, you mean my grandmother-in-law?" asked Shelby amiably. "She's one of those cuckoo-bird people you lot like to go on about. Not a big fan of them as a species, me, but I'm quite fond of Angela as an individual, since she's not charging us rent to live here with her. Can't stay forever, but for now, it's really quite pleasant."

"Ma'am," said the first operative. "We're going to have to ask you to come with us."

"Don't think so," said Shelby, and hit the ground just as Alex, who had come up behind the pair while she kept them distracted, stepped forward and pressed the handguns he was holding to the backs of their necks. He had one in each hand, giving him plenty of leverage to bring them both to a frozen stop.

"I could shoot her," said the one who'd already raised his gun.

"You could," agreed Alex. "Don't think I'd like that much. Don't think I'd be able to keep myself from returning the favor as soon as you pulled the trigger. You wouldn't even have time to see if you'd hit."

There was a terrible pause before the gun sagged toward the floor. Shelby bounced back to her feet and stepped forward to grab it and its twin, yanking them away from their former owners.

"I'll have those," she said, accent dropping back to a much less exaggerated level. "Mary, I'm guessing you're why the kids stopped howling? Thanks for that."

"The silence was actually what woke us up, before the gunfire," said Alex.

I quirked a very faint smile, allowing my appearance to slide back toward my normal. "Spoken like a true parent," I said. "What are we going to do with them?"

But one of the operatives had already stiffened, head tipping back until the barrel of Alex's gun had to be digging painfully into his neck. The other was drooping.

Then they both collapsed, spasming, to the floor.

Alex sighed and kicked one of them. "Verity warned me about this," he said sourly. "When they send out small teams, they send them with poison pills, just in case they're taken. Especially if there's a chance they might encounter a cuckoo."

"They can't be wearing proper anti-telepathy charms, or Isaac wouldn't have picked up on their presence," I said. "So they're prepared to die, just not to survive?"

"Imagine having the kind of numbers where you can treat your own people as cannon fodder," said Shelby with disgust, and prodded the closer operative with her foot, then knelt and removed their face mask, revealing a pale, unbreathing man with dark hair. His eyes were closed, and foam marked the corners of his mouth. He'd done a good job swallowing most of it. They were disciplined, these Covenant people, even if they weren't used to encountering monsters that actually fought back, even a little.

"The children are all right?" asked Alex.

I nodded. "Isaac started yelling for me as soon as he picked up on the intruders, and he shushed Charlotte when he realized there was real danger in the house. He should probably get extra dessert tonight."

"I will bake that child a tomato pie," said Shelby fiercely.

"How did they even know to come here?" I asked. "You've always been careful not to lead trouble home. But they were already in the house when I showed up."

"The Fringe," said Alex grimly. "They hit it this morning, shortly after we all got off the call. Dee called to tell me she wouldn't be coming to work."

"How does that give them your address?"

"How did they get the address for the Fringe?" countered Alex. "According to Dee, the elders were convinced I must have sold them out to save my own skin. She was doing her best to talk them down. Hopefully the fact that the Covenant came here too will convince them that I didn't give out their location."

"Who knows about both places, but isn't here?"

"Sarah," said Shelby.

I shook my head. "I was just with Sarah. She's in New York. Even if she were inclined to betray her own family to the Covenant, she wouldn't be in New York if she had."

"Plus she's still too emotionally fragile to have gone through with something like that," said Alex. "Making the decision to betray your family takes time and thought and effort. She's been a little too scattered for me to believe she's capable of that just now."

No one was foolish enough to say that Sarah would never do such a thing. Almost anyone is capable of almost anything, under the right circumstances, and pretending otherwise wasn't going to do us any good. If the Covenant operatives hadn't committed suicide upon being cornered, they would have been dragged outside and shoved into the trunk of a car before being driven out into the woods and shot. You don't leave enemies standing when you're in the middle of a war, no matter how much it offends your sense of being a good person to eliminate them.

"There's one other person I can think of," I said slowly. "Who might have been a target for known family associations, and would be able to lead people to both the Fringe and the house. Has anyone spoken to Megan recently?"

Neither Alex nor Shelby said a word.

The Fringe was an off-grid community of Pliny's gorgons who had gotten tired of lurking at the edges of the human world, never putting down roots or sure of where they'd be tomorrow. Instead, they'd taken the money they'd been able to earn by working under the table and off the books for people who needed odd jobs done, and used it to build their own settlement on land they actually owned, where they farmed, raised livestock, and did their best to raise their families away from prying human eyes. It was almost Amish in some ways, and blazingly modern in others. Dee, Alex's assistant at the zoo, was a resident of the more-transient community that existed outside the Fringe, but her brother was its founder. Her husband served as doctor to both groups, seeing them through injuries, illnesses, and childbirth.

And her daughter, Megan, was a medical student who had roomed with one Antimony Price at Lowryland. Annie had been going by the name "Melody West" back then, but she'd attracted the attention of the crossroads even so. The crossroads, and the cabal of human magic-users who'd been secretly using the Park to harvest luck from unwitting tourists, stripping them bare and tipping them out into the world with no way of knowing how ugly their lives were about to become. It had been a tidy little racket, right up until Annie wrecking-balled in and destroyed the whole thing.

Megan was still at med school, still playing human, still feigning a reality that wasn't her own for the sake of getting the training her species really needed her to have. Gorgons are synapsids, not reptiles, and a surprising number of human diseases have shown the ability to spill over into their population. This, combined with their forced proximity to human civilization, means that trained doctors are forever at a premium among their communities. Any education Megan received would be carried straight back to the gorgons and built upon.

Assuming she survived to graduate, which was far from guaranteed. And if the Covenant was tracking us down through our allies, she could be in serious trouble. "Alex, do you think Dee will take your calls?"

"If she knows what's good for her, she will," he said.

Shelby, meanwhile, was prodding the nearer corpse with the toe of her boot. "D'you think whatever they took will make the animals sick if we take them to the zoo?" she asked. Meaning she wanted to go with the time-honored local method of body disposal, "Feed the dead assholes to the occupants of the reptile house at the zoo." If forensics ever took a serious look at the fecal waste that place produced, they'd become convinced a serial killer was hiding in central Ohio.

"It might," said Alex. "Better to bribe the guards down at the crematorium."

Shelby sighed heavily. "Right. We'll tuck them down in the basement until Angela's available to go over with me."

Angela wasn't a receptive telepath, but she could project, meaning she could convince people to do almost anything she wanted. They'd take care of the corpses easily enough. I looked to Alex.

"I need to get back to the kids," I said. "You want to call Dee while I'm taking care of them? I can go over with you if she says you need to come to her."

"Sure," he said, and frowned. "Shouldn't you be heading back to Portland? Verity's going to freak if she thinks you're not taking care of Livvy."

"Verity's going to have better things to worry about, and so are you, so go ahead and make your calls," I said, and vanished.

Technically, as the youngest, Olivia *is* my primary charge. But no one would fault me for making sure Charlotte and Isaac were okay before I went back to her, and they might fault me if I *didn't.* All children are important, always.

I reappeared in the nursery the pair shared. They were still where I'd put them, clinging to each other. Charlotte sniffled when she saw me.

"Bad mans go?" she asked.

"Bad mans gone," I agreed, moving to scoop her into my arms. Isaac's eyes were no longer shining white, and as I watched, he rolled onto his back, staring at the ceiling. He looked exhausted, poor mite. I walked over to stroke his head with my free hand, holding Charlotte against my hip with the other. "You did really well, buddy," I informed him. "Good job keeping everyone safe."

He looked up at me and smiled the weary, innocent smile of a child, then closed his eyes as he slipped quickly into a doze. I turned my attention back to Charlotte.

She beamed at me, fear apparently forgotten, and locked her arms around my neck. I squeezed her in answer, taking a moment to enjoy the warm solidity of a child. She and Isaac were both seriously behind expected milestones in terms of verbal development, but that seemed to be due to Isaac's being able to translate most concepts telepathically. When Sarah transported all the cuckoos on Earth to a dimension filled with giant spiders—just roll with it—she met quite a few cuckoo children, including a girl named Morag who was being raised by her cuckoo grandmother in Ireland. The grandmother, whose name was Caoimhe, was in regular contact with Angela these days, the two of them sharing parenting tips and experiences, and between the two of them, they had determined that vocal delays were common in this sort of situation.

Mark and his sister Cici had probably experienced something similar, his semi-controlled childhood telepathy reaching out whenever she needed something, and the two of them growing up in a symbiotic tangle of ask-and-answer. Looking at the two of them, it was hard to lend any credence to Shelby's claim that they couldn't stay forever. I thought the whole family would be moving to a larger house before they'd be able to separate the children who were, effectively, siblings, and probably about as psychically entangled as it was possible for two small children to be.

"You'll have to talk more soon, though," I informed Charlotte, and kissed her forehead. "You'll be starting school before too much longer, and when you're around human kids, they're going to need you to use your words."

She reached and patted my cheek. "Mary," she informed me.

"Yes, well done. I'm Mary."

The nursery door opened. Charlotte squealed in wordless delight, reaching toward the person who'd just come in.

"There's my little ankle-biter," said Shelby happily, swooping over to pluck Charlotte from my hip and cuddle the child to herself. Charlotte squealed again, snuggling into her mother, as Shelby looked at me over her head.

"Alex would like to speak with you before you head out," she said. "If you wouldn't mind."

"Of course I don't mind. Where is he?"

"The kitchen."

The living room was directly beneath us. I nodded and stopped telling the world that I was a solid person who could stand on a solid surface. Promptly, I dropped through the floor to the room below, where I informed the world I was solid again before I could fall farther down and wind up in the basement. I landed with a thump and was briefly, smugly pleased with myself. That sort of trick is advanced ghosting. Baby ghosts can't drop through the floor unless they want to walk back from the center of the Earth.

There are no dinosaurs down there, by the way. Or giant caverns filled with amethyst crystals, no matter what Sarah's favorite bad science fiction movies might try to tell me. Just all the different colors and varieties of molten rock the world has to offer. There are far too many, and none of them are fun to trudge through. I did see some cool fossils, though. Not worth the trip, but still, pretty nifty.

One of the living-room windows had clearly been jimmied open from the outside. It was closed now, but the frame was ever so slightly askew, and the lock hadn't been flipped back into position. I willed myself invisible and moved closer to the window.

There was a van parked across the street. It claimed to be from a local tree service, but I'd been haunting this neighborhood off and on for years—ever since Kevin and Evelyn got married—and I'd never seen that service before. The font looked more like something you'd find in the Birmingham area than in Columbus. There aren't rules about local business font choices, but they tend to cluster, and most people can recognize a local business by the shape of the lettering on their signs, even if they couldn't articulate exactly how they know. Everything about this van said "not from around here" to me, even though there were no major flaws in its camouflage.

Maybe more damning, there were no workers. If they were a tree service, there should have been workers. Maybe not many of them, maybe just a few men with trimmers or rakes, but still, a van, sitting alone, wasn't going to get any work done. Hmm.

I walked through the wall and started across the lawn toward the street. The trees in our own yard were positioned such that no one would have seen my little abuse of the laws of physics unless they were standing in the driveway, so from the perspective of the people in the van, I was just walking from the direction of the house. That was good. Maybe they wouldn't try to drive away before I could get their license plate.

I changed angles as I got closer, to be sure I could do exactly that, taking note of the alphanumeric string and continuing onward, to knock on the driver's side window. The man behind the wheel jumped, more than he should have if he was just a law-abiding citizen sitting in his tree service van, and turned to stare at me with wide eyes. Another junior operative. I managed, barely, not to roll my own eyes. The Covenant was either scraping the bottom of the barrel or completely underestimating the threat we collectively posed.

Or, third, and more terrifying possibility, the Covenant knew exactly how dangerous the family was, and was holding their heavy hitters back while their expendables sniped at our fringes, knocking us down and wearing us out. Anyone can seem bumbling when they want to, but they had managed to endure for centuries, and it would be arrogant to think that they did it by accident, or because they had the Prices and Healys on their side. We needed to stay careful.

I knocked on the window again, and motioned for the man inside to roll it down so we could talk. Somehow, I didn't think pushing my face through the glass was going to make him a better conversationalist.

Haltingly, he did. "Can I help you, ma'am?" he asked.

"Whose trees are you working on?" I chirped.

He blinked. That was, apparently, not the answer he'd been expecting. "Uh . . . theirs?" He gestured to the house he was parked in front of.

"Yes, but what are their names? Where's your crew?"

He glanced, involuntarily, to the house behind me. Well, yes. That was where at least part of his crew was located, at least until it was safe to move the bodies. Recovering, he focused on me, and said, "In the backyard, trimming trees, and I don't like your tone, young lady."

"Trimming trees, huh? These are those new sonic tree trimmers I've been reading about? The ones that don't make any sound?" I craned my neck like I was trying to see around the house, then smiled at him. "They're not inside the house across the street, looking for the occupants? I know there are cars in the driveway. That doesn't mean everyone's home."

Again, that glance at the house, this time followed by a thinning of his lips and a measured gathering of his dignity. "I don't know what you're referring to, but I don't like your tone."

There are disadvantages of being a teenage girl forever. People assuming they can condescend to me because they're older is one of them. This guy was in his early twenties at the most, chin still spotty and skin around his eyes still smooth and firm. He wasn't that much older than I appeared to be. He was absolutely not older than I actually was. That wasn't going to stop him.

"I'm referring to the two Covenant operatives in full tactical gear that you sent into our home looking for evidence of a cuckoo nest," I said, with blithe sweetness. "They were very well armed, but ultimately unprepared for the babysitter." Shelby would be annoyed that I was taking credit for her confrontation, but she'd understand once I pointed out that I'd only done it to keep the children safe.

The man paled. "I don't know what you're talking about," he said.

"And I don't see your radio," I replied. "Which means you weren't a team of three. One second."

I took a step backward, and he seized the opportunity to roll up his window. I had to wonder about the Covenant budget, if they couldn't even provide their field team with a van new enough to have automatic windows. I flashed him a smile and a little wave, then turned and walked through the side of the van, emerging in the dimly lit back.

It wasn't the clutter of seats and equipment that I would have expected to find if I'd been harassing a real tree service, which was something of a relief; I try not to be an asshole to Angela and Martin's neighbors. They don't need a reputation for being jerks, not when they already have something of a reputation for being giant weirdoes. Unavoidable, given them, not something I needed to make worse.

Instead, the back of the van had been gutted and rebuilt, transformed into a mobile computer lab, with monitors and screens taking up the walls. A brunette woman in charcoal gray was seated there, speaking into a headset, partitioned off from the front of the van by a noise-dampening wall. That was why I hadn't been able to hear her before, and more, why she hadn't been able to hear my discussion with her friend. Too bad for her. She might have appreciated the warning.

"—report," she was saying. "I repeat, please report, over."

"If you're looking for your field agents, they're not going to report," I said. "They're a little busy being dead."

She stiffened, then slowly turned to face me. I smiled at her.

"Hi. I'm the babysitter. And you scared my kids."

I'll give her this: she was fast. Her hands moved almost too swiftly for me to follow, grabbing something from the desk next to her and aiming it at the center of my chest. I had time to register that it was a gun of some sort, and then she was pulling the trigger, sending a stream of water arching toward me.

I blinked as it splashed off my shirt, soaking in at the same time, then looked at her. "You know, most people answer 'hi' with a similar greeting, not by trying to initiate a wet T-shirt contest. Am I missing something?"

"Yes!" She lowered her water pistol—which was, of course, one of the deluxe ones that looked like a real gun, capable of really killing people, because why would the Covenant ever carry something that looked like a *toy*? It might undermine their overall aura of grim serious grimness. "That was holy water mixed with salt, thyme, and dill. You should be banished back to the hell you spawned from, spirit."

"Maybe, if I'd been spawned from a hell." As far as I know, there is no hell. There are various dimensions that people tend to *call* "hells," either because they're full of things that humans recognize as imps and devils, or because they're on fire all the time. But there's no single level of the afterlife corresponding to "hell." What would we even call it? The firelight?

Humans like naming conventions. We like them a lot. So that would probably be the name, and we'd all have to snicker every time we said it.

Right. Focus, Mary. I scowled at the Covenant woman. "I am not a demon. I am not a devil. I am a babysitter, and you endangered my charges with your reckless attempt to breach their home. I'm here to tell you not to do that again."

"Or what, you'll haunt me?"

"Yes," I said, with surpassing calm, and waited for her own calm to visibly waver before I smiled a thin, razor's-edge smile and leaned forward, finally allowing the water that had soaked into my shirt to fall through me to the van floor. "I'll haunt you every day for the rest of your life. You won't be able to receive a single piece of confidential intelligence without me being right there to hear it; you won't be able to take a shit in peace. Everything you know, I'll know, including what you ate for dinner."

She drew back. "That's disgusting."

"But that's what happens if you force my hand." I shrugged, watching her. "The ball's in your court. You can go back to the Covenant, tell them there was nothing here, and ask for another assignment. Or you can go back to the Covenant, tell them there was nothing here, and walk away. Things are about to get really unpleasant for anyone who doesn't walk away. I'd hate to see you stuck in the middle of what's about to go down."

"If I have to die for the glory of the human race, so be it!"

"Oh." I sighed. "You're one of those, aren't you?"

By now, Alex would have glanced out a window and seen the inexplicable tree-service truck parked across the street. He'd be on his way out to meet us, and the longer I could keep the person who was watching the cameras distracted, the better.

"What do you mean, 'one of those'?"

"I mean one of those people who think humans are better than everybody else, just because of their genetic makeup." I shook my head, watching her face. "No one chooses who their parents are going to be, or what species they're going to be born as. People are just people. It's what they do that matters, not how they're born."

"God gave this world to the human race," she countered.

"Lady, every species I've encountered has gods. Even humans have more than one, depending on where they're from and what they're hoping to get out of their religion. Even the dead have gods. Just because you say one god handed the world over on a platter, why does that mean none of the other gods get a say?"

Someone hammered on the outside of the van, and I smiled.

"Maybe you should have prayed to a better god," I said, and disappeared.

Ten

> "Everyone thinks their way of doing things is the best way of doing things, no matter how much evidence they're presented to the contrary."
>
> —Juniper Campbell

Standing outside a creepy surveillance van in Columbus, Ohio

ALEX DIDN'T BLINK WHEN I appeared beside him, just went back to hammering on the side of the van. The driver's-side door opened and the driver emerged, a short baton in one hand. He was holding it low by his hip but was clearly ready to swing if necessary.

Alex looked at him, unflinching. The man appeared faintly nonplussed at being stared down by a bespectacled man who had visually settled into his profession as a herpetologist and reptile keeper without a single word of complaint or attempt to look like he did something more interesting with his time. Alex was a man who'd been born to study things, and was quite happy knowing that he'd be able to spend the rest of his life doing it.

He was also, when pressed, his father's son, and that made him a lot more dangerous than most people realized on first glance. His eyes were narrowed behind his glasses, and he was standing with an easy looseness that could quickly translate into whip-fast motion.

"What the hell, man?" demanded the driver.

"Surveillance kit's in the back," I said. "They're definitely Covenant."

That was either the right or the wrong thing to say, depending on your perspective. The driver put two and two together at once, identifying Alex as a threat, and swung his baton hard for the side of Alex's neck, apparently seeing it as a soft, exposed target. It would have been, if he'd had any chance of hitting.

See, every modern member of the family has been encouraged to take up some sort of physical hobby that can translate into a combat discipline. It lets them train without risking Covenant attention, since they were likely to be watching the mixed martial arts and boxing communities for signs of Price survival, but not the dance studios and the roller derby courts. Alex, when he was younger, had been a remarkably active member of the Society for Creative Anachronism, voluntarily traveling back in time every weekend to an era before the Covenant had been quite so successful at their "holy mission."

He made a lot of contacts in the cryptid community through his time in the past, and he became a dismayingly good fighter. Sure, he used a padded foam sword instead of a steel one, but they treated their historical stakes like they were the real thing, and when someone hit you with a fake sword, you were supposed to go down. He got very good at not being hit. The baton swung, and Alex wasn't there, leaving it to slam into the side of the van, making a dent in the paneling.

The sound must have been incredibly jarring inside. I turned to watch the back doors, waiting to see if the surveillance tech would appear, and thus missed whatever Alex did next. But I heard the driver yelp, and the clatter as his baton hit the pavement. When I glanced back over my shoulder, Alex had him pressed against the van, one hand on the back of his head, the other engaged with twisting his arm up and behind his back at a painful angle.

"Hi," said Alex. "I'm Alexander Price. That's my house you just sent your flunkies to break into. My daughter is in that house. She's very young, and doesn't understand danger yet. She could have been hurt. People get hurt when you do things like this."

The man made a pained squeaking noise, his cheek squashed against the metal and preventing him from speaking clearly. Alex gave him a harder shove, grinding him against the side of the van.

"Now," he said, voice very low. "This is what's going to happen now. I'm going to take you inside, and we're going to ask you some questions. As a family. And if we don't like the answers, you're going to join your friends in the basement, waiting for our next run to the dump."

"What keeps this one from going the way of the last two?" I asked.

"They don't tend to equip the observers with suicide pills," said Alex. "Too much chance they'll bite down by mistake. The risk/reward balance doesn't check out."

"Ah, good."

The van's rear door swung open, and the woman who'd been

working the cameras sprang out, a new gun in her hands. Unlike the previous one, this appeared to be a real gun, capable of firing actual bullets, not over-seasoned holy water. She yelled as she charged out into the open, apparently thinking this was some sort of action film. I stepped in front of her. As I had hoped, she hesitated, trying to pull back in time to avoid a collision. Instead, she fell forward and passed cleanly through me, stumbling out the other side of my insubstantial form and right into Shelby's fist, the Australian having emerged to join the family brawl already in progress.

Shelby hit her squarely in the chin, with enough force that I heard the crack of knuckles against bone. The woman went down like a sack of laundry, hitting the ground hard and insensate. I clapped, slow and deliberately halfway mocking, then looked to Alex.

"You got him?"

He nodded.

"Okay. I'm going to head back to Portland. Do you . . . do you have your phone on you?"

He blinked at me before he nodded again. "I do. Mary, what's going on?"

"It's not my place to say," I said. "We'll call you, I'm sure. Right now, you should call Uncle Mike. Get him out here, so you'll have some backup on the ground."

Then I was gone, not giving him the chance to say anything. There aren't many things I would say aren't my business, where the family is concerned—I may not have been a blood relative, but I've been around long and consistently enough that there's very little that's off-limits for me to tell a family member. I've done the sex talk and the puberty talk and the where do babies come from talk, but I've never done the "I'm sorry, your aunt is dead" talk. That was one I was going to leave to his parents, because I was caught up enough in my own grief that I couldn't handle it.

You might think being dead would make death easier for me to deal with. You would be so very wrong. Being dead means I know exactly how much life matters, and how much it sucks to have it taken away. I didn't even have the cold comfort of being able to visit Jane in the afterlife: she had gone somewhere I couldn't follow and would never have been able to. She was as lost to me as she was to the rest of the family, and I ached knowing I would never see her burn pancakes or wrestle with her complicated thoughts about the family profession again. She had been a unique, complicated woman, and she was gone, and I didn't want her to be.

As I had when facing the Covenant operatives in the hall outside the nursery, I felt a pang of longing for the crossroads. They had been horrible, and no one sensible would want them back. I didn't want them back, not really, but I wanted the power they had given me—the power that would have allowed me to *do* something to avenge my friend and charge.

The crossroads never gave anyone anything for free, but they were always very generous with me when what I wanted was to do harm. Seeing me give in to temptation and fall into the habit of hurting people seemed to delight them. I think they may have seen it as the gateway to me truly becoming their creature, breaking the ties that were holding me to humanity, and as I shifted myself across the country yet again, I didn't *care*. The Covenant killed Jane. They deserved to pay for what they'd done.

And they *would* pay. They *would*. There was no way the rest of the family let them walk away from this. They were hurting people all across the continent, and while their strike-and-retreat tactics might seem amateur, they were allowing them to test our defenses and weaken our reserves. They had us outnumbered, based on everything I knew about their current organizational status. If this was going to be a battle of attrition, they would win, in the end.

We just had to find a way not to let them.

No one in Portland was actively calling me, and so I landed outside in front of the house rather than next to anyone in need. That was fine. I took a deep breath to center myself and started toward the door, my clothes re-forming around me as I walked. By the time I reached the porch, I was wearing a white blouse with a Peter Pan collar and a knee-length plaid skirt, with polished black patent leather shoes and knee-length socks. A bit immature by modern standards but perfectly acceptable by the fashions of the day I'd lived and died in, and comforting in their vintage familiarity.

I reached for the doorknob.

"Mary!" called a voice.

I turned.

Sally was standing near the corner of the house, face drawn tight with anxiety, a spear in her hand. That made sense. Sally had spent years stuck in a brutal bottle dimension with Thomas, and during her time there, her favorite spear became something of a surrogate teddy bear. If things were tense inside, it was reasonable that she would have raided the armory for a polearm she could cling to.

She beckoned me urgently toward her, and after a momentary

pause, I went, trotting through the ankle-length grass to her side. "What is it?" I asked.

"You don't want to go in there." She punctuated her words with a sharp, decisive shake of her head.

"Why not?"

"They're all . . . well, they were all yelling at each other, and now everybody's crying," she said. "You were with them, right? At the carnival?"

"I was."

"Did Jane really . . . ?"

I nodded.

"Dammit. I just met her, but she seemed okay, and James is pretty broken up about it."

"Is he out here with you?"

Mouth making a complicated shape somewhere almost exactly between a smile and a frown, Sally nodded. "He wants to be upset about Jane, like everybody else is. He really considers himself a part of the family now, and the family is upset, so he should be too. But he's all swallowed up by being happy that I'm here, and not really believing that I'm here, and giving me little pop quizzes about things that only Sally Henderson would know, which he expects Sally Price to have somehow miraculously forgotten—or more likely, never have known. It's like he doesn't *want* me to be real."

"Oh, he wants you to be real," I said. "He just can't risk accepting that you are, and being wrong. If you're not the actual, honest-to-God Sally he lost back in New Gravesend, then you're going to break him, because he can't handle losing you twice. If he's being weird, that's probably why."

"That sounds about right for James," she said, and sighed. "But anyway. Thomas is too busy being broken up over his *real* daughter to want his surrogate one hanging around not being dead at him, and that makes him feel guilty, and that's not good for him right now. James and I came outside because staying in there when we weren't grieving like everyone around us seemed like a sort of asshole move, and now you don't want to go in there unless you're ready to be hit by a giant tsunami of people having feelings."

"I'm pretty good at feelings, Sally, but thanks for the warning, and I need to talk to Kevin."

She waved with her free hand as I turned and walked back to the house, then through the wall, not bothering to backtrack all the way to the door. Passing through the wall put me in Kevin's office, which looked so much like his maternal grandfather's office that it always made me ache a little. Alexander Healy was a Covenant man until he realized the Covenant way was the wrong one, and when that happened, he traded in his life as he knew it for the chance to make something better in America. He'd walked away with his wife beside him, leaving everything he'd ever known behind. But he'd never quite managed to shake the building blocks of his training, and he'd spent his adult life blissfully surrounded by books, doing the bulk of his research in a room perfectly designed for his needs. Alice had packed her grandfather's office into boxes long before Kevin built the compound, and yet Kevin had somehow managed to recreate it in his own image.

A large leather armchair dominated the space not occupied by desk or lamps, making this the perfect place to retreat for reading or research. I trailed my hand along the arm of the chair as I walked toward the door and, not wanting to break my streak of defying the laws of physics, through it.

The yelling period Sally mentioned had definitely come to an end. Evelyn was clinging to Kevin on the loveseat, both of them weeping helplessly, while Elsie sat on the couch with her hands over her face, shoulders shaking from the force of her grief. She didn't look up as I entered. Arthur was sitting next to her with one hand on her back and a perplexed expression on his face, like he didn't quite know what he was supposed to be doing right now, or how he was meant to go about doing it.

Sarah wasn't in the room. Neither were Sam and Antimony. They were probably out at the barn, swinging in the rafters—literally, they both do trapeze work, and they're more likely to climb things when they're unhappy, meaning I didn't expect to see either of them on the ground for a week or more—and waiting for the worst of the shock to fade before they came back inside to deal with the rest of the family.

Alice and Thomas were standing near the back of the room, both of them dry-eyed. Thomas still looked sorrowful, but almost distantly so, as if he knew he *should* be weeping, but wasn't sure quite how to bridge the gap between "ought to" and actuality. Alice, on the other hand, had clearly *been* crying. Her eyes were red and the skin beneath them was puffy, and her nose looked raw, like she'd been blowing it almost constantly since I'd last seen her. Her expression was hard, barely contained rage and the burning need to point it at someone. I wouldn't have wanted to be on the other side of that look.

Out of everyone in the room, she was the first to notice my arrival.

She pulled away from Thomas, who let her go before looking almost helplessly at his hands, and strode across the room to grab my shoulders.

"Where did you *go*?" she demanded.

I turned insubstantial enough to back out of her grip, leaving her holding nothing, and answered, "New York, to start with. I needed to find Sarah. She'd gone to the hospital to sit with Mark and tell him what a terrible person she was, for not managing to keep Leonard from breaking out of her control. She was supposed to be coming here next, to get Greg and join the rest of the family. Have you not seen her?"

"Not yet."

"Huh." She could easily be outside with her spider, James, and Sally, but she might also have changed her mind and gone somewhere else.

Well, it wasn't like I could go playing *Where in the World Is Carmen Sandiego?* with Sarah in the middle of a family emergency. She'd show up, or she wouldn't, and we'd cope with it either way, the same way we always did. If there's anything we're collectively good at, it's rolling with the punches and seeing what may come.

"What do you mean, 'huh'?" demanded Alice. "My *daughter* is *dead* and you disappeared to chase after someone you didn't even bring back with you! Where have you *been*?"

"New York and then Ohio and I will thank you not to take that tone with me, young lady," I snapped. "I changed your diapers when you were a baby and I'm going to change them again when you're too old to remember who I am, and you do *not* talk to me like I'm a child."

"I'm sorry, Mary," said Alice, instantly contrite. It wasn't feigned, either; I knew her well enough to see that the shame in her eyes was sincere. She bowed her head, shoulders sagging. "I'm just . . . Jane's *dead*. We're all upset."

"I know, honey." I looked past her to Kevin and Evelyn. "There have been two more attacks. One in Chicago, on the Carmichael—Rose told me about it. I doubt there were any survivors among the Covenant forces. The second was substantially smaller, in Ohio. They were after the Bakers. I think the Covenant wasn't quite sure what they were walking into, so they just sent a small team—two field agents and two handlers. The agents got into the house."

Evelyn gasped, clapping her hand over her mouth. Kevin stood up a little straighter, expression bleeding out of his face and leaving him cold and neutral.

"Was anyone hurt?"

"Both field agents," I said. "I managed to lead them away from the kids' room, and then they ran into Shelby."

Evelyn lowered her hand, cracking a brief and somewhat pained-looking smile. "I cannot wait for him to marry that girl," she said.

"They're not married?" asked Thomas.

"No, Dad, they're not," said Kevin. "They were working on wedding plans, and then Shelby found out she was pregnant, and they decided to hold off." His tone all but challenged Thomas to have a problem with that.

Thomas only nodded and said, "Good for them, putting the health of the baby before a wedding."

Under the circumstances, it wouldn't have been appropriate for me to laugh, and so I satisfied myself with a very brief smirk. If Kevin was hoping to find disapproval from his father, he was going to be working a lot harder than that. Thomas had been sleeping with Alice long before they were married—he'd actually needed to propose several times before she noticed, and they'd barely managed to get married far enough in advance of Kevin's birth to keep people from counting on their fingers.

"The team in Ohio has been neutralized, but I need to talk to Annie," I said. "Do you know where she is?"

"She and Sam took Jane's . . . took Jane out to the barn," said Kevin. "We're going to organize a funeral, and bury her at the back of the property."

I nodded.

Kevin's original plans for the family compound included a small, bespoke parcel of land for a private cemetery. Part of what had led him to settle in Oregon rather than Washington, which had a higher population of several friendly cryptid species, was the legality of home burial. We could lay Jane to rest here, and her family would never be very far away from her. We couldn't have done that in Washington.

Alice still owned several plots in the Buckley Township cemetery, near her parents and grandparents, but Jane would never have wanted to be buried there. Buckley had only ever been her home in the most technical of senses. It was where she'd been born. That was all the claim it had over her.

"Why do you need to talk to Annie?" asked Evelyn.

"Because whoever dispatched that team to the house in Ohio hit the local gorgon community first. The one they call the Fringe? And the only person who might have known about the Fringe *and* the house is Alex's assistant, Dee, but she was at the Fringe when they were attacked, and she's too smart to think she can play with the Covenant and come away unharmed. Her daughter, on the other hand, was Annie's roommate while she was working at Lowryland, and she's been off at medical school, unprotected by the rest of the gorgons. If someone could get the info on *her*, they'd be able to use her to track down the gorgons *and* her mother's employer. It's all a matter of following the threads."

"So you want to ask Annie if her old roommate would have sold her out?"

"No. I want to ask Annie if she knows where Megan is. She's not family, so I can't just go to her—I lost that ability when the crossroads went away. They needed me to be capable of haunting literally anyone at a moment's notice, and so I was a lot better at aiming for non-family when they were around. We need to check on her, both for her safety and because if she's been taken, that puts us all in danger."

"And you're *sure* no one was hurt?"

"The two dead Covenant field agents might not agree with that, but our people are fine," I said firmly. "Alex's calling Uncle Mike to see if things in Chicago are settled enough to let him come play backup. To be honest, I think Uncle Mike will appreciate having somewhere to aim all that anger he's carrying after the attack at the Carmichael. One of you needs to call Alex. He needs to know what's happening here."

"We will," said Kevin. "I promise, we will. We're just waiting to catch our breath before we do that. I don't . . . I don't think any of us can say it yet."

"That's understandable."

"You didn't tell him?" asked Evelyn.

I shook my head. "It didn't feel like it was my place. I'm going to go look for Annie now. Thank you for telling me where to find her."

"James has agreed to keep the body cold enough that we can put together a funeral," said Evelyn. "He can't buy us forever, but he can get us a few days. That should be enough."

"No," I said. "It shouldn't be. It should take us years to put together a proper memorial for that woman. But it's going to have to be, and we're going to make it work."

I turned then, and walked back out through the wall, heading for the back of the property, and the barn. There wasn't anything else for me to do inside, and we weren't magically going to solve this if I hung around and grieved with the rest of the family. All the tears in the world weren't going to bring Jane back.

It wasn't surprising that Thomas wasn't crying. He'd barely known her. They'd met for the first time earlier today, although there had been a few awkward phone calls before this, and while he'd always known there was a second child on the way at the time of his disappearance, she'd never been more than an abstract idea to him, a person who might exist. All her complexity and contradiction had happened far away from him, and he was mourning the possibility of their relationship more than anything real.

I had little doubt that as the family gathered and the funeral preparations got underway, he'd come to know her better, and his sorrow over what he would now never have the chance to experience firsthand would grow until it engulfed him. He was as capable of mourning as anyone else. He was just oddly outside this most intimate of familial rituals, at least for now.

Stepping through the back wall of the house into the yard brought me into sight of the firepit and the obstacle course. James and Sally were seated at the former, the fire unlit and Sally shivering slightly, while James looked perfectly comfortable despite the chill in the air. Elemental sorcerers are annoying that way. James looked as shaken as everyone inside, although from the hungry, almost-desperate way he was looking at Sally, I could guess that it had more to do with someone returning from the dead than it did with Jane's death. I kept walking.

Motion caught my eye as I passed the obstacle course. I looked up and saw the top of Greg's bristly head moving behind the low wall that was used as a final challenge for people doing the rope climb. It was no challenge for him, of course; he was a spider. Climbing things was basically his purpose in life. I paused to cup my hands around my mouth and call, "Sarah! You up there?"

Yes, Aunt Mary, said Sarah's mental voice, meekly. *Do you need me to come down?*

"No, honey," I said, trying to think the words clearly as I spoke them. "I'm going to the barn to check on Annie and Sam. You're fine where you are. Just come inside or go to the firepit if you start feeling lonely, or sad, or like any of this is your fault." I paused. "Is Olivia still with you?"

Evie came and got her when everyone got back from the carnival. She needed grandbaby hugs.

Small mercies. "All right, then, sweetie. Take care of yourself."

Okay, Aunt Mary, she replied. *And thank you.*

"I love you too, Sarah," I said, and resumed my trek toward the barn.

I've done a lot more walking since the crossroads died. It's slow and it's boring and compared to popping in and out of existence, it can feel like a waste of time. Since I'm dead, it's not even like I get any benefits from the exercise. But when weighed against an eternity of subservience to an unspeakable force from outside the bounds of natural reality, I'll take the long walk every time.

The barn loomed ahead of me, and I walked through the wall, looking up as I did. The makeshift trapeze rig that webbed the rafters was sitting motionless, clearly not having been used any time in the recent past. I blinked, and took a more thorough look around.

It wasn't until my second pass that I spotted Sam and Antimony. They were up in what would normally have been called the hayloft, but was entirely devoid of hay, used instead for equipment and taxidermy storage. Maybe that was why I'd missed them the first time. In his natural form, holding perfectly still, Sam could be mistaken for a badly stuffed trophy of some sort. Annie wasn't moving, either. She was balled up against him, her knees drawn up to her chest and her arms wrapped around his torso, holding him as tightly as he was holding her. I couldn't see her face. He, however, looked completely miserable.

Right. He was a member of my family, and I could generously interpret this expression to mean he needed me. I took a deep breath, closed my eyes, and vanished, reappearing in the hayloft right next to him.

He didn't jump, just turned to me and said, wearily, "Hi, Mary."

"Long way from the kid who freaked out because a dead girl might be watching him shower," I said, and sat down next to him on the edge of the loft, letting my legs dangle.

"Oh, I'd still be upset if I thought you were watching me shower," he said. "I'd just tell Annie, and she'd take care of it."

I leaned forward a bit, to look at her. "She okay?"

"No," he said, simply, and squeezed her tighter for a moment. "I don't think she really believed her family was mortal. Not the way most of us do. They do this ridiculous shit, and maybe they get hurt, but they walk away from it. Every time. That's what Prices *do*."

"That's the Kairos that Franny brought to the family," I said. "It doesn't make them lucky, not the way we normally understand luck, but it makes them *fortunate*. When they flip a coin, it will coincidentally almost always come up the way they need it to."

"So how did Leonard manage to get Jane with just one shot?"

"There's a word in there that this family likes to pretend doesn't mean anything," I said. "'Almost.' A normal person might win the coin flip fifty times out of a hundred. Someone with Kairos ancestry could win it ninety-nine times out of a hundred, and start feeling like they can't lose. But that hundredth time, they will. Jane just got unlucky with where she fell in the coin-flip order."

Leaning over, I very gently stroked Annie's hair with one hand. "I'm sorry, sweetheart. I'm so, so sorry. But I need you to pull yourself together enough to talk to me, okay?"

She sat up enough to crane her head around and look at me, not loosening her grip on Sam. "Leonard Cunningham killed Aunt Jane," she said, voice dull. "I'm going to kill him."

"Yes, he did, and I'm not going to stop you," I agreed. "He's a bad man, and the world will be better off without him in it. But Annie, I need to know: why was he able to shake off Sarah's mental control?"

"He's pretty high up in the Covenant," she said. "Important enough that they actually care about him, in a way they don't care about a lot of their foot soldiers. He's supposed to take the whole thing over one of these days. I'm guessing that means he carries anti-telepathy charms, just in case."

"That worries me," I said.

Annie frowned. "Why?"

"Because Rose told me the Covenant hit Chicago when she answered my call in Iowa. And I was just in Ohio, and the Covenant went after your brother and his family—they're *fine*, we caught the intruders before they could do anything, Isaac heard them and called for me and no one was hurt except for the Covenant. But they knew where the house *was*. They also attacked the gorgon community near there. So they know things they shouldn't know, and they were looking for cuckoos."

"I thought you said you were careful to make sure they didn't see or remember Sarah when you were all in New York," said Annie.

"We were. Which means they're getting their information somewhere else. Have you heard from Megan recently?"

"No," said Annie, slowly. "She was off at medical school the last time we spoke, but it's been long enough since then that she's probably graduated by now. If she's not in Ohio, she's going to be with another gorgon community, or near one. And it doesn't matter, because she would never sell us out to the Covenant."

"I didn't say she sold us out, just asked if you knew where she was," I said. "I don't think Megan is their only source of information. But hitting two gorgon communities and Alex in the same day starts to paint a picture I don't like. If she's been compromised, or captured, she could be in danger, and they could be leaning on her to learn more about you."

"These people are real assholes," said Sam. "I hope you know that."

I nodded gravely. "Oh, we've known for a long time that the Covenant was an organization comprised almost entirely of assholes. And now they've gone too far, and we're going to have to make them stop, whatever that looks like."

"But there are so *many* of them," said Annie. "I was at Penton Hall. I saw their resources. They have the manpower. They have the weapons. If they know how to find us, they're going to pick us off one by one, and there's not going to be anything we can do about it."

"Optimistic," I said. "But presumably inaccurate. Look, we're not out to destroy the Covenant. I mean, it would be nice, but you're right—they have the numbers, and they're not going to go down easy. So we don't want to destroy them. We just want them to agree to stay the fuck out of North America and leave us alone."

Sam scowled. "My dad's in China," he said.

"We're one family," I said. "Asking them to concede a continent is about the limit of what we can hope to achieve. Even that's going to be pushing things."

"Why does North America get to be the one that's spared?"

"Because that's where we live, and where all our stuff is," I snapped. "Technically, right now, there's already one continent spared, and that's Australia. If we want to do more than this, we're going to need to focus. We've never had the numbers, or the freedom of movement. For a long time, only the Covenant thinking the whole family had died out made it even halfway safe to do silly things like 'going to college' and 'having kids.' Well, that's over now. Now we start fighting in earnest."

"This sucks," said Sam.

"It does," I agreed, and vanished, reappearing on the barn floor.

They had laid Jane out on one of the stainless steel work tables, still in her clothes from earlier, now with a sheet pulled up to her shoulders, covering the bullet wound in her chest. There was a little blood dried in her hair. Apart from that, she could have been taking an afternoon nap, serene and relaxed. I'd already seen her walk away into whatever waits beyond the various levels of light, but I was still hoping, in a distant way, that I'd find some trace of her when I approached. There was nothing. This was just a hollow shell, a place where Jane had lived for a while, but would never live again.

Ghosts—my kind of ghosts—don't cry, but I swear I felt my eyes burn with the need to shed impossible tears, and I rubbed them as I turned away, looking up toward Annie and Sam at the same time.

"Well?" I called. "Are we going to deal with this, or what?"

Sam gathered Annie in his arms and jumped down. It was easily twenty feet from the hayloft to the ground, but he made it look easy, like everyone should be leaping whole stories like it was no big deal. He landed with his feet spread and his knees bent to take the impact, lowering Annie's own feet to the floor.

She punched him in the shoulder as she pulled away. "Ow," he said, with neither heat nor force. She clearly hadn't hit him that hard.

Antimony wrinkled her nose. "Don't jump off roofs without warning me, you dick."

"It wasn't a roof, it was the hayloft," he protested. "Mary, did you screw up her flashcards when she was little-little, if she can't tell the difference between a roof and a hayloft?"

"You're an asshole," said Antimony blandly, but she was smiling as Sam looped his arm around her waist and tugged her back over to him.

"Your relationship dynamic is mysterious and strange to me," I said. "Annie, do you have a current number for Megan?"

"Yeah, we've stayed in touch," she said, and dug her phone out of her pocket. Then she frowned at it, and passed it to Sam, digging for a second phone. I was sure there was a reason, and she'd tell me if it was important, so I didn't ask.

The second phone, she unlocked and dialed, raising it to her ear. "What did you want me to ask her?" she asked. "I can't exactly lead with 'Hey did you sell us out?' It's rude."

"Ask if she's seen anything strange, or if anyone's been sniffing around who shouldn't have been."

Annie nodded, returning her attention to the ringing phone. Then she frowned, sharp and sudden. In a reasonably pleasant tone, she said, "Hey, Megan, it's Mel. Give me a ring if you get this, okay? I'm a little worried about you."

She lowered the phone, hitting the button to disconnect as she looked at me. "Straight to voicemail," she said. "I'll text, in case she's on rounds or something and just not in a position to answer the phone."

Most people Annie's age default to texts. Annie, sadly for her occasional attempts to blend in with her own demographic, knows enough about computers to understand that texts can be recovered and read by people other than their intended recipient. If she wants to maintain operational security, she needs to stick with voice. Even recorded messages can be a risk.

One good thing about the Covenant knowing we're here and declaring open hostilities: while we still need to be careful if we don't want to lead them home, we no longer need to pretend we don't exist. That was probably going to open some options up for the younger generations.

Annie tapped briefly away at her phone, then locked the screen and put it back into her pocket. "There," she said. "Hopefully she calls back sooner than later."

"And if she doesn't?" asked Sam.

"Then we start getting really worried." She looked at me. "I swear, Megan wouldn't sell us out. She's good people, and she wants to keep her community safe. And even if she *did* want to sell us out, she doesn't know much. I was Melody for most of the time I was around her. She didn't find out who I really was until the end."

"But if she knows her mother is working for a Price, that makes her a useful source of information about two members of the family, even if most of her information about you is inaccurate or filtered through a cover story."

Annie's phone began to ring. She pulled it out of her pocket again, glaring at the screen for a moment. "Blocked number," she said, looking back to me. "Do I answer?"

"Is that your real phone?"

She shook her head. "That's why I used it."

"Answer."

She raised the phone to her ear. "Hello?"

Almost immediately, she flinched, lowered the phone, and put it on speaker.

"You killed my aunt, you worthless fucker," she spat.

"Now, is that any way to talk to the man who's going to marry you?" asked the carefully cultured voice of Leonard Cunningham.

"Funny," said Sam. "She's never called *me* a worthless fucker."

"I don't know when you upgraded your stupid plan from 'Bring me back into the fold' to 'Marry me,' but it's still not going to happen," said Annie. "Even if I'd been looking to trade Sam in on a newer model, I don't date boys who shoot my relatives. It's a rule of mine."

"Ah, but what about men?" countered Leonard. "Annie, be reasonable. I only shot her because she was trying to kill me. You wouldn't want her to kill me, would you?"

"Only because having a Covenant asshole I recognize is better than the alternative," she said. "You killing my relatives doesn't endear you to me. How do you have this number?"

"I don't think that's any of your concern. May I assume you've taken your aunt's body to her final resting place?"

"You may," she snapped. "How did you get this number?"

"Really, Annie, you need to work on that temper of yours. The woman who was with you in the tent, I've seen her before. She was on television with your sister, wasn't she? During the incident which brought your family back to our attention, with the snake god."

"It wasn't a god, it was just a snake," she snapped.

"Snakes do work their way into places where they don't need to be, don't they? Slither, slither, through the cracks, whether they're cracks in reality or your defenses. Hard to keep them out, when you really get down to it."

"Leonard, you're a smug asshole, and I'm going to take great pleasure in putting a bullet between your eyes."

"I wouldn't make threats if I were you," he said, voice dropping into something less playful, more serious. "Your window of opportunity for changing sides is growing narrower by the moment, and I think you'll have some genuine regrets if you allow it to close while you're still standing in the wrong position."

"I was never going to choose your side, Leonard," she said. "And then you started shooting my relatives. I take that personally."

"That woman was Alice Healy, wasn't she?"

Annie said nothing.

"She didn't die, somehow, and she's stayed young enough that I almost didn't recognize her. I could tell she had the Carew look about her, but they bred like rabbits in their day—we still have plenty of Carews running around the place, bleeding on the floors and getting underfoot. Then she showed up again, and she didn't like it when I shot the little blonde. She didn't like it at all. There were always questions about the circumstances surrounding her death. If her children survived, which they clearly did, then why shouldn't she have done the same? Dark magic explains the agelessness nicely. It also explains why we're going to wipe you from the face of the Earth. You don't deserve to live here any longer."

"How are you not *dead*?" demanded Annie. "Grandma shot you. She doesn't miss."

"She did shoot me, and she didn't miss," said Leonard. "But she shot me in the chest, and unlike the relative of yours I apparently killed, I was wearing decent body armor. I stayed down because that beast you call a boyfriend was rampaging."

"How. Did. You. Get. This. Number?"

"It was easy to copy from the screen of the phone next to me."

Annie paled. "I swear to God, Leonard, if you hurt her—"

"You'll what? Say more nasty things you don't mean? Fuck your monster boyfriend while you think about me? Set some things on fire? You're going to do all those things anyway."

"She doesn't have anything to do with this," said Annie. "Leonard, please."

"Oh, now you'll demonstrate manners? When I might have a friend of yours in my power? I see how it is." It was impossible to listen to him and not interpret his tone as mocking. "Take me off speaker."

"I don't think—"

"Take me off speaker right now, or I swear to God the abomination dies. Don't test me on this, Annie. You know I won't hesitate to correct the cosmic error of its existence."

With a hopeless glance at Sam and me, Annie took her phone off speaker and raised it to her ear.

I didn't hear what he said next. But I saw her pale further, and wobble like she was about to collapse. She grabbed Sam's arm with her free hand, using him to hold herself upright. "You *wouldn't*," she spat.

He said something else. She turned to Sam, expression just this shy of hopeless, and asked, "How long?"

A reply.

"That's not enough time."

Pause.

"I understand."

She hung up the phone and turned to me, eyes blazing. Literally—they had lit up from the inside, like her pupils were suddenly aflame. "Mary, how much can you lift?"

"That is not a question I like," I replied. "Why?"

"Because *Leonard* wanted to give me one last chance to pick the winning side in our little conflict. One last opportunity to cross no-man's-land and save myself." She turned his name into a curse, twisting each syllable into a mockery of the very concept of the name. It was a neat trick, and probably something she'd learned from the Aeslin mice. "But seriously, how much can you lift?"

"If I don't have to carry it all that far, maybe eighty pounds. If I don't have to carry it at all, a lot more."

"Shit." Her expression turned hopeless, the fire in her eyes not quite guttering out, but dying back to ash and embers. "The bullet Leonard used to shoot Aunt Jane had a GPS tracker in it."

"They can *do* that?"

"They can do a lot of things with heat-protective casing and miniaturization these days," said Sam, grimly.

"They don't have a fix on our location yet," said Annie. "They *do* have Megan, but we can worry about that in a little while. Leonard wanted me to know that they'd have a location on us within the hour, and if I wanted to get my family out of range of the airstrike, I needed to start moving."

I turned to stare in horror at Jane's body, serene and silent on the table.

"An hour isn't enough time to get everyone out of here," I said. "The mice alone . . ."

"I know. So *how much can you lift*?"

Her meaning suddenly came clear. This was how I could help my family, even without the crossroads bolstering my natural capabilities as one of the unquiet dead. I lunged for Jane, jerking her body into an upright position and wrapping my arms around her torso in a parody of an embrace.

"Baby, I'm sorry," I said, and blinked out of the world of the living, pulling her with me into the realms of the dead.

Eleven

"Sooner or later, we all say goodbye. Sometimes it's just a matter of timing your exit so it feels natural, and not like a crime against the universe."

—Laura Campbell

Dropping into the twilight, arms around a dead woman, because that's a normal thing to do

ROAD GHOSTS LIKE ROSE spend their time skipping between the twilight and the daylight like it's no big deal, crossing the boundary so regularly that they're effectively dual citizens, equally at home in both places. That has never been an accurate description of me.

Oh, I've always had *access* to the twilight—every ghost does—but when the crossroads were still around, if I passed through the veil, I would usually find myself in an endless field of corn, the sky above me the gray-white colorlessness of the dead of winter. I always hated that sky. Even void would have been better. At least the void would have been honest about its desire to swallow me whole.

Of course, that sky's still with me. It's in my eyes. Everyone who looks at them tells me they're a different color, usually something that isn't a color at all. The most complimentary descriptions tell me I have graveyard eyes. The least say that looking at me is like looking at a hundred miles of empty highway, with nothing pleasant waiting at the end.

Either way, that space is gone now, taken over and transformed by the anima mundi, who has yet to invite me over for a chat, thank Persephone. I never want to go back there. Bad enough that I carry the sky with me.

Instead, when I pulled Jane into the twilight, we landed in the middle of a seemingly endless forest, with no signs of the barn or the compound around it. I didn't know the names for most of the trees around me—we had different trees in Michigan, where I was young and innocent enough to care about things like the naming conventions of trees—but I knew they were very old and had been cut down long ago.

Longer even than when Kevin bought and cleared the land for the compound. These were the trees that had been loved here before the Europeans came to America, before it *was* America, when this land had gone by other names, and the future had been nothing but a dire and distant dream. I eased Jane's body to the mossy ground, panting from the effort of yanking her so far, and straightened to take a look around me.

We hadn't traveled backward through time. The sky was wrong, for one thing; it was banded in colors like a piece of fordite, blue and red, silver and green. The sun bobbed in the middle of it all, a smiling cartoon disk. Literally smiling: it had a face, eyes wide and eager to study the land below, mouth stretched in a broad smile. I gave it a wary look. At least this iteration of the twilight sun seemed to be a friendly one. They're not, always.

Rose likes to say that everything we see reflected in the twilight is something that was loved long enough to be grieved for, once upon a time. The forest around us was probably the lingering grief of the native people of Oregon, possibly mixed with the broken hearts of a few settlers who'd been less interested in destroying the natural world for the sake of their own comfort and ease. This long after the primal forest's death, there was no easy way for me to tell.

A zeppelin drifted lazily by overhead, above a flock of passenger pigeons, their wings a smudge against the smiling sun. The twilight can get a little weird sometimes.

Jane's body lay motionless in the green, as inert as any dead thing. That was a bit of a relief. I've carried corpses through the twilight before, when I didn't have a better option, and none of them have ever reanimated, but I'm always afraid they will. My limits are simple, straightforward, and annoying:

I can take anything I can lift, and I can't take anything living. We know from past tests that if I try, bad things will happen. Living things wind up dead, and when I pretend to be a power lifter, I can seriously hurt myself. What does injury look like for a ghost? Nothing great. Fading, loss of control . . . disapparition, if I push it far enough. I've always stopped before I reached that point, and hopefully the survival of the world will never depend on my ability to lift an anvil. Jane was right up on the edge of what's easily possible for me, and worked only because I *could* lift her. Just not very high, and not for long.

I certainly wasn't going to be able to move her again.

Hoping there were no phantom predators around here waiting to come and make a nice snack of tasty, tasty dead girl, I smoothed her top, straightened her arms, and turned to walk away, heading in the direction that seemed most likely to have people in it. There might not be anyone haunting this specific stretch of forest just yet, but Oregon was pretty big. It was almost certainly haunted.

Distance can get sort of squishy in the twilight, as the land adjusts to the desires of the people in it. I've never really loved long walks, and so I reached the forest's edge long before I felt I should have, stepping out onto the edge of a sleek black river of asphalt running from one end of the horizon to the other. This was I-5 as she saw herself, the mighty interstate highway of the West Coast, younger sister and pale second to the Ocean Lady. She was almost a thousand miles shorter than the Lady had been in her prime, and more, she wasn't revered the way the Lady had been. Still, people loved her, people lived and died on her body and bled out on her banks, and she was remembered in story and in song. One day she might claw her way to godhood.

If that happened, I would hopefully be well away from her as it was going down, outside the reach of her nascent divinity. In the moment, I was wildly grateful to see her, because if the I-5 was here, that meant I was within shouting distance of Portland. Oh, in the daylight, it would have meant no such thing, but like I said, distance gets squishy in the afterlife.

I stepped onto the road, relieved when it held my weight and didn't suck me down into its tar-choked depths, and started walking in the direction of the city. I tucked my hands into the pockets of my high school letter jacket as I walked, keeping myself from making any sort of gesture that could be interpreted as hailing a ride. I'm not a road ghost. The road is always hungry, and the fact that I didn't belong to it wouldn't stop it for flagging me as its next meal if I attracted its attention too directly.

It felt weird, walking away from one of my kids—and Jane would always be one of my kids, no matter how dead she was; she would have been one of my kids at ninety, while I was technically babysitting her great-grandchildren—when they were defenseless. It was arguable whether Jane really needed me anymore, but her body was in the twilight because I'd yanked it here, and that meant it was my responsibility to make sure it got back to the daylight in one piece.

Still, helping her meant getting someone who could help *me*, and that meant getting somewhere that I could find people. Other ghosts or the various sort of human magic-user who could move through the lands of the dead, it didn't entirely matter anymore. Beggars can't be choosers, right?

A vast old farmhouse loomed to my left, one of those antediluvian pseudo-mansions that some of the logging families built during the early days of the state, the ones that were largely destroyed by "accidents" like fires and earthquakes when Oregon started trying to bury its racist origins. The state had been founded as a haven for white citizens fleeing the specter of reconstruction, and a daunting number of them had really believed they'd be able to close the gates and keep the world out forever. This architectural monument to the romantic idea of the American South broadcast its origins to anyone who cared to look, and I started walking just a little faster, not particularly wanting to meet the occupants.

Which is, of course, why the occupants came out to meet me. I was barely halfway past the property before the front door slammed and a man in coveralls emerged, a rake in one hand and a grim expression on his face. He started walking toward me, briskly, and the malleability of the twilight started working against me at the same time, as he was getting closer faster than I was getting down the road. I stopped where I was.

Might as well get this over with. Besides, I hadn't done anything to offend the I-5 recently, and if she wasn't mad at me, she wouldn't let me be dragged off of her. She didn't need to be a goddess to afford me that much protection.

"Stop where you are," he shouted, as he got close enough to make himself heard.

"I already stopped?" I said, somewhat bewildered.

He came right up to the edge of the highway, eyeing me suspiciously. "What are you doing here? You some sort of runaway? Or vagrant?"

"Sir, I'm dead, just the same as you are," I said. "As to what I'm doing, I'm walking the I-5 to the city. I have a right to do that. You don't own the road."

From the way his face puckered, like he'd just bitten into something sour, he knew he didn't own the road, and he resented it. Men like him always wanted to own the world, dead or alive, and being reminded that he didn't offended him. I eyed him and took a step backward, closer to the middle of the highway. Better to get hit by some phantom rider who wasn't looking where they were going than to be grabbed by some old homesteader and dragged off into the fields to be part of some antiquated wicker man routine.

Ghosts in the daylight can be injured, can get hurt, but are very rarely in any actual danger. The twilight is another matter. This man was armed, even if only with a rake, and he could hurt me in ways it would take me time to recover from. Time I didn't currently have.

"This is private property!"

"Maybe where *you're* standing. *I'm* standing on the I-5, the Rainbow Road from Mexico to Canada, and she's never been private property. And I don't have time for this."

He took a step toward the edge of the road, almost hesitant, still scowling. I didn't like that look.

I had four choices. I could flip myself back up to the daylight, without Jane, and hope I'd be able to find her again when I came back. I could drop down to the starlight, and really, that would be the same situation, moving between planes of reality without a guarantee of coming back here. I could run, and hope he wouldn't be able to catch me.

Or I could flag down a ride.

I didn't want to attract the attention of the road, but right now, that felt safer than staying where I was. I pulled my right hand out of my pocket, already balled into a fist, thumb jutting upward, and stuck it out in near-imitation of the family's other resident ghost. Rose was made to hitchhike, shaped by the needs and requirements of the road. I wasn't. I just had to hope, in that moment, that the I-5 was feeling generous and I'd been around the Healys for long enough that a little bit of their ridiculous luck would have rubbed off on me.

The man took another step toward me, onto the road itself. It held his weight, and he smiled, ever so slightly, as he advanced toward me.

I held my ground, fighting the urge to flee, whether on foot or to another level of the afterlife. I needed to be here, with Jane. I needed to figure out how I was keeping her body from being weaponized against her family. And I needed to do it without abandoning her in the woods to rot. I kept my hand firmly in position, thumb jutting toward the sky.

And in the distance—not the far distance, either—someone leaned on their horn. I glanced over my shoulder. A truck was bearing down on me, the driver honking to tell me I should get out of the way.

I looked back at the advancing homesteader and shrugged broadly, trying to look like I was sorry to have our unwanted conversation cut short. Then I backpedaled toward the other side of the road, waiting for the truck to pass between us, hoping against all hope that it would stop.

It stopped. The passenger side door swung open, and the driver beckoned for me to get inside. "Come on," he called. "Jolene and me don't have all day."

I hesitated for barely an instant, then ran toward the truck, grabbing the bar above the door to swing myself up and into the seat. The door closed without my touching it, and the seatbelt slid across my shoulder and waist like a living thing, some sort of sleek, boneless serpent.

As this happened, the driver laughed, saying, "Not all day, but all eternity. Come on, old girl, let's get this young girl where she's trying to go."

The truck's engine revved, almost like it was answering him, and we went shooting off down the highway, leaving homestead and homesteader behind us. I relaxed, marginally. "Thank you, sir," I said. "I really appreciate it."

"Oh, he harasses all the dead who come along this way," he said, easy as anything. "Man's been gone a century, still thinks he owns the road just because it cuts through what used to be his land. Poor bastard doesn't understand his kids sold off the acreage and moved to Seattle as soon as he was in the ground. They didn't want anything to do with him or his poisoned roots." He guffawed with sincere delight, seeming to think this was the funniest thing that had ever happened.

I squirmed in my oddly warm seat. Trucks this old don't normally have heated seats, but this one felt like it did, almost like I was sitting on the back of a living creature. "Yeah, people move on," I said. "I'm Mary. You are?"

"I'm Carl," he said, and patted the dashboard like a pet. "This here's Jolene. We're right glad to meet you, Mary. A pretty little thing like you shouldn't be tussling with nasty old ghosts like him. And before you start worrying that I'm being kind because I've got some sort of ulterior motive, don't. I couldn't do anything to you if I were inclined in that direction, which I'm not." He gestured to his denim-clad thigh like it held the answer to the mysteries of the universe.

I looked a little closer, seeing the seam where his jeans melted into the truck's upholstery, and maybe that did hold the answers. I glanced back up at his face. "Coachman?"

"Yup."

"You don't seem old enough to be a coachman."

"Funny. That's what everyone who knows that word says. But even the oldest types of ghost sometimes start a fresh haunting, and I guess I loved my girl enough that we're really married now, on the other side of the grave."

". . . huh." Coachmen used to be common, but they were fading out even as long ago as my own death, no longer nearly as likely to arise from deaths on the road. They're ghosts who loved their methods of conveyance—whether horse and carriage or engine and chassis—so much that they carried it with them into the afterlife, and then became one with it. Which also explained a bit of his evident disdain for the old man with the rake. Homesteads are ghosts who loved their stationary homes so much they pulled the same trick, and they never leave their properties. They're not haunting houses; they *are* haunted houses, in a sideways sort of way. So was Carl. He was just . . . a haunted house on wheels.

"I can tell by looking at you that you're not a road ghost, and you're not newly dead, either. What brings you to the Rainbow Road, Miss Mary?"

"I'm a caretaker," I said, hesitantly. He was such a young coachman, as coachmen went, that he might never have heard of them, and from his blank expression, he hadn't. "I haunt a family, and I take care of their children."

"All right . . . ?"

"One of those children died today." I didn't need to explain that Jane was a grown woman, had lived a good life and had children of her own before the gunshot took her life; none of that mattered, here in the twilight. She was a child in my care, and she was gone, and that was all the justification I needed to go anywhere I damn well pleased.

His face fell. "Oh, I'm so sorry."

"Me, too. Anyway, I had to bring her body into the twilight to protect the rest of the family, and now I need to move it to a different location in the land of the living, but she's too heavy for me to move on my own." I looked at him critically. "I'd ask you for help—Jolene is certainly big enough to haul her somewhere far away from here, but she's in the woods, and I'd never be able to get her out on my own, or you deep enough in to load her up. I'm going to the ghost of Portland to look for help."

"It's not Portland here," said Carl, "But otherwise, that's not the worst idea. I can get you to the city limits."

"If it's not Portland, what is it?"

"Stumptown, most days. The Clearing, some others. Depends on which city's ghost is at the forefront."

"Ah." A lot of phantom cities work that way, draping themselves in the burial shrouds of past names and past identities. I didn't know much about either past version of Portland, only that they existed, and that I'd always been enough outside the local ghost communities that I'd paid them no real mind. Who needed the dead when you had never pulled away from the living? Some days, I felt like I was more attached to them now than I'd been before my death, more connected to the daylight world.

Carl kept driving, and the road accommodatingly shortened itself to carry us along, trees and rivers and the occasional house flashing by outside the windows. I was almost surprised when Jolene came sliding to a stop, and Carl gestured toward the window on my side of the cab.

"We're here," he said. "Looks like Stumptown today. That's the Portland Hotel over there. Be careful of the saloons and the like. It can be pretty rough for a girl who looks as young as you do."

"I think most older ghosts can tell what my job used to be from my eyes, and they'll give me a pretty wide berth," I said, opening the door and sliding out.

Carl blinked. "What your job used to be?" he asked.

I looked at him gravely, and stopped trying to mask the miles in my eyes, letting him see the long and empty highway that waited there. "I served the crossroads for more than fifty years, before they were destroyed," I said. "It's nice to have met you, Carl. You and Jolene drive safe now, okay?"

He flinched away, pressing himself against the driver's-side door, but managed to nod and say, "All right. It was nice to meet you, Miss Mary."

"Bye now."

I didn't need to close the door: Jolene did it for me, and her engine roared as I walked away, the truck already gathering speed as it raced off down the road. I walked toward the hotel Carl had indicated, a tall, elegant construct of iron and glass, swooping lines and nineteenth-century flourishes making it a centerpiece of the skyline around it. Stumptown was lower to the ground than Portland, not yet graced by the towering fruits of modern architecture, although I could see pops of that modern world showing through: recently lost establishments that had been beloved enough to worm their way in here, into the collective memory of the city.

I let my clothes change as I walked, adjusting themselves to the time period, hems getting lower and sleeves getting longer. My hair remained a loose white cloud around my shoulders, rising into the air slightly to hang around me like a corona, one of those impossible styles accessible only to the dead—or to those who don't mind keeping one hand on a live electrical wire. I looked eerie and unworldly as I stepped through the hotel doors and into the lobby beyond.

I had never been to the Portland Hotel, and I had no idea whether the elegant, light-filled room in front of me looked anything like the original. Cut-glass chandeliers hung from the ceiling, their crystalline arms blazing with little bulbs, while ghosts lounged on leather couches or stood in small clusters, talking. Most of them looked more modern than I did, recently deceased Portlanders who were playing historical recreationist in the older versions of the city. Some were rougher around the edges, and as I looked around, I spotted a cluster of lumberjacks by the bar, their axes over their shoulders and their meaty hands engulfing their bottles of beer. If I'd been in the starlight, I would have taken them for Sasquatch. As it was, they had definitely been haunting these parts for a while.

I shifted trajectories to head for the group, weaving around furniture and other ghosts as I walked. It's considered rude to walk through things in the twilight, if it's even possible—everything on this level of reality was a ghost, whether the ghost of a person or the ghost of a couch, and ghosts can't always pass through each other. Just one more wrinkle to deal with as I made my way to help.

The men looked around as I approached, regarding me with only dull interest. I looked at them more openly, trying to figure out what kind of ghosts they were. The axes were a good indication that they might be able to manipulate the physical world in some way; lumberjacks who couldn't would probably still manifest their axes out of habit, but they wouldn't be likely to bother with them while they were inside drinking.

"Excuse me, gentlemen," I said. "I was wondering if I might have a moment of your time?"

All five of them focused on me, and I felt abruptly as if I were being stared at by a pack of wolves or something equally large and predatory. Their eyes were flat and cold, assessing me and dismissing me as any sort of threat. The shortest member of the pack stepped forward, expression not changing as he looked me up and down, then said, "What do you want?" in a surprisingly high voice.

Some people die young. I'm unliving proof of that. "My name is Mary Dunlavy," I said. "I'm a nanny for the Price family, and we just had a family member die. Unfortunately, her body has been compromised such that it can't safely be near her family, and I don't have the strength to move it by myself. I left her in the trees. Can you help me move her?"

"What's in it for us?" asked another of the men.

"I have living family in the area, and they know about the twilight," I said. "They can do you favors in the land of the living, or I can, if it's something a ghost can accomplish. And you'd be doing us a real solid favor. I don't like leaving her there alone."

"Wait," asked a third. "The Prices? You mean the crypto-whatsits? The ones who take care of the other people in the woods?"

From his tone, I guessed that he was distinguishing "people" from "humans." I nodded. "That's the ones."

"Which one died?" he asked.

"Jane."

Saying her name here, in this haunted hotel, made me wish all over again that she hadn't been quite so quick to head into whatever comes after. This would have been easier if she'd been with me, if she'd been able to help me ask these men to move her body.

"That's a real pity," he said. "She was kind to my Abilene after I died, when not enough folks were. I can help you move her wherever you need her to be, if you can carry a message to Aby."

"I can do that," I agreed. Carrying messages for the dead who've lingered but don't have an easy time manifesting in the physical world is one of the easiest forms of currency we have. "If any of the rest of you have messages, I can take those down, too, once we have them. For now, though, I need to get her body to whatever this town has for a doctor. She has a tracking device inside her, and we need to take it out."

There was no way I was abandoning Jane's body somewhere when I could take her home for a decent burial if I could just get the bullet out. If I'd been thinking more clearly, I would have asked Annie to grab a scalpel before I moved the whole body, but panic had been in charge in that moment, and I was committed now.

"So you want us to go with you, fetch the body, bring it back here, get the tracker out, and take her back to the woods so you can put her back wherever you stole her from?" asked the short one.

I nodded.

"We can do that," he said, looking to the other lumberjacks. All of them nodded. "It's something to do, anyway, and not something we did yesterday or the day before, which makes it more interesting than standing around here drinking. How far away is she?"

"A ways down the road," I said. "Past one of those big logging houses with a creepy old guy inside. He came out with a rake when he saw me walking by."

"Ah, you met old man Miller," said one of the lumberjacks, as the whole group began moving toward the door. Their social gravity carried me with them; I followed almost without intending to, and we were in the street before I knew it. "He employed a few of us, before we died. His whole place burned down around, what, eighteen eighty something? And then his kids sold off the land and split for the hills. Not sure he knows he's dead, really."

"We live out in the woods," said another lumberjack. That's pretty common, ghosts in the twilight saying they live one place or another; we don't have the language to say "exist and have experiences that lead us to grow and change without actually being alive." Talking around it is awkward and annoying. We use "haunt" in the daylight, but in the twilight, it's infinitely easier just to use the words we already know. "There's about eighty of us, all told. A few move up and down the coast, visiting the other lumber camps, but we're usually around here."

"Huh." That explained why some people insisted the trees between Portland and the compound were haunted. Enough ghosts gathering there without the living distraction of a city would inevitably become something people noticed, heavy enough to distort the daylight. "You just . . . like haunting the woods?"

"Most of us weren't what you'd call the social sort," said one of them. The others snorted and chuckled, agreeing with him. "John and his Abilene is about the only word you'll hear of a romance, and they were doomed from the start—she was a Sasquatch lady, and they don't get the same afterlife the human ghosts do. But when we died, we kept our axes, and we kept our trees. Even got a few we'd already chopped down back, and we can cut them down every night if that's what we want to do. They come right back in the morning. It's something to do. Keeps us from getting bored, or thinking too hard about what comes next."

"Elwood started asking a bunch of questions about whether this was heaven or hell or purgatory, and then one day he just looked off into the woods like he saw something the rest of us couldn't, and dropped his axe and walked away," said another lumberjack. "He vanished before he was more'n ten feet gone, and we've never seen him again."

"Sounds like he got tired of lingering in the twilight and decided to move along," I said. The city was falling behind us now, a brief detour that had served its purpose, and we were walking along the smooth black back of the Rainbow Road. The lumberjacks, I noticed, stayed well away from the edges, walking straight down the middle like the whole thing had only ever been intended for pedestrian use. It was odd, but I didn't comment on it, only watched them and tried to understand without asking.

Then I realized the trees we passed were moving. Their branches twitched and sometimes coiled back, tense as the striking arms of a praying mantis. I stepped closer to the nearest lumberjack, who glanced over, picking up on my tension.

"Oh, that's normal," he said. "These aren't the trees we worked while we were alive. Those trees know us, and know we were always respectful, even though our lives were spent ending theirs. They don't blame us for what we had to do. These trees, though, they just see men with axes, and they don't want to be cut down again."

"Huh," I said.

"So we stay out of reach, or else they give us a pretty good thumping, and we're in a hurry."

Indeed, that hurry was translating, again, to the contraction of the space around us, and in less time than it had taken Carl to drive this stretch of road, we were passing Mr. Miller's homestead, the old homesteader himself coming out onto the porch to glare menacingly as we walked by. I-5 wasn't just a nascent goddess in this part of the state; she was a safe passage through potentially hostile spaces. She was going to reach godhood on the back of grateful ghosts alone, with no aid from the routewitches.

I wondered whether she would ever be able to challenge the Ocean Lady. Would she rival her sister sufficiently in power to get a Queen of her own, a strange division of rulership to split the continent in two? Did the restless dead gods of the twilight care about that sort of thing? It really didn't matter, but it was something to think about as I signaled the lumberjacks to slow and reduced my own speed to match theirs.

"There," I said. "I came out of the woods there."

"You're sure?"

My heart was in my throat as I nodded. "One of my kids is that way. I'm sure."

"Then we'll be right back," said John, settling a heavy hand briefly on my shoulder. "You stay here. You don't need to see this."

I wanted to argue with him. I couldn't find the words. Because he was right—I didn't need to see this. This was the nightmare that had been haunting me since the day Alice was old enough to run off into the woods under her own power, and while I had always known that it was lurking, I had started to foolishly believe that I might be able to keep putting it off forever. That I might see my kids die safe in their beds, taken away by extreme old age.

That my punishment for serving the crossroads as long as I had was never actually going to come due.

The lumberjacks trooped into the woods, and only a few of the trees waved their branches at the group of broad-shouldered men, and I stayed where I was, arms wrapped around myself, alone on the road. I hated everything about this. I hated it as they walked away, and I kept hating it when I heard them coming back. I dropped my arms and strained to catch a glimpse of them, rising up onto my toes and only dropping back down when John emerged from the trees with Jane in his arms, cradled close against his chest. Her arms dangled, but he was supporting her head, and that helped keep me from feeling too uncomfortable seeing her carried that way.

"This is a little weird," he said, walking back over to me. "I've been dead a *long* time, but I think this is the first time I've touched a dead body, unless you count the time before I toppled out of my own."

"Not a lot of dead bodies in the twilight," I said, somewhat weakly. The other lumberjacks had followed him out, and we formed an unsteady processional line as we turned to walk back toward the city.

Nothing had changed about the route, even down to Mr. Miller and his rake, but when we approached the city itself, I saw how much *that* had changed. The buildings looked older, the architecture rougher, like they had been put together by people who were only concerned with function, and had never considered that form might matter. The roads were unpaved, save for the Rainbow Road, and the people looked as rough as their surroundings. The modern splashes were fewer, and more subdued; despite their brighter colors, they looked almost hidden in the scene, like they were trying to evade notice.

"Welcome to the Clearing," said the short lumberjack. "This is the oldest version of Portland that's remembered enough to appear in the twilight. Not much in the way of booze here, but plenty of fights, if that's your thing. Doctor's this way."

"Do you only have the one?"

"Not that much call for doctoring when everyone around you is already dead," he said.

I considered that as we walked into the city proper and down a side lane that couldn't be called a street by even the most charitable interpretation. Everything around us looked like it was made of wood, and I didn't recognize the layout of the streets at all. That, at least, made sense: like so many other cities, Portland had a bad case of burning down at one point, and the municipal authorities had been able to rebuild with a little more intent than their original semi-organic settlement.

We stopped at a small office with a shingle outside that read DECLAN MARK, DOCTOR OF PHYSIC.

The short lumberjack stepped forward and knocked. A moment later, the door swung open and a headless body in a white coat stepped out.

"Can't talk when you don't have a mouth, doc," said the lumberjack. "We have Miss Mary here, and she has a corpse that needs some doctoring done."

I stepped forward in turn, to address the figure, who I presumed to be a Dullahan. The headless spirits dwell mostly in the starlight, but some of them settle in the twilight. It made sense for a Dullahan with medical aspirations to set up shop to treat the things that actually *do* live here, in the lands of the dead—things like beán sidhe and the washers at the well, creatures that were born down in the midnight and move freely through all the levels of our world.

"My name is Mary Dunlavy," I said, and gestured to Jane. "This was Jane Price. She was shot by men who placed a tracking charm in the bullet, and I pulled her body into the twilight to keep those men from finding the signal and using it to close in on the rest of my family."

The doctor held up a finger, signaling for me to hold on, then turned and went back inside. When he came back, he was holding his head, which looked perfectly normal, dark-haired and bespectacled, except for the part where it wasn't attached to a body. "Are you telling me the family you haunt is aware of your presence?" he asked. "I know there aren't rules as such dictating how human ghosts interact with the living, but that seems a bit unwise, if you ask me."

"I'm a caretaker," I said.

He frowned, then snapped the fingers of his free hand. "Dun*lavy*," he said. "Of course. You're the crossroads escapee. We were all very impressed when we heard what you'd accomplished. Bring the girl inside. I'll get the tracker out."

"Thank you," I said, and stepped through the door, John behind me with Jane. "I want to take her home so she can be properly buried, and that means I need her body to be untraceable."

The office was almost a stock photo out of a western movie, with shelves of equipment and odd fluids lining the walls, a framed diploma, and a large polished wood table covered by a white sheet. "I hate it when we shift to the Clearing," he muttered, motioning for John to put Jane on the table. "All my good equipment is in Stumptown." He set his head on the stump of his neck, turning to face me. "I can remove the tracker for you, if you don't mind the small matter of my fee."

"How much do you charge?" I asked.

"For post-death surgery on someone this freshly deceased? A kidney," he said. "She's been gone too long to be an organ donor, and it's not like she'll miss it at this point. It'll just be one additional incision."

Bartering with someone else's body seemed wrong; bartering with Jane's body seemed even worse. At the same time, he was right, and she wasn't going to miss the kidney. The real deciding factor, though, was that he was a Dullahan; he wouldn't give the kidney to anyone else. It wouldn't exist to be passed on. "All right," I said.

He smiled—a perfectly normal expression that wouldn't have looked out of place on a human face—and took a tray of instruments down from one of the shelves. "I'll understand if you don't want to watch this," he said. "I wouldn't, if this had been a friend of mine."

"I'm not going anywhere," I said, even as the lumberjacks who'd followed me in mumbled that they'd wait on the porch and filed back out of the office, leaving me alone with the doctor and the corpse.

"All right." He picked up a scalpel and a small set of forceps, and bent over the body.

What followed doesn't bear description. But true to his word, removing a kidney was only one additional incision, which he made with quick efficiency, and digging the bullet out of her chest only took him a minute. It would have been quicker, but the bullet had fragmented upon entry, and he needed to find the pieces in order to be sure the actual tracker had been removed. There was no point in taking her back without doing what we'd come here for.

He dropped the tracker into a tray, and slipped the kidney into his mouth, swallowing without bothering to chew. I watched the whole thing. When her brother asked me what had happened while we were in the lands of the dead, I needed to be able to answer him with complete honesty. Finally, Dr. Mark turned to face me.

"She's ready for you," he said. "Do you want me to put the bullet fragments into a bag?"

"Please." Odds were good the transition into the twilight had been enough to short out the tracker, rendering it nicely inert, but on the off chance that it hadn't, I was going to take the damn thing and throw it into the sea. Leaving it here wouldn't do any good.

He picked up the pieces, dropping them into a plastic baggie entirely out of time with the things around it, and offered it to me. I took it with a nod, tucking it into my pocket.

"Thank you again," I said.

"It's not often I get to operate on human bodies, alive or dead," he said. "If you have another one, please, feel free to bring it by."

"I will."

The lumberjacks were all still gathered on the porch, and came back inside when I opened the door and beckoned them, John proceeding to the table where he scooped Jane back into his meaty arms. She dangled there, an empty vessel that would never be filled again, and I finally allowed myself to look away.

"All right," I said. "Let's take her home."

Twelve

"There's no fate. There's no destiny. No one's chosen. It's just a matter of who's standing in the right place at the wrong time and catches the attention of the universe."

—Apple Tanaka

Hauling a corpse back into the lands of the living, since it's not like I can leave it in the land of the dead

THE BARN WAS EMPTY when I dropped back into it, arms and back aching in a way that seemed entirely unfair, considering I was already dead. I couldn't hoist Jane back onto the table without help, so I lowered her gingerly to the floor and blinked out again, transiting through the space between like a stone skipping across a lake to reappear on the coast of Maine, standing on the edge of a high cliff. New Gravesend was only a few miles away, the town where the crossroads died and the world changed forever, even if most people didn't know it. I pulled back and flung the tracker into the sea, watching it fall to disappear into the waves below. This accomplished, I vanished again, heading for home.

No one was actively calling me. That silence was still jarring. It used to be that either the crossroads were calling me or one of my kids was, almost always. I got very little in the way of self-guided time, because the crossroads didn't want me to. Now, unless the kids needed me, I was almost always free. I would probably get used to that eventually. Not yet, though.

Bringing Jane out of the twilight had just been a matter of getting her body back to where we'd arrived and then flipping us into the daylight. Getting myself back to the compound was more difficult. No one actively needed me, which meant I couldn't precisely control my arrival. I blinked in next to the firepit, where James and Sally were still seated, although someone—probably Annie—had come along and lit the fire for them at some point. Sally was sitting as close to it as she could manage, eyes closed and a beatific expression on her face, while James watched her with the air of a man whose prayers had all been answered, and was waiting for the bill to come due.

I knew that face. It was the face of far too many people who'd made their bargains with the crossroads, and only knowing he couldn't possibly have done that kept me from rushing over to him in a panic. The rest of us were in freefall, but he'd just been given everything he'd ever wanted, and he was still drunk on the reality of it all.

Sometimes the world is kind, even if that kindness never seems to last. I looked toward the obstacle course. If Sarah was still up there with Greg, she had shifted positions such that I couldn't see either one of them; she might have gone inside, or she might just want to be left alone.

"How long have I been gone?" I asked, voice surprisingly loud in the quiet air.

Sally turned to look at me. "Annie came tearing through with her hands on fire about two hours ago," she said. "Said something about a tracking device? She wasn't making a lot of sense."

"That sounds about right," I said. "You two doing okay?"

"A little stressed, and a little guilty about not being as worked up as everyone else, but for the most part, yeah," said Sally. James nodded, but didn't speak. "You?"

"Exhausted. And we're not done yet. Call if you need me." I turned and walked toward the house, then through the back wall into the family room.

Ted was the only one there, sitting on the loveseat with his shoulders pressed to the cushions and his head tilted all the way back, leaving him to stare at the ceiling. I stopped.

"Hey, Ted," I said. "Where is everyone?"

"Annie came inside a few hours ago, said the Covenant had placed a tracking device in Jane's body and you'd taken it away to the ghost world." He paused long enough to swallow hard. "Kevin and Evelyn are in the security room, watching for any sign that the signal was picked up before you took the tracker out of range. Alice and Thomas are patrolling the perimeter, with Annie and Sam for backup. Arthur said he was going to take a nap, and Elsie went with him. Did you . . . did you bring . . ." He stopped there, apparently unable to continue any further.

I nodded, moving to stand beside the loveseat. "I brought her back," I said. "I found a doctor in the twilight who was able to remove the tracker, and I threw it off a cliff in Maine, right into the Atlantic. If taking it into the twilight didn't short it out, the Covenant can say hello to a kraken or two. They probably got enough information to tell them West Coast, but they'd be here already if they'd picked up much more."

"Maybe we'll get lucky and they'll all get swallowed by the horrors of the deep," he said, and chuckled, thickly, the sound turning into a sob as he folded forward, put his hands over his face, and started to cry again.

That explained a bit of why he was sitting here alone, and why James and Sally were staying outside. As an incubus, all Ted's bodily fluids had the potential to cause people to experience extreme and uncontrollable physical attraction in people who had the potential to find his gender sexually attractive. Which is a really convoluted way of saying "If Ted cried in front of James or Sally, he might find himself getting pursued by someone who didn't want to be pursuing him, any more than he wanted the pursuit." Sally, I knew, identified as a lesbian, but if she had any latent bisexual tendencies, an incubus's tears would drag them out of her in a way none of us were going to enjoy.

Direct blood relatives of Frances Healy had a degree of resistance inversely consistent with how far removed they were from her. Alice could probably have comforted him for hours without a twinge of arousal, while Kevin would succumb much more quickly. But it was a complication we didn't need right now, any more than we needed to be telling Ted not to mourn.

I put one hand on his shoulder, doing my best to lend what comfort I could, and he grabbed my wrist, holding it tightly enough that it would probably have hurt if I'd still been something that could *be* hurt in that way. He made a noise that was somewhere between a sob and a bray, a broken sound of grief that would have been comic if not for the circumstances surrounding it. I started to rub his back in small, concentric circles, trying to lend what comfort I could.

Ted raised his head and looked at me. "I want to hate you," he said. "It would be so *nice* to hate you."

I blinked. "Come again?"

"You're a ghost. You were one of the first things Janey mentioned when she was trying to make me understand how weird her family was—not the missing parents, not the talking mice, you. Because you made her feel safe, and if we ever had kids, you'd make them feel safe, too. So she told me about her ghost babysitter, and how wonderful it was to know that she'd be taken care of, no matter what happened. You died, and you still got to stay."

I knew what he was going to say next even before he said it. I knew, and there was nothing I could do to stop it, or help him stop feeling that way. So I just took my hand off his back and stepped backward, giving him room for his uncoiling rage.

"Why?" he asked. It was a small word, quietly asked, the question of a child. I still winced. "Why did you get to stay, and she has to go? Why are you still here, and my Janey isn't? How is that fair?"

"It's not, Ted," I said. "When my father died, even though I had stayed for him, he didn't stay for me. To be fair, he didn't know I was dead, and he'd never asked me to stay, but that just means he died and left his supposedly living teenage daughter all alone. It broke my heart. Daddy dying was worse than when I'd died, because I had time to grieve for him."

I paused to take a deep breath, choosing my next words with care. "But it would have been cruel to ask him to stay. Most ghosts aren't as flexible as I am. Or, to put it another way, most ghosts aren't nearly as good at playing alive as I am. They're one-dimensional, defined by their unfinished business, and over time, it warps them into something they would never have asked to be. Jane didn't want to make you watch her go through that. She didn't want to stay if it was only going to cause her family pain."

"So why did you stay?"

I stiffened. "You're in pain, so I'm not going to take that as badly as I would otherwise, but when I died, my father had no one else. Jane knew you'd have Elsie and Arthur and the rest of the family. This isn't one of those cases where the widower gets bounced out the door as soon as he's not married to a living relative, and you know it as well as she did. You're stuck with these weirdoes, forever, and that's not going to change. I stayed because he needed me, and because I was a child, and I was afraid, and the crossroads offered me a way to do it. I won't say I'm sorry I stayed, because it gave me this family, but I wouldn't have done it if I'd had a better understanding of what I was getting into. Jane made her choice because she understood the situation. She didn't want to go. She didn't mean to die. Implying that I should have forced her to turn herself into a haunting is unkind. It's unkind to her, it's unkind to me, and it's unkind to yourself."

"Mary, I didn't mean . . ."

"Yeah, you did. But that's okay. We all mean something terrible sooner or later." I took a step back. "I'm so sorry for your loss. At least I was able to bring her body home."

I winked out again then, vanishing and shifting myself elsewhere on the property. Olivia was likely to be in her room upstairs, and so I appeared there, unsurprised when Evelyn rose to meet me, Olivia bundled warm and drowsy against her hip.

"Mary, dear," she said. "Were you able—?"

"Jane's in the barn, although someone needs to get her off the floor; I couldn't lift her on my own. The tracker's somewhere in the Atlantic Ocean. Sally says I was gone for about two hours?"

"Closer to two and a half."

Meaning the Covenant would have arrived already if they'd been able to home in on their tracking signal before I blipped it out of the land of the living. I relaxed, just a little. "Any sign of them?"

"The Covenant? Yeah." She bounced Olivia on her hip, causing the girl to yawn and stretch. "Some of our allies in Seattle have seen the field teams showing up. They've declared a general lockdown, and they're doing their best to get everyone out of harm's way."

"Meaning they got as far as 'the West Coast' before they lost it," I said, grimly. "What are we going to do?"

"We're well outnumbered, so we're not going to shoot them all," she said. "I'd say we had to make North America too expensive for them, but they're mostly sending their low-ranking soldiers and recruits over here. I think we could kill everyone that they have on this continent without costing more than they're willing to pay."

I paused, standing up a little straighter. "We have to find a way to make the fight too expensive. We have to escalate our own assault."

"How do you suggest we do that?" Evelyn bounced Olivia again, then carried her over to the bed and lowered her down to the mattress. Olivia went without protest, rolling onto her side and closing her eyes.

"I don't know yet," I said, somewhat glumly. "It's a concept in progress."

"Well, I hate to be a nagging Nancy, but you need to conceptualize faster if you possibly can," she said, voice still the same serene lilt that it always was. I shot her a surprised look. "I know you know how bad this is, Mary. I won't insult either of us by pretending that you don't. Jane's dead. Ted's basically useless, and most of us can't go within fifteen feet of him without the fear of doing something we'll regret. Kevin's holding together as best he can, but he's going to fall apart the second the pressure's off. Sarah . . ." She sighed heavily. "Sarah's not well. Sarah hasn't been well for some time. She may never be entirely well again."

I couldn't argue with any of that, much as I wanted to try. Sarah's current condition wasn't any sort of secret. It hurt to see her this way. That didn't mean we didn't have to factor it into any plans.

"Basically, until we find a good way to break this stalemate, we're fighting a holding action at best, a slow loss at worst," she continued. "We may have gotten them to aim themselves elsewhere for the moment, but how long before Annie and Elsie head for Seattle looking for a little payback?"

"We can't scatter farther than we already are," I said. "It's bad enough that we're distributed across three different locations, with allies in half a dozen more."

"Makes us harder to take out with one hit," said Evelyn.

I straightened. "I need to talk to Annie," I said, and vanished.

I found Annie in the attic, sitting cross-legged on the floor with mice from Jane's priesthood sitting on her knees and looking at her gravely. She jumped when I appeared, and the knife she had produced from inside her shirt whipped through the space my head seemed to occupy, imbedding itself in the wood of the wall. I crossed my arms, looking at her silently.

"Sorry, Mary," she said.

"What have I told you about throwing knives at everything that startles you?" I asked.

"That it's antisocial and doesn't make me a very good neighbor," she replied.

"And what did you just do?"

"Threw a knife at my babysitter."

"Uh-huh." I nodded, taking in the scene in front of me.

The compound's attic had been built with the mice in mind, and never used for storage. The walls were a series of in-built shelves and cubbies, which the mice themselves had long since filled with their residences and structures, constructing homes and temples out of raw materials supplied by the family. Their streets were lined with glass stones from the craft store and highly polished pennies and dimes, pressed into modeling clay as a sort of cobblestone trail. Everything was made to their scale, but there were patches of floor, such as the one Antimony was sitting on, intended for use by the human-sized members of the family. There was even an armchair in one corner, surrounded by mouse construction but not covered by it, that had been put in place during Evelyn's first pregnancy, to allow her to visit when she could no longer sit on the floor.

"What's going on?"

She grimaced, gesturing to the priests on her knees. One began to groom its whiskers, which were long and black, matching the fur on its body. The other simply continued to watch her politely. "I'm trying to make them understand what's going on, but it's like they don't want to listen to me," she said, frustrated.

"It's been just as long for them as it has for me," I said, and walked over to kneel beside her. "Do you mind if I try?"

"Be my guest," she said, leaning back on her hands and making space for me to address the mice.

"Hello," I said. "Do you know who I am?"

"HAIL!" shouted the mice. "HAIL TO THE PHANTOM PRIESTESS!"

"Excellent," I said. "So you know I've been here for the departure of two Priestesses and two Gods, when they passed from this world into the next."

"We do, Priestess," squeaked the black mouse. "For did not the God of Uncommon Sense say, 'I Don't Know What I'm Going To Do Without Her' before the burial of the Patient Priestess?"

"I oversaw his departure as well," I said. "And the departures of the Violent Priestess, and the God of Unexpected Situations. They were all known to me, and are known to me still, living in the chambers of my memory."

The mice murmured agreement, acknowledging my place as a family authority.

"The Precise Priestess has come before you to tell you a great and terrible truth," I said. "Why do you refuse to hear it?"

"Because, Priestess, if the Silent Priestess has departed, it will change everything," said the other priest, a brindle mouse with a large white blotch over one eye. "She was ours and we were hers and we will always be hers and she will always be ours."

"Yes, but she'll be yours in a different place," I said. "I'm so sorry, and it's not fair, but the Silent Priestess has departed for the lands beyond this one, and all the faith in the world won't bring her back to you. Like the Violent Priestess before her, she has not chosen to linger here, but has made her departure in quickness and ease."

The mice drooped, whiskers sagging.

"I was with her at the very end," I said. "After her body had died, as her spirit was deciding whether or not to stay, as I've done, and haunt her family. And she said, 'Tell them you found me, and tell them I'm okay; tell them I loved them so much it hurt sometimes.'" Those weren't her last words, but her actual last words felt private, like they were meant to be reserved for me alone, and I didn't want to share them. Especially not with the mice, who would never let them go. "She chose to move along, and not to haunt the living. She lived a good life and she died a good death, and her afterlife is hers alone to do with as she wills. We honor her by respecting that choice."

The two priests of Jane's order drooped, further and further with every word, until they were down on all fours like ordinary mice, their noses pointed at the denim-covered flesh of Annie's leg.

"We are left," said one.

"She is lost," said the other.

"Woe," wailed all the mice as one, and it should have been comic, almost, should have been one of those cartoony moments to hang a laugh upon, but it was somehow heartbreaking and tragic, the sound of nonhuman intelligences trying to express inexpressible grief. The two priests scampered down the sides of Annie's legs to join the rest, and were quickly swallowed up by the crowd of the congregation. I leaned closer to Annie, offering her my hand.

"We should go."

"What? Why?"

"Because this is where they begin their mourning, and it's not for us," I said. "They need the space to be sad without us projecting our human sadnesses on top of them, and they need to decide what they're going to do next."

Annie took my hand, and together, we stood.

"The family histories say the priests of a dead god or priestess sometimes take their own lives."

"Yes," I said, although I privately questioned the word "sometimes." I had never known a senior priest to outlive their chosen deity by more than six months. The grief swallowed them alive, and snuffed out the fire in their tiny hearts. Aeslin mice are smaller than people. They sometimes seemed to have room for only one feeling at a time. And right now, grief was taking up all that space. Everything else would have to wait its turn.

The mice began beating the drums inside their temples, and wailing filled the air as the news of Jane's death passed from home to home. I led Annie quickly to the exit, and followed her down the ladder to the floor below us. She glanced up as I pushed the ladder back into place.

"That was harder than I expected it to be," she said. Then, suddenly seeming to realize what my presence meant, she asked, "Did you . . . ?"

"She's in the barn," I said. "I need some help getting her back up on the table. She's too heavy for me to lift alone."

"She'd smack you so hard if she heard you say that," said Annie, sounding halfway amused.

"Yeah," I said. "I guess she would. Anyway, can you come help me? I need to talk to you."

Casting a curious look in my direction, Annie started for the stairs. I followed her, choosing to do things the slow manual way, rather than popping around and risking winding up in the wrong part of the house. We stayed quiet as we walked down, the distant sound of drumming fading away behind us. The mice knew exactly how far the sound of their various rituals carried through the house, and were careful to keep their mourning rites as close to private as possible. Anyone on the third floor would know, but the second floor and below would be none the wiser.

We walked along the hall, passing the closed doors of various private rooms, and made for the front staircase. Going down that one would put us by the door, and avoid an awkward trip through the family room, where Ted was presumably still lost in his own grief. The mice might send an envoy down to invite him to join them after a little longer, and to be honest, I hoped they would; it would help him a lot to not be alone right now, and there just weren't enough options for people who could grieve with him safely.

Annie waited until we were outside on the lawn before she turned to me and asked, "What else do you want?"

"What do you mean?"

"I mean, you could have asked anyone to help you get Aunt Jane on the table. I would have asked Sam, if I were you: he's strong and he's not as emotionally attached to her as the rest of us, so he'd have been able to do it without crying. Whereas I'm probably going to cry on you. So you must want something else. What else do you want?"

"I need to talk to you about your time in England."

Annie frowned as we started walking across the yard, heading for the back. "What about it?"

"I was talking to your mother before I came looking for you, and we agree that this fight is too expensive for us and too cheap for the Covenant," I said. "They have the numbers to just keep throwing field teams at us, and even if they lose a whole team for every Price or ally they manage to pick off, we're still taking heavier losses, proportionately speaking. They can do this forever. We can't. If we want this to end in anything other than a mass funeral, we need to make the fight more expensive for them. We need to make ourselves unattractive as a target."

"And how are your proposing to do that?"

"Something your mother said, about how us being scattered across the continent makes it harder to take us all out with just one hit," I said. "That made me think . . . obviously the Covenant is scattered, but most of their leadership isn't going to be going out into the field. They're going to be staying where they feel safe, and ordering other people to die for what they claim to believe in. Where do they feel safe?"

"Penton Hall," said Annie, without hesitation. "In England."

"How well do you know the place?"

"Better than I want to, and Grandpa probably knows it even better than I do, since he grew up there," she said. "It's one of those big old country homes like you see in BBC miniseries about Jane Austen. The estates that used to host massive balls and employ half the village and barely aren't castles."

"Okay. So we talk to your grandfather and we figure out how we're going to bring the fight to them, in Penton Hall."

Annie stopped walking to stare at me.

"What?" I asked.

"It's in *England*," she said.

"I got that the first time."

"It's fortified like a prison. The walls are solid stone, and at least two feet thick. Plus we'd have to take a plane to get there, and we already know they have surface-to-air munitions. We'd just get shot out of the sky."

"Ah, but that's where you're wrong," I said. "Sarah and I don't need a plane to get there." I wasn't as certain about that as I was trying to sound. Sarah could pop back and forth between New York and Portland with what seemed—to me—like relative ease but was much harder than it looked from the way she described it.

"And . . . ?"

"And if Sarah can get the location of Penton Hall out of your head, she can go there and call for me, and I can go after her," I said. We were drawing close to the firepit, where James and Sally were still seated, still talking quietly. "That gets the two of us inside."

"What are you going to do then?"

"I'm still working on that part, to be honest. But we need them to stop coming after us, and we need to do it in a way that leaves them too weak to immediately pivot to going after the dragons. I'm pretty sure they know about William. This is as much about getting to him as it is about getting rid of us. I don't suppose you have any ideas about what we should do in Penton Hall?"

"You can't carry living things through the twilight, or I'd suggest unleashing a few colonies of social huntsman spiders, but that would probably just upset them, not make them stop," said Annie.

"True enough, and yet still fun to think about."

James, seeing us, waved. Annie shifted our trajectory to take us closer to the firepit, calling an amiable "Howdy, kids, what's good?"

"I'm the same age you are," said James, with a sort of complicated relieved annoyance in his tone. Anyone who questioned whether he had accepted his role as Annie's brother just needed to listen to him, because that was the "put-upon brother secretly very glad to see his sister but not sure how to admit it without making things weird" voice. I used to hear it from Alex a lot, and from Kevin before him. James was still turned partially toward Sally, but sometime in the time when she'd been missing, she'd gone from comforting and familiar to strange and new, while Annie was now something safe and easy. Watching him try to balance that was going to be fascinating—or would have been, if we'd had the time for it. Right now, I just wanted to tell him we needed everyone at full functionality.

But that would have been cruel. None of us were operating at full capacity, and we wouldn't be until the worst of our shock and grief had faded into the rearview mirror. Grief keeps its own timetable, and it doesn't care what else is going on. When Fran died, I put on a brave face for Alice's sake, but I cried every night for well over a year. If something had attacked during that time, I would have been useless. It wasn't fair that none of us were going to get the time to mourn for Jane that way.

Sally looked Annie mildly up and down, then said, "If you're the same age as James, you're the same age as me."

"I had to time travel to kill the crossroads," said Annie, unflustered. "That makes me older. Hi, kids. What's going on?"

"I liked Jane, but I didn't know her long enough to love her the way everyone else did," said James. "I felt weird staying inside and not being sad enough, so I came out here."

"I just met her today," said Sally. "I wasn't really managing to be sad at all. Pissed on her behalf, and on the boss's, since I know he'd been really looking forward to meeting her, but that's not the same as sad. I didn't want to intrude. And I did want to spent time with James, so I came outside with him, so we could start catching up. We have a *lot* to catch up on."

"Yeah. 'Hey, buddy, sorry I sold myself to the crossroads and went off to become a warrior princess,' not a conversation you expect to have with your best friend from high school," said James.

"You're not much better, Mr. 'I turned out to be one of the X-Men, and then I got pressganged into an adoption by another X-Man, so now I'm a superhero, and also the guy who kept you alive in your hell dimension and basically adopted *you* is technically my grandfather now.'"

"Fair," agreed James, with a shrug.

"We're going to the barn," I said. "I was able to get Jane's body back out of the twilight, but I need Annie to lift her onto the table. Do you two want to come along?"

"It's a little nippy out here, even with the fire," said Sally. She stood, dusting her hands against her jeans. "James?"

"Sure," he said, and rose. The two of them fell into step with Annie and me, and the four of us proceeded onward.

I stopped as we were passing the obstacle course. "I'll catch up with y'all," I said. Annie glanced at me, then at the high platform, clearly guessing what I was doing. She nodded, then resumed walking, urging James and Sally along.

There were various ways to reach the obstacle-course platforms. The "right" way was usually difficult, scaling a sheer wall or climbing a waxed rope, something that stood a generally decent chance of dropping you into the mud pits below the structure. But the whole thing had been built with the expectation that it would be largely used by children, who are better at shimmying *up* things than they are at getting down. Even if Kevin had wanted to build it so that there were no easy ways for the kids to get down, his wife and sister would have killed him.

Every platform was thus built to be accessible by a low-impact ladder or stairway, for those times when you absolutely had to get to a higher point than your skill levels allowed, or needed to come down in a hurry *without* choosing Verity's method of playing chicken with gravity. True to form, the kids had looked at those easy ups and downs and immediately turned using them into the cause of much mockery and hazing within their small pack. Adults were allowed to use the stairs. *They* were not. As long as they didn't go beyond teasing, there wasn't much we could do about it, and so they'd been left to sort things out among themselves.

(The big game-changer in regards to making them act less like feral assholes had been starting elementary school and meeting kids who *didn't* view putting themselves through *American Gladiator* training every afternoon and weekend as "perfectly normal." They'd never been able to bring their new friends over for a visit, but having those friends had given them enough of a different perspective that they'd started being slightly less horrible to each other.)

I remained solid as I climbed up to the first platform, pulling myself along the steps by holding fast to the rails, which were less stable than I wanted them to be. It had been easier when the kids were younger, and I'd still had the incredibly fine control over where I reappeared that came with serving the crossroads. Now, however, I had to climb, and remind myself with every step just how god-awful dangerous this thing was. And we allowed *children* to use it?

"What the hell is wrong with this family?" I asked aloud, and started up the ladder to the next level.

Likc thc housc, thc obstaclc-coursc tower had four levels, but the lookout at the very top was too small for Greg, and so I wasn't surprised when I reached the third level and found Sarah smooshed into one corner with Greg pressed low to the platform in front of her, his head resting in her lap. His many multifaceted eyes seemed to gaze at her adoringly, even though that was more human emotion than he was physiologically arranged to display. I suppressed my shudder and stepped onto the platform, crossing to crouch down next to her.

"Hey," I said. "I was hoping I'd find you here. How are you feeling?"

"Sad," she said. "I've got so much sad in me that I'm scared to be where anybody else is, because my sad on top of their sad might be too much sad for them to carry, and that's not fair to do to people who didn't agree to it. So I'm staying out here, where I can keep my sad in just me and Greg, and Greg's a spider. He doesn't feel sad the same way we do. Mostly he feels a sort of fuzzy melancholy, that makes him think about prey he ate a long time ago and wishes he could eat again, or how much he'd like to meet a lady spider someday."

She stroked Greg's head as she spoke, tone apologetic. Greg would never eat the prey of his spider childhood or meet a female of his species; he was in the wrong dimension for that, and while Sarah probably *could* open a passage back, she wasn't going to. Anyone who knew her knew that.

"It's okay to be sad, sweetie. You just lost someone." I sat down next to her, still solid, which made the space surprisingly tight. It really hadn't been intended for two full-sized women and a giant spider. "Everyone is sad right now. We're all going to miss Jane."

"Artie isn't sad," she said, looking down at Greg. "Artie's confused, like he doesn't understand everyone else's sadness. He knows he *should* be sad, because she was his mother, but the actual sadness is just . . . not there."

"Oh," I said, too stunned to say anything else.

Lilu, like Ted and his children, are natural empaths. It's part of the whole package, along with the narcotic blood and the irresistible pheromones. Arthur didn't get the persuasive telepathy or the ability to influence people's dreams—that all went to Elsie. Instead, he got a double dose of empathy, and a tendency to pick up on the emotions of the people around him, whether he wanted to or not. Like Sarah, he sometimes had to retreat to keep his own strong emotions from stepping on those of everyone else around him.

Sarah glanced up again. "Do you understand now? Does that help you see what I actually did to him? He has all the pieces of his life, as seen from the outside. He knows she was his mother, but he's only working up the level of sad that he'd have if she were a character in a book or on his favorite show. I snapped all the emotional ties between them, and I just don't have the skill to re-tie them, even if I had permission to go back into his head."

"He'd give you permission if you asked, sweetheart," I said.

She shrugged. "That's why I can't ever ask him. I know he'd give me permission. I don't want him giving me things I shouldn't have. He has good reasons not to trust me ever again. I'm not going to try to make him change his mind."

I recognized the signs of her becoming well and truly entrenched in her position. She'd always been prone to absolutist positions, especially when they supported her inherent belief that she was the one who'd done something wrong. This was an argument I wasn't going to win. I decided to pivot.

"Do you think you can hold the sad inside enough to be around other people for a little while?" I asked.

Sarah turned to frown at me. Her pupils were solid black, meaning she had her telepathy dialed as far back as it would go. "I already am," she said. "Can't you tell?"

"Ghost, remember?" I waved a hand in front of myself. "I don't tend to pick up on what you broadcast unless you're actively targeting me. I don't have a physical brain for you to broadcast into."

"Oh." She sighed, giving Greg's head one more careful stroke, then stood. "I can hold the sad back for a little while," she said.

"Good." I pulled myself to my own feet. "Then I need you to come with me, all right?"

"Where are we going?"

"To the barn." The others had continued walking while I was talking to Sarah. I could see them approaching the barn doors, rendered small by distance and perspective. "We need to get Jane back onto the table, and then I need to talk to you and Annie about how we're going to make this stop."

"Okay, Aunt Mary," said Sarah, docilely enough. I wanted to trust it. I couldn't, quite. She was miserable, and she was blaming herself for not keeping Leonard under control when she grabbed the rest of the field team, and she needed to feel like she was being punished.

I couldn't bring myself to do it, even in pantomime. Sarah had been through enough.

We all had.

Descending the platform was easier than climbing up had been: I just stopped keeping myself solid and fell through, dropping down until I stopped myself just above the ground. Sarah climbed down the more-ordinary way, while Greg leapt after her, demonstrating with one mighty motion why he was called a jumping spider. He waved his pedipalps at her as she reached the ground, seeming pleased to be moving again. Together, we followed the others toward the barn.

Surprising as it had been to find Annie alone in the attic, it was entirely unsurprising when I stepped into the barn to find that Sam had rejoined her, and was standing beside her as she looked down at Jane's face. They had already hoisted her body back onto the table, and the four of them were standing in a loose circle around her, watching her as if they expected her to open her eyes and tell them to give her some space. James looked around as Sarah and I walked into the barn, Greg following close behind us, and Sally turned, following his motion. Then she squeaked, tensing.

"It's just Greg," said James. "He's Sarah's ESA."

"I met Sarah in New York," said Sally. "She did *not* have a fuck-off giant spider with her. I would have noticed."

"Greg doesn't like the city," said Sarah gravely. "Even the big spaces are too small for him, and he can't be with me most places, so he doesn't understand why he can't just stay here or in Ohio and keep roaming around in his woods, the way he wants to. He's happier when he's with me, but he's happiest when he doesn't have to go in the city.

He's my emotional support animal, and I'm his. I try not to upset him when I don't have to."

"That's . . . surprisingly sensible," said Sally. "I always hated it when some of the ladies at the Hendersons' church would bring their 'emotional support' dogs to services, even though it clearly made the poor things completely miserable. If Greg doesn't want to go to Manhattan, he shouldn't have to. He's still a giant spider, though."

"I noticed," said Sarah.

"So did the rest of us," said Annie. "Greg's harmless, as giant spiders go. Okay, Mary, we got Aunt Jane off the floor. Thank you for bringing her back."

"I didn't really think I had a choice," I said. "I wasn't going to leave her in the twilight, and I couldn't leave her somewhere else in the daylight. It wouldn't have been fair to anyone. Especially not Ted."

"Or Elsie," said James.

Sally blinked at him. "That's the cousin with the pink hair?"

"Yeah," he said. "She was the token queer kid until I came along, so she and I spend a lot of time talking. She never really *got* her mother, but she loved her a whole lot. She's going to be a mess for a while. Where is she, anyway?"

"Elsinore is in the library, reading books about how to raise the dead," said Sarah. "She's very unhappy, because all of them indicate that it's a terrible idea, rarely works the way you want it to, and requires a willing spirit. As Aunt Jane has already passed outside the layers of death that Mary can access, it seems unlikely that she would be classified as a 'willing spirit.' I expect her to give up soon and cry herself to sleep."

"Okay, that's bad," said Annie. "This is all terrible. Nothing about this makes things better. Mary, you had what sounded like the start of a plan?"

I nodded. "I did. I mean, I do. I mean, it may not work, and it might be a truly terrible idea, but it's still worth looking into. Sarah, if Annie lets you into her head, can you extract the location of Penton Hall?"

"I can gather what she knows, and extrapolate from there," said Sarah. "I should be able to locate the facility."

"Okay. Good. If you know where it is, can you go there?"

Sarah nodded. "England is no trouble."

"I was worried it might be outside of your range."

Sarah blinked, then laughed, briefly. I raised an eyebrow.

"You want to tell me what's so funny?"

"I don't normally hop from here to New York by going across

North America," she said. "Shorter distances are substantially more difficult than long ones."

"Meaning?"

"Meaning I customarily make the trip by going from here to New York the long way around."

I stared at her for a moment, trying to reconcile the distance she'd just cited with my assumptions. It didn't work. In the end, I had to let it go, because trying to wrap my head all the way around it would have taken too much time. "Fine," I said. "You can get to England. Are you willing to go once you know where you're trying to wind up?"

"I came here, I can go there," said Sarah. "Why do I need to go there?"

"Because if you go there and you shout for me, I can come to you, guaranteed," I said. "My aim isn't that great anymore unless I have someone I'm aiming *for.*"

"And why are we going to Penton Hall?" asked Sarah.

"So we can make the Covenant sorry," I said, grimly. "So we can make them stop."

"I'm coming with you," said Annie.

Thirteen

"People have some pretty wild ideas about what life after death is going to be like. And I'm telling you, a lot of it is like watching paint dry, forever."

—Rose Marshall

Standing in the barn, trying to make sense of what I just heard

FOR A MOMENT, WE all stared at Antimony, even Sarah, who was generally unflappable these days. I guess learning how to rip holes in dimensions will do that for you. Sam recovered first.

"Like fuck you are," he said.

Antimony turned to glower at him. "Don't tell me what to do."

"Oh, you mean don't tell you to go back to the den of the assholes who want to kill your entire family, now that we know for sure that they know who you are and how to spot you on sight? Don't tell you not to take a pointless risk when the dead lady and the girl who no longer respects linear space are perfectly happy to take it for you? Don't say how much I prefer you alive and breathing?"

"You don't have any right to tell me what to do, Sam. I love you, but—"

"Will you marry me?"

Antimony stopped dead.

"What."

"Here." He produced a little black velvet box from inside his pocket, holding it awkwardly toward her as he got down on one knee. "I mean, fuck. I was planning to do this over the weekend—it's why I made us dinner reservations at that steak place you wanted to try. I was going to take you somewhere nice, feed you too much protein so you couldn't run away, and then talk you into it. I'm convincing when you're slipping into a meat coma."

"Sam . . ."

"But now you want to go and commit a really elaborate form of suicide, and you're not going to do that without me, so will you marry me? Like, actually marry me, so you can't say things like I don't have any right to tell you not to go die messy?"

"Marriage isn't some sort of tether that means you get to tell me what to do," said Antimony.

"I know," said Sam. "But it is a promise that you'll let me try to be there whenever I can, and you won't go off without telling me. So even though this is a shitty version of what was going to be a really nice proposal, will you *please* marry me?"

"Will you get up if I say yes?"

"Yes."

"Okay, yes. I'll marry you." She took the little black box out of his hand and opened it, revealing an equally black ring in a braided knotwork pattern, with several small diamonds set into the band. "Diamonds, Sam? Really?"

"They're the strongest gemstone in the world, and they're pretty heat-resistant," hc said, standing and taking thc box back in order to remove the ring. "The band is tungsten. It's the *most* heat-resistant metal used in jewelry, and one of the strongest. May I put this on you?"

"Dad helped you with this, didn't he?" she asked, holding out her hand to let him put the ring on.

"Yeah. It's not like I asked his permission or anything—we both knew that would just piss you off—but I asked for his help, which was a way of getting his permission without wording it in a patronizing manner." He slid the ring onto her finger, where it fit perfectly. "I love you, Antimony Price."

"I love you, too," she answered, and embraced him. "I'm still going to Penton Hall."

"I know," he said, glumly. "I'm not so delusional I thought I could change your mind about that. I just hoped I could give you a good reason to come back, if you couldn't take me with you."

"She can't," said Sarah. "If Antimony is set on going with me to Penton Hall, carrying her will complicate the math to such a degree that it becomes dangerous. Bringing her back will collapse the channel behind us, and prevent me from going to that location again for an indefinite period of time. Trying to transport two people at the same time . . . I can't take you both. We wouldn't make it back."

"That's what I was afraid you'd say." He looked at me. I raised my hands.

"Hey, no," I said. "Dead stuff only, and I have to be able to lift it. I can't lift you, and if you weren't dead when we left, you'd be dead when we got there."

"No killing my fiancé," said Antimony firmly.

"Why do you want to go, anyway?" asked Sam. "Isn't the plan to go to Penton Hall and do something horrible but as yet undefined that probably causes a lot of property damage and loss of life? You being there won't make it any nastier than whatever Mary already had in mind."

"Because there's a colony of Aeslin mice there," said Annie. "They stayed behind when my great-great-grandparents left the Covenant. That's where Mork comes from. I found him in Penton Hall, and he came home with me to join the colony here. They're innocent. They've been living in the walls, keeping track of the remaining family members, and they don't deserve to die there. Even if they did, we need the genetic diversity. They may have started as a splinter of the colony we still have, but they've had time for genetic drift. Maybe not much. It could still buy the species as a whole a few more generations."

We fell silent as a group, considering the weight of what she'd just said.

One of the quietly unspoken truths of the family is that the Aeslin are destined for extinction. So far as we know, the family colonies are the last ones in the world, apart from the colony in the walls at Penton Hall. We can protect them from a lot of things. We can't protect them from inbreeding.

And much as Sarah looks human but isn't, Aeslin mice look like mice but aren't, not really. Even if it wouldn't have been the pantheistic rodent equivalent of bestiality, reproduction with ordinary mice simply isn't an option. They're not the same species.

"She's right," said James. "She has to go to Penton Hall. Mary, what's your actual plan?"

"I go to Uncle Mike—Mike Gucciard, he's a friend of the family in Chicago, although I'd guess he's most of the way to Ohio by now—and ask him for the biggest explosive device he thinks I can reasonably lift. Then Sarah takes Antimony to Penton Hall, Antimony collects the mice, and Sarah yells for me to come to her. I pick up the bomb and take it through the twilight to Penton. It's not alive. I know fuses and incendiary devices can make the transition without shorting out. All I need to do is lift it. I don't have to take a step."

"Then when you get to Penton Hall, you drop the bomb, and . . . what? Nuke half of England?"

"No." I shook my head. "Uncle Mike doesn't have access to nuclear weapons. At least I hope he doesn't have access to nuclear weapons. I guess he might. I'm just looking for the biggest non-radioactive yield I can get."

"Penton Hall is an old building," said Antimony, a note of growing excitement in her voice. "If we put the bomb in the boiler room, we can undermine a lot of the structure. Some of the blast will go downward instead of out, but that'll crack the foundation, and we should be able to collapse several floors. If we do it during a training period, the loss of life will be devastating."

"Which is what we need," I said. "We need them to lose so many people that they can't *afford* to keep coming over here and harassing us like it's a normal thing to do. We need to buy the dragons time to move William somewhere safe. That means we take the fight to them."

"That plan isn't completely tactically insane," said Sally slowly. "It's still riskier than I like, and it depends on some factors I don't like—we don't have blueprints, and it's not like we can predict what size bomb Mary will be able to lift before she tries—but it might make this all go away, or at least make it less immediately pressing."

"So now we just have to convince everyone else," I said.

"And make sure they know that I'm the one the mice will come out of the walls for," said Antimony. "They know me. They'll trust me enough to come when I call."

"Can Sarah transport you when you're carrying the mice?" I asked.

"If she can't, I'll just have to trust my ability to absorb the fire before it reaches them," said Antimony.

"A bomb's effectiveness is primarily measured in concussive force," said Sarah. "Or, to put it in more universal terms, you are resistant to fire damage. This is force damage. You would be pulverized. Yes, I can transport the mice. It's mass, not minds, when I'm running the numbers."

"Excuse me, but how was that more universal?" asked Sally.

"Dungeons and Dragons *is* universal," said Sarah serenely.

"I'm not sure that's—" I began, and stopped, clutching the side of my head, as Verity's screams echoed through my mind. My connection to the family isn't the same as Sarah's telepathy: she gets words and fully formed ideas, at least within a limited range. I don't have a range. The only thing I've ever found that interferes with my ability to hear the family calling for me is them being in a dimension where the laws of reality are sufficiently different to keep me from manifesting there. I think my lack of hearing in those cases is self-defense—whatever controls my afterlife understands that if I heard them, I'd try to go to them, and if I went to them, I might cease to exist. At the same time, there's really no other way to describe the way it feels when they call me. I hear their voices in my head. I hear their need.

It hurts.

"Mary? What's wrong?" asked Antimony.

Verity was still screaming, so loud I could barely hear anything else. It was the loudest thing I'd ever heard in my death, even louder than Alice screaming when she'd seen Jane fall. And it felt unfair to compare those two sounds, because they were both very much born out of trauma, out of a moment of pain so all-consuming that there was nothing left in the world but wailing. There were no words. If anything, this felt like the preverbal calls I received from infants, when they knew need and discomfort and very little more.

I kept clutching my head as I staggered away from the group. Antimony followed me, her concern written clear upon her face. She reached for my shoulder, and her hand passed straight through; my grasp on solidity had slipped at some point, and I couldn't muster the focus to get it back. All I could focus on was the screaming.

"Tell your parents something's wrong," I gasped, looking at Antimony. "Tell them Verity's in trouble."

And then I was gone, hurling myself into the echoing absence of transit, following the sound of soundless screams.

I appeared in an alley, Verity nowhere to be seen, but a large bloodstain splashed across the bricks in front of me. I spun around, looking for a sign of her, and saw nothing but dumpsters and the sort of fire escapes that made her view New York as the ideal urban environment, perfect for climbing and leaping from.

She was still wailing inside my head, which made it virtually impossible to pick up on subtler sounds nearby. But unless my aim was getting suddenly and rapidly worse, she was here—she'd called for me, she had to be nearby. I walked toward the nearest dumpster, and was rewarded with a human foot barely peeking out from behind the corner.

It was a man's foot, not Verity's, larger and square and clad in a sensible black tactical boot, perfect for running or finding traction on slippery rooftop surfaces. There was no tension in it. The owner was either completely relaxed or profoundly asleep.

Or dead.

That was when I knew, really, but I didn't want to admit it, even to myself. Verity's heartbroken wails were still ringing in my head, making it hard to hear the absence of another family member. In that moment, there was no one but Verity. She was the sole member of my family remaining in the world.

I forced myself to continue forward, rounding the corner of the dumpster, and was heartbreakingly unsurprised to find Verity on the ground in her charcoal-gray tactical suit, clearly dressed for the sort of roof-running infiltration she excelled at, blood in her short-cropped hair and streaking her cheeks, sobbing as she tried, desperately, to pull the man in front of her into her arms. There was so much blood that her hands kept slipping on the sodden fabric of his jacket, leaving him to slump back against the wall.

Dominic had always been somewhat darker than Verity, with a naturally tan complexion. His skin was still lightly browned, but there was an ashen gray undertone to it now, leaving him looking almost waxen, like he was a badly sculpted replacement for the real thing. I moved closer, still struggling to fully solidify.

My intangible feet made no sound as I approached. Verity's head still whipped around as she caught my movement out of the corner of her eye, and her shoulders dropped, some of the tension going out of them as her screams inside my head abruptly cut off, leaving me in a ringing silence. The small patch of family tree that belonged to Dominic was empty; if I'd been harboring any hopes that the situation wasn't as bad as it seemed, that silence would have washed them away.

Verity must have seen my face change, because she looked back down at him, bending forward to slide one arm behind his head. She didn't make any attempt to boost him up, just stayed folded almost double, her blood-matted hair hanging across her face, her shoulders starting to shake with the force of the wails she was working so hard to swallow.

I continued walking toward her, and discovered I could force myself solid enough to bend and rest my hand on her shoulder, trying to be a comforting presence. Instead, my touch seemed to do the opposite: she threw her head back and keened, a long, wailing noise that sounded like it had been physically ripped from her throat. She kept making that horrible sound until she ran out of air, then inhaled sharply and started again. I tightened my fingers on her shoulder, refusing to break contact. It wasn't much comfort. A dead woman's touch never is. It was the only thing I had to offer.

This time, when the keening faded, it was replaced with a series of harsh, sharp coughs, like she was attempting to expel the remains of the mourning from her lungs. She turned her head enough to look at me, bloody hair still hanging in her eyes, and in a small voice asked, "Is he gone?"

"Physically, yes," I said. "If you mean 'Has his spirit elected to remain,' I don't know. Do you want me to go and check?"

I didn't want to. I really, *really* didn't want to. People who die violent deaths almost never linger as anything good. When they linger, they tend to become poltergeists, or the sort of twisted apparition that gives all the other ghosts a bad name. They torment and they kill, and they resent the rest of the world for not being as dead as they are. I didn't want that for Dominic. I didn't want that for *Verity*.

Maybe most of all, I didn't want that for Olivia, who was too young to truly remember her father as more than a beloved presence that had been there until one day, suddenly, it wasn't there anymore, but who was still a Price. She was going to grow up to hunt the sort of thing her father would become if he stayed here. I wanted her to have a better future than that one.

"Yes," said Verity, spitting the word with the force of a gunshot. "Check."

"All right. Promise me you'll stay right here, okay? Can you do that? Because I'm not going to go if you can't do that."

"I promise," said Verity, almost sullenly.

"All right," I repeated, and let go of solidity, let go of tangibility, and let go of the land of the living. The transition to the twilight was almost instantaneous, and I found myself standing in a funhouse reflection of the alley where Verity knelt over her husband's cooling body. The bloodstain on the wall was even more visible here, rich red and dripping down the brick in thick rivulets, like the reaching tendrils of a hungry slime mold. The ground was covered in garbage and debris, broken glass and human waste. The ghosts of rats moved in the shadows of the dumpsters, unafraid.

What's loved endures. What's hated endures almost as long, buoyed up through the twilight by the sheer weight of the mental and emotional energy people pour into it. There are a lot of pockets in the afterlife like that alley, shadowy terrors drawn from real horrors, the ghosts of events and nightmares rather than once-living people.

What there wasn't in this terrible place was Dominic, or any sign that he'd stopped for even a moment on his way out the door. I looked at the filthy ground. There were no footprints. No one had been through here in some time.

Which was more likely—that Dominic had died and immediately found the presence of mind to walk around the various puddles of ooze and goo, or that he'd died without manifesting in the twilight at all?

Just to be sure, I dipped down to the starlight, where the alley appeared in much better condition, ground free of unspeakable substances if still scattered with trash and debris, rats replaced by the skittering spirits of tailypo and basilisks. I looked around, satisfying myself that he wasn't here, then bounced all the way back to the daylight in a blink.

Verity was still on the ground where I'd left her, cradling Dominic's body against her chest. She wasn't keening anymore, but tears ran ceaselessly down her cheeks, cutting channels in the blood.

"They caught us on the rooftops," she said, seeming to sense my appearance—and maybe she could. It's never been entirely clear to me where Fran's gifts interact with the family's day-to-day existence. "We were conducting a pretty standard patrol, just the two of us, watching for signs of Covenant teams. We met for the first time on that rooftop over there." She jerked her chin toward a building that looked like all the others around us. "He'd set a snare, and he caught me. What an asshole."

She laughed a little, the sound thick with snot and tears. "So we were running along, looking for traces, because the dragons are scared and the bogeymen are scared and hell, Mary, everyone's scared. *I'm* scared. I swear we were paying attention to where we were going, but we hit a roof and everything went to hell. They were waiting for us behind the elevator house. A whole team. Five operatives. Dominic's good. I'm amazing. That's not arrogance, because it's true. But they had us on the ropes from the moment they attacked."

Verity turned to look at me, eyes wide and wet with tears. That Carew look—blonde hair and big blue eyes—definitely does lend itself to looking like a hopeless damsel searching for a savior. "Three of them went after me. They harried me and pinned me down, so I couldn't get to Dominic while the other two engaged with him. And then one of them slashed him on both sides of his neck, and the other shoved him off the edge of the building. I killed them."

The statement was made with the simple ease that someone might use to say "I made a sandwich" or "I didn't like the play." She made it sound like it was nothing of importance, like it was easy. "I killed all five of them. The three who were keeping me occupied didn't know what to do when I got angry enough to stop fighting defensively, and the other two weren't prepared for me to take them down."

I could picture it so easily. Verity seeing her husband go down, and tapping into that vein of irrational love that seemed to run so hot and strong through the Healy line, using it to motivate herself to do the impossible. I've seen Alice when she loses her temper. I couldn't imagine anyone who wasn't braced for that to happen would be able to stand up before that kind of rage.

"It was a long fall," said Verity, continuing without a pause. "He would have broken almost every bone in his body, but if he'd survived the impact, I could have taken him to St. Giles's. Dr. Morrow's a Caladrius. Broken bones are nothing to him. He can fix anything. He could fix a broken spine. And Dominic got hurt trying to protect the cryptid communities of this city. They owe us a little medical care."

"But he didn't survive the impact," I said.

"No," said Verity, with almost surprising fierceness. I blinked at her. She shook her head. "He was dead before he hit the ground. Look at the blood splatter."

I turned to look at the wall. The blood was splashed across a wider surface area than I would have thought possible, even if Dominic had been attacked on the alley floor—which Verity was now telling me he hadn't been. There was more blood on the ground than I had noticed at first, and the blood on the wall looked like it was dripping down from the top, not originating from a central splash.

"He bled out while he was falling?" I asked.

Verity nodded.

I looked up.

If Dominic had been dead before he hit the ground, that might explain his absence. His spirit could be anywhere between the roof and here, assuming it was still around at all—which I didn't want it to be. I didn't want to raise Verity's hopes, and I didn't want to think about him trapped here, bound by some undefined, unfinished business.

She was still watching me when I looked back down, that yearning plea for rescue in her eyes. "I left their bodies on the roof," she said. "They must have been watching us, to learn our patrol routes. There are four other elevator houses suitable for hosting an ambush that we could have gone running by."

The request was simple, and easy to understand. "Can you tell me where they are?"

"I can."

"My aim's not what it used to be. This may take me a while."

She nodded. "I know."

"If I go looking, will you be all right?"

"I need to call the bogeymen to come and get his . . . come and get him," she said, looking down at Dominic's face like she was trying to memorize every bloodstained inch of it. "His immigration status is questionable, and the false IDs we created for him won't stand up to someone running his fingerprints through an international database. The last thing we need right now is for the Covenant to find out that they just killed Dominic De Luca when he's supposedly been dead for years. I won't be alone for long."

"And you won't . . . hurt yourself?" I have a long history with Healys and the way they respond to losing their loved ones. I watched Alice try to throw herself into a rift in reality to keep Thomas from slipping away from her.

Verity shook her head. "I won't. I swear. Olivia needs me."

That made her the first member of her family who'd had the sense to see that. "All right," I said. "Tell me where to go."

She lifted her head, looked me in the eyes, and did exactly that.

My aim may not be what it once was, but unlike Sarah, moving from one place to another isn't exhausting unless I'm carrying things with me. I appeared on the first rooftop she had identified as a possible ambush site, and immediately wished they'd come this way. There were three Covenant operatives gathered behind the elevator house, none of them more than twenty-five, all of them clearly terrified.

I strolled over to them, hands in my pockets and a bright, false smile on my face. "Hi," I said, once I was close enough, and was gratified to see two of them jump while the third flinched, all turning to look at me.

They were clearly terrified. Hardened field agents, these were not. If this was the quality of people the Covenant was throwing at us, I didn't understand how even three of them had been able to distract Verity for more than a few minutes. Which meant, given the fact that I couldn't deny what had happened to Dominic, that they'd been expecting Dominic and Verity to encounter that particular team, and had been watching them long enough to have a good sense of their patterns.

That was horrifying.

"What are you doing on my roof?" I asked.

One of the agents screwed his courage to the sticking place and stepped forward, demanding, "What do you mean, your roof? How did you get up here?"

"I live here," I said, with as much disdain as I could muster. "This is *my* building. And I've never seen you before."

The Covenant agents started to look even more nervous. One thing about dealing with secret societies: they *really* don't want you to do things like call building security on their people because you don't think they should be wherever they are. Another agent straightened, apparently recovering from the shock of my initial appearance. "Ma'am, you need to move along."

"Oh, you're going to appeal to my presumed desire to obey authority?" I crossed my arms, glaring at him. "I think the three of you need to move along. Preferably over the edge of the roof."

"What?" asked the first.

I said nothing, just allowed my mask of normal, living girl to slip, cheeks going hollow, eyes sinking, and hair beginning to lift up from my shoulders in a spectral wave. My eyes, I knew, would be terrifying without me making any attempt to hide them, all those empty miles stretching out into infinity. I moved closer to the trio, and was gratified when they fell back at my approach, making space for me to step closer still.

"You are not welcome here," I said. "Not on this rooftop, not in this city, not on this continent. This is not your place, and it never will be."

"Phantom," snapped one of the agents. "Everyone, as you were. It's just a ghost."

"Just a ghost?" I asked. "*Just* a ghost?" I moved closer and closer, until I was looming and they were pressed against the elevator house, staring at me like I was the nightmare they'd been having since they were children huddled in their beds, waiting for the sun to rise on another day of Covenant indoctrination. "How *dare* you."

"Depart, spirit," said the agent.

"I shall be there when you die," I responded. "And I'll see you very, very soon." I disappeared into invisibility, winking out like an extinguished candle without moving from my position, and watched as the trio began to argue, squabbling about what my appearance could have meant, what I was doing there, what they might have done to offend the local ghosts. I made note of their location, and moved on to the next spot Verity had identified as a potential ambush.

All four of the locations she'd given me had Covenant teams waiting. Two were like the first one I'd encountered, clearly half-trained and out of their depth, scared out of their minds by the thought that they might actually see combat today. The other two were like the team she described meeting with Dominic, older, better armed, and clearly prepared for a fight. One numbered five, the other seven. The Covenant didn't get lucky. They got *prepared*.

I didn't harass the other three teams. The first one had been correct that I couldn't do anything to them, and while I might have haunted them anyway on another night, for the fun of it all, right now, that felt less important than getting back to Verity. I let go of my position atop the last building and willed myself back to the alley, appearing to find myself alone.

Verity wasn't there, despite promising to stay. For a moment, I thought I might have blinked back into the wrong place, but as I turned to look at the walls, the bloodstain was still there, still exactly as it had been before. I moved over to where I'd left her. The place where Dominic's body had been was surprisingly devoid of blood, probably because he'd lost so much of it while he'd been falling; there hadn't been much left to pool on the ground. I still crouched down, scowling at the pavement like it was somehow going to tell me what had happened.

In a way, it did. While I was glaring at the ground, there was a scraping noise behind me. I whirled around. A manhole cover was sliding slowly out of the way. I straightened and walked toward it, peering down to see Kitty, Verity's former employer, looking up at me, concern and sorrow written on her grayish face. Like all bogeymen, she was long-limbed by human standards, with impossibly spindly fingers marked by extra joints. As long as she wore foundation makeup and kept her hands behind her back, she could have passed for human.

At the moment, she wasn't even trying. "Mary," she said, with some relief. "Verity told me you'd be coming back here. Come down?"

I have nothing to fear from a sewer. I walked over to the manhole and released solidity, dropping through the street and into the tunnel below. I stopped when my feet would have passed through the sewer floor, and waited there as Kitty pulled the manhole back into place and descended the ladder.

"The dragons have been compromised, and we're out of aboveground bases, but the bogeymen have remained secure, and hidebehinds were willing to let us share their tunnels for the time being," she said, stepping onto the sewer walk and gesturing for me to follow. "We can get almost anywhere under the city if we're clever about it."

"About the dragons . . . this is all about William, I'm almost sure of it," I said. "The Covenant needs a big showpiece to prove that the world still needs them. What better than a living dragon?"

"That's our assumption too," said Kitty. "We're trying to find a way to move him, but it's hard. He's been under the city for a long, long time, and there aren't any openings large enough. Still, we're on our guard."

That might need to be good enough. "If you're that secure underground, why were Verity and Dominic on roof patrol?"

She made a complicated face. "Partially habit, and partially because some of the locals refuse to go underground. They have their homes—some of them have rent-controlled apartments—and they have biological needs that require access to the open air. The harpies have been running a sort of sanctuary for the city griffins, getting them into aviaries before they can run afoul of the Covenant, and you can't keep griffins underground. They go wild and will injure themselves trying to get free."

I thought of Alex's beloved lesser griffin, Church, and nodded. "That makes sense."

"They're still part of the cryptid population, even if they're being stupid about a bunch of birds," said Kitty. There was a bitterness to her voice that told me she was speaking more out of grief and fear than actual anger. She glanced back at me, and we kept walking. "Verity and Dominic went out to make sure they were clear to fly for tonight."

"But the Covenant was waiting for them."

"Yes." Kitty made a sound, half-choked, that I was pretty sure counted as a smothered sob. She put a hand over her mouth, ducking her head a little even as she kept walking. "Dominic was a bigoted bastard when Verity first brought him home. He'd been raised to think that people like me weren't people at all. That we were monsters, and deserved to be treated like monsters by the *real* people—a category that conveniently enough included him, and just about everyone he loved. Not that he loved many people. They raised that boy like a rabbit in a hutch, or a dog on a chain. The Covenant never taught him how to be anything but a weapon, and then they pointed him at Manhattan and let him go, figuring he'd bring them back a few trophies for their wall, a few kills for their sacred books, and maybe not die in the process. Instead, he didn't come back at all, because Verity stole him."

"She did," I said. "She gave him everything they didn't, and she taught him how to have a home, not just a place he happened to be living. She found him, she liked him, she took him, and the Covenant never got him back."

"No, but they broke him so no one else could have him, either." Kitty stopped at a section of wall that looked just like everything around it, pressing her hand flat to the concrete. There was a grinding sound. The wall slid inward several inches, and she pushed it with more force, sliding it to the side and revealing an opening a little bigger than a standard door, leading into a long, dark tunnel. "Come on," she said, stepping through.

I followed.

We walked through the dark for a long, long time, Kitty occasionally making a turn or opening another hidden door. They were simple machines of a kind, weights and pulleys, carefully balanced pressure points, and they slid back into place behind us as we continued onward, continually closing off the path in our wake. It would be difficult verging on impossible for someone who didn't already know the way to follow us, and Kitty never paused or faltered. She moved with the ease of someone who knew exactly where they were at all times, and the darkness didn't slow her down.

It wouldn't. Bogeymen are almost entirely nocturnal and don't require much light to see perfectly well. Full daylight is painful for them, rendering them virtually blind, and as a consequence, their communities are almost entirely underground. Like everyone else, they need money if they want to live in or around human society, and that means bogeymen like Kitty, who own businesses in what most people consider the "human world," are not uncommon. They're just almost always cash businesses that allow them to keep the hours that are the most comfortable for them, meaning they rarely have to be in the office while the sun is up.

Some witches have found a way to make darks for bogeymen who need them—the magical equivalent of lights, but instead of illuminating a room, they cast it into total darkness that can't be pierced by most natural means. I wouldn't have been surprised to find out the hidebehinds had installed some of those down here, concealing them among the more-ordinary lights to dissuade sewer workers from doing maintenance. Any tunnel with a healthy hidebehind or bogeyman population would be meticulously maintained without the intervention of human authorities. The city was probably safer because they were here.

"Almost there," said Kitty's voice, reassuringly. It's a little odd to think of a bogeyman in the dark as something comforting, but my existence has been a little odd since I failed to get out of the path of an oncoming truck on Old Logger's Road. This was nothing new.

A door opened in the dark ahead of me, letting a slice of watery light into the tunnel. The outline of Kitty stepped through, beckoning me to follow her, and I did, moving quickly to stay close. The door shut behind me, leaving us in a cavernous chamber filled with shadows and lit around the edges by flickering candles. Clusters of bogeymen occupied the space, all turned to watch us. Other figures seemed to move in the shifting candlelight, and I didn't try to look too hard at them. Those were the hidebehinds, one of the more reclusive types of cryptid.

We suspected they existed but weren't actually sure until a sewer worker dropped his phone and the hidebehind community discovered the internet. They quickly turned out to be friendly and gregarious people, just unwilling to be seen by outsiders. It seemed to be somehow biological, like the weight of a non-hidebehind's eyes was crushing to them. Given that gorgons can petrify with a gaze, it wasn't as farfetched as it might have felt at one time. They were just people, people who didn't want to be seen and deserved the respect of having their wishes honored.

Kitty led me across the chamber to another door, and paused to murmur, "Open it carefully," before stepping aside and letting me pass.

The door was unlocked, the knob turning without resistance. I paused, then let it go, glancing back to Kitty. "Or not at all," I said, and stepped through, into bright white light.

I stopped just on the other side of the door, blinking as I waited for my eyes to adjust. It seemed unfair that out of all the things about a living body, this was one of the things my eyes insisted on emulating. But replicating eyes well enough for them to work meant replicating the musculature and retinal structures, and sudden bright light still burned exactly the way it had when I was alive. At least it wasn't painful.

I finished blinking the brightness away, and saw that I was once again in the waiting room at St. Giles's Hospital. A bogeyman was sitting in one of the hard plastic chairs, a makeshift sling holding his clearly broken arm to his chest, and a harpy was sitting in another chair with a large cat carrier in her lap, its occupant making loud squawks and croaks of protest.

A female Caladrius in nurse's scrubs stood behind the desk. She perked up at the sight of me, waving for me to approach. I walked toward her.

"Miss Dunlavy," she greeted me. "We've been expecting you."

"Is Verity here?" I asked. It was no real surprise that the bogeymen had their own entrance to the hospital. Honestly, it would have been more surprising if they hadn't. A special entrance meant they could bring their people in without exposing them to light if they were already injured. I had little doubt they had some sort of signaling system for when they needed to ask the hospital to dim the lights in advance, just to keep everyone safe.

Human hospitals have it easy. They just have to deal with one species. A cryptid hospital is more like a veterinarian that specializes in treating intelligent, communicative animals. Dr. Morrow had to know the anatomy and biology of a few dozen species of cryptid, and be flexible enough to deal when someone brought him something he *didn't* know intimately. It probably helped that as a Caladrius, he had certain preternatural healing abilities, and could work around what he didn't know. It was still a challenge most human doctors would never need to face, and might not be able to rise to if they did.

The woman behind the desk nodded. "She's in the . . ." She hesitated.

"The morgue?" I asked.

The woman nodded again, clearly relieved. "Yes, the morgue. I'm sorry. I wasn't sure if that was a sensitive word around posthumous people."

"We prefer 'ghosts,'" I said. "May I go to her?"

"Please do," she said.

"Thanks." I turned, then, and walked through the nearest door, heading deeper into the hospital.

Some cities have cryptid funeral parlors. Others have cryptid-friendly funeral homes, where people can take their loved ones for a respectful interment as necessary. Manhattan's last cryptid-friendly funeral home closed down in the nineties, when even cryptid community funds couldn't stand up to the rising tide of local real estate prices. So St. Giles's fills the gap.

They have a mortician on staff who's fully licensed to prepare bodies for burial in New York state, and can embalm well enough to prep them for transport all across the continent. He's a ghoul, but no one holds that against him, and whenever he needs to eat parts of his clients, he takes the cost off his final bill. It's very respectful, really, and reminded me a little of the Dullahan who'd taken Jane's kidney.

Not many cryptids have a hunger for human flesh, but the ones who do try to find jobs that give them access, mostly because it's easier than getting corpses the do-it-yourself way. Sure, some people enjoy murder, but it tends to have bad consequences when they inevitably get caught, and it's a hell of a lot easier to become a mortician, or get a job in hospital janitorial, or any one of a number of other corpse-rich professions.

The halls were largely empty, although the lights were on above more of the doors than had been earlier in the day, and more of the nursing staff were bustling back and forth, some looking downright harried. The Covenant had been busy.

I continued onward.

My journey eventually brought me to the morgue, and I walked through the door into a cool room where the air tasted like dust. Stainless steel tables dotted the space, some of them occupied by sheet-draped figures. One such table was also occupied by the blood-streaked form of Verity Price, curled tight against the table's shrouded and rightful occupant.

Right. Not surprising. Not great, either.

I walked toward her, taking in the absence of the morgue attendant as I did, and stopped a few feet away from the table before I said, "Hey, Very, that doesn't look terribly comfortable."

She didn't move or respond.

"You know you can't stay in the morgue all night, right? This isn't a hotel."

Still no response.

I sighed and walked over to rest my hand on her shoulder, turning intangible when she tried to shrug me off. "Sweetheart, I know you're hurting right now. I know you don't want to think about what happens next. But tomorrow's going to come, and you're still going to be here, and Olivia's still going to need you. You can't give up now."

"What the hell do you know?" She finally turned her head to look at me, glaring viciously. "You died when you were a kid. You never fell in love. You never even dated. You don't know what I'm feeling right now. You don't know how much this hurts."

"No," I said, with artificial calm, trying to swallow how much her words stung. "I don't know from experience, because I didn't have the opportunity to learn. What I do know is that I've watched three generations of Healys and Prices grow up, and figure out who they love, and fall in love so hard it hurts, and stay in love even when it kept on hurting. I've watched you marry and I've watched you mourn, and nothing about this is new, and nothing about this is fair, and it's not right but it's the way things are. I can't change it any more than I can go back and not get hit by that truck. I don't even know if I would have fallen in love if I *hadn't* died. I know a lot of ghosts who've fallen in love after death, and it's just never happened for me. Not the way you mean. But I've fallen in love with your whole family. You're my family. You're *mine*, in a way that words don't really have the strength to describe. You make me feel like this world has a purpose. You make me feel like I'm still on this side of whatever's next for a reason. You make me want to stay. If that's not love, I don't know what is."

Verity was crying again, tears following the channels already worn along her bloodied cheeks by the tears that had come before; her eyes and nose were red. She was normally a reasonably attractive crier, one of those girls who could weep without smearing her eyeliner or getting snot all over her upper lip. Not right now. Right now, she was a mess, and that was somehow well and good and entirely correct, because this was her time to mourn. Her grief would last after this, and probably for a good long time. It would never be this raw again. I wouldn't tell her not to be sad, not when she had every right to be.

She sat up, putting one hand on the chest of the shrouded figure next to her, and looked down at him with tears dripping off her nose to pool on the shroud in a damp, red-tinged stain. "I never really fell in love before him, you know? I dated, and sometimes I thought I was in love, but it always went away the first time we fought. None of them ever understood me. Even Blake didn't see why I didn't want to come out of the field and join the normal world, and he was a cryptozoologist in training. We could have been good together, if he hadn't been so determined to make me into someone else by loving me hard enough."

"I know, sweetie."

"And then I was in New York, and I wasn't looking for a relationship. I wasn't even looking for a friend with benefits. I was just trying to help the community, and learn more about urban cryptids, and find a way to distinguish myself from the rest of my family. I wasn't *looking*." It came out almost like a plea. "I wasn't looking, and he was there, and he danced with me. He danced with me, and he fought with me, and that would have been enough. He could have been the kind of friend I needed in my life. But his life was so . . . so empty. The Covenant didn't give him anything but the mission. They thought that was all he needed. So I tried to show him there could be a better way, and somehow that turned into the two of us, and bribing the mice to keep quiet, and— The mice. Mary, how am I going to tell the *mice*?" Her tears, which had almost stopped during her recollections, started again in earnest. "They loved him almost as much as I do. They're going to be heartbroken."

"You'll tell them the same way you tell them anything. Carefully and in words you can handle hearing echoed back, because they're going to repeat whatever you say forever." I paused. "Verity . . . have you spoken to anyone from the compound since this morning?"

"No." She shook her head. "There hasn't been time. Is everyone okay?"

"I . . ." I paused, unsure exactly how to finish that. "You should call home when you get the chance. You need to talk to your mother."

"My mother . . . God, Mary, she loved Dominic too. Once she got over him being Covenant, she said she couldn't imagine me finding a more perfect partner." She looked at me, desperation in her eyes. "I know the crossroads are gone, but is there any way . . . ?"

"No. And even if there were, I wouldn't. I couldn't. They never had the ability to raise the dead. Not like that, baby. You wouldn't want what they could give you, even if they were still here to do it."

"When does it stop feeling like I'm the one who bled out in that alley?"

"I don't know," I said, honestly. "For your great-grandfather, it never did. And you saw what your grandmother did to her life. Love is a powerful thing. It's also a pretty poison. You've been drinking deep, and now you get to pay for it. The thing about love, though, is that you'd do it all over again if you had the choice. That's what makes it powerful. That's what makes it good."

"I want to make them pay."

"I know. But you have to think of Olivia. What happens to her if you go off on a mission of revenge and don't come home? You saw what that did to your father and aunt. She needs at least one parent to stay with her. She needs to feel like she's enough."

"Then you have to make them pay." She turned to look at me again, eyes huge. "Will you make them pay, Mary? For me? For Dominic? For what they did?"

"We're already working on that, sweetheart, I promise. They're going to be sorry as hell that they ever messed with us. But I need to get back."

"Can you . . ." She looked down again, swallowing hard, then glanced at me. "Can you not tell Mom and Dad? I want to tell them myself."

"They need to tell you some things too," I said. "Please call as soon as you feel like you're up to it. I love you, bug. I know this is hard, and

I know this is horrible, but your family is here when you need us, and we always will be. Dominic would want you to keep going, for all of us, and for him."

"I know." For the first time since I'd found her in the alley, she wiped the tears from her cheeks, smearing the remaining blood in the process. The end effect was ghoulish but hopeful. "I'll come to Portland as soon as things are stable here. I want to hug my daughter."

"I can ask Sarah if the numbers have unsnarled enough to let her bring her back?"

"No!" Verity's response was immediate. "If it's not safe for me to leave, it's not safe for her to come, either. I'm dealing with this, whatever that means, and then I'm coming home."

"Okay, baby," I said. "I'll see you there."

She wiped her face again, offering me a weak, wavering smile. I wanted to tell her she didn't have to force it for me. I wanted to tell her she was allowed to be sad. And she was; she just wasn't allowed to fall into the wallowing despair that had claimed so many of her ancestors. If I could break the cycle I had witnessed for generations, I would consider my time with the family to have been more than well spent.

I blew her a kiss, and I was gone.

I still had work to do.

Fourteen

> "Children aren't pets or projects. They're people. We can tell them who we want them to be, but we can't force anything. No matter how much we may wish we could."
>
> —Eloise Dunlavy

Skipping through the twilight, on the way to another destination, sure I'm making about a dozen mistakes but not sure how to stop

I APPEARED IN THE middle of the produce section of a Whole Foods Market, standing between a display of assorted apples and a cart with a baby in the basket. The adult associated with the cart had her back to me, attention on the two zucchini she was weighing in her hands, studying them with the focus most people reserved for active surgery. The baby stared at me, eyes enormous but somehow unsurprised. Everything was strange and new—why shouldn't people appear out of nowhere? It was just like peekaboo but with a stranger's entire body, rather than Mama's face.

I was probably going to be responsible for this kid taking an extra few weeks to develop proper object permanence, and I would have felt bad about that, if I'd done it on purpose. As it was, I waved to the kid, causing them to flap both arms in excitement, then walked out of the produce department and around the corner of the nearest aisle, where there were no witnesses. Once there, I vanished again.

This lack-of-reliable-aim thing was getting old. I couldn't exactly ask my family members to distribute themselves evenly across the continent and call for me precisely when I needed them to, so I was going to have to figure this out, no matter how impossible it seemed.

This time, I appeared on a suburban street corner, the street around me lined with charming brick houses and beautifully maintained trees. A squirrel chattered at me. I chittered back in pale imitation of its indignant protests, and vanished a third time, trying to focus harder on where I was going.

It worked. I appeared on the back-porch step of an unassuming duplex apartment that looked exactly like every building in the row around it. The door was closed, but through the glass panel at eye level, I could see the dining room and a slice of the kitchen. There was no one there, which just supported the decision to appear outside. Inside, the motion detectors were probably on, and while the home security system had no defenses that could do me actual harm, that didn't mean I wanted to set them off. Instead, as solid as a Girl Scout hoping to unload a backpack full of Thin Mints, I raised my hand and rapped on the glass.

Motion on the other side of the glass answered me almost immediately, as a short, curvy woman with blue streaks in her brown hair came pounding down the stairs with more speed than a simple knock deserved, all but throwing herself into the kitchen. Her left bicep was heavily bandaged—an affectation, since her body was even more on the "mostly water" side of things than your average human. She slowed as she approached the door, slicking back her hair with one hand and composing her face into something that wasn't quite so grim. She still looked like she was going to attend a funeral; she just looked less like she was going to facilitate the need for one.

Then she saw me through the glass and the grimness bled away completely, replaced by surprise and concern. She hurried the last six or so feet to unlock the door, pulling it open. "Mary! You could have just come in, you know. We don't have any shielding against ghosts."

"I'd be concerned if you did, since I don't think I've given you reason for it," I replied. "It's good to see you, too, Lea. I figured after the attack on the Carmichael, you'd have brought any extra defenses the house had online. Is Mike in Ohio at this point?"

"He left as soon as Alex called," she confirmed. "I convinced him I should stay here. I'm more useful by the lake than I am in a landlocked area."

Aunt Lea is an Oceanid, a sort of plasmoid shapeshifter that can move between liquid and solid forms. In their liquid form, they're all but indistinguishable from water, but are actually more like extremely large, impossibly complex amoeboid life forms, capable of dissolving their own cellular walls for the sake of losing unwanted rigidity. In their liquid forms, they have a degree of control over the water around them, which makes them terrifying opponents when they're anywhere near a decently sized body of water. Like, say, Lake Michigan, which was less than a mile away.

Oceanids like Lea who choose to live near freshwater tend to be smaller and more human-like than saltwater Oceanids; the lack of salt means they can only maintain coherence up to a certain size in their liquid forms. That also means they're more likely to live among humans, as she had quite dramatically chosen to do when she married Mike Gucciard and settled with him in a suburb of Chicago.

No, I don't know how any of this works, and I don't care enough to try to figure it out. I'm a dead babysitter with a high school education. I'll leave the complicated questions like "How does a puddle get a social security number, an accounting degree, and a husband who doesn't mind her needing to sleep in a bucket?" to the members of the family who care about that sort of thing, and I'll just focus on trying to keep the rest of them alive.

"I was hoping that would be the case," I said, and watched her flip a switch that appeared to do nothing. That, I knew, would shut off the motion detectors in the kitchen and make it safe for people like me, who didn't know exactly where to step to avoid setting off the alarms. If I did set off the alarms, they would send a message to Uncle Mike, and I really didn't want to cause him another panic attack after the day he'd already had. "Him leaving, not you staying behind. How did you convince him, anyway?"

Her smile was thin and cruel and filled with the bodies snarled in the weeds at the bottom of the lake. "I pointed out that if the Covenant tried to come to the house, I'd punch them with the lake. As many times as I had to. Ever been punched by a lake?"

"No," I said.

"Good. Keep it that way."

"Sometimes I forget how terrifying you are," I said. "Everyone okay at the Carmichael?"

Her face fell. "The hotel was seriously damaged, and the Covenant knowing it exists means we have to seriously question whether it can stay open. We lost three gorgons and a pair of bogeymen who stood to fight rather than running to their rooms."

I grimaced. "I'm so sorry. And I'm sorry to have to ask you this, but how long ago did Mike leave?"

"He called to tell me he was at the house twenty minutes ago," said Lea. "Not that I don't enjoy your company, but Mary, what are you doing here?"

"I don't have a phone, no one in Ohio is currently calling for me, and you seemed less likely to freak out if I suddenly showed up than most of them did," I said. "Can you please call Uncle Mike and ask him to summon me?"

She gave me a sympathetic look. "Aim's not getting any better?"

"It took me three jumps to get here." It didn't help that Uncle Mike and Aunt Lea were only satellite family members—I couldn't sense them the way I could the core of the family, and while I'd hear if they called for me, the summons wouldn't have the same burning need to reply that I got when it was one of my kids.

"That's better than it was last year," she agreed. "Do you think it's going to continue to improve?"

"I definitely hope so, but for right now, much as I enjoy your company, I need to get to Ohio, and that means I need them to know I'm coming, and to call me there. Please."

She blinked, then nodded. "I'll call him. Come inside."

I stepped into the kitchen. It was, as always, meticulously clean. Uncle Mike and Aunt Lea liked everything to be just so, perfectly in its place and never askew for longer than it took to use. It was part of what made them so excellent as organizational allies. It was also part of why I was glad neither of them had ever wanted children. Biological children were impossible for them as a pair, of course, but adoption would have been an option, if they hadn't recognized that it wouldn't be healthy for anyone involved.

Lea moved toward the phone. They still had a landline, for whatever reason, and it was reassuringly familiar as she picked up the receiver and dialed, then waited for an answer. After a moment, her face relaxed into a smile.

"Mike, hey," she said. "All is well? Good. Yeah, all's well here too, no sign of Covenant activity. I'm at home, and I have Mary here with me. Could one of you give her a summons so she can get to Ohio without bouncing all over the Midwest? That would be fantastic." She paused. "Love you too, see you when you get home. All the alarms are on. I'm staying in unless I get a distress call or have to go out for groceries." She hung up, then turned to me. "He's going to call."

"Great."

"Now be honest—were you aiming for Chicago? At all?"

I shook my head. "Nope. But once I hit the downtown Whole Foods, you were the closest family member, so I came here before I went any farther. Thanks for calling him."

"Any time." She looked at me searchingly. "You wouldn't have shown up here by mistake if you hadn't already been thinking about us. What do you need?"

"I was worried about the Carmichael, and I need Uncle Mike to get me a bomb."

Again, she blinked. "That's a new one."

"Yeah, but he's the only one I believe can. And we need to stop this before we all get picked off."

"You're dead. You can't be picked off."

"I'm a babysitter. If they kill all my charges, they might as well have killed me again. I already died once. That was more than enough."

Lea nodded. "So a bomb is the answer?"

"Not usually. This time, maybe."

She frowned, opening her mouth to answer, and stopped as she saw me flinch. "He's calling?"

"No. That would have been too easy. Alex is calling." Which meant it was louder and more urgent, jangling my nerves and making an already overlong day feel even longer. I tuned her out to focus on the call. "He doesn't feel like he's in active distress, which is a good thing, but I should go. Thank you for your help."

She gave me a concerned look. "You know you're welcome any time, Mary. I don't see you enough."

"It's baby season right now," I said. "Hard to find a lot of time for social calls when everybody's making more kids for me to take care of. But I'll be sure to come for a visit when all this is over. Let my folks know they should hire someone living for a week or two. Everyone gets vacations, right?"

"Right," she agreed, concern fading into a smile.

She was still smiling as I vanished, hurling myself toward Ohio with all my phantom heart.

On arrival, I appeared in the kitchen of the house where Alex and Shelby lived with Angela, Martin, and the children, often including Sarah. All four of the resident adults were present when I popped in, along with both children, Alex's griffin and Shelby's garrina, and Uncle Mike, who was leaning against the counter with his thick arms crossed across his black-clad chest. He looked like hired concert security that had wandered afield of his actual assignment, and he nodded as I appeared.

"Mary," he said.

Shelby, meanwhile, threw herself out of her chair and wrapped her arms around me with surprising force, yanking me into a hug that could just as easily have been delivered by a grizzly bear. I squeaked with surprise, the wind knocked out of me by the gesture, and hugged her back as she kissed me on both cheeks, repeatedly.

"Mary," she said. "Brilliant Mary. I can never thank you enough for what you did."

"They're family," I said, a little uncomfortable with the intensity in her tone. "They're my responsibility, and I would be a pretty lousy babysitter if I didn't come when my kids called."

"Even so, brilliant Mary," she said. "I shan't forget this."

I remembered, belatedly, that Shelby's older brother, Jack, died in a cuckoo attack before she came to America. He was part of the reason she'd started dating Alex—she had recognized Angela's species, and wanted to protect what she saw as another cuckoo victim, only to fall in love. The fact that Shelby now lived with two adult cuckoos while helping to raise a cuckoo child really said something about how much she'd healed since meeting up with Alex, or how good this family was at convincing people that second chances were a necessary kindness. It was difficult to say which was the case.

I leaned back, and Shelby took the hint, letting me go. Stepping over to Alex, I ruffled his hair the way I used to when he was a little boy hurrying to show me some horrible thing he'd pulled out of a hole, and he smiled up at me, tired but unharmed.

"You dispose of those bodies?" I asked.

"I did, after we ran some quick tests to make sure their flesh wasn't contaminated enough to be toxic," he replied. "We bled them out, then split the meat between the Komodo dragons at the zoo and the lindworm nest we've been monitoring out by the Fringe. They're small enough that they haven't started hunting people yet, and we're hoping we can discourage them from getting started. They'll be dangerous when they're fully grown. Those woods could use a few dangerous things, to keep the locals at bay."

"Is that safe?"

"Nope," he replied. "Lindworms can't be domesticated. But they can be worked around, and there's something to be said for predictable, territorial apex predators."

"Is the something 'Ahh no, stop, run'?"

He smiled, crookedly. "Love you too, Mary."

I looked around the table. No one seemed upset enough to have heard about any of the day's losses. I winced. It still didn't feel like my place to inform them—I've been a part of this family for decades, but I'm not really *part* of the family. I'm the babysitter. I'm not the one who's supposed to handle the big announcements, whether good or bad.

Unfortunately, being the babysitter meant they knew me as well as I knew them. Alex frowned at the expression on my face. "Mary?" he asked. "What's wrong?"

"I . . . You *really* need to call your mother," I said. "There are some things you should know, and it's not my place to be the one to tell you."

He froze. Then, in a very careful tone, he asked, "Was it Annie or Very?"

I shook my head.

"Then I can call and keep myself together enough to stay useful," he said, rising from the table. He paused to kiss Shelby on the temple. "I'll be right back."

I doubted that, but I didn't say anything as he walked out of the room. This needed to happen, and then it would need to happen again, after Verity called home. Sometimes, knowing things is hard. I still generally like it better than the alternative.

"Lea said you were looking for me," said Uncle Mike. "What's up?"

I walked over to stand near him. "I need a bomb."

He blinked. So did Angela and Martin. Only Shelby looked unflapped, as if me looking for heavy explosives was the most reasonable thing in the world. She seemed more concerned about Alex, glancing after him before looking back to me. Isaac, who had been contentedly pulling on Crow's wing, looked up and focused on me, saying, "Mary sad. Why Mary sad?"

"Why *is* Mary sad, Isaac," I replied. "Use your verbs."

"It's a struggle getting him to use his words at all," said Angela. "I've never dealt with a cuckoo as young as he is. He makes me wonder how any of us normally learn how to talk. He finds it so much easier to just communicate telepathically with Charlotte, and then both of them expect us to read their minds the same way he can read hers."

Isaac was still looking at me with earnest, faintly glowing eyes, waiting for my reply. I sighed. "Mary is sad because it's been a very hard day, Isaac. I've seen a lot of bad things happen, and I've seen some people get hurt."

Shelby sucked in a sharp breath, clearly making the connection between my telling Alex to call his mother and people getting hurt. She leaned toward me.

"How bad is it?" she asked.

"Pretty bad," I said. "Terrible. It could be worse, but I.'m not exactly sure how." Except that I was sure how, and all the ways I could think of involved even more bodies hitting the ground. The Covenant was still active in New York, and Verity was going to be a lot less careful now, a lot more inclined to rely on her luck and her momentum to carry the day. We still didn't have accurate damage reports for the Fringe or the other carnivals, and it sounded like Leonard might have Megan locked up somewhere.

It was bad enough. It didn't need to be any worse to break my heart.

As if on cue, Isaac started crying. Charlotte followed suit, barely a moment later. The two children reached for each other, latching on and holding tight as they cried, sobs escalating into wails in a matter of seconds. Shelby looked at them, her eyes growing wide, then launched herself from her seat and ran after Alex. Angela and Martin rose in turn, walking more decorously after her.

"What just happened?" asked Uncle Mike.

"Alex called his mother," I said. "Now, about that bomb."

"Right." He focused on me. "What do you need?"

I explained the layers of the afterlife to Uncle Mike a long time ago, and once he determined that he and Aunt Lea would go to different places without my help, he got a lot more eager to help me out with whatever issues I might have. Normally, I didn't like to exploit that. These weren't normal circumstances. "I need an explosive device, non-nuclear, large enough to do as much damage as possible, small enough for me to lift it," I said. "I don't have to be able to physically carry it anywhere, as long as I can pick it up."

"What are you trying to level?"

"Big, very old building."

"How old?"

"British, pre-World War II."

"Can you get belowground?"

"I should have access to the basement. And someone to call me so I wind up in the right spot when I get there."

"That's the important thing. A lot of buildings survived the Blitz because the bombs weren't ground-piercing, and those places were built sturdy as hell. They're supposed to stand up to centuries. You want to take them out with an explosive, placement matters more than almost anything else you can come up with. You'd be better off with more than one."

"Can you *get* me more than one?"

"It's going to take some doing. I'll have to pull some strings, burn a few IOUs that I was saving for a rainy day, but—yeah. Give me three days, and I can get you either three or four Mark 81s. They'll each weigh about two-fifty, but you should be able to budge that for at least a few seconds."

"I should," I agreed. It was going to hurt like hell, and I was probably going to do the dead-girl equivalent of pulling a muscle, but there was no reason I couldn't grab one bomb, jump to where Annie was calling me, and then return for another one, as long as I had someone on that end to call me back. I would ping-pong from my starting point to Penton Hall and back again, and we'd blow those fuckers to hell. "Is there any way you can get them delivered either here or to Portland? Because I'm going to need a family member to summon me in order to come collect them—I could probably show up on my own, but the keyword there is 'probably,' and we're going to be on a countdown as soon as I say go. I need the anchor to be sure."

"Guessing I wouldn't be good enough?" he asked, without any rancor. He and I had discussed my ties to the family in the past, and which ones I heard the most loudly. He was so focused on operational security in most situations that it was important for him to know exactly what he was working with. I think he was the happiest person in the family, apart from me, to hear that I was no longer obligated to answer when the crossroads called. My connections to an incomprehensible, presumably hostile intelligence had never sat well with him.

"Sadly, no," I said. "I need someone I've officially been the babysitter for. Alex could do it, or Kevin."

"Your other charges not available?"

The question was mild, but I could hear the subtext loud and clear. I looked him dead in the eyes. "Some of them are," I said. "Some of them aren't. Some of them are going to be with me while I'm setting the explosives, both to anchor me to the location and because they have goals of their own to accomplish. Alex and Kevin I can safely expect to be stationary."

Uncle Mike blew out a heavy breath. "Yeah," he said finally. "I can get the bombs to whatever location you think is best, if you can deliver them to the target from there."

"Thanks," I said.

The children were still clinging to each other and crying. Much as it pained me to ignore them while they were distressed, the sound of their cries had been enough to keep us from being overheard. I stepped over to the kitchen chair that they were sharing, even though it was rapidly becoming too small for the two of them at the same time. The pillows they were sitting on had been knocked entirely askew and were on the verge of falling to the floor.

Charlotte reached for me when I was close enough. "Mary," she wailed. "Mary, Mary. Daddy's so *sad*."

"I know, pumpkin," I said, scooping her up and bracing her against my hip with one arm while I offered the other to Isaac. He shook his head and stuck his thumb in his mouth, shrinking back against the pillows.

Cuckoo powers work better when there's skin contact. He was old enough to be figuring that out. While he probably didn't find Charlotte's thoughts overwhelming with as much as they lived in each other's heads, wanting to avoid touching someone else made sense. He was old enough to have the beginnings of bodily autonomy, while also being too young to have fully grasped what it meant for me to be dead; he didn't know that my thoughts would never get any louder, and I wasn't going to push the issue.

"Uncle Mike will stay here with you," I informed him. "Is that all right?"

He nodded as he sucked his thumb, tears running down his cheeks. He'd only met Jane twice, but the size of Alex's grief was enough that he had no defenses against it. Poor kiddo. The perils of having a baby telepath around the house.

Charlotte firmly on my hip, I followed the path of Shelby's flight to the living room, where I found her kneeling next to Alex, who was seated on the couch with his glasses shoved up onto his forehead and his hands pressed over his eyes. Charlotte immediately whimpered and reached for Shelby, who was rubbing Alex's back with one hand.

"Can you take her?" I asked quietly, looking at Shelby.

She glanced up at me and nodded. "Of course. Come here, mite." She reached for her daughter, who transferred willingly into the safety of her mother's arms as I sat down next to Alex on the couch.

"I'm so sorry," I said.

He shifted positions, pressing his face into my shoulder as he dropped his hands, and sobbed like the child he'd been during our time together, like he had never known anything in this world but grieving. I stroked his back with one hand and his hair with the other, making quiet shushing noises as I tried to lend what comfort I could. Shelby, bouncing Charlotte to soothe her, took a step back and watched us.

My relationship with my adult kids is an interesting one. I'm not a parent—I'm the childhood nanny who never grew up, a strange combination of Mary Poppins and Peter Pan. But that means they all turn to me for comfort in times of stress, often over their own spouses, and that's something the spouses in question have to learn to be comfortable with. It's sort of the second test, after "Can you handle a colony of talking pantheistic mice?"—"Can you handle the fact that my babysitter is still around?" In Alex's case, I had also been his first crush, even if he'd never done much beyond blushing and stammering and handing me toads.

They'd been some pretty nice toads, too. Thankfully for everyone involved, Shelby took my existence, and everything it included, in stride. She was generally a pretty mellow person until she had a reason not to be, and she wasn't threatened by the resident dead girl. She just watched as I stroked Alex's hair and murmured nonsense syllables, waiting for him to calm down enough to speak to me.

Eventually, he raised his head and met my eyes, tears still running down his face. "She's dead," he informed me, as if I might somehow not have known. "She was . . . and now she's gone."

For an instant, a pang of terror lanced through me, making me question whether I might *not* know, whether he might be talking about someone else. But when I reached for the network of my connections to the family, everyone else was strong and stable. Dominic and Jane were the only missing pieces—and "only" felt like a misnomer there, a terrible attempt to downplay something that couldn't be downplayed, to minimize a loss too big to focus on.

"I know, baby," I said. "I'm so sorry."

"Was she . . ." He stopped, not quite able to continue, and I sighed.

"I was there. She was scared, but it was all very fast, and she didn't have time to suffer." I said. "I saw her, after, down in the starlight, and she said she knew she had to go. She wasn't going to stick around and haunt people when her time was finished."

"How do I tell the *mice*?"

That was a question I was getting pretty good at fielding. "Just tell them. Whatever you say is going to be repeated to you forever, but you have to tell them. Especially if you have any members of her clergy here. They deserve to know."

Alex nodded, a pained expression on his face. "I guess I have to."

Charlotte's sobs were tapering off, replaced by hiccups, as Alex got his grief under control and Isaac stopped bouncing it to her quite so loudly. She clung to Shelby, not yet to the point of reaching for her father, and he sighed, wiping his eyes with the back of his hand.

"It's always been a risk," he said, pulling his glasses back into position. "We go out into these fields, we do these—sorry for the language—these damn stupid things, and we just count on luck to keep us safe, but luck doesn't hold forever. Everybody has a bad day. Eventually, I'm going to have a bad day, or Shelby is, and then where will we be?"

"You'd think for a family that has proof of life after death, we'd have less existential fear of dying," I said, and bumped his shoulder with my own. "Where you'll be on that unlucky day is on the other side of the twilight, and then you'll call my name, and I'll come, and we'll decide together whether you want to stay or go. If you want to stay, I'll do whatever I can to help you figure out how that's going to work, what it's going to look like, what kind of haunting you have it in you to be. And if you want to go, I'll carry your final message back to your family, and tell them you're at peace, and that this was your choice. Luck isn't forever. The babysitter is."

"When you die, you'd best move along, you wanker," said Shelby, with her customary lack of anything resembling sympathy. "I intend to remarry rich, and be able to buy half the privately owned land in Queensland so I can set up a proper wildlife sanctuary. Hard to do that with my dead husband's ghost haunting my underwear drawer."

"Yes, dear," said Alex, and actually cracked a smile.

"Where are your grandparents?" I asked, looking around the room.

"They went upstairs," said Alex. "I'll have to tell them, too. Grandma Angela really liked Aunt Jane." His face fell, and for a moment, it looked like he was going to start crying again.

"All right," I said, and stood, giving him one last pat on the shoulder. "I'm going to head out. I think you should stay here."

"What? But the funeral—"

"Won't be for at least a week, and hopefully by then, this will all be over," I said. "It's too dangerous for you to travel right now, and we still need to find out how they found the house, or the Fringe." Megan, it was Megan, and telling him that would do no good. "You have work to do here. Annie and I are going to take the fight to the Covenant."

"Please don't let my baby sister get herself killed," said Alex, with grim serenity.

"I won't," I said. "I promise."

Turning, I walked back to the kitchen, where Uncle Mike was waiting, to finish arranging for the acquisition and delivery of the bombs I needed. Just another ordinary day for a dead girl in the middle of a war most of the world had yet to notice.

Sometimes I really wish the dead could drink.

Fifteen

"Nothing wrong with handing your kids to a dead girl so you can get a moment's peace. You need the patience of a corpse to raise kids."

—Jane Harrington-Price

Returning to the barn, ready to continue

MY AIM WAS GOOD enough to get me to the compound, if no better: I appeared in the barn, alone. Jane's body was still on the table, and the air around it was colder than it should have been, a sphere of James's magic holding her in a sort of cold storage that would keep her from decaying before we could call people together for the funeral. As someone who preferred to work with the social side of the cryptid world, Jane had a lot of friends, allies, and acquaintances who were going to want to be there when she was buried, if only because it was the only way some of them were going to believe she was actually dead.

Everyone else was gone. I moved toward Jane's body. She wasn't there—no one knew that better than I did—but there was still a strange comfort in addressing her as if she were. I leaned over and brushed a lock of her hair back from her cheek, smoothing it into place.

"Hey, Jane," I said. "We're taking care of things. I know it won't bring you back, but we can stop them from doing this to anybody else. Then we'll start getting things together for the funeral. I know you wouldn't want us to drag our feet on that one. Everyone's going to be there. It'll be the social event of the season." My voice broke on the last word, and I bowed my head, eyes burning with unshed tears. I'd known this woman since she was a screaming baby placed in my arms by Laura, who had still been bloody from the home delivery. I held her before her own mother did. I saw her through skinned knees and first crushes and first loves and real love and her own courtship, marriage, and children. I had watched her do everything in her power not to grow up anything like her mother, and in the process, become more like her mother than she could ever have dreamed she'd be.

And I had loved her every inch along the way. Gods and goddesses, but I'd loved her. She hadn't chosen to stay, but I was still here, and I still loved her, and I always would, forever.

I leaned down to kiss her cold forehead, then straightened and walked out of the barn, leaving her behind. A corpse is nothing scary to someone who's already dead, but I had living people to talk to, and plans to make.

As I had almost expected, I found all five of my companions around the firepit, as well as Greg, who was curled up at Sarah's feet like a parody of a big, fluffy dog. He was keeping his limbs well away from the fire, but seemed to be enjoying the heat. James and Sally shared a log, while Antimony sat on the ground, leaning back on the log where Sam sat, his knees flanking her face and his tail wrapped around her ankles. That would make getting up interesting, when it happened.

Sally saw me first, and waved for me to come over and join them. I walked over and settled on one of the open logs.

"I wish we had some marshmallows," said Antimony, idly. "I know I shouldn't be hungry when I'm grieving, but I am, and this seems like a marshmallow-toasting sort of day."

"You think every day is a marshmallow-toasting sort of day," said James.

"Yeah, and I'm pretty much always right," said Antimony. "Hey, Mary. Everything good?"

My throat went dry. "Not really," I said. "Verity's fine. I'm sure she'll call home soon."

Sarah raised her head, eyes widening and flashing white in the same instant as she stared at me. Antimony scowled, looking between the two of us. "You're not telling me something," she accused. "I don't like being left in the dark."

"Would you be happy if I went inside right now and told your parents Sam had proposed? If I decided I got to be the one who spread that news around, whether or not you were ready?" I kept my eyes on Antimony until she shook her head, shoulders slumping as she backed down. "Then you'll wait for Verity to call. What I know isn't for me to share. Or for anyone else to share." I shot Sarah a hard look. She wouldn't be able to read my expression, but she'd be able to understand my intent. Face-blindness and telepathy is a good combination for actually knowing what's going on.

"Okay," said Antimony. "But you know that just makes me want to know even more."

"Can't be helped," I said. "Sorry."

"Did you find Uncle Mike? Did you talk to him about the bomb?"

I nodded. "I did, yes. We have a plan, but it's going to take three days for him to get the bombs to me. The Covenant isn't going to back off and stop harassing us because we're waiting on our munitions."

"No," said James. "But they are going to be pulling back to calculate their own losses. They don't have the manpower to stay on the offensive forever."

"Maybe, maybe not," I said. "The more time they have to regroup, the worse our position becomes."

"Three days gives us time to find Megan," said Antimony. "She shouldn't be a part of this. We have to save her."

"I'm positive Leonard knows her location," said Sarah. "If we can locate him and get me close enough, I can extract it, and we can retrieve her."

"That sounds like the start of a very dangerous plan," I said. "How are we supposed to find him?"

"I can call Megan's phone again; I'm sure he'll pick up," said Antimony. "He has a weird obsession with me. If he can bring me back into the fold, I prove the veracity of his leadership. If I seem like I might be willing to listen, I bet I can get him to tell me where to meet him."

"And I bet you're not going," said Sam.

Antimony gave him a disgusted look. "Of course I'm not going. I just want to convince the asshole that I *might* go, so we can go and yank the information we need out of his stupid head."

"Charming as it is to watch your relationship dynamics in action, I don't see where this is the best idea," I said. "While you try to get information out of Leonard, Leonard's going to be working to get information out of *you*."

"Do you have a better idea?"

"Find a complicated but valid way to declare Megan a member of the family, and allow Mary's connection to extant family members to locate her?" suggested Sarah.

"I . . . don't think that would work," I said. "I didn't start picking up on Sally or James until after I'd been introduced to them *as* family, by a *member* of the family. I can't just decide someone's going to be my responsibility now."

"What if her mother hired you to babysit for her?" asked James, with sudden interest.

I frowned at him. He shrugged.

"Sorry. Natural-born rules lawyer."

"That might work," I said, carefully. "But I'd have to talk to her mother, and there's just been an attack on the Fringe—she's not likely to want to talk to *me*."

"She'd probably talk to Alex," said Antimony. "Can't you ask him for help?"

I paused. "That might actually work," I said.

"We have three days," she said, and shrugged. "I know you just got back, but it's worth trying. Honestly, I think everything is worth trying at this point."

"Your mother just finished telling him about your aunt. He's not going to pick up the phone right now, and I'm tired of hopping around the country like a jackrabbit on a hot tin roof," I said. "Are you *sure* this is what you want me to do?"

"Right now, I don't think anyone is sure of anything," said Antimony. "But we need to know where Megan is, and we only have three days. If Leonard feels like he can't get anything else out of her, he might kill her. I don't think we can get another routewitch to give us a ride, not after asking twice in one day, and we can't fly when we aren't sure where the Covenant is or what they're watching. That's going to mean about a day and a half in the car if she's near the Fringe, and possibly longer if she's being held elsewhere."

"Or maybe this one isn't your fight to finish," I said. "Depending on where she is, I may need to get someone else to help."

"Providing it doesn't conflict with an existing collapsing spatial tunnel, I will bring Antimony to your location as necessary," said Sarah, voice serene. "My apologies, Samuel, but I lack the mathematical acumen to bring you both. The higher-level calculations are still in progress."

"You did just fine when you abducted her *and* James to Iowa," said Sam sourly. He didn't mention that she'd had a third passenger for that journey. We all tried not to mention Artie around Sarah more than absolutely necessary. It wasn't like she was going to forget what she'd done.

"I also moved us forward in time a week, because I had to sacrifice accuracy on either the dimensional length or the dimensional time. My method of bending space moves all four relevant dimensions. Would you like me to accidentally hop us to the end of this battle, and hope none of us are needed for a victory?"

"Wait," said Sally. "Is the telepathic wasp-girl talking about *time travel* now?"

"Yes and no," said Sarah. "The only time travel I can accomplish is the same kind everyone's capable of—forward. It's just that I can get there faster than you can, if I really want to."

Sally sat back on her log, looking stunned. It was odd that she was out here instead of inside with Thomas, but nice to see that she was already fitting in with her peers. It was even nicer to see Antimony not trying to needle her or otherwise test her suitability as James's friend. I guess "sold herself to the crossroads so he could have a better life" was enough of a display of good friendship that Annie was willing to accept she might be worth keeping, even if she still wasn't going over to make friendly overtures to Sally directly. Not quick to warm up to new people, is our Annie. Honestly, if I hadn't been there to witness it, I would still have had issues with the idea that she was engaged.

I stood.

"Where are you going?" asked Annie.

"Inside, to talk to your grandfather," I said. "If we're going to blow up Penton Hall, I figure I should ask him whether he has any advice about how to get the best bang for our buck. They may have changed operational standards, but there's no way they changed the basic blueprint of the building while he's been gone."

"And you'll go to Alex after your talk? To ask him about getting Megan's mom to offer you a job?"

"I will," I said solemnly. "Now, you lot try not to burn the compound down while you're having quiet time out here."

"No promises," said James, and several of the others laughed. It was a comfortable, convivial atmosphere; I was happy to see how well Sally was already fitting in with the others. Her experiences weren't going to make it easier for her to find a peer group.

It was a problem I'd navigated before, first with Alice, then with Jane and Kevin, who'd at least had the other children at the carnival to keep them company, all the way up to the current generation. It's hard enough for normal people to make friends. My people, much as I adore them and always will, are not normal people.

I walked back to the house, trying not to think too much about the fact that they wanted me to jump, *again*, to Ohio. Sort of like it's easy for the dead to say things like "It's my life" or "the high cost of living," language facilitates using movement words for the way we get around. And for some of us, it *is* movement, always—Rose, for example, can't just vanish from somewhere in the twilight and reappear wherever it is she wants to be. She has to travel along the roads, and she has to hitchhike at least part of the way, or there can be consequences. She walks a lot.

I can go from family member to family member, and have some fine control over where around them I land, but that's not *moving*. I just decide I'm done being in one place, and I appear somewhere different. Situations like my journey to Stumptown are unusual, and I avoid them whenever I can. The bomb plan would never work if there was actual *movement* involved; picking up the bombs and trying not to fall over before I put them down was about the extent of my strength. There isn't a word for what I actually do. I tend to use words like "jump" and "throw," because that's almost what it feels like—like I'm picking myself up like a dolly in a dollhouse and hurling myself to wherever it is I need to be. Only when the crossroads died, I started having to throw with my eyes closed, which is why I keep missing my targets unless I have someone waiting to catch me.

And I still get tired. I may not be *moving*, but I'm exerting effort, in a strange metaphysical sort of way that I don't entirely understand. After bouncing back and forth so many times in one day, I felt like I'd been running laps in PE before I died, circling the track until my joints screamed and my tongue tasted like desert.

At the same time, I might have to, because there was a more-than-solid chance that Alex was *not* going to answer his phone right now. Not with two crying children seeking comfort and a dead aunt hanging on the edge of his awareness. I knew him well enough to not even ask.

Inside, Kevin and Evelyn were in the living room, with Arthur and Elsie sitting in the dining room, some sort of overly elaborate board game spread out across the table. Arthur looked like he was enjoying himself as he peacefully rolled dice and moved pieces, and that was the only reason I could think of for Elsie to be tolerating the activity so soon after their mother's death. He seemed as normal as he ever was, a little stiff, a little awkward in his motions, like he had never quite figured out how his body was supposed to work after getting it returned to him. She, on the other hand, looked abjectly miserable, eyes red, corners of her mouth turned firmly down. If I hadn't already known that something was wrong, her face would have told me. There was no way Arthur hadn't noticed.

But from the way he was playing, he hadn't. We'd been trying to pretend there was nothing wrong with him, but it had always been just that: pretending. Because something was clearly very, very wrong.

I walked over to where Kevin and Evelyn were sandwiched together on the loveseat, her head on his shoulder, his hands in her lap, clasping hers. They both looked up as I approached; they had both been crying.

"Hey," I said, softly.

"Verity just called," said Kevin, looking past me to where the cousins played. His expression, already grave, turned downright funereal. "I don't know how to start telling them, and until I figure it out, I can't tell the mice. Once the mice know, it's public news."

"I know," I said. "I'm sorry. I got there right after it happened, and I didn't know what to say, either."

"Excuse my terrible manners, Mary," said Evie, wiping her eyes. "What can we help you with?"

"Where are Thomas and Alice? We may have the start of a plan, but it would be better if I could discuss it with Thomas before I bounce back to Ohio to start looking for a missing gorgon."

"Poor Mary," said Evie, with what sounded like genuine sympathy. "We're running you ragged today, aren't we?"

"Comes with the territory," I said.

"Ted went up to one of the guest rooms to have a little nap and be alone without actually being *alone*. Thomas and Alice are in the library." Evie paused, shaking her head. "I've known for a year that they were planning to come back here, but that still feels so odd to say, you know? Like it ought to be impossible."

"A lot of things ought to be impossible," I said, and walked deeper into the house.

As I approached the library, I heard a familiar sound that had been absent for so long that I had to stop for a moment to just listen, letting it wash over me.

Alice and Thomas were arguing about a book.

They weren't angry, just disagreeing about the text, and expressing that disagreement in their respective ways. She sounded annoyed; he sounded exasperated; together, they sounded like a trip back in time, to a world that had been so much less complicated. For a moment, I wished their arguing *would* take us back in time, would let us try this all again.

But going back would have meant giving up the people I'd come to love in this time, the people who were my family. I shook off the illusion and walked into the library. "Am I interrupting something?"

"Just someone who doesn't want to accept that some of the basic texts have been updated since the 1960s," said Alice, with a fond, exasperated look at Thomas.

"Some things aren't broken," said Thomas gravely. Then he paused, looking at my face. "Mary? What's wrong?"

"The Covenant hit again in New York," I said. These were members of my family, yes, and they knew Dominic, but they didn't love him the way everyone else who knew him did. They didn't have the bonds that Kevin and Evelyn had formed with their son-in-law, or that Annie and Alex had formed with their brother-in-law. They were the next ring out of grief.

Alice looked at my expression and winced, closing her eyes. "Oh, God, poor Verity," she said.

"How . . . ?" asked Thomas.

"She wouldn't be this calm if it had been Verity who went down," said Alice, opening her eyes and looking at her husband. "She wouldn't look like this if it had been someone who wasn't family."

Thomas glanced to me for confirmation. I nodded. "Dominic," I said. "A Covenant field team ambushed them while they were patrolling. He was dead before he hit the ground." There was something unforgivably final about saying it aloud, like I was betraying his memory by treating his death like a historical fact. Even though it was. History is anything that's already over, and can't be changed.

"Poor Verity," repeated Alice.

Thomas, meanwhile, lowered his head in what looked like a moment of genuine grief and regret.

"Tommy?" I asked. I hadn't been aware Dominic had made such a deep impression on him.

"I'm sorry," he said, raising his head to look at me. "I can mostly pretend I didn't lose as much time as I did, that it doesn't matter in the greater scheme of things, but then something like this will happen. I had some time to talk with Dominic when we were in New York. Did you know he was the last of the De Lucas? I never knew his parents. His grandparents, on the other hand—his grandfather was one of my roommates at Penton. I was so *pleased* to hear that Orlando had survived to adulthood, and managed to marry and have a son of his own before his death. I'd always hoped he might have the sense to break away, as I had done, but I couldn't blame him for sticking with what he'd always known; sometimes the easy route is the only one you can see."

Alice reached over to put her hand on his arm, comforting him. He sighed and folded his hand over hers, holding her where she was.

"I suppose I'm going to hear more and more of these stories as we clash with the Covenant," he said. "Boys and girls I knew all grown up to become the monsters we were warned against, and then going one step further to become *dead* monsters. It's just a bit of a shock to know that not only is my old friend gone, his whole family's gone as well."

"Not all of them," I said. "Olivia is still here."

"I suppose that's true." He quirked the slightest of smiles. "An unholy amalgamation of Healy, Carew, Price, and De Luca. She's going to be a spitfire when she's grown."

"Yeah, she is," I agreed. "Funny you should mention Penton Hall, but I was actually looking for you because I wanted to discuss it."

"Penton Hall?" asked Thomas, blankly. "What of it?"

"It's the Covenant's main training facility, isn't it?"

"In England, yes. They have other facilities elsewhere in Europe, and I believe a few others in other locales—they were never as successful with the satellite branches as they were with the ones constructed when the dragons were still a known threat, before their own success made their holy mission a harder sell in most places."

"And they've been there forever?"

"Oh, not forever," said Thomas. "The Covenant didn't acquire Penton until the 1700s, when the original owners were eaten by manticores. It's a very tragic story, really, and one we used to recite on the anniversary of their deaths. Despite the fact that it provided us with a secure place to train our children, it was still a blow to the human race, and—" He stopped himself. "And you don't want to hear about that just now, do you?"

"Not particularly," I said. "In your experience, how often do they renovate?"

"Not often," he said. "A building that old, you're limited by the walls you can't move and the improvements that have already been made over the years, ad hoc as they'll almost always have been. Just wiring the place for modern electricity was a bone of contention when I was young, with some people insisting that the people who wired the hall for light and heating had been committing a blasphemous act, and others claiming we needed to fully modernize if we wanted to survive. I have no idea who will have won the argument by now."

"But the basic blueprint will have remained the same?"

"Yes . . . why? What are you thinking?"

I looked to Alice. She had never been to Penton Hall, but she was really our explosives expert. There had been a time when it looked like Annie was going to follow in her footsteps, but then Annie had started setting fires with a touch, and had wisely moved away from heat-sensitive munitions. If you wanted something to blow up good, you needed to talk to Alice.

"Uncle Mike can get me a couple of Mark 81s. They're small enough for me to lift, as long as that's all I do—I'm not carrying them anywhere."

"They're not ground-penetrating. All you're going to do is blow out some windows and piss the Covenant off even more."

"Not if I place them in the basement." I looked to Thomas. "What do you know about the Penton Hall anti-ghost measures?"

"I know they're powerful enough to prevent any sort of casual haunting, but I also know various Covenant-employed witches have been able to summon spirits within the grounds," he said. "If you had someone to summon you, I believe you would be able to make your way inside."

"That part isn't going to be a problem," I said. "So I can get in—that's good. And I can get the bombs into the basement. If I crack the foundation, how much damage am I potentially doing to their organization?"

"A substantial amount," said Thomas. "They train there, yes, but they also school there."

Meaning a big explosion would potentially squish a bunch of Covenant kids. "Oh."

"Yes. It's part of why they've always recommended keeping the children near to the training grounds. It not only gives them something to aspire to as they grow older, it discourages attacks on their stronghold—most cryptids intelligent enough to formulate a plan to come after the hall will also frown upon attacking children."

"Not a level of discretion the Covenant has ever been inclined to extend in reverse," said Alice.

"No, sadly. But the fact remains: any attack on Penton will come with unanticipated casualties."

Great. One more thing for me to worry about. Maybe it's heartless of me, but they had already attacked two locations containing my kids, and if it was mine or theirs, I'd prefer to avoid any further casualties on our side. "If we do it anyway, if we take the fight to them, how much do we damage their operation?" I asked. "Would they have to withdraw their American attacks?"

"I think, if we were to ensure they knew we were behind their troubles, they would pull back to regroup, if not abandon the idea of attacking us entirely," said Thomas, words slow and deliberate, like each one was being selected with the utmost care. "There is a point beyond which the cost of their choices would seem to be too great."

"That was my thought on the matter," I said. "Can we sit down and talk about Penton for a little while? I'll do my best to figure out how we can minimize collateral damage, but this has to stop, and the only way it does is by them accepting that attacking us is too expensive. We need to put ourselves out of their price range."

"All right," said Alice. "Let's talk."

Alice had never actually been to Penton Hall, but she was used to laying traps and—more importantly—setting detonation charges, and proved surprisingly helpful at identifying the weak points in the structure Thomas described to the pair of us. She took notes the whole time, pen moving fast over a plain white notebook, leaving instructions behind. Thomas stole peeks at what she was writing and occasionally offered mild corrections, the two of them falling back into the patterns of research they had developed during their years together in Buckley. It was incredibly reassuring to see. If they could find their way back to each other and then all the way home, it felt like there was a chance for all manner of impossible things to happen.

Maybe, for all our losses, a happy ending would eventually be something we could wrest from the world. Maybe we could win.

We talked for about an hour, me asking questions and Thomas giving answers while Alice wrote everything down, and by the time we were done, I felt much better about our chances of success. It was still going to be a long shot, but at this point it was a long shot with a big bull's-eye we could aim for. I rose from the chair where I'd settled, looking between them.

I *really* didn't want to go to Ohio right now, and if there was any chance Alex was going to pick up, I'd take it.

"Does either of you have a phone?" I asked.

"I do," said Alice. "New one from Uncle Al. No GPS or trackers on it."

"I still don't understand how you're all so casual about carrying private communication devices with you everywhere you go," said Thomas, somewhat dourly. "I remember when Alice couldn't even call me for fear of the operators listening in and ruining her reputation, and now you're running around with portable telephones that are so common you've started using them as tracking devices."

"Which means they can still ruin your reputation, it just takes a bit more work," said Alice, fishing the phone out of her pocket. She offered it to me. "Lock screen is three-five-three-two," she said. "Kids, biological grandkids, adopted grandkids, great-grandkids."

"Where are you counting Isaac?"

"Adopted grandkids," she said. "If he's going to be Sarah's brother—"

"Which we're pretty sure he is, biologically speaking," I said.

"—it makes sense to put him in the column with her," she finished.

"That does actually make sense," I agreed, unlocking the phone. The wallpaper was a picture of Thomas and Sally standing outside a gas station with a desert landscape stretching out behind them, Nevada at its finest—and driest. I smiled briefly as I pulled up her address book.

As I'd been more than half-hoping, she had already input all the grandkids' numbers, and I was able to select Alex's name without needing to take the time to key it in. I clicked, raised the phone to my ear, and waited.

There are some ghosts who can travel via phone lines, becoming disembodied voices in the ears of their targets. If that's something you can learn, it's not something I've ever really seen the point in doing; I get around just fine without it, thanks awfully. The phone rang. I waited.

Alex picked up just before his voicemail would have kicked in. "Hello, who is this?" he asked, voice dull despite its interrogative tone.

"This is your grandmother's new number, but it's your babysitter calling," I said. "How are you, buddy?"

"Holding it together as best as I can," he said. "Verity doesn't want us to come to New York. Says it would be dangerous for the children, and she's probably right, but she's also my baby sister, and I want to be there for her. I hate this, Mary. I hate everything about it. Make it go away."

"We're working on it," I said, as soothingly as I could. "I called because I might have an opening for a new client—do you have a number for Dee?"

"My assistant, Dee? She doesn't have any kids, and she's a little busy at the moment . . ."

"But she does. You're proof that I don't have an age restriction, upper or lower. I can take care of Lottie *and* your octogenarian grandmother. Megan's her kid. If she hires me, that makes me responsible for Megan's welfare, and Megan can call for me. More generally, she can call for help, and I can answer."

Alex paused. "Do you really think that will work?"

"I honestly don't know, Alex. We're clutching at metaphysical straws here. Can I take on more clients, or am I the sort of haunting that only happens to one family at a time? I'm not concerned about breaking my tie to our family by forging another one—if that were going to happen, I would have started losing people a long time ago, right around when Angela decided to bring a stray home from Lowryland. What I *do* know is that there was an attack on the house, the Carmichael hotel, and the gorgon Fringe, which implies that someone with intimate knowledge of the gorgon community has been compromised, and Megan's known as an associate of Annie's."

"What does Annie have to do with any of this?"

"The man who shot Jane is named Leonard Cunningham," I said bluntly. "He met Annie when she went undercover with the Covenant, and figured out who she was. He followed her to North America, and she's intersected with him at least twice. He was the leader of the team that attacked the Spenser Family Carnival, and he was in New Gravesend when she killed the crossroads. He wants her. He thinks he can convince her the Covenant is a better choice than staying where she is."

Alex barked a short, sharp laugh. "He'd have an easier job convincing her that she's a lost princess from the moon."

"I know. I think he may know too, by now, but that hasn't stopped him from trying. We know he's been tracking Antimony. If that included backtracking once he had a known location, he may have found out about her time at Lowryland. Which could lead him straight to Megan."

"Which would explain how the Covenant knew to hit us here," concluded Alex. "Bastards."

"No one's disputing that, although I think the Covenant generally prefers it when their operatives marry before they reproduce; helps to keep the lines of inheritance clear," I said. "Can I have Dee's number, or can you call her for me? If Megan is officially one of my responsibilities, I should be able to find her. Hopefully."

"She's not likely to want to talk to a stranger, or be in the mood to answer her phone," said Alex. "I'll go to her. If I can convince her to hire you, I'll call you to come join us."

"All right," I said. "Hopefully see you soon." I hung up the phone before passing it back to Alice, who looked disappointed.

"I was hoping to say hello," she said.

"There will be better times to say hello," I said. "Less brutally difficult ones." I turned toward the door.

"Where are you going?" asked Thomas.

"To check on Olivia, and then probably back outside to hang with the grandkids," I said. "They're a lot closer to my responsibility than the two of you are. If this works, I'll know."

And if it didn't, I was sure someone would tell me eventually.

That was how this whole thing worked, after all.

Sixteen

"I like gorgons. You shouldn't get into staring contests with 'em if you have a choice, but on the whole, they're good people."

—Frances Brown

Back out at the firepit, which may not be exciting, but hey. That also means it's not trying to kill anyone

OLIVIA WAS AWAKE, AND had been for some time. I hadn't picked up on it because she was in the attic with Elsie, happily telling the mice her version of what had happened over the course of the day. I made a silent note to set up a conference call between Verity's mice and the mice here at home before we wound up with a religious schism over the two exceedingly different stories of the day's events. Elsie flashed me a weary smile when I popped my head into the attic, but didn't move to greet me or to hand Olivia off.

'Thank you,' I mouthed, before heading back down. Elsie liked kids well enough to have spent some of her own teen years as a neighborhood babysitter, and she'd keep Olivia alive, even if she wasn't up for promising much beyond that. It wouldn't have been fair of me to ask for more. She'd just lost her mother, and her brother seemed incapable of grieving with her.

But that's the thing about grief. It hits everyone differently. Ted couldn't stop crying; Elsie was briskly taking care of anyone who seemed to need it, starting with Arthur and now extending to Olivia; and Arthur was playing board games and wandering the house, lost in his own version of reality. None of them was doing grief *wrong*. There's no way of doing grief *wrong*. There are just different flavors of doing it right.

I made my way out of the house without going through the living room, not wanting to face Kevin and Evelyn again, or to deal with Arthur, and trudged across the lawn toward the firepit, where hopefully the others would be waiting. I was almost there when I heard Sally yell for someone to calm the hell down and I stopped dead—no pun intended. She sounded genuinely angry.

Sarah's pulse of "Mary I need you" hit me a bare instant later, and I blinked out, reappearing at the firepit's edge. Sarah was no longer sitting on her log. She was on the ground behind Greg, who had clearly shoved himself in front of her, protective as any large dog. He was standing on six legs, his second pair from the front raised high in an attempt at looking menacing. And his attention was focused on Arthur, who was standing between Greg and the fire, hands balled into fists, glaring at Sarah. James, Sally, and Antimony were staring. This must have happened so quickly that they hadn't had a chance to physically react yet.

"You have to fix it," Arthur snapped, just as I appeared. "This isn't *right*."

"I'm sorry," moaned Sarah. Her eyes were blue, powers quiescent for the moment. "I didn't do it on purpose."

"And that doesn't matter as much as you want to pretend it does," said Arthur. "The people you've hurt are still hurt even if it was an accident."

"All right, that's enough of that," said Antimony, standing up and stepping right into the middle of the bonfire. The leg of her jeans began to smolder. She ignored it as she grabbed for Arthur's arm. He pulled it out of her reach, shooting a glare at her.

"This doesn't concern you," he snapped.

"It does." She stepped out of the fire again, now on the side with him, Sarah, and Greg. "I was there, all right. In the dimension where this happened to you. I was *there*. I saw Sarah struggling to do the math that would get us home alive and in one piece. I saw how close she was to collapsing. And I saw you grab her arm. I don't know why you did it. Unlike Sarah, I'm not a mind reader. But I know she was so deep in the equation to get us back here when it happened that she *can't* have compelled you to do it, and I know she didn't tell us to touch her, and I know it wasn't an accident. You didn't trip or brush against her. You grabbed her, with intent. And yeah, she fried your brain."

Sarah turned her face away, guilt writ large across her features. But Annie wasn't done.

"She fried your brain, and that sucks, and we're all so sorry it happened, but Artie—Arthur—whoever the fuck you are now, she didn't do it on purpose, and she didn't reach for you to make it happen. You were a participant in this as much as she was. And when she understood what had happened, she did everything within her power to make it right, just as quickly as she possibly could. She tried to put the pieces back together."

"My mother is *dead*," he snapped. "I know she was my mother. I remember her as my mother. I remember loving her. But I'm not sad that she's gone. I'm not even managing to be upset about it, except that it's upsetting everyone else to see how much I don't care. I can feel them being disgusted and unsettled and this isn't right. This isn't how it's supposed to be. I want my brain back."

"I'm sorry," whispered Sarah. Her eyes flashed white, and she and Greg were gone, leaving Artie glaring at empty space while Annie stood beside and slightly behind him, the leg of her jeans still smoking.

"That was shitty, Arthur," she said. "I get you're having big feelings right now, but we all told you what happened, and you know she didn't do any of it on purpose."

"I just wanted to be sad," he said, turning to look at her plaintively. "I just want to grieve for my mother. Why does that make me the bad guy?"

"Because that was a rotten way to ask for what you need," said Annie. "Your mom just died, so we're not going to be dicks about it, but maybe you should go back inside now."

Artie looked to James and Sally, seeming briefly like he was going to argue. Then he turned, shoulders slumping, and began to trudge back toward the house.

I walked over to the trio. "Where's Sam?"

"That was . . . a lot," said Sally. "Someone's going to explain all of this eventually, right? I'm not going to feel like I started reading a series in the middle forever?"

"Just store up all your questions, and I can answer them tonight when we go to bed," said James.

The babysitter in me was stirred to say, "Sally's going to have her own room tonight."

"Am not," said Sally. "Okay, maybe am, but you can't make me stay there. Jimmy and I have a lot to catch up on."

"And it's not like you have to worry about her compromising my virtue," said James, almost primly. "That ship has sailed, hit an iceberg, and pulled a Titanic all the way to the bottom of the metaphorical ocean."

"Right, don't try to keep the queer kids from keeping each other awake all night, what was I thinking." I looked around, then repeated my question: "Seriously, though, where is Sam?"

"He was getting worried, so he went to call his grandmother, after he made me promise to stay here until he got back," said Annie. "He's such a worrywart."

"Can you blame him?" I felt a strange snapping sensation at the back of my mind, like the sound a cathode ray television makes when turned on somehow translated into a physical feeling. I blinked.

Then, with surprising fierceness, Alex's voice called, "Mary, I need you." "That's my cue," I said, to blank looks from all the people who hadn't been able to hear what was going on inside my head—which was to say, everyone. Even Sarah couldn't read me casually the way she did everyone else. "Alex just convinced Megan's mother to hire me," I explained. "I felt the connection with Megan snap into place, and Alex is calling for me now. I'll be back as soon as I reasonably can be."

"Try not to be too terrifying, okay?" asked Antimony.

"No promises," I said, and blinked out, throwing myself back toward Ohio. It was much easier, now that I had someone actively calling my name, providing me with a rope to pull myself across the void. Really, the less I thought about the mechanism that let me move around, the better. Trying to understand it too deeply just left me more confused.

Then I was standing in a double-wide trailer I'd never seen before. It was one of the ultra-fancy ones, the ones that make you question why anyone would consider living in a mobile home to be a bad thing. The carpet was thick and plush, the furnishings were well used but well maintained and clean, and the ceiling was high. There was a woman in front of me, wearing a nice blouse and a pair of fitted jeans. She would have looked perfectly normal almost anywhere in the world, if not for the snakes writhing atop her head where hair would normally have been. Like so many of the people I'd been dealing with today, she had clearly been crying, and her eyes were rimmed in red.

Alex was standing beside her, his face turned toward the wall and his back to the woman. That made sense, given I could see her eyes. She squeaked in surprise when I appeared, then fumbled for the dark glasses on the nearby counter, trying to unfold them and slide them on. I raised a hand.

"It's fine, honestly," I said. "I'm dead. You can't petrify me."

"What?"

"Hi, Mary," said Alex, sounding deeply relieved.

I kept my eyes on the woman but smiled, and replied, "Hey, bud. Is this Megan's mom?"

"She is."

"Great." I focused more intently on the woman. "Alex explained who I was when he said he was going to call me, right?"

"He did, but . . ."

"But you've never dealt with a physical ghost before, right. Okay, well, we're immune to gaze-based effects. You're looking at me, but you're not looking at my body, because that's buried in Michigan. I guess if I stared deep into your eyes for long enough, you might turn my bones to stone, but that's about it."

"I'm a Pliny's gorgon," she said, sounding ever so faintly baffled. "Our gaze isn't petrifactive. Our venom is."

"So you're worried about me seeing your eyes because . . . ?"

"Our gaze is paralytic."

"Ah. I'm immune to that, too. Being dead comes with a few benefits, to counterbalance all the ways in which it kinda sucks. Why aren't you worried about paralyzing Alex?"

"I'm not looking her in the eye, and she needed to finish cleaning herself up before you got here," said Alex. "I know how to handle myself around gorgons."

Understatement of the year. "Okay. That makes sense and we may not have a lot of time, so let's get down to business. You're hiring me to babysit your daughter, yeah?"

"Megan," said Dee, tone almost reverent; it was like she was describing the most important person in the world, and to her, maybe she was. It was clear from the fact that she'd been able to hire me that they had a strong relationship—maybe I was being overly optimistic about the way the world works, but I had the distinct feeling that an estranged parent wouldn't have been able to pull the same trick. I could be used to hunt down the beloved, not the intentionally absent. "She's a doctor, you know."

"Is she working at a cryptid hospital?"

Dee's face fell. "No. I told her to wait until one of them had an opening for an intern, I *told* her, but she made human friends while she was in medical school, and I work for a human, and she wanted to experience the whole process. She matched with a hospital in Seattle. Made a lot of terrible jokes about a television program called *Grey's Anatomy*, bought a sweatshirt for the hospital from the show as well as the things she'd need for her posting, and went off to finish her studies. I didn't like it then, and I don't like it now. She's not supposed to be so far away from home."

In a human parent, that might have caused me to look at her askance. In a gorgon parent, that attitude made a lot of sense. They're fairly critically endangered, and they don't reproduce any faster than humans do. It's uncommon for kids to settle very far from their parents, just because they lack the distributed support structure that many humans have.

Alex grimaced but didn't say anything. This was Dee's daughter, and Dee's story, and he was only here to facilitate.

"So there wouldn't have been any unusual security," I said, thoughtfully. "Do you have any other kids?"

"No."

"All right. Last question: may I hold your hand?"

Dee looked startled. "How is that going to help?"

"You've hired me to sit for Megan. Normally you'd introduce me to the child right after I agreed to work for you. Obviously, we can't do it that way right now, so I think the solution is for me to bring myself closer to you. The families I sit for are just that—family." And it was "families" at this point. The Prices might slap the "aunt" and "uncle" label on everyone who slowed down in their vicinity, but Drew wasn't really family to anyone who lived in Portland, except for Evelyn. He was his own branch, and he shouldn't have registered for me. But he did, because Sarah was one of my kids, and he was her uncle by adoption. I usually thought of them as one big, coherent family, but they hadn't been for a long time, and there was nothing wrong with that.

Uncertainly, Dee reached over and took my hand.

"Tell me about her."

"Megan's wanted to be a doctor since she was a little girl. Her father's our doctor, here at the colony, and she wanted to be just like him. She wanted to keep gorgons safe and healthy and happy. She used to find animals that had been hurt and nurse them back to health—when she was twelve, she found a turkey vulture who'd been blown into some power lines by a bad storm, and she saved his life. He was in love with her for years, would follow her around when she was outside, just like a puppy. He flew away eventually. All children fly away eventually." Her lips twisted, expression turning pained.

"What does she like?" I prompted.

"She loves ice cream, and boardgames with too many rules, and Lowry movies. She always said they were better than Disney because they didn't have the budget not to be—they couldn't afford the most fluid animation or the most impressive celebrity voices, so they had to have the best stories. She got a Princess Aspen dress for Haloa when she was six, and wore it until it literally fell apart around her. When she got accepted into the Lowryland college program, it was like all her dreams were coming true at once, even if she considered it a crime that she couldn't let her snakes sunbathe in the Florida sun. She's had two steady boyfriends, but never reached the seriousness level of a courtship."

I was starting to feel a dim flicker of presence from the west, farther north than Portland, as Megan became a part of my mental map. She was alive, then, and still in the Seattle area.

"Now," I said. "About my rates."

Dee blanched. "We aren't what you'd call 'wealthy,' by human standards," she said. "I get a salary from Alex, but mostly we barter among ourselves for what we need. I give most of my actual money to the community for necessities, and—"

"I know it's expensive, but I charge a whole dime an hour, because I have a lot of experience for someone my age, and your children will be so safe with me, it's worth the money for the peace of mind," I continued, not letting her stop me. Dee's mouth snapped shut, and she stared at me, confused. "I don't know a lot about how this all works, since I've done the bulk of my work for one family for the last ninety years, but I'm pretty sure I have to give my rates, and you have to accept them, before I'm formally hired."

"A—a dime an hour? Ten cents?"

I nodded.

"I can do that," said Dee.

"Then we have an agreement," I said, as the feeling of Megan's presence snapped into sudden clarity. I knew where she was. Of course I knew where she was. She was my responsibility, and I'd be a pretty lousy babysitter if I didn't know where the kids I was supposed to be taking care of were. "I'm going to go check on Megan now. Is it unreasonable of me to ask for my first hour's pay in advance?"

One thing you learn after being dead for a while: when something seems like a good idea, it's almost always better to just go with it. The twilight has reasons to ask for the things it does. Dee frowned, digging a hand into her pocket to produce a crumpled dollar bill. "I don't have any coins on me," she said. "Can I pay you for ten hours?"

"That would be fine," I said, and took the dollar. The feeling of presence from the west got stronger, Megan truly becoming my responsibility. I would be able to find her now; I was sure of it. "It was nice to meet you," I said, and flashed a quick smile at Alex. He smiled back, and I disappeared.

The world blurred around me, and I was standing in a small, dark room, the windows covered by heavy canvas curtains that let only the barest edges of the light in, the walls draped in plastic sheeting. What looked like a dentist's reclining chair was set up at the center of the room, a figure strapped into it, head lolling insensate. I hurried over to the woman I already recognized as one of my charges.

She was clearly unconscious, only kept in place by the straps holding her to the chair. She was also taller and broader than I was, meaning I wouldn't be able to support her if I undid the straps. She'd fall. I turned her face toward me, and while her eyes stayed closed, lids not even fluttering, a few of the snakes that were her hair stirred themselves to lift their heads and flick their tongues at me, testing the air. Their eyes were dull, and more than half of them weren't moving. As my eyes adjusted to the lack of light, I realized their motionlessness was due to something far more dire than mere unconsciousness; several of them were missing their heads, while others had twisted, bloodied lips, showing the raw places where their fangs had been extracted.

Rage bubbled up inside my chest, the kind of rage that could motivate a girl to go full poltergeist on the nearest targets. Gorgons don't regrow their snakes, or their fangs; Megan would be dealing with the consequences of her captivity forever. If we could get her to Dr. Morrow, he might be able to seal over the stumps where the heads had been removed, and either amputate the remaining portions of their bodies or stabilize them such that they wouldn't rot away to nothing. I didn't know enough about gorgon biology to say what the solution was going to be.

I was suddenly very glad that Megan was still unconscious, even as I cast around the room for some sign of where we were. There were no helpful signs or abandoned pieces of mail with the address written clearly on the front. Scowling, I started toward the door.

—and stopped dead, again, no pun intended, as my left foot stuck to the floor. I stumbled back and looked down.

I was standing in a Seal of Solomon. To the living, it would have looked like a geometric doodle on the floor, but to me, its silvered lines gleamed, glittering from within with the brutal strength of their intent. It had been painted with a mathematical precision that made me suspect stencils had been used in setting this trap. It didn't matter. The Seal of Solomon is one of the ghost-hunting tools that don't hinge on intent—it's all about the crispness of your angles, the precision of your lines. A machine can catch a ghost as well as a mesmerist can, if they're given the right instructions.

With my feet stuck inside the Seal, I couldn't go more than about a foot in any direction—the distance from the center to the edge. I tried to vanish, to put myself back beside Megan, and nothing happened. That was another change. I used to be effectively immune to any ghost trap that didn't need a human sacrifice to set up properly; even if I got caught, I could always dip and go to the crossroads, who were big and bad enough to supersede whatever it is that powers things like Mesmer cages and Seals of Solomon, But the crossroads were gone, and I was caught.

Even as that terrible truth was sinking in, something moved in the far corner of the room, where the shadows had been too deep for my eyes to adjust. A figure rose from a sitting position and moved toward me, becoming more visible with every step.

"Hello, ghost," said Leonard Cunningham, tone almost mocking. "With as often as you've interfered, did you really think we hadn't factored you into the equation?"

"I hoped," I said, standing up as straight as I could and trying to look intimidating. Not easy for a sixteen-year-old stuck to a circle. "And the name's 'Mary,' not 'ghost,' unless you want me to call you 'asshole.'"

The jibe didn't appear to bother him. "Ah, yes. Mary Dunlavy. You would never have been among our priority targets, but your association with my sweet Annie meant researching you began to seem like a good idea. We already had your name from the reports filed by a former field agent of ours, Gwendolyn Brandt? She seemed to think you were in a relationship with Thomas Price, which clearly wasn't the case, as dead women bear no children and Annie is very much his, but what she left was enough for us to track you down. We know your name, where you were born, where your parents' bodies were buried—all the information we could possibly hope for. And we know how many people you've hurt."

I blanched. "What are you talking about?"

"You're a greater monster than any I've ever hunted, and I don't know how you were able to fly beneath the surface of our surveillance for so long. Do the people you claim to care for know what you are? What you've *done*?" Leonard's voice was calm and evenly modulated, the voice of a man asking a simple question, not the voice of someone hurling unfounded accusations. "We can make a guess at when you died, based on how old you look and when the stories started, but your death has never been confirmed. Did you know that? They still list you as a missing person in your hometown."

I said nothing. Anything I said could be used against me.

"But you started to pop up all over the world, for the people who know how to look. Brokering deals with the crossroads, leaving devastation in your wake. You were single-handedly responsible for hundreds of ruined lives, and uncountable deaths."

"That was the crossroads. I'm just the babysitter," I said. "I'm here for Megan. You have no right to hold her captive."

"She's a monster who had the audacity to go among humans as if she belonged there," snarled Leonard, his mask of calm reason dropping for a moment. "Horrible deceitful *thing*. Nothing we can do to her balances out the damage she's done."

"There's nothing you can do to me," I said, voice cracking at the end of my sentence. Leonard took another step forward, smiling, and I fought to stand my ground rather than shying back to the outline of the Seal. Two things were clear in that moment:

He was a true believer in the cause of the Covenant, and like all true believers, he thought anything he did in the pursuit of his cause was justified by the sins he had accepted to be true. Worse, at least for me, he genuinely thought he was doing the right thing.

"Annie is a good person," he said. "Loving. Kind. Devoted. She's got a huge amount of potential when it comes to helping humanity cleanse this world. It was always meant to belong to the human race, and with her by my side, it will finally be ours. She's being held back by the monsters around her, but she'll be glorious when she's free. All we have to do is release her."

"You're *not* a good person," I spat. A little childish, maybe, but it felt like something he might actually acknowledge, as opposed to the many things he was happy to just gloss over.

"True enough," he said instead, "I'm not. But then, neither were you."

He pulled a small black box from his pocket and pressed a button at the top of it. Speakers around the room came on with a hiss of static as Latin chanting began to fill the air, sonorous and archaic. I smiled.

"The Christians may have stolen the idea of the exorcism, but that doesn't mean Latin is the language of the dead, no matter how much you try to make it happen," I said. "Latin isn't even going to give me a headache."

"Wait for it," he suggested, sounding far too smug about the situation. The chanting transitioned to Hebrew, with a contrasting voice providing a fluid line of ancient Sumerian. I didn't understand a single word. It didn't matter. Every one of them hit me like a flung stone, bruising and shredding my spectral flesh. I screamed but couldn't blink away, couldn't vanish, couldn't do anything but cover my ears and drop to my knees, struggling to remain coherent.

"I'll tell Annie you quit," said Leonard serenely, and then I was gone, breaking into a thousand pieces, into starlight, into silence.

Into silence.

Seventeen

> "It never does much good to decide 'oh this is who I am, this person right here' and try to hold yourself to it. Everybody changes. You're dead if you stop changing."
>
> —Enid Healy

Who even knows anymore? Somewhere, presumably. Something is happening

EVERYTHING WAS DARK. BIT by bit, I realized it was because my eyes were closed. I was curled into the sort of tight, fetal-position ball that terrified children default to, my knees up against my chest and my legs pulled in close to my body. I forced myself to uncurl bit by bit, and sat up, opening my eyes.

I was sitting in the middle of a vast field of golden wheat, ripe and ready for harvest. A faint breeze blew by, smelling of herbs and flowers, like a perfect dream of a summer night in farming country. I uncurled the rest of the way, pushing myself to my feet as I turned to look around.

The wheat extended seemingly forever in all directions, and the sky above it all was a deep blue, spangled with stars bright enough to see by. There was no moon. I frowned. An exorcism is supposed to throw a spirit into the deepest level of the afterlife they can resonate with, but this didn't look like anything I knew in the twilight *or* the starlight, and if I'd somehow developed an affinity for the midnight, no one had bothered to tell me about it.

I cupped my hands around my mouth. "Hello?" I called. "Hello, is there anyone there?"

No one answered. I scowled, dropping my hands, and tried to return to the daylight. It didn't work. Nothing changed. The wheat rippled around me, bowing its many heads for a brief moment. I turned in the direction of the breeze. There was a woman standing behind me in the grain. I jumped, not because I didn't know her, but because I did. I didn't know how, but I did.

"Hello, Mary Dunlavy," she said, voice ringing and oddly accented, as if she were trying to speak with every accent in the world at once. Her appearance rippled like the wheat around her, hair long, then short, then long again, straight and curled and tangled and brushed to gleaming perfection. Her face shifted in the same manner, cycling through every possible combination of form and features. It should have been disconcerting, alien, even, but it was somehow perfectly normal and mundane, like the beating of a heart.

She was wearing a long, simple sheath dress the color of the very ripest wheat. It hugged her body like a glove, even as her curves shifted and changed to match the rest of her, now skinny, now fat, now every size in-between. She looked at me with infinite affection and even deeper sympathy.

"First time banished from the mortal plane?" she asked.

"I used to have a pretty nasty bodyguard, ma'am," I said. "And when I wasn't working for said bodyguard, I was taking care of kids who may have *wanted* to banish the babysitter but didn't know how until they were old enough to understand why they shouldn't. So I never really ran into a serious attempt at exorcism. Ma'am."

She smiled, and her pleasure was a poem I could have spent the rest of eternity trying to memorize. That was a terrifying feeling. The desire to make this woman happy was so powerful it was almost overwhelming. It was also a distraction.

"Pardon me, ma'am," I said, with all the politeness I could muster under the circumstances, "but can you tell me which way takes me back to the mortal world? I need to get back. I have responsibilities."

"It's amazing how often the dead want to use that as an excuse, or a reason they should get special treatment," she said, smile fading. "Looking at the length of you, I suspect you've had more than enough special treatment."

I was starting to feel as if I'd been here before and just forgotten somehow, after I walked away. That, more than all the other evidence, told me where I was and who I was talking to. I pressed one hand over my heart like I was getting ready to recite the Pledge of Allegiance, and bowed at the waist, deep and respectful. "It's lovely to see you again, milady," I said. "I don't know why it took me this long to realize who you are, and I apologize for any insult my slowness may have offered."

"Oh, don't worry, my Mary," she said, waving my words away with a sweep of her hand. "I took the knowing away when last you left me. There are some secrets mortal souls were never meant to carry. But when banished, this is where your soul returns. Always."

I looked around at the field of wheat. "Why?"

"Because the parasite in my place claimed you here, and made you here, and you were reborn here, into death and duty," she said, mutable appearance melting into one I hadn't seen in far too long, until it was Frances Healy standing in front of me, speaking to me. "I am the anima mundi, and while you may have chosen your living family before me, you are still my creature at the core of you."

I wasn't sure I liked the sound of that. I also wasn't sure it would do me any good to argue. I took a deep breath. "Then send me back."

"It's not that simple, my Mary. You were banished fairly, according to the rules that bind your kind."

"Megan is *mine*. I need to get back to her."

"She's yours through a loophole at best, and a fine illustration of why you shouldn't be going back. Your former employers were very fond of loopholes. As it seems you've inherited their tendencies, shouldn't I keep you here for everyone's safety? Shouldn't you come back to your old position, serve me, and spare the world?"

"Everyone looks for loopholes," I said, desperately. "They're not breaking the rules, they're just . . . understanding the rules well enough that you can use them to your own advantage. Loophole or no, Alex convinced Dee to hire me, and Megan's mine now. I have to save her."

The anima mundi yawned. "Why is this girl so important?"

"She's in danger because of what Antimony did. Because Antimony saved *you*." I looked her in the eye, trying to seem intimidating. "Leonard only has her because she was Annie's roommate at Lowryland. She deserves better than this. She deserves a future. Let me help her achieve it."

"If I do, what stops you coming begging favors again?"

"Not sure I could arrange an exorcism if I wanted to, and that hurt like a mother," I said. "Also, I saw what happened to Rose when she spent too much time among the gods. I'm happy with my current haunting. I'm not going to go dancing with the divine so often that it gets me transferred to a different celestial department. I have no desire to beg your favors, ma'am. The only reason I'm asking for one now is because I'm not done yet. I have a family left to serve."

The anima mundi frowned thoughtfully, still wearing Fran's face.

"I can't decide whether you're foolish or heroic, little ghost. I'm not sure you understand the difference."

"I understand bedtimes and brushing teeth and listening to adolescent woes," I said. "I understand that it's the babysitter's job to keep their charges alive until the sun comes up, and I realize that I've failed twice this week, and I don't want to fail again. Please. I just need to get back to Megan."

"Then you shall have two favors from me, Mary Dunlavy," said the anima mundi, ponderously. "I'll return you to where you were, and I'll chase thoughts of the gorgon girl from your opponent's mind, at least for the moment. He'll remember her when reminded, so you won't have much time to work, but I can give you a little. Make good use of it."

"And the Seal?" I asked. "Going back does me no good if I just get exorcised again."

"Already broken," she said, with a careless wave of her hand. "I'd stop asking for favors now if I were you. You've already had more than your fair share."

"Yes, ma'am, thank you, ma'am," I said, with almost embarrassing eagerness. "Please, just send me back. I can handle all the rest."

"See that you do," she said, with utter mildness. She didn't snap her fingers or make an arcane gesture with her hands. She just turned her back, leaving me alone in the endless wheat, waiting for a miracle.

There was no miracle. And then, without transition or preamble, there was no wheat. There was just a small, dark room with an insensate gorgon strapped to a chair, and no sign of Leonard. The Seal was still on the floor, but broken, rendered inert by a footprint across its lines. Guess he didn't think he needed to worry about more than one ghost, or about the same ghost bouncing back from an exorcism.

I ran my hands quickly down the memory of my body, checking the phantom lines of my figure. Nothing had changed. I glanced down, and confirmed that my clothing hadn't changed either. If the anima mundi marked me in some way, it wasn't something I could find for myself.

Megan wasn't moving, but she was breathing, and a few of her snakes twitched as I watched, verifying that she was still very much alive. Good. That gave me a moment before I unstrapped her. I turned myself half-solid to avoid noises if I bumped into anything and began to move around the room, searching my surroundings.

Leonard was Annie's age, and this looked like it had been a corporate office before it received a horror-movie makeover and became a slaughterhouse-in-waiting. One fixture of the corporate office: the landline phone. Boxy, reliable, and so cheap that even when an office was emptied out, the phone would often remain. What's more, kids these days don't necessarily recognize them for what they are. I hate the phrase "kids these days." It's a beautiful combination of shame and regret that doesn't do anyone any good under most circumstances—it says both "How dare you be younger than I am" and "Everything worth experiencing has already happened; you lost the game before you knew you were playing."

But that doesn't mean there's not truth to the concept that every generation knows something new and forgets something old. I made my way over to the plastic-shrouded bulk of the desk and began picking around in the clutter beneath it, pawing through cast-aside staplers and hole punches until my hand passed through the solid black rectangle of an industrial-grade touch-tone telephone. I knelt, turning solid, and pulled it into my lap.

"Come on, universe, do a girl a solid," I muttered, and lifted the receiver.

There was a dial tone.

I swallowed a shout of exultation that would have impressed even the mice, settling for punching the air and hissing a sharp "Yes" under my breath.

One fun thing about looking like a kid today but actually being an old lady: I still memorize the important phone numbers. I never got out of the habit, and it's not like I can reliably carry a cellphone. Passage through the twilight kills things. That often includes batteries. Not always, which was why I couldn't just blip Jane there and then back to kill the tracker, but often enough that it's not really a safe option.

Settling on the floor where the desk would block me from view if Leonard came back, I tried to figure out where Sarah would have gone. She'd taken Greg with her, which meant it was likely to be somewhere rural or at the very least suburban; hiding a giant spider isn't always an easy ask. But she'd been fleeing from Artie, which meant she didn't want to be found quickly, and she hadn't gone to Ohio.

She knew I was going to need her to get Megan out. Where could she have gone that was suburban enough to hide Greg but accessible enough that I'd be able to find her? I frowned, brow furrowing, before dialing experimentally and raising the receiver to my ear. The characteristic trilling ring of a landline rang out, soft enough that I could hope no one would hear me.

After the fourth ring, the answering machine picked up, and Uncle Mike's gruff voice said, "If you called, you had a good reason. Explain it." There was a loud beep, followed by dead air.

"Lea, it's Mary," I said, keeping my voice low. "I know you're there, listening to the machine. I need you to pick up, please. This is an emergency."

There was a click as the receiver was picked up on her end. "Mary? What's wrong? Why are you calling?"

"You mean instead of coming over? Well, for one, I just got back from an exorcism, and I suspect my aim would be even worse than normal right now—I'd rather not appear in the middle of a park and scare the crap out of a bunch of nannies." The kids would be fine, by and large. Children are much calmer about ghosts than adults tend to be. "For another, I'm in a room with an unconscious, beat-to-shit gorgon, and I'd rather she not wake up alone. Is Sarah there with you?"

"Yes. How did you know?"

"I was guessing," I said, sagging with relief. "She's not in Ohio, I don't think she'd go to New York right now, but she's always liked you, and you have an excellent basement for Greg to scurry around in like a big furry nightmare. Can I talk to her?"

"Hang on. I'll ask." There was a soft scuffing sound as she presumably covered the receiver with her hand, followed by the sound of her voice, muffled and indistinguishable. A few seconds passed, and then she was back, saying, "She'll be right here."

"Great," I said. "Civility says 'no rush,' but I think we're more in 'big-time rush' territory right now."

"Got it. Where are you?"

"Seattle." I looked around. "Looks like the upper floor of a hospital. Which makes a certain degree of sense, since Megan was doing her internship in a Seattle hospital. Grab her, drug her, haul her someplace where no one's going to be looking for her, don't worry about evading the security cameras to get her out of the building."

"And based on what we've learned from Antimony, the Cunninghams have the sort of money that could make massive donations and buy themselves some freedom of movement around the building," said Lea. "Here's Sarah."

There was a scuffling as the phone was passed hand to hand, and then Sarah's voice was saying, "Hello? Mary?"

"Hi, Sarah. Needed a little time away from all those negative thoughts, huh?"

Silence, and a soft sniffle that told me I'd guessed close to the mark—but not exactly right. There was something more that I was missing, and it was going to bite me in the ass if I didn't figure it out soon.

"I found Megan."

"Antimony's friend?"

"Yes. The one who must have told the Covenant where to find Alex and Shelby, and where to find the gorgons in Ohio. She's here in Seattle, and I need to get her out. But she's alive, so I can't take her through the twilight. Can you find me?"

"Seattle is quite large," she said, dubiously. "Can you narrow it down at all?"

I looked at the phone. It didn't have any identifying marks. "Hang on a second," I said, and put the receiver down as I started shuffling through the discarded papers on the floor. Halfway down the pile, I hit paydirt. I picked the phone back up. "Sarah? Are you still there?"

"I'm here," she said. She sounded drowsy, almost disconnected. With Sarah, that was probably a sign that she'd begun extending her mental awareness to cover more of her surroundings. That would allow her to serve as an early-warning system for both Covenant agents and other cuckoos. If Lea was in immediate danger, Sarah would know in short order.

"Okay. I have a piece of letterhead here that says I'm at University District General, in the surgical center."

"All right. I'll look up the address. Stay where you are."

The line went dead. I eased the receiver back into the cradle and rose into a crouch, listening intently for signs that Leonard might be coming back. When I didn't hear anything, I straightened up and walked quickly back over to Megan.

She still wasn't moving. That was getting a little worrisome. But more of her snakes were awake and alert, shying away as I approached. Only about a quarter of them had lost their heads, and the others twined protectively around the remaining trunks, seeming to cradle them close, like they could understand what was happening. No one's ever been quite sure how smart the snakes on top of a gorgon's head really are; they have some awareness of their surroundings, they eat independently, and they have preferences regarding what people they choose to trust versus strike at. But they're not fully sapient, and it was questionable whether or not Megan's snakes could really understand.

"Hi," I said, voice very low. "I'm your . . ." What were they? Was Megan their host, or were they an intrinsic part of her? If they were an intrinsic part of her, I was their babysitter as well. That felt right, and so I forced the kind of smile I'd normally reserve for a child Olivia's age or younger. "I'm your babysitter."

I'd never been a sitter for a child whose language I didn't speak before, and as more of the snakes turned toward me, their tongues flicking at the air, I had to wonder how this was going to work. Then one of them extended itself in my direction, moving with a sort of sinuous grace. I raised my hand without thinking about it, holding it out for the serpent to twine around. Its scales were smooth and warm against my fingers, and its tongue tickled my skin.

I got a deep feeling of relief and hope from the snake, like it was trying to tell me it had been afraid for a long time, and now felt like it could start to relax. I looked up, startled. More of the snakes were stretching in my direction, and they joined the first one in tangling around my hand. I sighed. They had all been so scared for so long, and I didn't know how I knew that, only that I did. I looked back down at Megan's face.

Her eyelids were starting to twitch with the effort of waking up. I pulled my hand free of the snakes and bent toward her, touching her cheek gently. "Megan?"

She made a small whimpering noise, and didn't open her eyes.

"Megan, it's Mary. We met at Lowryland. I'm here to get you out."

She did open her eyes at that, revealing irises that could have passed for human even in an optometrist's office. She flinched when she saw how close she was to my face, glancing away.

"Hey," I said. "It's all right. You can't hurt me. You can't— Why didn't they blind you?" It suddenly seemed like a very important question. While she'd been unconscious, focusing on her lack of sunglasses would have been a waste of time, but now, their absence meant she could have hurt me if I'd been human.

"Hard lenses," she rasped. "In my eyes."

"You're wearing special lenses?"

She nodded.

"And they didn't try to take them out?"

Megan coughed before offering me a wan smile. "Told them I was a lesser gorgon. They couldn't tell the difference."

"Ah."

There are three types of gorgon. Megan's variety, the Pliny's gorgon, is middle-of-the-road in terms of venomousness and danger. She could paralyze with a glance and petrify with a bite, but she couldn't petrify with her eyes. That privilege is reserved for the greater gorgons. Lesser gorgons can also paralyze with a look, but the paralysis is less intense and doesn't last as long. If the Covenant agents who'd grabbed Megan believed she was a lesser gorgon, they might have accepted her claims to just have a weaker-than-average gaze, thus sparing her eyes.

Still . . . "Why did they cut the heads off some of your snakes, and not the rest?"

Megan winced, looking miserable. "They had a plan," she said. "They were going to keep me alive until they were absolutely sure they couldn't get any more information out of me, cutting off as many bits as they thought I could survive losing—a few snakes, some toes, the little pieces—and then they were going to set me loose in downtown Seattle so they could heroically recapture and detain me. Let me scare some of the locals before they came charging to the rescue. If they'd cut off all the snakes' heads, I would have just looked like a woman in a rubber wig, and not a properly terrifying monster."

"I'm so sorry," I said.

Before she could answer, Sarah stepped out of the air into the room, her eyes glowing incandescent white. It could be easy to ignore how bright that bioluminescence was, when she was in a well-lit room. Here, it was like she had replaced her pupils with LEDs, and it was unnerving as hell.

"Hello, Megan," she said, calmly. "I know your mother quite well. She is very nice, and once bought me a Ring Pop when I was sad. It was green apple–flavored, although I've never had a green apple that tasted like that. Do you suppose there is an orchard somewhere that grows apples that taste the way the candy-makers think apples are supposed to taste?"

Megan blinked, several times, then shied as far away from Sarah as her bonds would allow, trying to press herself into me. The intact snakes on her head rose and hissed at Sarah, fiercely defensive.

"It's okay," I said. "Sarah's on our side. She's Antimony's cousin."

"She's a *cuckoo*," hissed Megan, as if I might somehow not have noticed. "If you think she's part of the family, she's—she's—she's been rewiring your head! I know how cuckoos work!"

"Keep your voice down," I said. "I love all the children I sit for equally, but I won't tolerate bullying, got it?"

Megan blinked, looking bewildered. The conversational ploys I use to calm misbehaving preschoolers tend to have that effect on people who aren't used to them. If I had to call for quiet coyote, it was going to blow her dazed, possibly concussed mind.

"Sarah, can you help me get Megan loose?"

"You could have done this part on your own," said Sarah, walking over to us, as serene as if Megan hadn't just implied she'd wormed her way into our family by abusing her telepathy. "The buckles are fairly straightforward."

"Yeah, but she's bigger than I am," I said. "If she starts to fall, I'm going to need you to help me hold her up. How did you get here?"

"I came to Seattle, and then eliminated hospitals by running a grid search for phantom minds," she said. "I found several dozen haunts, but you were the only one with your particular frequency. From there, it was a simple matter of modeling the three-dimensional manifestation of the hospital itself, and coming into the room where I would find you."

I blinked at her. "Oh," I said. "Nice and easy, then."

"Yes," agreed Sarah, not catching my sarcasm—or maybe just ignoring it. "I was glad when you said you were somewhere well away from the compound. It allows me to avoid the weakened areas created by my tunneling that have not yet had time to recover. Further, it means both that the Covenant has not yet narrowed in on the rest of the family, and that . . ." She tapered off.

"That you didn't have to go back yet," I concluded. "No, honey. You don't have to go back. You can go just about anywhere else you want to be. But right now, I need your help getting Megan out of here. We're taking her to St. Giles's."

"My mom . . ." said Megan weakly.

"Understands that you need care more than she needs to see you," I said. "I'll make sure she knows where you are. All right? Sarah?"

Sarah cocked her head, apparently considering the situation. After an unnervingly long pause, she said, "All right. I can get her to New York, and you can meet us there."

"Thank you," I said, and eased Megan's weight onto Sarah's arm as we got the gorgon medical student to her feet. Sarah staggered, just a little, before she smiled and vanished, taking Megan with her.

I stayed where I was, waiting for the call to come. Only a few seconds later, I heard Sarah's voice calling me across a continent to family and safety. I closed my eyes, let go, and followed the beacon of her voice.

Eighteen

"Everything costs someone. If you think it doesn't, that just means you've never been the one who had to foot the bill."

—Juniper Campbell

In the grain. Again. Which was not the idea, and is not terribly welcome

I APPEARED IN A field of grain, under a dark and star-spangled sky. Looking around in bewildered dismay, I did the only thing I could think of: I stomped my foot like the teenage girl I still appeared to be, balling my hands into fists, and wordlessly shouted my frustration into the void.

When I was finally exhausted enough to stop, a single star fell from the firmament above me, leaving a glittering trail across the dark as it dropped toward the horizon. I held up my middle finger, showing that glorious astronomical event exactly what I thought of its ineffable beauty.

"That's not very kind," said a chiding voice behind me.

"I was sort of in the middle of something," I said, turning to face the anima mundi. She looked at me with amused patience, and I flashed briefly back to speaking to Megan like she was a child. The age difference between the anima mundi and myself was even greater; to her, all of us were children, bratty, badly socialized children raised in the time of the crossroads, and now in need of a firm hand to set us back on the right path.

"You were following your family from Seattle to Manhattan," she said. "I pay attention."

"Then you must understand why I need to get back."

"Why are you in such a rush? You've been with them for decades without being in a position to be this active. Now you're here, there, and everywhere, and acting like they can't accomplish this without you. Don't you think that's a little arrogant?"

"I would have been this active from the start if I'd been able to," I protested. "I haven't been neglecting my duties because I wanted to. The crossroads kept me busy most of the time."

"The crossroads was a cruel master, abusive and alien, and the things they asked of you were not things that should be asked of any spirit of the earth; I failed you in my absence, and it is because of that failure that we're here now, which is why I would like to speak with you before I make decisions in which you have no say. When I look back along the line of your fate, I find a fascinating quirk. Do you know what that might be?"

I did my best to release my irritation without allowing it to morph into fear, as it so very much wanted to. "No, ma'am," I said.

"When you died, Mary Dunlavy"—and she waved her arm and we were no longer in the grain under the stars; we were in the scrubby corn growing along the verge on Old Logger's Road, the corn that no one loved or tended, and the sky was smudged yellow and gray with the impending sunset. I knew this cornfield, and this road, far better than I wanted to admit. This was where I'd died, and on the few occasions when I'd worked up the nerve to openly defy the crossroads, this was where they'd hurled me, leaving me to consider the mind-crushing nothing of haunting a cornfield for eternity. I shuddered, wrapping my arms around myself.

The anima mundi didn't appear to notice. She simply continued, calm and serene: "There was nothing about you that should have allowed you to become any sort of manifest ghost. Oh, you had the love and the longing to anchor you to the land of the living for as long as you wanted to stay, but you should have been a shapeless haunt, a spirit of place and tragedy, wailing your grief to the wind as your humanity leeched slowly away on the prevailing winds. The crossroads offered you another opportunity—a bargain, if you will—and pinned you here through artificial means, making you over as something they could claim and control."

"I know all this," I said.

"But do you know why manifest ghosts are so rare, Mary Dunlavy? They cost. Oh, how they cost. They cost the pneuma of the world every time they walk in the world, because they have to be powered by something. And a ghost like you, who has no clear service to refuel them, why, you are a very expensive haunting to maintain."

I shot her a surprised look. "What?"

"Not long after you were anchored, your line was spliced with something very old and very long forgotten. It wouldn't have been possible, had not the hand that held the scissors belonged to a daughter of an equally forgotten line. The Kairos change fates when they have the cause to do so, and while she knew not what she did, Frances Healy changed your fate. She made you less expensive by giving you a purpose beyond the crossroads."

"Great," I said. "Then I'm the babysitter, and I'll go do my job now."

"Not so fast, Mary Dunlavy. When you tend to the children, you're a babysitter. When you cleave to the ill, you're a nanny, and that, too, is a part of your purpose, clean and ancient enough to incur no additional costs. But when you exploit the ill-defined rules of your existence to add more people to those who can spend your presence freely, I have to make sure you understand how precarious your position is."

The anima mundi was suddenly much taller than I was, towering over me. She bent forward, placing her hands on her knees, and looked at me sternly. "There will be no more cheating, Mary Dunlavy."

"Er. Yes, ma'am," I said. "In my defense, though, the woman I just helped to rescue knows too much about my family. I couldn't just let the Covenant have her without leaving all of my family exposed to attack."

"Yes, and that's why we allowed the manipulation, clever as it was, to succeed, rather than restricting you to a single family, as it would have been in days of old. We simply want you to refrain from trying again."

"Yes, ma'am."

"As to this continual back-and-forth, we thought you would have realized, as the passage grew more and more difficult, that we would like you to stop moving according to your own whim. Go where you are summoned, little caretaker, and leave the unclaimed road to others. Our lands are open to you between times of need, if you tire of the starlight and its wonders."

"Generous an offer as that is, ma'am, I do have one more big jump planned." I looked up at the anima mundi. "I've arranged it so I'll be summoned on both ends, but it's not a short distance. Please. I need to do this, or the Covenant won't stop, and more members of my family will die."

"The Covenant . . ." The anima mundi sighed. "We can't play favorites, Mary Dunlavy. The predator is as beloved as the prey. But they, like you, have tried the bounds too many times, have reached beyond their grasp, and now begin to damage the balance on which the world depends. We made many wondrous things because we wanted to have them."

"I'm sorry, I don't follow." The anima mundi, as far as I knew, was the spirit of the living world. It couldn't pre-date life on Earth, or have influenced its creation in any way: when life was getting started, the anima mundi didn't exist yet.

Then again, as a force, it seemed to have some pretty flexible ideas about the flow of time. Maybe it *had* been there, and I just didn't have the capacity to fully comprehend how. I quietly added one more item to my list of reasons being dead sucks: it's debatable whether or not I really have a head, what with the whole "no more physical body" thing, but I definitely had a head*ache*.

"Because you act now to correct an imbalance we would never have allowed, had we been in our proper place, we will allow it," said the anima mundi. "But when this matter is concluded, you will move only at the pace of the living, or when summoned by your charges."

"That's fair enough," I agreed. It was still a massive limitation compared to the way I'd been doing things, but as long as I could help blow up Penton Hall, it was something I could accept. It left me with my family. That was all that really mattered.

"Then we have an agreement, Mary Dunlavy," said the anima mundi, with aching solemnity. "I will give you no aid but this, and you will not try me again."

"Yes, ma'am," I said, fighting back the impulse to salute. "Not on purpose, anyway."

"And no more trying to use the rules of your existence to your own advantage." The anima mundi looked amused for a moment. "Even if we *were* somewhat impressed when you thought to extend your client base for the sake of saving a friend, it's not something we can tolerate going forward."

"Yes, ma'am." Megan was safe. That was what mattered here.

"Then go, and fight this battle with our blessing. It's been waiting for some time."

I stammered for a moment. The blessing? Of a divinity? That wasn't something I wanted to have. Pushing aside anxious thoughts of Rose and her fate—she had been actively seeking the favor of three different divinities, not having a crossroads negotiation with a single one—I nodded, and then I was gone.

I appeared in the waiting room at St. Giles's, popping in to find the space much more active and occupied than it had been on previous

visits. Dragons, bogeymen, and assorted other cryptids filled the hard plastic chairs. Some of the children were crying. In one corner, a spotty-faced teenager who I recognized as the babysitter through some odd commonality of body language and the way the children were watching them, stood up, did a little turn, and transformed into a wolf. The children cheered, setting themselves to petting their now-canid babysitter, whose tail waved vigorously as they licked the children's faces.

Wulver make great babysitters, when they can find cryptid families to sit for, and don't get painted with the same brush as werewolves. They're not the same thing, even remotely. Wulver are a stable species of therianthropes, and werewolves are people with a disease. Wulver have been complicit in spreading lycanthropy, because they can survive it longer than most victims, but that's where their relationship with the situation stops.

The Caladrius woman from before was behind the desk again, seeming substantially more harried. Her wing feathers were in disarray; it looked like she was on the verge of a molt. I stopped politely in front of her, waiting my turn.

She kept typing frantically on her computer keyboard for several more seconds before she glanced up and jumped, apparently startled by my appearance.

"Um, hello?" I ventured, trying to sound friendly and not terrifying.

"M-Mary!" she squeaked. "I didn't think we were expecting you."

"Sarah should have just come through, with a semi-conscious Pliny's gorgon," I said. "I need to go to them."

Once I was sure Megan was all right, I could go home and wait out the rest of the time before my bombs were available with my kids. Even if there was more drama than I necessarily liked at the homestead right now, being around that many members of my family would be restorative, and would hopefully help me put back some of whatever energy the anima mundi had to expend to let me do the things I did.

The woman blinked, very slowly, color draining from her cheeks. "Yes," she said. "You really should."

"Okay, what am I missing?" I asked. "Because you're reacting to me as if you'd just seen, pardon the expression, a ghost. I *am* a ghost, but I don't normally get that level of 'Oh no a spookiness has occurred,' especially not here. What's going on?"

"Miss Zellaby arrived yesterday with Miss Rodriguez," said the woman, folding her wings tight against her back in her anxiety. "She seemed to think you would be here immediately after, and when you weren't, she became quite agitated. She's sleeping now, but we weren't sure . . ."

"Oh," I said. From my perspective, I hadn't even been in the wheat for an hour. Clearly, I was going to have to talk to the anima mundi about how incredibly attached humans were to the linear and consistent flow of time. "Can someone take me to them?"

"Yes, of course." She pressed a button on her desk, and the doors behind her opened, a petite woman in nursing scrubs emerging and approaching the Caladrius, who looked at her with clear distress, and said, "Miss Dunlavy is here to see Miss Zellaby and Miss Rodriguez."

"Come with me," said the woman. She flashed me a sunny smile, and beckoned me to follow her back through the door into the hospital halls.

There was a certain lightness in her step, a buoyancy that implied a lower-than-standard density. I walked a little faster to draw up level with her. "Sylph or spirit?" I asked.

"We don't have any hospital ghosts in residency at the present time," she said. "Sylph." Then she flashed me another smile. "Most people can't spot us that easily."

"I babysit for someone—human—who has a very close friend who's a sylph."

"Fascinating." The woman stopped in front of a closed door. "Miss Zellaby locked it from the inside, but I don't anticipate you'll have any issues with that," she said.

"No, I shouldn't," I said. "Thank you for your—" But she was already walking briskly away down the hall, heels clacking against the linoleum with every step. I turned back to the door. "—help," I concluded, to no one at all, took a deep breath, and stepped through the wood.

The room on the other side was fairly generic. It wasn't the room I'd found Sarah in before, thankfully; Mark wasn't here. Instead, the bed at the center of the room held Megan, now connected to an array of beeping monitors and machines, bandages swaddling her arms and head. Sarah was sitting next to the bed, one of Megan's hands held in her own, their fingers twined together to maximize skin contact. I stopped before coming any further.

"Hi, Sarah," I said.

She didn't look around. "You weren't here," she said.

"I know. I'm sorry."

"I got Megan to the hospital, and I was very tired, and I needed to go lay down until my head stopped ringing like a bell that had just been struck, and you weren't here to explain what was going on." Her voice took on a sharp, childish edge. "I didn't like that."

"You can't threaten to wish me away to the cornfield right now, Sarah, I just got out of the wheat."

She did lift her head at that, turning to blink at me in bewilderment. "What?"

"The anima mundi wanted to have a chat with me about tricking the universe into treating Megan as one of my charges. Apparently I'm not supposed to do that sort of thing." Which didn't stop me from feeling just a little smug about having figured it out. Megan might be direly injured and on some sort of complicated life-support system, but the key word there was "life." She was alive. She had survived her captivity, and would have the opportunity to recover.

"Oh. And she got the math wrong for traversing the fourth dimensional axis." Sarah's expression melted into one of thoughtful relief, and I realized for the first time just how much reined-in anger she'd been swallowing before. It was a daunting revelation.

"Sure. So I'm sorry I wasn't here sooner, but she nabbed me as soon as I left Seattle, and I couldn't exactly tell her that wasn't a good time."

"No, I suppose not," said Sarah. "I'm glad you weren't late because you didn't care."

"Honestly, Sarah, does that sound like me? How's Megan?"

"According to Dr. Morrow, she suffered blunt-force trauma to the torso and abdomen, and bruising of her internal organs. Did you know lungs could be bruised? She will recover. She just needs rest, and time. She's currently in a medically induced coma to assist with that recovery."

I glanced at Megan's bandaged head. "Those snakes didn't look like blunt trauma."

"Ah. No," said Sarah. "That was very sharp trauma in most cases, although the surrounding serpents tell me that a few of their fellows were crushed before they were decapitated, to add to Megan's distress. Dr. Morrow is working to regrow the lost appendages."

I blinked repeatedly. Caladrius are among the greatest healers the world has ever known, which is part of why we have so few of them left; they were hunted down, butchered, and sold as panaceas for centuries, and formed much of the basis for Christianity's obsession with angels. Pretty people with big white wings who can cure the sick will do that, but I had never heard of them sparking regeneration.

"According to Dr. Morrow, the biology of gorgons is closer to that of lizards than any other currently extant reptilian clade," explained Sarah, with the air of someone who was sharing knowledge that they themselves had only recently received. "Normally, the regenerative ability of gorgons is dormant in adulthood, although they tend to heal without scarring. By adding his own abilities to her natural healing process, he can coax her body into restoring the snakes she's lost. He can't regrow the fangs that were pulled from the snakes that weren't severed, and the new snakes will be shorter than the originals, but it's better than remaining as she is."

"I guess so," I said, wonderingly.

"I can't wait to see what changes in the thought patterns of the restored snakes versus the originals," said Sarah. "The ones she has are simple by human standards, but they're as old as she is, and they understand more than people assume they do; presumably, the new snakes will have new brains, and may need to be taught manners and proper behavior from the beginning."

"Have you called Megan's mother?"

"I did, after she was stable and it was clear you weren't coming," said Sarah. "Dee is occupied with cleanup at the Fringe, and while she would like to be here, neither she nor Frank can leave the community before they've decided whether they will have to move."

I hadn't even thought of that. The gorgon Fringe where Dee lived and Megan had grown up was unusual in that it was a semi-permanent gorgon settlement. Gorgons often prefer to live near humans, but can't always live among them, for obvious reasons. They've been pushed to the edges of the world, and past a certain point, there hasn't been any farther for them to go. The Fringe was an attempt at a stable, planned community, close enough to humans to access the resources they needed, but self-sufficient and isolated enough to let the gorgons who lived there enjoy a natural—for them—life. And now that was all in danger, because the Covenant had been able to capture one gorgon girl and dig the answers out of her mind.

"I understand," I said. "We can call her again later. Have you spoken to anyone else?"

"Yes. Alex is grateful that we were able to find and rescue his assistant's daughter, and Antimony is adamant that as soon as I find you,

I dispatch you to Seattle to, quote, 'get ready to burn those bastards to the ground.' She's very angry. I don't want to go to Seattle."

"That's okay, sweetie; I'm going to go without you. It's only been a day, right?"

Sarah nodded.

"Well, then we still have about two days before Uncle Mike can get me those bombs. Once I have them, we'll be able to end this. Are you staying here?"

"For now." Sarah squeezed Megan's hand. "She's very scared and confused, and being asleep doesn't make that go away, it just makes it harder for her to push against. So I'm trying to help, by being here."

"All right. Can you make sure someone—me, or Antimony, or even James—knows where you're going if you decide to move along again? I don't want to lose track of you." Almost as much as I didn't want to annoy the anima mundi by doing things the fast way.

Sarah nodded, a bit reluctantly, but agreeably enough, and I relaxed. If she was willing to help me with this, we could still finish what we'd started. "Has there been any sign of Leonard?"

"No. There were a few attacks in Seattle, but nothing major, and Annie says it looks like they went for easy opportunities on their way out of the city; the Covenant is on the move again. But there's nothing to indicate they're moving toward Portland."

"Small miracles," I said. "How's Verity?"

"Sad. So sad I can't go to New York right now—I'm too attuned to her, and I can't block the sadness out, no matter how hard I try. She loved him a lot. She still does."

"Love is one of those things that don't end just because one of the people involved dies," I said. "Love keeps going, even when there's nothing to anchor it."

"That's terrible."

"I know. But it's true."

Sarah sighed deeply. "Yeah. I guess it is."

I hesitated. "The anima mundi doesn't want me hopping around at my own discretion anymore, so we're sticking with the plan where you and Annie go over first and I meet you there," I said. "I'll call the hospital when I need you to summon me so we can get the bombs to Penton Hall."

"Blowing up the Covenant's house isn't going to bring back the dead or get rid of the field teams," she said.

"No. But it's going to scare them, and stop them from getting reinforcements for at least a little while, and maybe that gives us the time we need to turn this fight around," I said. "I'll see you soon, Sarah."

"Bye, Mary," she said, and I was gone.

This time, I made the journey without being waylaid into the endless field of wheat, although I couldn't help feeling as if I were being watched by something ancient and implacable. The eyes of the anima mundi were upon me, and I just had to hope she approved of me making this journey on my own.

I appeared in the room that was serving as Olivia's makeshift nursery, surrounded by the evidence of time passing: a surprising number of toys littered the floor, some fresh from the box, still more brought out of the storage loft above the garage and unpacked for the enjoyment of the latest generation of Prices. There was a moth-eaten taxidermied jackalope on the bed that I recognized from Alice's childhood, hauled out for one more round of tea parties and wild backyard adventures.

But there was no Olivia, sleeping or otherwise. I frowned as I looked around the room, then crouched down and went for the one guaranteed method of getting an update.

"Hello," I said. "This is the Phantom Priestess, and I could really use some revelations."

It's rare for there not to be an Aeslin mouse in eavesdropping distance when you're in one of the compound interiors, and this time was no exception. I had barely finished talking before three tiny heads popped out of a hole in the baseboard, their whiskers quivering with excitement. "Hail to the Phantom Priestess," they chorused, in politely restrained unison. One of them pushed forward, a dark brown male wearing the livery of the Pilgrim Priestess. "Truly?" it squeaked, all but overcome with ecstasy.

"Yup." I sat down all the way, resting my elbows on my knees. "I've been unintentionally out of the loop for days, and I need you to fill me in on what's been going on around here."

"Hail! Hail to the recitation of the recent events," intoned the mouse.

I gave it a quizzical look. "Is there a reason you guys are so quiet?"

"Two of the faiths are in mourning, priestess," squeaked another mouse, this one in the traditional attire of the Violent Priestess, Fran.

"The litanies of the Silent Priestess and the God of Hard Choices in Dark Places transition now from cultivation to preservation."

"Hail," said all three mournfully.

"And did not the Thoughtful Priestess say, Love the Enthusiasm, But That Child Needs Her Sleep, So Keep It Down In Olivia's Room or Else?" asked the third mouse, who wore Evelyn's livery and recited her commandment with the zeal of a true believer.

"Good to know Evie's on the case," I said, and settled back to watch the rodent recreation of the last day.

Aeslin mice never forget anything, and as a consequence, they never leave anything out. Their recitations tend to unspool a little faster than real time unless they're explicitly asked to slow down, and they skip over periods where nothing is happening—"Sleep Held No Surprises" is their usual phrase for that—but they still go through the minutiae in agonizing detail.

After I'd left to find Megan and Sarah, Antimony and Sam had come inside from the firepit to get some lunch for themselves and the rest of their group, and found Evelyn and Kevin weeping in the kitchen, having just gotten off the phone with Verity in New York. A family meeting had been called after that, to bring everyone up to speed with current events, including where people were and who was dead.

To be honest, I was a little glad not to have been there for that one. Family meetings that include funeral arrangements are never anything I would consider a good time. Jane would be buried here in Portland, of course; Dominic's final resting place was a little more up in the air, and might be either here or in Buckley, where he could find a home among the bodies of our lamented dead. Either way, they weren't with us anymore.

Olivia was now expected to be at the compound for an extended visit, and Evelyn was already drawing up plans to convert one of the guest rooms into a long-term bedroom for the girl, somewhere she could feel safe and secure and adjust to the difference between our wooded isolation and the city where she'd spent her life to date. Elsie had apparently suggested contacting the dragons in Vancouver to see whether any of their kids wanted to take the train down for a playdate, figuring Olivia might do better when buried in a pile of semi-identical blondes. I wasn't sure she was so wrong about that.

As for Elsie, she was still profoundly sad, but she had gone home to sleep last night, and managed to convince her father and brother to go with her. Ted was brokenhearted and mostly sitting listlessly around the front room, moving to the library when he couldn't control his tears and risked flooding the house with his pheromones. Unlike Arthur, who didn't affect anyone he was directly related to, Ted was only a blood relation of his own children, and could send the whole household into a bacchanal if he wasn't careful.

Alice and Thomas had mostly been out in the barn, drawing up tactical plans for the attack on Penton Hall and, one suspected, spending a few final hours with their daughter before she was taken away forever. They'd missed their chance with her. There was no way to pretend they hadn't, not now that she was dead and gone. But at least they were trying to make up for it, in their own somewhat stunted way.

Arthur still wasn't grieving. He didn't seem to know how. He'd come back with his father and sister, more because he didn't want to be alone than because he wanted to be a part of the planning, and had been moping around the fringes of the household ever since.

As for James and Sally, they had yet to let one another out of sight. She slept on the floor of his bedroom, and he snapped awake every time she got up to go to the restroom in the night, both of them seemingly convinced the other was going to vanish at any moment. That was something they were going to have to work on, but everyone needs a therapist when they're living in a war zone. That's just the nature of the situation.

On the whole, it sounded like things had held reasonably steady while I was gone. I waited for the mice to finish their accounting, then bowed my head with polite respect to the mouse in Alice's livery, which I guessed as their senior.

"Thank you for revealing to me the mysteries," I said, with deep formality. Then I looked around. "Where's Livvy?"

"Did not the Thoughtful Priestess take the child of the Arboreal Priestess down to the Room of Life, that she might be enlightened as to the familial structure of sharks?"

"Oh, Verity is definitely going to thank her mother for *that* one." I stood up, leaving the mice on the floor. They waved after me, as happy to be left behind as they would have been to come along. That's one of the things about Aeslin mice: they're generally in good spirits.

And as none of these three had followed either Jane or Dominic, they had reason to be in good spirits. The colony would be in turmoil for the next few weeks, as they transitioned the now-finished faiths from "cultivation to preservation," meaning there would be no new scripture, no new mysteries, only the endless study of what already existed.

It was a normal, natural part of Aeslin religious development, one that I had witnessed multiple times before, once for every lost member of the family (but not for Laura, never for Laura. Her faith, small and secretive as it was, remained in cultivation, eternally hopeful that their prophet would return). I had even witnessed the beginnings of Thomas's faith being brought back to life, a slow, stuttering, utterly baffling process that currently seemed to involve the mice poking him daily with a pin, to verify that he was actually alive.

The mice would be fine. It was the non-rodent family I needed to worry about right now. I released my hold on solidity and sank through the floor, descending slowly down into the living room, where I turned solid again before I could get a tour of the basement.

Olivia was indeed sitting on the floor, raptly staring at the screen on which a small cartoon shark was swimming its little yellow heart out, pursuing a school of deeply concerned pink fish. Evelyn was sitting on the couch nearby, watching her granddaughter rather than the screen. She tensed when she caught my arrival out of the corner of her eye, one hand going to her waistband even as she turned to look at me and melted into relief.

"Mary!" she exclaimed, standing and striding over to sweep me into a firm, maternal hug. "*There* you are! Where have you been? We've been worried *sick*."

"Sarah said she called to update you," I said, hugging her back.

"Yes, and Sarah said that you were missing." Evelyn let me go to step back and put air quotes around the word "missing." "Forgive me for getting worried when one of the family ghosts goes 'missing' for no apparent reason."

"Sorry," I said, and truly meant it. Worrying Evelyn was almost never my primary goal. "The anima mundi wanted to have a little chat, so she grabbed me while I was in transit. And she doesn't seem to have the best grasp of linear time just yet, so she kept me longer than I think she intended to before she put me back."

"Excuse me?" Her eyebrows spiked sharply upward. "Are you saying that the living soul of Earth wanted to have *a little chat* with you?"

"Yeah, pretty much. But she let me go when we were done, and now I'm here."

"Why is that not entirely reassuring?"

"Because you've met me, ever." I looked over at Olivia. "How's she doing?"

"She misses her parents. This is technically below her age range, but I think she's seeking comfort in the familiar right now, since everything else is so strange. Verity says she'll be here as soon as she can be—I'm leaving the rest for her to explain."

Meaning Olivia didn't know yet that her father was dead, assuming that would even be something that could be explained to her. I thought it was. Little kids are better at understanding death than people tend to assume they're going to be, as long as you're honest and upfront with them about it. If anything, the hard part would be making her understand that Daddy wasn't going to come and haunt her the way that I did.

Olivia finally looked around from the shark's aquatic adventures, perking up at the sight of me. "Mary!" she exclaimed, bouncing to her feet and running to hug me around the thighs. "You came home!"

"I did."

She reached for my hand, tugging me with her back toward the TV. "C'mon. We're watching *videos*." She made it sound like the activity that would save the world, the secret key to survival.

I laughed and let her lead me, and as I settled with the little girl on the floor, her scooting her way into my lap, I couldn't help thinking this was what life was meant to be like, always: children and television and thick carpets and safe homes. This was what I was willing to fight for, for everyone.

This was what we were going to protect.

Evelyn returned to her own chair, and together we watched the songs of the sea as they played out on the screen, and for a little while, I could pretend that everything was fine.

Nineteen

> "Family is a thing you choose, and the minute you stop choosing it is the minute it all gets swept away."
>
> —Laura Campbell

In the kitchen of a small, suburban house in Columbus, Ohio, two days later, preparing to bring this whole damn adventure to an end

Uncle Mike had, in his pragmatic way, decided he wasn't going to bring questionably legal explosives to his own home, not when it was just as easy to bring them to Ohio and make them Alex's problem. What was easier for him was also easier for me, since as soon as he'd appeared on Alex's doorstep, Alex had started yelling for me, and even under the anima mundi's new restrictions, I was allowed to answer when he called. So here we were.

Three unassuming gray metal cigars lay on the kitchen floor, each of them dull with some unspoken dread, as if they understood on a primal level that they were weapons of mass destruction, intended for nothing but exploding. Shelby had taken one look at Uncle Mike's delivery and removed herself to the park, along with both children and Angela, leaving Mike, Alex, and Martin to stand in a rough semicircle in the kitchen, looking down at the bombs, which somehow managed to give the impression that they were lurking while being entirely motionless and also inanimate.

I stood on the far end of their circle, looking at the bombs right along with them. I glanced up at Mike. "What do I owe you?"

"Eh." He waved a hand. "Call it a lifetime's worth of birthday gifts I never gave you. We're square. You've done more than enough to protect me and mine over the years."

I wanted to argue. I wasn't going to. He understood his finances better than I did, and we needed these bombs more than just about anything. I circled them, careful not to bump against the men, and asked, "All right. How do they work?"

"You pull this pin"—he crouched down and indicated what he meant—"then you turn this crank until it ejects the safety disks. At that point, your bomb is armed to fire. These are normally dropped from altitude, and they explode on impact. You can set them off manually with a hard-enough hit to the cap, or with sufficient fire."

"Right. Antimony on deck," I said, trying to sound optimistic. "This is going to go just fine." The bombs being at Alex's place meant he could call me back for the other two after I transported the first. I flashed a smile at all three men. "Thank you so much."

"You're already dead, or I'd ask you to try not to die," said Martin.

"I'll try not to vaporize my corporeal form, how's that?" I asked.

Alex, unexpectedly, stepped over and hugged me. I tensed for a moment before I hugged him back, patting him on the shoulder with one hand. "Hey, kiddo," I said. "It'll be okay. We have a plan. It's a good plan, even. It's going to be just fine."

"I don't like this," he said, giving me another squeeze before releasing me and stepping back. "I don't like sending my sister and my babysitter and my cousin off to the enemy stronghold with a bunch of bombs and hoping that they'll come back in one piece."

"Your sister is a human flamethrower, your babysitter is a ghost, and your cousin respects the laws of physics only as a courtesy and not out of any obligation," I said. "We'll be fine."

He forced a tremulous smile. "I suppose so."

"Text Annie now."

Her calling me back to Portland was an essential starting step. Alex nodded as he pulled out his phone. "I'm setting a timer," he said. "I'll start calling you back here in ten minutes, got it?"

"Got it," I agreed, and looked to Martin. "I'm going to be in and out for a while. That okay?"

"As long as it ends with my kitchen free of explosive charges, that's more than fine by me," he said.

"Great. Thank you all." I looked at the three men, managing one last smile, and disappeared as Annie's call of "Mary, I need you" echoed through my mind.

Annie and Sarah were in the barn, next to the table where Jane's body still waited in frozen stasis. James had to re-freeze her every twelve hours or so, but as long as he did that, she would stay the same, not changing, not starting to decay, held exactly as she was until it was safe for us to bury her.

My poor Janey. Ted didn't come to the barn anymore; he'd been banned after the second time we found him sitting next to her body with a vodka bottle in one hand, weeping so furiously that it had rendered the area unsafe for non-relations for hours. Ironically, Ted's shattered condition had proven useful by giving Arthur something to do: as long as he focused on taking care of his father, he wasn't stalking the grounds looking for Sarah so he could yell at her some more.

Sarah was uncomfortable being at the compound, because Arthur could walk in any time. As I reappeared, she was leaning against Antimony, the two holding hands, Sarah's head resting on Antimony's shoulder. I scuffed my toe against the ground, making enough of a sound to hopefully catch their attention. They both turned in my direction, Annie's free hand suddenly holding a knife. How a quick draw could be genetic, I had no idea, but every Price or Healy born I'd ever known had mastered the ability to seemingly conjure knives from nowhere before they'd mastered algebra.

"It's just me," I said, putting my hands up before Antimony could fling a knife through my head. "I come in peace. You two ready to go?"

"No one's too thrilled about this plan, but yeah, we're ready," said Annie.

"Oh, believe me, I know." In the last two days, I'd heard every argument possible against our plan, from "What if something goes wrong?" to "What if the Covenant has shields against transdimensional mathematics?" In the end, however, our various family members had been forced to concede that this wasn't going to end unless we hit the Covenant hard enough to *make* it end, and we really didn't have another method of doing that.

"You ready?"

"I think so. Uncle Mike gave me the instructions for arming the bombs. We're going to set them and arm them, and then you're going to fill the place with fire to set them off."

"And I'll pull myself, Antimony, and the mice out when necessary," said Sarah.

"I have a cat carrier." Annie bent to pick it up, then held it up for my inspection. It was, indeed, a cat carrier, half-filled with alfalfa hay and scraps of colorful fabric. "For the mice."

"You really think they'll come with you?"

"I hope they will. They're in extreme danger if they don't."

And they would provide a valuable source of information on the Covenant if they did; getting the mice out would have been a reasonable excuse for going to Penton Hall, even if we hadn't been trying to bring this whole stupid conflict crashing to a close. I nodded.

"So it's go time," I said, and pushed my hair back from my face with both hands, trying to look brave. "Alex is going to call any second now, and we'll get this party started."

"Maybe next time, send a card instead?" suggested Sarah.

I laughed.

A moment later, Alex called for me in the back of my mind, summoning me back to Ohio. His voice lacked the urgency it would have held if he'd really been in trouble, but even when I served the crossroads, I'd been allowed a certain degree of flexibility around coming when called. Sometimes a kid just needed to see their babysitter, to be reassured that they were still loved and cherished and important. So when Alex called, I was allowed to answer.

I vanished from the barn, hurtling across what I could now see was an endless field of golden wheat, and was in the kitchen in Ohio, looking at three men and three bombs. Alex didn't even blink when I appeared. "Can you tell Annie I love her, when you see her again?" he asked. "I'm worried I won't get to."

"You will," I said solemnly. "No one else dies today." No one outside the Covenant, and some of their deaths would be regrettable ones—we had no way of evacuating the children without playing our hand, and no possible pattern of charges would avoid the part of the building where Thomas said they were kept. One way or another, innocents were going to die today. I hated the Covenant for pushing us to this point, and I was so, so sorry, even as I understood that it couldn't be avoided.

I moved to the first bomb, crouching down to lever it off the floor and upright, wrapping my arms around it like the world's most dangerous teddy bear. It was heavy, and cold, and I hated it, even as I silently thanked it for being the answer to our current dilemma. Straining as much as I could, I was able to get the base a few inches above the floor, and held it there, waiting for the bell of Annie's voice at the back of my head. Just holding it was hard enough that I could feel the burn in muscles that didn't exist anymore, the idea of my body objecting to what I now understood was an increased draw on the anima mundi's power. I didn't have adrenaline to spike or muscles to strain. I had the living world, and it hurt to pull on it this hard.

Annie called with more urgency than Alex had, probably because she was already in enemy territory. I took a deep, unnecessary breath and threw myself, bomb and all, into the nothingness that would take me to her.

My flight above the grain was slower this time; I could actually look down, could actually see what lay beneath me in all its ripe and golden glory. The presence of the anima mundi hung heavy in the air, and I had the sensation that she knew exactly what I was doing, was entirely aware of my every move. She approved despite the strain—thus far. But if we deviated at all from the original plan, she might take that approval back, and I wasn't at all sure what would happen then.

Nothing good, of that much I was sure.

The basement of Penton Hall was as large as an auditorium, gray slate floor and brick walls stretching out as far as the eye could see. Structurally key pillars connected the floor to the low ceiling, and a bank of boilers occupied a chunk of the space. But only a chunk. The rest of what I could see appeared to be the Covenant archives, box after box of documents and stolen cryptid artifacts extending in all directions.

Antimony and Sarah were standing right in front of where I had appeared, their mouths open as they stared around themselves. "Grandpa didn't mention this when he was helping us find the weak spots in the structure," said Annie.

"He thought about it," said Sarah. Annie shot her a scandalized look. "He didn't say anything because he recognized, correctly, that you might be reluctant to move forward with the plan if confronted with the reality of how much scholarship and history would be destroyed alongside the Covenant warriors we were trying to harm, especially not when you were already conflicted over the projected loss of life. It was a calculated choice."

"Oh he did *not* decide he got to withhold information from me because I might not do what he wanted," said Annie, audibly furious.

"Excuse me," I said. "Dead girl with a bomb, here. Where do you want me to put this?"

Sarah swept her eyes around the visible portion of the room, doing some sort of elaborate mental calculus, then indicated a position at the base of the nearest support column. "There," she said.

We had appeared almost on top of the point she was, well, pointing at. I leaned over and released the bomb, which promptly fell over with a ringing clang. If any Covenant archivists were down here, we were going to meet them shortly. Both Sarah and Antimony flinched.

"Don't worry," I said. "It's not armed."

"Because arming mechanisms *never* malfunction," muttered Annie, crouching down. She set the cat carrier on the floor and opened the door before shrugging out of the bulky backpack she was carrying and unzipping the top flap. She began withdrawing blocks of clay-colored plastic explosive, packing them in around the bomb. I blinked.

"What's this?"

"Insurance," she said, glancing up at me. "If one of the bombs fails, or the walls are thicker than we think they are, this gives us a little extra boom."

"A little extra? That looks like you're trying to bring down the British Museum."

Antimony stopped what she was doing, looking briefly stricken. "If we were planning to blow up the British Museum, we would have hired a team of art thieves to clear out all the priceless cultural artifacts before we set the charges," she said. "But that's essentially what we're going to do here, and we haven't had time to loot the place yet. Can we do this? Morally speaking, can we *do* this?"

"We've already come to terms with killing noncombatants for the sake of our own side. Can we survive this war if we don't do it?" asked Sarah. She bent down, addressing the open carrier. "Your priestess is having a crisis of faith. Your wisdom would be welcome."

Two heads immediately popped out of the bedding, oil-drop eyes focusing on Sarah. "We live to serve," squeaked one, and the two mice skittered out of the carrier, then up Antimony's leg to climb onto the arm that was still extended toward the pile of plastic explosives. They didn't shout or exalt. That was odd enough behavior for an Aeslin mouse that I frowned at them, perplexed.

"They're following the scriptures," said Antimony, in a more normal tone—normal for her, anyway. From anyone else, it would have been the beginnings of a lecture. "Mindy here came with me to Penton the first time, as my living black box, and had to agree to strict vows of silence unless invited to speak. Mork was originally from the resident colony. Silence is ingrained in him at this point."

There was something tragic about an Aeslin mouse who defaulted to silence over celebration, but I didn't have the time to focus on that. Instead, I focused on the mice themselves. "We have to destroy this place," I said. "We don't have a choice. Mork, you grew up here. Does your colony have any knowledge of what things should be preserved?"

"That is the province of the clergy of the God of Bitter Honesty," squeaked one of the mice, presumably Mork. Ears flat and whiskers pushed all the way forward, he continued, "If any would know, it would be the priests of that litany."

"The God of . . . ?"

"Charles Healy," supplied Antimony. "Great-Great-Grandma and -Grandpa's older son, the one they had to leave behind when they came to America. Mork, can you find us a member of that clergy?"

"We will go, Priestess," said Mork, barely concealing his eagerness. Both mice darted off into the shadows of the basement, disappearing quickly.

I turned back to Sarah and Antimony. "While they're doing that, we should set the second charge. Where does it go?"

"Over here," said Sarah, and started walking.

The basement was large enough to be internally subdivided into smaller areas, although they weren't rooms so much as chambers, distinguished by a few interior walls and an archway, no actual doors. Sarah led us through one of those archways, indicating another support pillar. "Here," she said.

"All right," I replied. Alex was already calling in the back of my mind, trying to summon me to Ohio. "Just let me bounce over to Alex, and I'll be right back."

With that, I vanished, flinging myself into the void. This trip was faster than the one where I'd been carrying the bomb, but still substantially slower than the norm, giving me plenty of time to watch the grain roll beneath me, and a sense of place and position that had never been a part of this transition before. The air was thick, like I was moving through maple syrup, and I was relieved beyond measure when I reappeared—not in the kitchen, but in the front yard, shielded by bushes and decorative hedges, but still outside.

I squeaked, going insubstantial, and basically ran inside the house, not going solid until I was safely back in the kitchen with Alex, Martin, and Uncle Mike. Alex and Martin were sitting at the kitchen table. Both jumped to their feet at the sight of me, Alex's eyes going wide behind the lenses of his glasses. "Well?" he asked.

"Well, what?" I moved to start levering the second bomb off the floor. They were the same model, but this one seemed heavier. I'm a ghost, and ghosts don't get physically tired, but I felt like no one had bothered to tell my body that. My arms and shoulders ached, and my lower back protested hiking the bomb into my arms in a way that would probably have been a promise of future troubles if I'd been alive. Lifting that thing *hurt.* I had carried heavy objects before. Never several times in quick succession, and never *this* heavy.

"Did it work?"

I managed not to drop the bomb as I stared at him. "Alex, we need all three bombs before we can set off the charges, or we're not going to do enough damage to do us any good. No, it didn't *work.* It hasn't *happened* yet. Have a little patience."

"And when it does work, it won't disperse the field teams immediately," said Martin. His voice, as always, was low and deep, and entirely out of place coming from the mouth of such a mild, ordinary-looking man. He sounded like a supervillain and he looked like an accountant. "They'll still be here, and while they may realize something's wrong when they lose contact with headquarters, they'll still be milling around for a while before they realize no more orders are forthcoming."

"So we stay vigilant, and we do cleanup, but they don't get reinforcements," said Alex. "Works for me."

"I'm going to go place this bomb," I said. Annie was already yelling in the back of my head, demanding that I get back over there, because she wasn't finished talking to me. "After that, I'll be back for the third one, and when I come back from *that*, I'll be able to tell you whether it worked or not."

"And if you don't come back?"

I looked at him levelly, trying not to let on how much that question scared me. "That means it didn't work."

Hauling the second bomb through the void was even more difficult than the first. The air wasn't just thick—it pushed back against me, like it was trying to shove me all the way out of the void and out into the daylight. I kept going, forcing my way through with a degree of effort that had never been present before, not once, not even when I'd been fighting the crossroads for the tiny scraps of autonomy I could wrest out of their clutches. By the time I dropped back into the living world in the basement of Penton Hall, my forehead was covered with sweat, my mouth was dry, and my heart was hammering. All signs of exhaustion in a living person who actually had a body.

The most upsetting thing was that I couldn't make it *stop.* Since my body is more a courtesy than a structure, I can normally decide whether I want to do things like breathe, or sweat, or have a heartbeat. I didn't feel like carrying bombs through the space between the twilight and the daylight was bringing me back to life, but I couldn't stop my body from mimicking the signs of life in extreme distress, either.

I dropped the bomb to the stony floor with a clang and caught myself against the pillar, propping myself up for the stability it offered. Sarah and Antimony both looked at me with obvious concern.

"Well?" I asked. "Get it where it needs to go."

I didn't help them as they rolled the bomb into place against the base of the pillar. Again, Antimony packed additional explosives around the bomb, stealing guilty little glances at the shelves around us the whole time. The mice hadn't come back yet. I wasn't sure how she was planning to carry out a full evacuation of a structure this size, but hopefully it would be possible.

Sarah didn't help, just stood back and watched, her pupils faintly filmed over in white. Once I thought I could stand up on my own, I pushed away from the pillar and moved over toward her. "You good?" I asked.

"I am monitoring our surroundings for signs that we've been noticed," she said. "There have been none, as yet. We are undiscovered. The mice are difficult to track—their minds are so simple that I have trouble distinguishing them from one another, and there are plenty in the walls here—but I believe they have reached their destination, and will hopefully return in short order. I have located the caretakers responsible for the school-age children, and implanted the idea that they want to take their charges for a moonlit stroll. Most, if not all of them should be outside before the bombs go off."

She sounded so calm that it was tempting to just believe her and decide that nothing could possibly go wrong. As Antimony finished packing her plastic explosives, she straightened, turning to the two of us.

"One more," she said.

"Yeah." I couldn't feign enthusiasm at the thought of making that trip again. It would have been daunting *with* time to rest. As it was, I sort of wanted to throw up, which was not a sensation I had any real lingering familiarity with. I shuddered, and fell into step as Sarah led us to the other side of the basement, and another support pillar.

"Here?" I asked.

She nodded. "Here. This is where we— Mary? Are you all right?"

I blinked. Sarah was staring at me, frowning deeply. "I'm fine. Why?"

"Your eyes," she said, voice gone slow and heavy with concern. "You're crying blood."

"Oh. That's just a thing that happens to ghosts sometimes," I said, waving her concern away. I wasn't lying, exactly; weeping blood is definitely a thing that happens to ghosts. Other kinds of ghost. Not me. Neither babysitters nor crossroads negotiators become more effective when we scare the living crap out of people. But I was yanking power out of the anima mundi like it was going out of style, and it made sense for it to be burning out a few channels in the process.

"If you're sure . . ."

"I'm sure." I was not, in fact, sure. But we needed to finish this, or everything we'd done so far would have been for nothing. I forced a smile I didn't feel and disappeared, back into the molasses-thick air of the void. This time, I could *definitely* feel the anima mundi watching my passage, and her sorrow as she did. She couldn't save me from the consequences of my own choices, and she couldn't help me except by allowing me this one final burst of freedom, but she could watch, and she could grieve.

Her grief was palpable enough to be disturbing. I was doing what I had told her I was going to do, with her permission and according to her rules. But it was eating me—not alive, but I guess eating me dead at the same time, and my mortal haunting couldn't contain much more. And I couldn't stop. I was saving my family. I was breaking the momentum of a war, even if I wasn't bringing the war to a true ending. I was serving her interests. And yet she watched me go like she was watching a star fall, burning up as it hit the atmosphere.

Panting, I dropped back into the kitchen in Ohio. Alex, who had been waiting there for me to return, recoiled.

"Mary, your eyes . . ." he said.

"Huh?"

He didn't answer in words, just pulled out his phone, opened the camera, and flipped it around so that when he held the screen toward me, I could see myself.

Sarah hadn't been exaggerating: I was weeping blood, thick red tears running down my hollow cheeks, only to vanish as they dripped from my chin. My shirt was clean, and I was obscurely relieved by that fact. I've known too many ghosts who somehow managed to stain the spectral idea of their clothes, and have had to wander around haunting people looking like they need to do their laundry. My mother would have been so ashamed if I'd become one of them.

The tears were distressing. My eyes were worse. They had gone a deep reddish-black from side to side, like clots of curdled blood. I could still see perfectly well, which wouldn't have been the case if I'd been alive, but what I couldn't see was how this was an improvement over my customary empty-highway stare.

"That's different," I said, refusing to let myself cringe away from the phone. Decades of seeing small children with naturalist bents through their infancy has left me remarkably able to summon stoicism when necessary. If I don't flinch at dead racoons or living bloodworms, I'm not going to flinch at some fucked-up eyeballs, even when they're mine. "But I have a job to do. Can you help me with the third bomb?"

"Mary, you look exhausted."

"I *am* exhausted. But we don't have anyone else who can do this. Even if she were here, the rules are different for Rose. Sarah's got to stay with Antimony and the mice, or she won't be able to handle the evacuation." If Sarah came to get this bomb and Annie was alone when the Covenant finally realized they had guests in their basement . . . No. My exhaustion wasn't an excuse for taking that kind of risk. It never could have been. "So please. Will you help me?"

Alex lowered his phone, looking at me with naked concern. "Mary, we don't know all the rules of your new kind of ghost yet."

"I know."

"We still need you. *I* still need you. You were the first woman I ever loved. You were my best friend and the only person who ever really understood me when I was a kid, and I don't want to lose you over this."

"I know." Alex's crush on me had never been as well concealed as he'd thought it was. There had been times when the crossroads implied, slyly, that if I were willing to exploit it, I might be able to strike the kind of deal that let me return to the lands of the living and enjoy the rest of the mortal life I'd been denied. Joke was on them, though. My loyalty to the family was and had always been such that I would rather haunt them forever than live a few short years at their expense. What's more, the thought of seeing one of my kids in that manner was revolting. I'd changed his diapers. I didn't need to share his adulthood.

Alex watched me for a few long seconds, then sighed and turned his face away. "But you're still going to do this."

"Unless you've figured out teleportation in the last few hours, I'm the only one who can. Now help me."

I sank to the floor, no longer trusting myself to do this standing up, and Alex half-rolled, half-dragged the bomb over to me, allowing me to hoist it up into my lap. I wrapped both arms and legs around it, clinging like a koala, and flashed him a watery, no doubt unnerving smile. "Love you, kiddo," I said.

"I love you too, Mary," he replied, and I was gone, and I don't know what he said or did after that.

Back into the anima mundi's void I went, motionless and moving very slowly at the same time, a falling star for the living spirit of our world to weep over. I could feel her watching me go, and I wanted to call out for her, to ask her for help, but I knew in some fundamental way that her help would take the form of plucking me from my passage and pulling me down into the grain, where she could keep me safely grounded. What I was doing didn't break the rules, but it bent them, twisted them so hard that it *felt* like they were being broken, even if I was still technically in the right. The universe doesn't like a rules lawyer.

It would be so easy, I knew, to drop out of the space that my mind insisted on interpreting as a sky, to let it go and descend into the grain where the anima mundi would be happy to take care of me, to leave my task unfinished. They had two bombs and however much plastic explosive Antimony had managed to scrounge. They'd be fine. They'd finish what they started and be home in plenty of time for dinner.

Unless they weren't. Unless they waited for me to come back until they couldn't wait any longer, and got caught by the Covenant; unless the charges they had weren't enough to knock the building down, and they wound up with a half-destroyed Penton Hall filled with even-angrier Covenant agents, who would now be on guard against similar guerilla tactics. This was our only shot. This was what we had to do. I couldn't leave them hanging now.

The air pushed against me like it was trying to blow me back to Ohio, and the bomb was so heavy I could barely hold it up, but I kept going, and then Penton Hall shimmered into view around me, dragged back into visibility aching inch by aching inch. I dropped this bomb, too, and it hit the floor more loudly than I would have thought possible.

I didn't really notice, since I hit the floor half a second later, my entire body throbbing like a bruise, stars bursting behind my eyelids, and the dark reached up and dragged me down, and everything was silence, and everything was still.

Twenty

> "People like me, who gain something by losing everything, we're the exception, not the rule, and we make things harder for everyone, because people look at us and think the universe is kind. The universe isn't kind. The universe is a hungry animal, and some of us don't taste good enough to eat. That's all."
>
> —Apple Tanaka

In the basement of Penton Hall, Covenant stronghold and extremely historic building that probably shouldn't be blown up, but what can you do?

EVERYTHING WAS PEACEFUL AND nothing hurt, mostly because nothing existed; I knew, on some level, that if I went back to where anything existed, then the states would reverse. Nothing would be peaceful, and everything would hurt. I didn't like that idea. Pain was never something I enjoyed when I was alive, and then I died, and pain became something that happened to other people, something *I* didn't have to worry about. Now it was waiting for me on the other side of waking up, and fucked if I was going to hurry toward it. The bomb was in place. My work here was done. I could stay in the comforting absence for a little longer.

Then there was something that was neither peace nor pain: a voice, echoing through the abyss. *Mary? Mary, can you hear me?*

Sarah sounded frightened, like she didn't understand what was going on and didn't know how she was supposed to deal with it. But she was definitely herself, and not some sort of weird hallucination; I hadn't been unconscious or dreaming in a very long time, and yet I knew there was no way I could have mimicked her so convincingly, even inside my own mind.

Mary, you're scaring us.

She sounded like she was getting closer, which was impossible, since she was definitely inside my head, and thus right on top of me. But maybe there's distance in dreams, somehow, miles measured in minds, and she was approaching through a mechanic I didn't appreciate or understand. Maybe I should answer her.

Mary!

Maybe I wanted to answer her. But maybe I didn't know how.

She made a small sound, like she was trying not to cry. *The children went outside, and the mice came, Mary. While you were gone, the mice came out of the walls, and now they're here, and they're helping Annie find the things she needs to take. They've read the files—we won't lose the information, just the artifacts, and Annie's picking through those as fast as she can. Please, can you wake up?*

So I hadn't vanished when I passed out? That was good to know. My kind of ghost normally needs at least a little effort to remain in the daylight; I would have expected to drop to the twilight at the absolute minimum, and possibly all the way down into the starlight. Better to stay here than to be knocked cold in either of those places, which have their own predators. The twilight under Penton Hall wasn't likely to be the sort of place I'd enjoy visiting.

Mary, I'm scared. I need you. Please can you wake up now? Please? Come back to us. Come to me, Mary, please.

Sarah's position in the family has always been difficult to articulate. It's not that she's adopted—we have plenty of adoptees, and they're all family, just as much as the ones who were born into the whole mess. It's that she's technically Evelyn's sister, making her Kevin's sister-in-law, and that's normally a distant-enough relationship to release me from my duties as babysitter. But because she was brought into the family so young and bonded so tightly with her cousins—who are really her nieces and nephews—she's still my responsibility, and the universe takes that as seriously as I do.

She called me, and when one of my children calls me, I come. The nothing dropped away, replaced by something, and the something was an amount of pain that I imagined I would have felt if the accident that killed me had left me to die slowly, instead of snapping my neck on impact with the ground. Every muscle I had ached, including some that couldn't possibly have been involved in lifting the bomb. My arms and back and abdomen, sure, but my ears? My tongue? This was a full-body agony that I wanted nothing to do with.

I opened my eyes anyway. Sarah needed me to open my eyes.

I was in the basement of Penton Hall, and pretty clearly on the ground. I sat up—or tried to, anyway. When I got my hands under myself and pushed, they sank into the floor rather than giving me any measurable leverage. Great. So I was solid enough not to sink to the center of the planet, but not solid enough to interact meaningfully with my surroundings. The worst of both worlds.

The second time I tried to sit up, I didn't bother using my hands. It took a little rocking back and forth before I managed to get myself upright, but I did it, and looked around at my surroundings.

Annie was moving along the wall of boxes, occasionally pulling one out and rooting around inside for a moment before extracting some doubtless priceless artifact and stuffing it into her backpack. There were mice on her shoulders and peering out of her hair, which was nothing unusual, except that these mice were naked, missing the colorful raiment that normally distinguished Aeslin mice from their wild, non-sapient cousins.

Sarah knelt nearby, her hands on her knees and her eyes very wide, and very blue. The white had faded from her pupils, leaving her as normal-looking as she ever was. When I sat up, she gasped and put a hand over her mouth. I turned to look at her.

"Hey, kiddo," I said, through gritted teeth. I was trying not to let on how much I was hurting. She'd pick up on it if she went back into my head, but she's not an empath like Elsie or Arthur; there was a chance I could navigate this without adding to the mountain of guilt she carried in her daily life. "Thanks for calling me back. That nap wasn't entirely planned."

She made a choking noise. "Mary, your *eyes* . . ."

So they hadn't changed back after leaving Ohio? That wasn't a surprise, but it was an annoyance. "I know," I said. "I think I did the ghost equivalent of pulling a muscle. It should be fine in a few days." I had no way of knowing whether or not that was true, but I hoped. Maybe the burn from excessive contact with the anima mundi was something I could sleep off. If not . . . if my eyes didn't go back to normal, I was going to be dealing with a lot more nightmares in the children under my care for a while. Maybe forever.

"I didn't—you reappeared, and then you just *collapsed*," she said. "You were flickering, like you were the lights in an old house during a thunderstorm. You just kept going on and off and on and off and it was . . . bad. It hurt to watch. Mary, are you all right?"

"Honestly, honey, I don't know," I said. "I hurt all over. Carrying that third bomb here was harder than I thought it could be. Are all the mice here?"

"Not all of them," said Sarah, gaze dipping momentarily downward.

I winced. "Some of the faith lines aren't willing to leave their gods?" I guessed.

"They haven't had real contact in generations, not since the era of the Obedient Priestess—that's what they call Ada Healy—but they've continued to worship the family, just more in secret than our colony does," she said. "They never lost faith. I don't think Aeslin mice *can* lose faith. And they've been talking since Mork left about what they'd do if Annie came back and tried to get the rest of them to go with her. A lot of the younger mice are excited to have a new adventure, and new gods who actually want to talk to them. The older mice, though . . ."

She stopped, and shook her head. "The older mice can't see anything good in leaving the place where they've lived and worshipped for so many generations. They've thanked us for the opportunity and sent us their children, and gone back into the walls to die."

So detonating these bombs would not just destroy priceless cultural artifacts, but kill an uncounted number of highly endangered cryptids? Oh, this just got better and better.

"I know what you're thinking," she said, and grimaced. "Not because I read your mind, just because Annie thought it too. Is it really worth doing this if it's going to have so many secondary costs? And I have to say it is, because if we *don't* do it, the costs keep coming, and they keep coming at home. They keep coming in Ohio, and in Seattle, and in Manhattan, and eventually, they come in Portland. The mice are making a choice. They're individuals, and they have the right to choose to stay here if that's what they want. But they sent us enough of their archivists that we're preserving more than we're destroying, and we're doing what has to be done to protect our own."

"You think that's the excuse the Covenant used in the beginning, when they still had people who thought hey, maybe becoming genocidal bastards isn't the world's best plan?" I groaned and rubbed my forehead. I still felt as solid as ever, when I was touching myself and not the floor, but my skin was cold and clammy, like the skin of a week-dead corpse. Honestly, that was going to be more of a problem than the eyes, if it didn't clear up. Babies will eventually stop being scared of funny eyes and bloody tears, if those things become common enough. They'll never learn to like being held by something cold and unpleasantly damp.

Sarah flinched. "If it is, I think they didn't have anyone who was willing to serve as a moral compass when they started going too far." She looked at me, lips curving in the faintest shadow of a smile. "They didn't have a babysitter."

"Luckily, you do." I stood, then, and my feet didn't sink through the floor, and I was grateful for that, even as I doubted my ability to interact with my environment in a more meaningful way. "Annie?" I called.

She looked around, shoulders dropping briefly in obvious relief, then trotted toward me, bulging backpack held in front of her. "You're awake!"

"I'm surprised you didn't hear us talking."

"You try hearing anything with this many mice shouting in your ears," she said. "I'm almost done grabbing the things they say are important enough to be a cultural crime to destroy. We can document them at the house, and then look at repatriating them to the cultures they were stolen from."

"Good to hear," I said. "You get the third bomb into position?"

"We did," she said. "Took the last of my plastique, but it's ready to go up."

"Not until we arm them, it's not," I said. "But that should only take a few minutes."

"Can you?" asked Annie.

"We'll find out." I could see one of the bombs from where I was. I walked over to it and bent to turn the crank. My hand passed clean through. Looking over my shoulder to Antimony, I said, "Nope. Come over here and do this."

"All right," she said, starting toward me. "Walk me through."

As soon as she got to me, I repeated the instructions I'd received from Uncle Mike, showing her how to arm the bomb. I stepped back and watched. They didn't need me for this part. They never had.

My kids were growing up. Eventually, they wouldn't need me anymore for anything—and given that neither Annie nor Sarah was likely to have children of their own, that not-needing would extend to not needing me to babysit for their own kids once this current lot was grown. There would be a period between Olivia and Charlotte and their peers and them being old enough to have their own kids, where I would be extraneous to needs.

I hurt and I was exhausted and in that moment, being extraneous to needs was a beautiful dream.

Once the bomb was armed, Annie went to recover the last few artifacts, while I followed Sarah and talked her through arming the other two bombs. And still no one came from above. If not for Sarah monitoring the hall, I would have been afraid it had been abandoned at some point, leaving us to demolish a haunted house and accomplish nothing but making the Covenant even angrier with us.

Sarah and I returned to the center of the basement after arming the third bomb, standing next to the cat carrier, which was now filled to bursting with enthusiastically chattering Aeslin mice. After a lifetime spent in silence, they were finally free to make themselves heard, and they were taking that opportunity seriously. Sarah stood between me and them, and we waited, her wrapping her arms around her middle like she was trying to stop herself from shaking apart, me wishing I had a mirror so I could check to see if my eyes were recovering at all. Abruptly, Sarah jerked like she'd been stuck with a pin.

"Annie," she said.

"I think she's in the next room," I said. "Want me to go get her?"

"I don't want you to go *anywhere*," she snapped, grabbing for my hand and flinching when her fingers passed through me. "Annie!"

"What?" Annie called back, sounding frustrated. "I'm almost finished."

"You *are* finished, because we have to go *now*," yelled Sarah. "Someone's coming!"

Annie came running into the room, mice clinging to her hair to keep themselves from being thrown off, and raced to join us. "I have to put this pack on," she said. "Please make way." Then she shrugged the backpack over her shoulders as the mice scurried clear of the straps, hurrying to avoid being squished.

"Sarah?" she asked.

"I have them," said Sarah, picking up the cat carrier. It must have contained hundreds of mice, all of them crammed in on top of one another until there wasn't any space left. The ones on the bottom must have been on the verge of being crushed. But none of them complained. They were doing this to please their gods, and because they wanted to survive. If not all of them did, they would still have better odds than the ones who'd chosen to remain.

"All right," said Annie. She raised her hands to roughly shoulder height and began opening and closing them, like a cat making biscuits on a blanket. The air in front of her started to shimmer with a heat haze. "When I let go, grab me and jump," she said.

Sarah nodded. This part of the plan hinged on her being faster than the fire.

Somewhere high above us and in the next room over, a door closed.

It was an ordinary sound, rendered loud only by how much we didn't want to hear it right now. Footsteps followed, an unlucky Covenant researcher descending toward us.

Annie kept kneading the air, the heat haze growing thicker and thicker. "*Now*," she snapped, and made a hard shoving motion, which turned into a wall of rolling flame that crackled menacingly as it advanced toward the bomb. People like to talk about fire like it's a living thing; well, this fire was definitely alive, in its terrible, magical way. Alive, and *hungry*.

Sarah grabbed Annie's arm, and they were gone, both of them stepping into a fold in the fabric of space, tesseracting away without another word said.

The fire would hit the first bomb in under a second, and from there, the blaze and blasts would handle setting off the other two. I didn't want to be here for that. Ghosts are notoriously hard to destroy, but "hard" is not "impossible," and standing at ground zero of a massive explosion felt like a bad idea all the way around. I blinked out.

Except that I didn't. I tensed in that way that had nothing to do with tension and everything to do with no longer being somewhere I didn't want to be, and nothing happened. The fire was still rushing forward—time had done me the immense favor of slowing down just enough to let me enjoy my failure—and so I did the next best thing, and dropped into the twilight.

Only I didn't do that, either. I remained stubbornly rooted to the spot, not quite material and not quite insubstantial, unable to change states or levels of reality. And then the flames hit the plastic explosives, and everything was fire and massive, concussive booms, and once again, the rest was silence.

Exit Mary, stage right.

Twenty-one

"This isn't the end of the road. This is just the start of a new adventure. So come on, and let me show you how far this highway goes."

—Rose Marshall

Who the hell knows anymore? Position: uncertain, time: unknown

THERE WAS NOTHING.

It wasn't dark; darkness would have been something. It wasn't light, either. Sarah described finding herself in a big white room when she was locked inside her own mind by a hostile cuckoo, and again, that's *something*. There was just . . . nothing. I gradually became aware of myself as a sequence of thoughts and memories, a whisp of information that believed it was an individual, but that awareness didn't come with anything else, not even the sensation of having a physical form. That wasn't as frightening as it would have been once upon a time; I'd been dead for decades, and ghosts are only questionably physical. Even down in the starlight, my body was more my idea of what I was supposed to be than anything real.

Which meant my body couldn't be hurt, right? Standing at ground zero of a massive explosion wouldn't be enough to do anything permanent to me—maybe enough to knock me out for a while, discorporate me and leave me drifting in an intangible void, but nothing more than that.

I was starting to get upset. I forced myself to slow down, reflecting grimly on the fact that in the absence of the physical indicators of upset—the racing heart, elevated blood pressure, clammy palms—it was hard to *stop* being upset. Those responses give a person something to focus on, something to calm. All I had were my thoughts, and the nothing.

Until, gradually, there was something: a breeze, blowing from the east. It was soft and warm and playful, in the way of little spring breezes, and I had no skin, but I could feel it all the same. I focused on the breeze, letting it remind me of the outlines of my body, like a bat using echolocation to find its way home. The breeze kept blowing, and bit by bit, my awareness of what my physical form was supposed to be came back. I still couldn't move what I felt, couldn't reach up to touch my face or make sure I had all the pieces of myself, but I *had* a self again, and it was impossible not to see that as an improvement.

After the breeze came a slowly building golden light, replacing the void with itself a degree at a time. I didn't know if I even *had* eyes at the moment, but if I did, the light came on gradually enough that they didn't need to adjust. I looked into it, and it shone around and through me, warmer than the wind but just as soothing.

Then, something new: a hand, touching my cheek, and with that touch, I had a cheek, unquestionably, and that meant the rest of me existed as well. It was like someone had touched the surface of my psyche and, through the ripples cast by that moment, called everything I was back into being.

"Mary, Mary, quite contrary," said a voice, distant and half-familiar, "what am I supposed to do with you?"

If I had a body, I could open my eyes. I did, seeing starry sky above me, blurred and indistinct. I blinked, repeatedly, until the stars became clear, and then I turned my head to look at the owner of the hand still pressed against my face.

The anima mundi looked back, unfazed by my sudden awareness.

"Hi," I whispered.

"I told you that you reached too far," she said. "I told you there were limits."

"You also said I had your blessing," I managed.

"I did, at that," she said, and sighed. "You pushed yourself far beyond what I thought you would achieve."

"So you're impressed?"

"I didn't say *that*," she replied. "You channeled more of my power than a simple spirit is meant to hold. I should have allowed you to disperse, to pass into the next stage of the afterlife as payment for the liberties you'd taken."

"Payment for you or for me?"

"Instead, I called you back together, because I *did* say you had my blessing, and you acted in good faith. You took what steps you could."

"So you fixed me?"

"I anchored you until you could fix yourself."

I struggled to sit up, the muscles of my abdomen protesting. The anima mundi pulled back and watched me, but didn't extend a hand to help.

"Can I go home now?" I asked.

"Are you sure you want to?"

I didn't know how to feel about that question. I frowned at her. "What do you mean?"

"I mean, you didn't come back together in an instant. It's been six months as they measure time among the living." She sounded so calm about that, like it was a perfectly reasonable thing to say. "Your family thinks the bomb discorporated you permanently."

"Then I should go tell them otherwise."

"Wait. Mary, this means they know they can survive without you. *You* know they can survive without you. You *can* choose to move on, if that's what you're ready to do. The parasite is gone. Your family is at peace. There's no unfinished business left for you."

I paused. Move on? I had never really considered that an option. First, there had been my father, and then Alice, and after Alice, her children, until I was needed more than ever. But was I, really? If they were doing okay without me, couldn't I go? Jane was right when she'd said that there would always be another excuse, another reason to stick around: if I didn't go now, when would I? Would I, ever?

Did I want to haunt the living forever?

"A family is sort of like a house," I said, slowly. "They have walls and roofs and closets full of things they'd rather not remember, skeletons in the attic and unspeakable horrors in the basement. And sometimes a house needs to be haunted, for the comfort of the people who live there. I don't want to move on.

"I want to go home."

"If that's your wish," said the anima mundi. "Remember the limits I've given you. Don't try me."

"I won't," I said.

"Close your eyes."

I did. She tapped my forehead, and there was a feeling of all-consuming lightness, as if the last of some terrible and lingering contagion had been swept out of me by an unstoppable wave. The breeze stopped blowing, and when I opened my eyes, I was standing by the firepit. It was extinguished and charred, charcoal and ash, with no sign of my people.

I turned toward the house and started walking. I was going to have to get used to that.

I was halfway there when the door slammed open and Sarah ran out, crying, "Mary!" in a joyful voice. I opened my arms. She hurled herself into them, and I held her close, letting her weep against my shoulder.

When she finally pulled back, I smiled, and asked, "Did you eat your veggies while I was gone?"

"I did," she said. Then, with a blink, she said, "Your eyes . . ."

"Are they still bleeding?"

"No. They're . . . blue."

"Well, I'm still dead, so I guess the anima mundi just decided I didn't need to carry the crossroads with me anymore," I said, as lightly as I could. Patting Sarah on the shoulder, I asked, "Shall we go inside?"

She sniffled and nodded.

So we did.

Read on for
a brand-new InCryptid novella
by Seanan McGuire:

DREAMING OF YOU IN FREEFALL

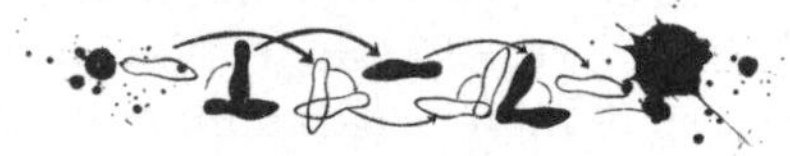

"I was born in Italy, raised in England, and brought to life in America. I'm not a man without a country. I'm a man with all the world."

—Dominic Price-De Luca

The morgue of the St. Giles's Hospital in Manhattan, New York

Almost too numb to remember how to breathe

MARY BLEW ME A kiss, the same way she always did: by kissing the fingers of her left hand and then resting the side of her hand against her face, like she was telling me a secret and the secret was how much she loved me. I caught it in one hand, the way *I* always did, and she was gone, one less ghost in a place that felt like it should have been full of them, and I was alone, and Dominic was dead, and he was never going to wake up, or wrinkle his nose at the things I was willing to put in an omelet, or dance with me again.

I was alone.

I stared at the spot where Mary had been, willing her to come back without allowing myself to escalate to calling for her. Because she'd come back if I did, I knew she would; she'd answer my need the same way she always had, since I was a little girl who thought she was invincible and let that dictate half her choices. And calling her back right now would be cruel. She was trying to fix this. She was trying to end this war.

But there was no fixing this. Dominic was dead, and none of the ways we had of bringing people back were going to be anywhere near good enough.

If he'd been willing to stick around and play the phantom, he would either be here in the morgue, with me, or Mary would have hauled him in by the scruff of the neck and ordered him to get haunting. The only form of physical resurrection I've ever known to actually work is the sort that was performed on Martin, a sort of human taxidermy crossed with kintsugi, where the damaged flesh was replaced with undamaged pieces of another body, and all of it melded together with a science so far outside the bounds of my comprehension that it became a form of magic. But that form of resurrection only works on bodies that don't have any scrap of their original inhabitants remaining, and it drives ghosts away.

Worst of all, it doesn't preserve the people who were there in the beginning. Martin is made up of several men, and while he says he sometimes has dreams he thinks may hold hazy memories from the past life of the body that donated his brain, that's it. The body that provided his heart, his lungs, his legs? It doesn't get any part in who he is now.

I loved Dominic's body, maybe before I loved his heart, because I saw him before I knew him, but that didn't mean I wanted the flesh without the man. Dominic's body without Dominic inside would just be a stranger who hurt to look at. I didn't want that.

He was gone.

He was really, truly gone, and he wasn't coming back to me. I hiccupped, starting to cry again, feeling the tears trickle slick and slow through the dried blood on my face, and I wanted to stop crying, because every tear that dripped off my chin to fall to the floor took another tiny fragment of Dominic away from me, and I wanted to shower for a year, until I had sluiced every bit of blood away, and those two desires were entirely incompatible, and nothing I did would make them stop. I allowed myself to look back at the shrouded form of the man who had been my husband, and the past tense in that sentence hurt like hell. "Until death do us part" wasn't supposed to be an instruction.

"Guess you got away from my crazy family after all," I said, and wiped my eyes, careful not to smear blood into them. "They really did adore you, you know. Not as much as I did, but no one ever adored you as much as I did. I love you, asshole. Even if you always did think you were Batman."

Standing here talking to a corpse wasn't going to get me any closer to that shower, or to snapping out of the shock I could feel settling over me like a warm, heavy blanket, smothering my senses and making my body feel alarmingly far away. If there's one thing I've always been, it's connected to my body. I know my physicality better than most people do, and I define myself by it. But now, I felt like I was wrapped in heavy cotton, dulling everything around me, making my limbs slow to respond to my commands, making everything feel very far away.

I wiped my eyes again. "I'm sorry I wasn't faster," I said. "I'm sorry I wasn't better. I'm sorry you won't be there to see our babies grow up, I'm sorry, I'm sorry, I'm sorry . . ." There was no chance I'd stop crying after that. The tears came hard and heavy, running down my face until it felt like they might drown me. My nose clogged up until I could barely breathe, which didn't help my fear of suffocation, and my knees slowly buckled, leaving me to sink to the ground next to the platform where Dominic was lying, silent and shrouded.

"I'm sorry, I'm sorry," I kept murmuring, until the tears were everything. The tile was cool against my forehead, and there was no air left in the slowly spinning room, there was only grief and the taste of salt, until I wept myself into unconsciousness, and even that was gone.

I hadn't been dancing much since Olivia was born. Oh, I'd been doing what I could to stay limber and avoid losing too much strength—there's no age where it's really safe for a dancer to neglect their core, but past the age of twenty-five or so, any ground lost is ground that may not be regained. So I'd been practicing and training every minute I got, but I hadn't been *dancing*, hadn't been throwing myself into the music and the arms of a partner the way I wanted to. First I'd been pregnant, and then I'd been recovering from my pregnancy—which hadn't been an easy one. People say you'll "glow" and look back on those days with joy and nostalgia, but I'd mostly seen them as a long series of aches and pains, my body feeling less like my own with every unrequested transformation, swollen ankles and loosened joints, all capped off by gestational diabetes combined with an insatiable craving for frozen hot chocolate, which really wasn't a compatible desire.

Honestly, I would have said that all those "easy pregnancy" stories were myths, designed to convince people to keep on having babies, if not for the fact that Shelby's pregnancy had overlapped with mine, and to hear her talk about it, had basically been a vacation crossed with a trip to the spa. She'd been radiant, hungry, and horny, with no real medical complications, and a fast, easy birth, making my own unplanned C-section seem positively unfair. If not for the fact that Dominic had hauled me off to St. Giles's as soon as I'd gone into labor, where Dr. Morrow had been able to heal my incisions in a matter of days, I would have been *livid*.

But Olivia made up for all the trouble she'd caused on her way into the world. Olivia was *wonderful*. I'd never been that excited about the idea of becoming a mother. If it happened, it happened, if it didn't, it didn't. Pregnancy isn't great for a dancer's career under the best of circumstances, and it's not that much better for a cryptozoologist's. Becoming slow and heavy is generally bad for a person's chances of survival in the field, and sitting out nine months of my life for the sake of allowing someone else to leech calcium from my bones just didn't seem like the best use of my time. And then the line on the pregnancy test had popped positive, and my nausea and aching breasts had taken on a whole new meaning, and the idea of a little person who was the best parts of me and Dominic mixed together had become more appealing than I could have believed possible.

And then she'd been more than just an idea. Then she'd been *real*, our Olivia, a fussy little bundle of opinions and ideas that didn't match up with mine, or with Dominic's. Her hair had been a shock to us both. The blonde in my family apparently comes from our Carew ancestors, and Dominic seemed to view their genes as completely dominant, to the point where both of us had been expecting a blonde child. Not that it mattered; she was perfect as she was, and I at least liked how much she looked like her father. I didn't fall in love with the man for nothing.

And at first, I'd been too tired to dance, too occupied with trying to keep this strange new miracle of mine alive and prevent her from grabbing and squashing the Aeslin mice, all of whom were way too casual about getting into baby-hand range. She had the grip strength of a gymnast when she couldn't even lift her head yet, and her tiny nails had been like razorblades. I'd been genuinely afraid that she would crush one of the mice, and worse, that when the rest of the colony ritualized the event, they'd decide it meant annual sacrifices. They'd have been happy to do it. Aeslin mice are always happy when they're following their faith. That didn't mean I wanted it to happen.

But then she'd been old enough to be away from me for a few hours, and she'd been sleeping through the nights, and I'd been going slowly out of my mind with idleness. I'd started to move again, training with all the fervor I could muster, but I hadn't been *dancing*. My kind of dancing requires a partner to feel like it's really happening, and not just another practice. Practice is essential. It just doesn't fulfill me the way real dance does.

So the fact that I was spinning and stepping in Dominic's arms now made me feel like I was whole for the first time in weeks. His hand cupped my waist, providing the anchor I needed while I went through my own steps, and the crowd outside the dancefloor made the appropriate sounds of pleasure and delight every time we successfully completed a trick. Dominic had never been a professional dancer, but he'd danced with me enough to know how to hold his own, and no one knew how to anchor me better than he did. I could dance for the rest of my life and never find a better partner.

The music swelled and stopped as he spun me out into a trust fall and spun me around the floor like he was using my body as a compass needle and needed me to find true north. Then the audience was applauding, and the judges were calling out their scores, but I couldn't hear them, because of that damn beeping.

"Can you make that *stop*?" I demanded, climbing off the floor and turning toward Dominic in my agitation. Then I froze, blinking blankly for several seconds before I screamed.

The audience didn't react, just continued to applaud while I screamed my heart out. Dominic, his eyes filled with blood that leaked down his cheeks in thin ribbons, blinked.

"Verity, what's wrong?" he asked.

This whole time, I'd thought he was wearing a red suit, but now I could see the dots of white at the cuffs, and understood that it was blood. It was all blood, dyeing the fabric, and my red dress wasn't red either—it was a sodden piece of gauze, wrapped around me to catch the blood and keep it off the dance floor. I screamed again. He let go of my hand and I stumbled back, still screaming.

"I'm sorry," he said, reaching for me. "I'm so sorry, Verity. I didn't mean to. I didn't mean to slip. I didn't mean to get hurt.

"I didn't mean to die."

The beeping got louder, until my ears were ringing. I staggered farther from him, evading his grasp, and clapped my hands over my ears, trying to block out the sound. It dimmed the beeping, but did nothing to muffle the sound of my own screams, which echoed inside my skull, ricocheting back and forth like a rubber ball dropped into a box. I dropped to my knees, and the dead man in my husband's suit stopped advancing, sparing me the touch of his bloody hand. His flesh was beginning to wither and pull away from his skull, rapidly making him unrecognizable.

I kept screaming, closing my eyes to shut away the sight, until everything was screams and beeping, and then the screams fell away, but the beeping remained. I breathed harder and harder, until I started to hear words through the beeps.

"—unharmed but dehydrated."

That was Dr. Morrow. I knew him. I trusted him.

"And her bill?"

The second voice was familiar, as well. Female, pitched somewhere above alto, with a hectoring note that told me who the speaker was more clearly than her words could ever have done: Candice, the dragon who was William's first and most loyal wife. She sounded furious, like she was on the verge of launching herself at the doctor.

"No bill," said Dr. Morrow. "The service she has done for this community and this hospital means her money is no good here."

"You take *our* money!"

"You have substantially more money, and have done less in the manner of community service," said Dr. Morrow.

"Is she going to wake up soon?"

"We hope so." He sighed. "We've done everything we can for her. Honestly, we don't have the experience working on humans that we wish we had. Prior to Ms. Price arriving in Manhattan, we never needed that experience."

"Humans get everything else; why should we accommodate them?" asked Candice, in a mulish tone.

"Because she keeps getting hurt in our service," said Dr. Morrow. "And because she could reveal our presence if she went to a human hospital. People say things when drugged or coming out of sedation; one poorly timed comment and a rumor of our location reaches the wrong ears."

"I'll take her from here," said Candice. "You're dismissed."

That was all the warning I had before she grabbed me by the shoulders and shook vigorously, hard enough that my head bounced against the pillow I was only just becoming aware of.

"Wake *up*, you big stupid mammal!" she snapped. "I don't have all day to hang around here watching you sleep."

Right. I opened my eyes. Candice was looming over me, face screwed up like she had just smelled something unpleasant. If she hadn't been making that face, she would have been quite pretty, in a deceitfully "All-American girl" kind of way. Oh, she fit both of those requirements—she had been born in America, so far as I was aware, and she was definitely the female of her species—but the people who coined that term were probably thinking of humans, not highly evolved synapsids masquerading as humans to avoid extinction.

Her hair was a rich caramel blonde, her skin was flawlessly clear save for a scattering of freckles across the bridge of her nose, which only added to her general "farmer's daughter" air, and her eyes were very blue. She looked like the kind of woman who knew the labels of every piece of clothing she owned, and didn't allow anything from a department store to touch her skin. A glance below the neck put that part of her appearance to bed; everything she was wearing had clearly been mended more than once, and had probably stopped off at a thrift store at some point in its life cycle.

Which was really what I would expect from a dragon. They're incredibly focused on money—obtaining it, retaining it, and transforming it into gold. I'm pretty sure that we could crash the world gold standard by cracking into a couple of well-established dragon Nests, which probably goes a long way toward explaining why the Covenant of St. George has managed to maintain such a high level of hate for them when dragons haven't been truly dangerous for centuries.

The thought of the Covenant was like driving a heated needle between my ribs, stopping barely shy of my heart. I closed my eyes and swallowed hard, only for Candice to shake me again.

"Wake *up*, you stupid human," she snapped. "I don't want to spend all night sitting around here waiting for you to get over yourself."

I opened my eyes again, sighing, and took a look at my surroundings.

I was in a hospital bed—no surprise there—with an IV bag hooked to my right arm, the needle taped down to the crook of my arm. It didn't hurt, but I could tell that it would as soon as I pulled it loose. I blinked, then looked over at Candice. "What happened?"

"You keeled over in the morgue, like a big drama queen," she said, studying her fingernails. "Only dead people get to nap there, mammal. Bad choices. And it turns out I'm still on your list of emergency contacts."

Dimly, I remembered filling that out as part of the paperwork when I'd been checked in for Olivia's birth. Candice was fifth from the top of people to call in an emergency. Dominic was first.

Dominic was no longer available.

I took a painful breath. Sarah was listed under him, but she was out of the state, and I didn't think she'd come back for a non-emergency emergency, not when she was helping Mary deal with the greater crisis. Istas and Kitty should both have been called before they worked their way down to Candice. My eyes widened as the facts of the situation sank in.

"Wait," I said, barely managing to resist the urge to grab Candice and shake her. It would just have been returning the favor, after all. "Are Istas and Kitty . . . ?"

"The waheela and the bogeyman are both as well as they ever are," said Candice dismissively. She whisked the blanket off of me and looked with disdain at my legs, exposed from the knee down by the hospital gown I was wearing. "Both were indisposed by other duties. I would also have been indisposed, but William objected. He said it would be a poor return on the friendship you've offered us since coming to this city."

"I'll have to tell him how much I appreciate it," I said, half-numbly.

"Oh, you're about to have the opportunity."

I blinked. "Come again?"

"We are returning to the Nest proper. William wants to speak with you." She sniffed. "I don't like bringing outsiders there under the current circumstances, but he was quite firm, and I try not to argue with him when I don't have to. It upsets us both. I'm much happier when I don't have to deal with an unhappy husband."

"That's pretty universal," I said. "Most people don't like it when their spouse is unhappy."

"Yes, but mostly people aren't married to fifty-foot-long predators who breathe fire," said Candice.

"Okay, I have to give you that one," I said, looking around for the call button. "Candy, can you do me a favor?"

"I'm already doing you a favor," she said sourly. "I'm collecting you and taking you back to the Nest, against my better judgement. What else can you possibly want from me?"

"I want you to find a nurse so we can get this IV out of my arm," I said. "Let's not keep the fifty-foot predator waiting, all right?"

"Fine," sniffed Candice. "Wait here." That said, she flounced out of the room, and I sighed, watching her go.

"I wasn't planning to do anything else," I said, to the empty air.

My clothes had been too soaked with blood to save; Dr. Morrow had ordered them burnt while I was still unconscious. Which was why I was now walking through the sewers in sweatpants and borrowed shoes, with a thin white tank top under an NYU hoodie two sizes too large swallowing my arms and torso. Candice, who knew the route between the Nest and the hospital well, led the way deeper and deeper into the network of tunnels beneath the city, occasionally pausing to beckon me along and make small, irritated noises over how slowly I was moving.

My legs felt like they were made of lead. My borrowed shoes technically fit, but they fit *wrong*, rubbing the sides of my feet in an unpleasant way. I wanted to stop and take them off, and the only thing that stopped me was the knowledge that if I did, I'd be walking the rest of the way barefoot.

Candice looked back to snap at me once more, and paused as she saw the expression on my face. She not only stopped walking; she took a few steps back, to meet me, and touched my arm. "Verity? Are you all right?"

"Not in this or any other universe, but why do you ask?"

"Because you're crying again."

I stared at her. "When they called you to come and get me, they told you what had happened, right?"

"Yes." She nodded, with something that looked like real sympathy sparking briefly in her eyes. "I'm sorry about Dominic. He was always very kind to us, once he got over his initial instinct to behave as if we were all horribly dangerous monsters. He was human, but he was good."

I wiped my cheeks with the back of my hand, saying nothing.

"I was unsure about you when you first came to the city," she said. "All of us were. Oh, we know you Prices say that you're not Covenant anymore, and you've been doing a decent amount to prove that over the past few decades, but what's a few decades against centuries? Your names are in our histories, and we don't speak of you kindly. Then you show up with a current Covenant member and expect us to trust you? It's a miracle no one stabbed you."

"It's a miracle no one *tried*," I sniffled, unable to let the comment pass.

Candice ignored me. "And then you find our sweet William, and you didn't tell anyone about him, you didn't rush to claim the greatest kill any Covenant member could possibly make. If your family was in exile against your will, taking his heart would have washed you clear of your sins in their eyes, but instead, you gave him back to us. You *saved* us, in a way I'm not sure you can fully appreciate as a member of a species that still has a functional gene pool. My mother spent her whole life dreaming of a husband, and the only thing I regret is that she died before we found him."

I wiped my cheeks again. "We had to give him back to you, and give you back to him. You're right—my family used to be part of the Covenant. Some members still are. We helped put the dragons on the verge of extinction. There was no way I could pass up an opportunity to pull you back."

"We didn't need a savior."

"I know. But maybe I needed a save."

Candice smiled thinly as she nodded, patting my arm. "You did good. And so did he. And yes, I know he's gone, but we don't mourn the way you mammals do. We haven't had that luxury in a long, long time."

Sometimes the reminders of what my ancestors did to hers could just sneak up on me, even when we were talking in circles around them. I winced. "Thank you for coming to get me."

"Like I said, William told me to," she said, waving off my gratitude with a flip of her hand. "Come on. We need to get out of the open."

It was hard to see any interpretation of our current position where the descriptor "open" would apply; we probably weren't as far beneath the city as it felt, but then, I'm essentially arboreal—hence the mice using it as my title. I'm not claustrophobic or anything, but I'm not super comfortable any time I can't see the sky. There was nothing remotely open about our current position. One earthquake and we'd be buried under so many tons of rubble that our bodies would never be retrieved.

But Candice turned away to hurry down the tunnel, and I followed her without objection. I didn't really have another choice. The hospital had been all too happy to see the back of me; they weren't going to welcome me back without a serious injury, and even then, they might be happier if I just didn't show. If I went back to the bogeyman community that had agreed to shelter us after the Nest was destroyed, I'd have to face the well-meaning sympathies of all the people who loved me . . . and worse, I'd have to tell the mice what had happened. Oh, God, the mice.

My family cohabitates with one of the last known colonies of Aeslin mice, a species of highly intelligent cryptid rodents who balance that intelligence with a hyper-religiosity that drives them to seek the divine in their daily lives. Generations ago, they found that divinity in us, and have worshipped us to this day. They believed Dominic was one of their gods. A whole branch of their church was dedicated to his worship. They *loved* him. This was going to break their little pseudo-rodent hearts, and I just couldn't deal with that yet. My own grief was too hot and raw to allow me to make space for theirs.

It had been a long time since we'd actually lost a family member. I'd never *actually* seen the Aeslin grieve before, and I wasn't sure I really wanted to. Not that I was going to have a choice. They had as much right to their grief as I did.

I stumbled, a wave of what felt like physical despair sweeping through me, rendering my knees weak and threatening to send me crashing to the ground. Candice paused again, looking back at me.

"Don't collapse now," she said, voice more sour than supportive. "We're almost there."

Gritting my teeth, I forced myself to keep on walking. The tunnel began to brighten around us, small motion-activated safety lights coming on in the niches near the top of the walls. They glowed with a clean, pale LED white, enough to see by, not enough to totally scramble our night vision, and I was grateful for them, even as I wondered at the security.

"We have motion-activated darks that we turn on when we're not expecting visitors," said Candice.

I nodded. Darks were developed by human witches in answer to the needs of the bogeymen and other dark-adapted intelligences; they did exactly what the name would imply, and when a dark came on, it deluminated an area as well as a light would illuminate it. If they balanced lights with darks, they were managing their security better than I had momentarily feared.

And I was focusing on the lighting because it was better than focusing on anything else. I was going to be in mourning for a long time. I didn't need to start it now, while we were in the middle of certain danger.

Candice motioned for me to follow as she adjusted her trajectory and walked toward a small service door set into the wall and nestled back in a deep alcove, where it was almost invisible unless viewed from the precise right angle. She approached the door, knocked twice, paused, then knocked three times more. The door cracked open, just far enough for someone to peer through and see her, then slammed shut again. Candice, unperturbed, took a step back and folded her arms, waiting.

There was a series of clicks as the locks were undone, and the door swung all the way open, revealing a slice of the cavern beyond. Candice stepped through, then turned to look at me.

"Well?" she asked. "You coming?"

I followed her.

The dragons of Manhattan had an aboveground Nest in the Meatpacking District for years, only to largely abandon it when they moved underground, then start using it again, this time as a preschool of sorts, when their birth rates spiked and they began seeing male children for the first time in centuries. That Nest was gone now, burned to the ground by the Covenant of St. George. The dragons would probably sell the land from here, since rebuilding would have been virtually impossible. Too much attention; too many prying eyes.

Fortunately for them, they still had their subterranean home. A natural cavern cut deep into the bedrock below the city, it had been there before Europeans came to North America, and long before the settlement that would be known as Manhattan. William had been very young when his sisters carried him with them on a boat to the "New World," sneaking him into the caves under cover of darkness and staying by his side as the city grew around and over them, inevitably sealing him off from the world outside. That was always the fate of male dragons, whose sheer size made it difficult for them to move around much once they reached adulthood. They could fly when they were very young, and hunt when they were reaching maturity, but by the time they were fully grown, they were better equipped to moving slowly through their hoards, counting their gold and courting their wives.

Everything we had indicated that, under normal circumstances, there was one male dragon born for every five to ten females, and one adult male survived for every twenty females. So far, that had been borne out in the births among the Nest since William's return; girls outnumbered the boys five to one, and they doted on their little brothers without question or compromise. They seemed to have a genetic predisposition to adore the boys, viewing them as protectors and something to take care of at the very same time.

It was an interesting adaptation, one that would encourage the comparatively defenseless females to cluster around the males, who were enormous and intimidating and could breathe fire, thus providing those same males with food when they needed it. The whole species benefitted, as long as a bunch of human monster-hunters didn't come along and throw everything all out of whack.

I have no idea what dragon culture looked like before humanity hit them. Humans are minimally sexually dimorphic, to the point where normal variance and the right jacket can make gender anybody's guess. We'd be miserable if we had to live that way. And dragons would be miserable if someone could mysteriously make them live like humans.

The cavern Candice and I had entered was William's original landing place in Manhattan, the underground home his sisters had chosen for him when they were trying to hide the last known male dragon. He didn't know much of his own life story, or what had happened to his sisters after he went to sleep: he knew that their father had been killed, and most of his brothers, in a violent Covenant offensive, but that one of his sisters had been entrenched in a local village as a weaver's assistant, and she'd been able to smuggle the youngest and smallest of the boys to safety wrapped in a bundle of textiles. From there, they had decided to flee Europe, a little family group of women and children crossing an ocean to try and keep the future of their species safe.

They'd been lucky to find the cavern, following natural caves deeper and deeper into the bedrock until they felt like they were safe, and then they'd spent several years feeding their brother and preparing him to hibernate, watching him grow larger and larger until he could no longer be moved. And then he'd gone to sleep, and stayed asleep until a group of human cultists tried to wake him up. Human cultists have a nasty tendency to assume that anything large and scaly is some sort of eldritch god and can give them infinite cosmic power.

Really, anything large and scaly enough to be mistaken for a god is mostly likely to give annoying human cultists a swift, unpleasant death, and William was no different. He'd been displeased to be woken up, until he discovered that a Nest thrived in the city above him, dozens of dragon females who had prayed he really existed every night of their lives, and who were ecstatic to learn that he was real. Best of all, none of them had smelled like his sisters.

With a low male birth rate and a tendency to travel in groups, dragons developed a remarkably sensitive nose for their own relatives. He might be mating with some of his great-great-great-great-grandnieces, but with the family relationship that far removed, it was no longer enough to register with his nose as a bad idea. A male dragon would never voluntarily breed with his own sisters or offspring, and so they were able to avoid genetic bottlenecking. Since the females could reproduce parthenogenically, that meant that even if we never found another male, we'd just managed to provide the species as a whole with generations of new males. Send a hatchling to another Nest where he wasn't related to anyone, let him grow up to have children of his own, then let him go to sleep for a few hundred years—which was, incidentally, how long it took for female dragons to stop laying eggs without the presence of a male. By the time he woke up, they'd all be distant-enough descendants to let him kick off another generation.

It wasn't perfect. By human standards, it was fairly horrifying. By draconic standards, this was the best things had been in centuries.

The cavern was about the size of an aircraft carrier, which made it large but not abnormally so for the local bedrock—so far as I was aware, nothing of this scale was even suspected under Manhattan, at least in part because who the hell would want to know? The city had been constructed before they had the kind of ground-penetrating equipment that would have allowed them to find something like this, and now all of the Big Apple rested above an air pocket that, if it popped, would do millions upon millions of dollars in property damage. What good would discovery do at this stage? Better to leave it alone so they could claim ignorance when the insurance payments came due.

The ground was smooth, rendered so by a combination of William's sisters with hammers and William's own willingness to melt irritating rock into slag. It wasn't quite as level as a constructed floor, but it was about as even as could be accomplished without modern tools, and it always impressed me. That floor was strewn with gold, in coin, jewelry, and knickknack form. The dragons hadn't been careful about where they tossed things when they dredged the gold out of the remains of the burnt slaughterhouse and dragged it down here to pile up around William.

William himself occupied the back half of the cavern, massive even with his head down and his wings furled. His scales were a healthy shade of green, like emeralds, and like emeralds, they varied in shade depending on where they appeared on his body, ranging from deep, deep green through a variety of near-yellows and green-blues. His eyes were open, large and luminescent, and a bright pumpkin orange that made them occasionally unsettling to look directly into.

In case looking into the eyes of someone with a head the size of a VW Bug wasn't unsettling enough. Which it was, as a rule.

Several small café tables and chairs had been set up around him, all of them wrought iron, and several with white cushions on them. I blinked, shooting Candice a curious look. William had a tendency to breathe fire on his surroundings. Cloth cushions seemed like a bad idea.

She saw where I was looking and made a small chuffing noise, like she was swallowing a laugh. "I wouldn't sit on those, if I were you, mammal," she said. "Asbestos is bad for your kind, and I doubt you'd find them very comfortable."

"Yeah," I said. "Yeah, that would suck, a lot. Where the hell did you find asbestos cushions?"

"It doesn't bother us, and what exists is remarkably cheap, probably because of how much it *does* bother you. So we use it for the spaces where we want to be comfortable near our husband, and he tries not to breathe directly on the furniture anyway. He can melt stone. You really think a little wrought iron is going to defeat him?"

"Remind me not to piss him off," I muttered.

There were other dragons in some of the chairs, or sitting in piles of gold, or curled up on the ground leaning against William, who seemed perfectly content to be furniture. Little blonde girls in patched dresses ran wild through the clutter, some of them chasing or chased by winged lizards the size of dogs, who fanned their wings and occasionally launched themselves into the air for brief flights before crashing down again.

I couldn't imagine being able to fly as a child and knowing I'd lose the ability as an adult. I would never have come out of the sky, not until the moment when gravity decided it was time to yank me down forever.

That thought brought my mood, which hadn't improved by all that much, plummeting back to earth, just like the baby dragons. Dominic was dead, and here I was making a social call like nothing had changed, like it didn't matter. But it did matter. It mattered more than anything else in the entire world.

And not that many people were going to understand how much had just been lost. Dominic grew up Covenant, and they didn't really encourage making a lot of friends, or developing the skills that would make somebody a "people person." And then he walked away, for me, and for himself—I could never have convinced him to leave if he hadn't already been starting to see how wrong the things they were asking of him were. He left because he was ready to be a better person, or at least a person who didn't attack innocents for the crime of being born.

I was going to miss him for the rest of my life. I was going to mourn him endlessly and extravagantly. My family might not grieve as hard as I did, but they were going to miss him, too—especially Mom and Alex, both of whom had taken to him with remarkable speed. His fighting style had been similar enough to Alex's for the two to spar, which was a rare treat, for both of them, really. And the mice, oh, the mice. Their grieving was going to be the stuff of Greek tragedies, world-ending and sky-shaking.

Olivia . . . my mind still refused to let me anywhere near the question of what this was going to do to Olivia, who loved her father completely and unquestioningly, and who knew what death was in the abstract way that children do, not as something that could come into her home and whisk her beloved Dada out of her reach. Maybe we don't do our kids any favors by having a ghost as our primary babysitter and expecting them to somehow understand that death is supposed to be forever.

But that was very nearly it. Ryan and Istas liked him well enough that they'd be sad when they learned that he was gone. Kitty had never been entirely comfortable with him, and while I knew she would support me in my own grief, I wasn't sure whether she'd have any sorrows of her own. It was selfish of me to want the world to grieve with me. It was selfish, and it was wrong, and it was . . . it was *small*, in the way my baby sister always accused me of being small. She liked to say that I thought about me first, myself second, and everyone else in the world a distant third, and she hasn't always been wrong.

Candice led me across the cavern to the dividing line between William's private space and the rest of the lair. It was just a line scratched into the stone about ten feet away from his crossed front legs, but no one was supposed to pass it without an invitation except for his wives and the children too young to understand why Daddy wasn't always available.

He raised his head as we approached, focusing on me. Once we were close enough that he didn't need to raise his voice, he rumbled, low and grave, "I'm so sorry, Verity."

I burst into tears. Not cute tears, either: big messy tears, the kind that no one looks pretty shedding. He looked, briefly, alarmed, which is no small trick for a giant reptile. Then he half-unfurled one wing and raised a clawed hand to gesture me forward.

"Come here," he said. "You look like you need a hug."

I threw myself across the line and against the warm curve of his neck. He wasn't rough like an alligator, but smooth like a snake, slick scales flat and broad over hard muscle. And much like a snake that had just been lifted off a hot rock, he was warm, radiating the heat from his internal fire. He folded one hand around my body and wrapped the trailing edge of his wing around me, blocking me from view. And I?

I pressed my face into his neck and bawled like I was dying. I sobbed and sobbed, until his scales were wet with tears and sticky with snot, until my knees went weak and I sank, still crying, to the floor.

Candice was there to catch me before I fell. "You should stop crying now," she said, with something I could almost interpret as real concern. "The doctors were giving you fluids because you had dehydrated yourself with excessive weeping. You can't afford to lose that much water. You mammals are mostly water, internally speaking."

I sniffled, blinking at her. I didn't know whether it was surprise at Candice showing empathy or surprise over the implication that dragons weren't mostly water, but my tears stopped. "Are you not?" I asked.

"Oh, we are," she said. "We're biological organisms subject to the rules of this reality. We need water to live. We just have the sense not to cry ourselves into unconsciousness."

"You would if I died," said William, half-reproachfully.

"Yes, because I would be a widow for the rest of my life, which would be very long and very lonely," said Candice. "Verity is human. She has uncounted options for remarriage, should she choose to mate again, and her life will extend another fifty years at most—probably less, given her approach to personal safety. She has less cause to grieve than I would have. She's weeping for herself. I would be weeping for my species."

I sniffled again, wiping my nose with the back of my hand. There was something charming about her blunt self-interest. I always knew where I stood with the dragons, and while it might not always be a flattering assessment, it was always an absolutely honest one. Wiping my hand on my borrowed sweatpants, I straightened and let go of the arm she had used to catch me.

"I'm very sad," I said. "Humans tend to mourn very intensely when we lose our mates."

Candice gave me a withering look. "You don't need to explain *humans* to me," she said. "You've been the dominant species on this planet for eight hundred years. We learned your culture and its rules and how to pass for part of it because we wanted to survive, and we didn't have another choice. I might need to explain myself to you, but you never need to explain yourself to me. We didn't have the luxury of ignorance."

"I'm sorry," I said, and wiped my nose again. Making a disgusted face, she produced a real cloth handkerchief and offered it to me.

At my surprised expression, she shrugged. "One handkerchief can be reused for years, and used for drying the tears of children as well as blowing your nose. A box of tissues is gone in a week, *and* it costs money."

Leave it to the cheapness of dragons to bring back the hankie. I laughed, the sound still thick with tears and snot, and accepted the handkerchief, using it to dry my eyes before wiping William's neck clean. I wanted to blow my nose, but by the time I'd accomplished those two things, the hankie was well and truly sodden. I turned back to Candice.

"Is there a hamper or something where I could put this?" I asked. "I don't think you want to just take it back."

"Well, you can't *keep* it," she said, sounding more horrified by the idea of me wandering off with her personal possessions than by the idea of being handed my snot-soaked hankie. Priorities. "There's a laundry hamper over there." And she pointed past the café tables to what looked like an iron lockbox.

"Fireproof," explained William. "I try to keep the flames under control, but sometimes a man gets excited, and well . . ."

"Say no more," I said—half-begged, really—and walked over to deposit the handkerchief in the lockbox.

We don't know how dragonfire works. We'd need a male dragon to dissect if we wanted to figure that out, and since William is the only available specimen, we're willing to settle for ignorance and observation. We'd always assumed it was a trait evolved for protection—a little extreme, sure, but there are lizards that bleed from their eyes and snakes that shoot venom. Breathing actual flames isn't that much more over the top, especially not when your species had a tendency to cluster in large, vulnerable groups protected by a single dominant male. And then we'd found William, and established friendly relations with a functional Nest for the first time since leaving the Covenant, and, well . . .

It was also a mating thing. Male dragons used their flames to sterilize an area before reproduction, guaranteeing that no other male's sperm would somehow work its way into the mix, and protecting their wives from contaminants and bacteria. This also raised the female's internal body temperature, and it was something about that heat that triggered the mechanisms for sexual, rather than parthenogenic, reproduction.

Somehow, thinking through the scientific mechanisms for dragon reproduction—as we had managed to figure them out without an invitation to a dragon orgy or something—helped to settle my nerves. I'm not the most scholarly of my siblings. I'm probably the least scholastic, and that includes my in-laws. Neither of whom has actually married in, but Alex and Shelby have a kid, and Sam is like a bear trap that snores. They're not going anywhere.

Scholarly or not, I enjoy the science. Focusing on it gave me something to think about beyond my grief, and so I kept thinking about it as I walked the hankie over to the laundry box and tossed it inside, onto a snarl of fabric ready for the laundromat. Or whatever sort of washer system the dragons had syphoning water off the city utilities, more likely, since going to the laundromat would cost money, and if there's one thing a dragon doesn't do if she can help it, it's spend money.

Their penny-pinching actually has a biological basis. All that gold they focus on collecting is biologically necessary. The mechanism is unclear, but without reliable access to reasonably pure gold, dragons fail to thrive. Worse yet, their birth rate drops, and for a species that's already holding on with a wish, a prayer, and a grappling hook, that's just not acceptable. Every cent they get, they keep, until they can turn it into gold. There are whole dragon communities dedicated to searching yard and estate sales for underpriced gold necklaces and rings, anything that pings their incredibly well-developed sense of the metal, which they buy for the below-market asking price and then sell on to their sisters at a reasonable markup. Every dragon we've ever asked about the system has been firm that the hunter Nests would never take advantage of the rest of them; gold is too important.

It's the center of their physical and spiritual lives, it enables them to survive, and it matters more than anything else, even money, which brought me full circle back to the laundry. A trip to the laundromat could be expensive, especially with the swarms of children the dragons had running around at any given time; a washer and dryer would be even more expensive, in the beginning, but I had all faith that any such appliances the dragons had would have been obtained second-hand, if not third- or fourth-hand, repaired, and then installed in some hidden tunnel where the dragons could make use of them, and also charge the local bogeyman and hidebehind communities for laundry services.

If there's an angle to be exploited, the dragons will find it, grab it, and squeeze it until it cries for mercy. I could admire that, a bit, even as I turned back to William and Candice, beginning to trudge back toward them. My legs felt too heavy, like they'd been swaddled in cotton laced with lead fishing weights, but I kept going, forcing myself not to stop. If I stopped moving, I might never start again.

I had almost reached Candice when a little blonde girl in jeans and a T-shirt advertising a 1993 Walt Disney World parade slammed into my hip, wrapping her arms around me and jerking me to a halt. I turned to blink down at her. She beamed guilelessly up at me, her grin revealing a missing front tooth with just the beginnings of its replacement poking out through her gum. A gamin grin if ever there had been one.

"Auntie Verity, where's Olivia?" she asked, in a bright, sweet voice. "We want to play with her."

My daughter was very popular with the dragon girls, who viewed her dark hair as a curiosity—dragons being uniformly blonde—and liked having a human child they could cast as the terrifying monster in their games of tag. Olivia didn't seem to mind, and would gleefully make hand-claws as she chased her draconic playmates around their shared space. I had expected the dragon mothers to be wary of her, in the beginning, but they had welcomed her with open arms, showing me considerably more kindness in the process.

"A human child is good camouflage," Candice had explained to me, when I expressed surprise over that strange fellowship. "A few dozen would be better. She'll teach them how to blend in more easily than the rest of us do, and their children will benefit for it."

It was hard to argue with logic like that.

"Sorry, kiddo," I said. "Livvy's with her grandparents for a few weeks, until all this business with the Covenant is over and done with."

The dragon child looked up at me, eyes wide and blue and fringed in thick golden lashes. She could have been a killer in print advertising; she had the sort of face that begged to sell me something. "It's going to end?" she asked.

I forced myself to nod, swallowing past the lump in my throat. "It's going to end. We're going to end it. I promise."

"And then Livvy will come back?"

"And then Livvy will come back," I confirmed.

She let me go, taking a step backward. "Pinky swear," she commanded.

I extended my hand, and she hooked her pinky through my own.

"One two three, promise me," she chanted. "So you've said, so it will be." She reclaimed her hand and skipped away, not looking back.

I managed a smile as I continued my walk over to Candice. "Cute kid," I said. "Who's her mom?"

"Don't know; we found her in the park one day, and thought she matched the decorating scheme." She laughed. "You should see your face. You totally bought it!"

"Sure, Candy," I said. "You'd risk the Nest by kidnapping random sticky, smelly human children."

She stopped laughing. "They *are* sticky. How are human kids so sticky? Do you roll them in jam?"

"I'll be honest—I don't know. Livvy was sticky before she was crawling. I think babies may secrete some sort of biological adhesive."

"It wouldn't surprise me," she said, and thawed. "Her mother's Madison, one of the dragons who came down from Boston after William got settled." The Nest was made up largely of dragons who could trace their relationships by two or three generations, sisters and cousins all living together to keep each other safe. William had added a new wrinkle by making sexual reproduction possible again, and so they had begun quietly making trades with other local Nests, keeping their population stable while dragons whose sisters had already been accepted as William's wives moved on to increase the local genetic diversity.

Again, if I tried to think about that in human terms, it seemed terribly wrong, but when I looked at it as a naturalist whose subjects could manage their own preservation, it made perfect sense. If William was going to impregnate two females, better that they not be sisters. They had to be smart about things if they actually wanted to revitalize their species rather than buying it the very briefest stay of execution.

"Right," I said, looking to William. "I'm sorry I got you all snotty."

"You wiped it off," he said. "And you're grieving. You're allowed to get a few things all snotty. If you don't mind my asking, what are you planning to do from here?"

"I . . ." I stopped, once again unable to swallow past the lump in my throat. I struggled for a moment to force it down, finally saying, "I can find a new apartment, once we're done driving the Covenant back. I should probably stay in New York for at least a while, make sure everything is okay before I go home to my family."

"But you will return to your family?" he asked.

I blinked. "Are you trying to get rid of me?"

"No. Entirely the opposite, actually. The Nest would be . . . willing, if not happy, to pay your housing costs if it meant you would remain in the area. We have many needs where interfacing with the human world is concerned, and you could serve as a negotiator where relations with other Nests are concerned. We've had more inquiries regarding adoptions, and some of them have been rather aggressively . . ." He paused, looking hopelessly to Candice for help.

"Smug," she offered. "Patronizing. Rude as hell. They assume that because the Covenant is in our city, we can't take care of our own husband. They want to buy our sons at a discount, because they'll be 'protecting them' from the dangerous risk of dragon-slayers. We've never been that careless. We've never endangered our boys."

That wasn't entirely accurate, but pointing it out wasn't going to do me any good. I nodded instead, and focused on William. "You really want to pay my rent? That's not cheap in Manhattan."

Candice grimaced. "We have some investment properties," she said. "Not as many as we used to—we've had to sell a few to balance the rising tax rates—but we could provide you with a place to live well below market rate." Offering me a bargain made her look, briefly, like she was going to throw up, which paradoxically made me feel better.

Knowing *why* dragons are the way they are about money doesn't make it any less fun to occasionally tease them about it, or any more rewarding to have them offer me fair compensation for my time. I kept my eyes on William.

"What would you need from me?"

"Negotiation services, and continued monitoring of the cryptid activity in the city to be sure that nothing dangerous to my family came to reside here in the absence of the Covenant's quelling activities. In return, we would provide you with housing and basic utilities, and sufficient free time for you to find another source of income to feed yourself and your child."

I nodded thoughtfully. Kitty was already talking about reopening the Freakshow once the current danger had passed. She had the funds—the only people who come close to the dragons for financial literacy and budgeting are the bogeymen, who have made fiscal responsibility one of the pillars of their culture and community. Kitty had been saving and investing since she was six years old, and could easily afford to find the club a new home. She just didn't want to do it when there was a chance the Covenant would firebomb the place again. They were good with their accelerants, and they had a vicious tendency to deploy them to make an attack look like an act of arson, which would block insurance payments. Insult and injury in one fell swoop.

If Kitty reopened the Freakshow, I could go back to working for her as a cocktail waitress-slash-dancer, and while that wouldn't be enough to live on under normal circumstances, it would be sufficient if I wasn't paying rent. This could work.

"I'll want to move back to Portland eventually," I said. "Livvy needs to grow up around her family. But I'd like to stay here for a little while before that happens. We can talk about it more, after this is over."

"I'm glad you're willing to at least consider a path that doesn't see you leaving us," said William, gravely. "You've been a good friend during your time in this city, and I owe you for bringing me my golden ones."

"Just paying an old family debt," I said.

One of the little boys turned around and snarled at a group of his sisters who'd been chasing him, producing a small spark and puff of smoke. He stopped after that, blinking in dumbfounded confusion at the dissipating cloud. Then he sat down hard in the gold coins on the floor and started to wail, the sound surprisingly human—that, or the sound of human babies was surprisingly draconic, and I didn't want to think about that too hard, so I shunted the comparison to the back of my mind and watched as two more adult dragons detached themselves from their conversations and ran toward the boy. The first to reach him swept him into her arms, while the other turned to begin talking softly but firmly to the girls.

"Livvy can still come play if that's all right with you," I said. "She's going to need community." The bogeyman kids were generally willing to play with her, but they preferred to play with the lights off, which was difficult for a human child. It would be better if she could have multiple friend groups for social situations.

William nodded. "Of course," he said. "She's always welcome here. I truly am sorry about Dominic."

Tears stung my eyes. For a few seconds, I'd been so distracted that I'd almost forgotten about the situation. Not good.

"I should probably get back to Kitty and the others," I said. "They'll be worried about me by now. Candy, can you walk me there?"

"Of course," said Candice. "It's not like I have anything better to do with my time."

"Candy," said William, in a chastising tone.

She sighed, and beckoned for me to follow her as she started walking back toward the door we'd arrived through.

We were halfway there when it slammed open and three immature dragons came tumbling through. The oldest would have passed for a human sixteen; the other two were younger-looking, neither more than twelve. All three had been crying, and the middle girl was missing a shoe.

Candice stopped immediately, eyes going wide with alarm. "Girls!" she said. "What is the meaning of this?"

"Mama!" wailed the girl with the missing shoe, flinging herself at Candice hard enough to knock the woman back a few feet. The other two followed her at a slower pace, stopping a few feet away rather than barreling into her.

"What are you doing here?" asked Candice, even as she wrapped her arms protectively around missing-shoe girl, holding her tightly.

"We were at the park? With Madi," said the oldest girl. "She was getting us some waffles from a food cart, and I was watching the littler ones chase pigeons, and then these two people in funny-looking gray sweaters came to stand to either side of her and they said something I didn't hear, but she looked real scared, and when she got our food, she left! With those people! She took them *and* all the waffles with her. She didn't even get her change!"

That last bit was what sounded like it had truly upset the child, and seemed to upset Candice just as badly. She stiffened, her grasp on the girl who'd called her "Mama" getting even tighter. I could understand her distress. For a dragon to buy waffles from a food cart was just reinforcement that they really *were* excellent parents, even if their parenting style wasn't strictly normal by human standards. For her to leave without her change was a sign that she was under extreme duress, and had probably been trying to keep those people from noticing the children she had with her.

I focused on the oldest girl. "Hi. I'm Verity. You are?"

"Alicia," she said, warily. Then she paused, wariness fading. "You're Livvy's mother, right?"

"Right," I confirmed. If my daughter being the playmate of her younger siblings could make this easier for her, then I would lean into it. "I need to get some clothes that fit me better, and then would you take me back to where those people led Madi away? Can you do that?"

She looked at Candice, clearly waiting for some form of permission. Candy, for her part, nodded.

"Yes," she said. "You can take Verity back to the park. She's a friend. Although she's a friend without socks right now, and we're going to have to fix that."

"I still have my gun," I offered. The staff at St. Giles's had been unwilling to return my bloodstained clothing, but they weren't foolish enough to stand between a Price and her weapons. Sometimes having a reputation can be helpful.

"That's not enough," said Candice crossly. "Come with me."

The dragons had a cavernous—no pun intended—wardrobe off the back of William's cavern. The floor was less even there, having been smoothed out entirely by erosion and manual effort, with no help from the massive reptile in the next room. Still, it was level enough for us to walk easily, and they had constructed a truly impressive array of racks and shelves. The whole place had the faint closed-in smell I normally associated with thrift stores, detergent, and slowly decaying fabric. No mold or mothballs, and no standing water: it was just entropy unraveling the cloth, one tiny stitch at a time.

I stopped in the doorway, staring, and Candice pulled me onward, into a series of racks of clothing in roughly my size. She never reached for a measuring tape or a size guide, just eyed me somewhat dubiously and began grabbing things, thrusting them into my arms, until I was carrying a full change of clothing. This done, she hauled me to the end of the aisle and virtually shoved me into a small cubicle with a curtain across the front.

"Change," she said.

I blinked at her, and did as I was told.

Her eye was good: she'd found me a pair of yoga pants in the correct size, with pockets set into the outer thighs and stirrups under the feet to keep them from rolling up around my ankles, and a racerback running top that only had a few expertly darned holes at the bottom. Combined with the bra I already had from the hospital, a pair of socks, and some decent running shoes, I felt almost normal again as I emerged from the changing room.

"You can leave the sweats," said Candice. "They look to be roughly equivalent in value, and if you do that, you won't have to pay for borrowing clothing from our supply."

"Thank you," I said. Then, because we were about to go back to where the children were, I asked, "Is there any chance this wasn't a Covenant grab?"

"There's always a chance, for almost anything you can imagine," she said. "Now, do I believe it wasn't a Covenant grab? No. If you tried to convince me of that, I would question your intelligence. They saw one of us alone and vulnerable, and I can only be grateful that they didn't see her far enough in advance of the waffle truck to realize that she had children with her. This could have been so much worse."

"Are you trying to convince yourself or me?"

"Myself." She offered me a watery smile. "How'm I doing?"

"You don't sound like you believe it yet. Keep trying."

We walked back into the main cavern, where a cluster of dragon children had formed around Alicia and her companions. One of the boys hissed at us as we approached, tail lashing.

"Stand down, buddy," said Candice. "We're not going to take the girls away from you."

He growled, tail still lashing, and looked for a moment like he was going to lunge and bite her. Candice gave Alicia a sharp look, and the girl knelt to take the boy's head in her hands, turning it so that he was facing her.

"You're very brave, and we're all very impressed by what a good job you've done taking care of us," she said. "But I have to go with Verity now, to make sure we get Madi back, and you need to stay here with Whitney and Angie, so they won't be scared."

Dragons live and die by how well they can hide in the human population. It shouldn't have been grimly amusing to me how many dragons have names like "Angie" and "Candice," but it is. Nice, generic, blonde-lady names for a society of nice, generic, blonde ladies. The boy probably had a name like "Trevor" or "Scout."

And I wasn't judging. They needed every scrap of camouflage they could possibly get, and if having solidly middle American names made them feel safer, I was all for it. They'd earned a little safety.

The two younger girls hugged Alicia, and the one with the missing shoe glared at me in a way she had very much learned from her mother, all furrowed brow and judgement. I had already failed her, according to that expression, just by choosing to exist in the lair while distinctly human. Anything I did from here would just be an attempt at a redemption I didn't deserve, but which she *might* be willing to grudgingly grant if I forced the issue.

"Cindy, what do we say?" asked Candice.

"See you later," said the girl, still glaring at me.

"Definitely your kid," I said softly, and Candice cracked the sliver of a smile as Alicia started for the door and I followed after her, leaving the rest of the Nest behind.

She waited until we were out in the hall before she looked at me, frowning without most of the heat Cindy had been serving up. "You're human," she said.

"Yup," I agreed.

"Those people who took Madi away, they were human too."

"That seems very likely."

"Why would you help us against other humans?"

There was no way she didn't know about the current situation with the Covenant. The dragons were as inclined to shelter their children as any other sapient species, but there's only so much sheltering you can do from a paramilitary organization bent on wiping out your entire species. She might not have all the details, but she knew the basics of what was going on, no question.

Unless she didn't, and Candy was going to kick my ass when we came back.

Well, at least she'd be kicking my ass with Madi safely home, and not kicking my ass with one of her own people missing. I took a sharp breath. "That's a complicated question," I said. "There are so many humans in the world that we don't put as much value in species solidarity. We don't have to. If a few dozen of us die, it doesn't affect our overall viability."

Alicia recoiled at the idea of anyone *not* practicing species solidarity. "So you're a traitor?"

I tried not to show how much the word stung. "That's what some people call my family."

"Madi says you used to be Covenant, and we shouldn't trust you."

"She's right that my *family* used to be Covenant, a long time ago, but I was never Covenant."

"Your husband was."

She didn't know. She didn't know, she *couldn't* know, and she wasn't trying to be hurtful. I breathed in and out through my nose, pushing back the grief and anger, until I felt like I could speak again without screaming. "Dominic was born into the Covenant. He didn't get to choose that. And when he came to New York and people like me, and Candice, and William started telling him the Covenant was wrong, he was willing to listen to us. He didn't have to do that. It would have been easier for him if he hadn't done that, because being part of the Covenant for him was like being part of the Nest is for you. When we decided he couldn't do that anymore, it was like if you walked away from all your aunts and sisters and your new little brothers, and knew that they would never speak to you ever again because of what you'd done."

Alicia looked stunned by the idea that anyone *could* do such a thing, much less actually would. "Why?" she asked. "Why would anyone decide to leave their Nest?"

"Same reason Madi left Boston," I said. "He fell in love."

"With you?"

"With me. I got lucky." I shrugged. "We both did, I guess, because I fell in love with him, too. And we've been really happy together, even when everything's been awful, and I guess that's all you can really ask the world to do for you. Just give you chances to be happy, and hope you can grab hold of them while they exist."

"Oh." Alicia frowned, and kept walking. "The Covenant's really scary."

"You're right about that."

"They scare you, too?"

"I'm a traitor to my species, remember? As far as they're concerned, I gave up the right to be treated like I was a human being as soon as I decided I'd rather help dragons than hunt them."

She looked stricken. "I didn't mean—"

"I know, kiddo. You're what, sixteen? You didn't know that you were saying something really mean."

"I did, though," she said. "I was trying to be mean, because I didn't want to go somewhere with a human, not after humans took Madi away."

So dragons had mean girls too? Well, that made sense. But I still wasn't going to get into a fight with a sixteen-year-old, regardless of her species. I had some *standards*. "Look, I'm not mad or anything. Let's just find Madi and get her home, and then if you want, you and I can have a talk about humans sometime."

"Why would I need to talk about humans?"

"Because they're the dominant species on this planet, and like Candy said when I tried to explain how humans grieve, you don't have the luxury of not knowing how humans operate. So maybe there are things that confuse you about the way we do things, and maybe you'd like to ask a human about them, in a safe place, where the answers won't be life-or-death."

Alicia nodded, thoughtfully. "That might be nice. Can I bring some of my friends?"

The image of me trying to teach a class on human cultural norms to a room full of adolescent dragons flashed across my mind's eye. I shrugged it away, and nodded. "Of course you can."

We had left the deep tunnels for a shallower system, one that doubtless ran much closer to the surface. It was still wide enough for us to walk side by side, and like so many of the sewer tunnels I'd seen, it was dry, making me wonder where, exactly, the city put its waste, but the lights overhead were strong and steady and no longer appeared to be under draconic control, bearing more of the hallmarks of the New York City Public Works Department, including cobwebs and the occasional missing bulb. I glanced at Alicia.

"Where are we?"

"Passing through bogey territory, almost to the park," she said, as carelessly casual as any city teen explaining their route to a popular hangout. "We have a good-passage agreement with them right now, and we're allowed to use this path."

That explained the lack of sewage, the presence of NY Public Works, and the speed with which she was moving. A good-passage agreement didn't mean the right to linger or loiter, especially not when she was accompanied by a human. Knowing both dragons and bogeymen as I did, I wouldn't have been surprised if the passage agreement had been monetary in nature, and escorting me through could come with extra charges. Candy had ordered her to take me back to the park, but if she got in trouble while she was doing it, the fees would come out of her pocket.

Like I said, I know dragons and bogeymen pretty well.

We followed the tunnel to a ladder set up against one wall, which Alicia and I both climbed easily, finding ourselves in a tunnel that somehow managed to seem gloomier than the ones below it. There was nothing *materially* different, except that this one had boxes and old equipment piled against the walls, turning it into a sort of storage area. I frowned as I followed Alicia to a door in the far wall, and realized the difference as she unlocked it.

The tunnels below had been part of people's *homes*. Hallways, maybe, rather than living rooms, but still homes where people lived, where they spent their time and energy. This room wasn't anybody's home. This was a storeroom, a place where things were put to be forgotten, and no one cared about it enough to think about the place when they weren't present. Of course it was gloomy. Places carry the impressions of how they're used.

Maybe that sounds like so much metaphysical nonsense, but consider the fact that my babysitter and my favorite aunt are both ghosts; I'm allowed a little metaphysical nonsense. Besides, it's true. A single good or bad event won't color a place, but pile up enough of them, and the walls start to remember. It lingers, like juice stains on your fingers after you've been picking blackberries for an entire afternoon. The tunnels below felt like homes, and this felt like a place you passed through on the way to somewhere that mattered.

The door opened in a narrow white-tiled hall that looked like the sort of thing that led into a hospital parking garage. It smelled, rather strongly, of urine. Alicia waited for me to exit, then locked the door behind me and pocketed the key before gesturing for me to follow her to a bank of elevators. I blinked.

"Where are we?"

"Mall parking garage," she said easily, pressing the call button. A few moments later, the elevator light came on, and the doors slid open. The smell from inside the car was even worse than the smell in the rest of the hall. Alicia stepped on as if she hadn't noticed.

"This level is supposed to be for management only," she said, waving for me to join her. "But someone cloned the override key a few years back, and now all sorts of people can get down here. They sleep in the storeroom sometimes."

"No deeper down?" The door we'd taken from the bogeyman stretch of tunnels hadn't been locked, either on their side or this one. It would be easy for someone looking for a private place to sleep to slip on through.

Alicia looked at me like I'd just said something profoundly stupid. "Deeper down is bogey territory," she said, in a slow and patient voice. "Most of them wouldn't risk it."

I stepped into the reeking confines of the elevator, fighting the urge to vomit on my newly acquired shoes. "Mmm," I said, to avoid opening my mouth.

Alicia's expression turned amused. "You mammals are such whiny babies about a little excrement," she said, and pressed the button for the ground level.

The elevator slid up more than a single floor—the parking garage was apparently at least two levels down—before opening on a busy urban street. The people hurrying by didn't spare us a second glance as we stepped out and joined the throng, letting it sweep us toward the corner.

No one's ever going to call the air in Midtown Manhattan fresh, but after the elevator, it was like we were walking through a summer meadow. I took several deep, greedy breaths through my nose, and Alicia shot me another amused look.

"You really don't care about looking cool, do you?" she asked.

"I used to," I said. "But then I jumped off a few buildings and got over myself. Those cloned master keys. How easy would you say they are to get?"

She looked briefly thoughtful. "For me? Very. For you? Very not. No one I know who has them will sell to humans. But humans can obviously get them, or we wouldn't have homeless humans sleeping belowground. I'd say difficult but not impossible. Why?"

"Just wondering." The proximity of bogeyman territory to the storeroom meant that I didn't seriously think the Covenant would have taken Madi belowground. They had multiple teams operating in the city, and they'd done some serious damage even without taking

Dominic into account, but going into bogeyman territory as hostile actors would be a particularly unpleasant means of committing suicide. I didn't think even the Covenant was inclined to be that stupid without a really good reason.

Alicia waited for the light to go green, then charged across the street to the small, wedge-shaped park on the other side. It wasn't the kind of park that had playground equipment or climbing structures; it was mostly just a narrow slice of greenery and open seating in the heart of the city, and for children who spent most of their time underground, it was probably a paradise.

Various office workers and tourists milled around the little tables, drinks and easy eats in hand. You could tell the locals from the visitors by the gawking they were doing. Locals didn't look up nearly as much, or jump when a flock of pigeons exploded near their feet. Not literally exploded—I think everyone would have jumped if someone had tossed a bottle rocket into a flock of pigeons, and because this was New York, they would have beaten the shit out of anyone who did something like that about five seconds later. No, this was a more ordinary explosion, pigeons launching themselves into the air in a mass of churning wings and flying feathers for no apparent reason. Locals were used to it. Tourists . . . weren't.

One man, sitting alone at a table with a latte in his hand, jumped. He was dressed like an office worker from one of the surrounding businesses; he shouldn't have jumped. A few pigeons should have been old news to him. He was scanning the park with quick, anxious motions of his head, and his attention seemed to linger just a beat too long on anyone blonde, from a group of middle-aged women having a book club meeting at one of the tables to a toddler gamely attempting to escape from her parents. Interesting.

"Go hang out on the other side of the park," I said to Alicia, keeping my voice low. "Find a nice spot in the shade. And *don't leave the park*. Not for any reason."

"Not even the Mister Softee truck?"

"We both know you wouldn't waste money on ice cream, try another one."

She huffed but nodded, and as I approached the man, she broke away and vanished into the crowd, heading for the back of the park. Good girl. It wasn't a large area, and being a little away from me wouldn't give her that much cover, but anything to keep her out of the line of fire was worth doing, however minor it might be.

The man didn't look my way until I was practically on top of him, pulling the open chair away from his table. Then he waved a hand, eyes still on the other side of the park, and said, "You can take it. No one's sitting there."

"I am," I said, and plopped down. "Subtlety" is not a word with which I am very often associated. "Wrecking ball" is a bit more in line with my usual approach. "You look like someone I should be talking to."

He turned in my direction, frowning and making an inquisitive noise at the same time. The motion gave me a chance to study his jacket, making note of the way it fell across his shoulders. It was reasonably well fitted, especially considering that it had been tailored to account for the sidearm he had strapped to his side, and needed looser sleeves than normal so he could access the brace of throwing knives around his right bicep. Just scanning him, I could spot five different ways to kill somebody, and I was sure a strip search would have given me more.

Like most of the Covenant operatives I'd had the misfortune of meeting, he had clearly been trained in multiple weapons and in close combat, and not in how to blend properly within a human city. They were still using a playbook that assumed most of their fights would take place in the countryside, brave knights riding against ravenous dragons, and they weren't keeping pace with the rest of the world.

I was just fine with that, since it gave me a reasonable advantage in most of the situations I found myself in.

There was no recognition in his face. "Who are you, miss?"

"An interested citizen who heard that you were looking for information." This part was a gamble. The Covenant couldn't tap into the bogeyman gossip networks the way the family could, which meant they were usually shooting in the dark. It was just that sometimes, shooting in the dark hits something that shouldn't have been hit. "About pretty ladies like me." I gestured to myself, and watched his expression change from politely schooled curiosity to blatant disgust.

He shifted in his chair to put another few inches between us, radiating revulsion. I risked a glance around. No one was paying attention to us. Which was good, since if any of the local police caught sight of the way he was looking at me, I was likely to get arrested for either public solicitation or panhandling. Not the way I wanted to end a day that had started with my husband dying.

If it was even the same day. My sense of time was pretty shot by this point.

I leaned toward him, still smiling, and said, "That bitch Madison didn't want to pay me for my silence. Well. You know what they say about dragons and money, don't you?"

"I don't think I do, no."

"Never stand between us," I said. "I know more than she wants me to, and all I asked for was a few hundred dollars, so I could take my egg and go off to start a Nest of my own. But do you know what she said? She said, 'I would sooner see you make an omelet than walk away with a penny.' Would *you* stand for that sort of disrespect?"

He blinked. "No, miss . . . ?"

"Alicia." She was staying out of this; she'd never know I'd borrowed her name. "If she doesn't want to pay me to keep quiet, I figured I'd come and see the other side, see if maybe you'd pay me for *not* keeping quiet, if you know what I mean. I know you work with witches. Surely one sweet, harmless little princess isn't such a stretch?" I batted my eyelashes, looking at him like he was the judge of a regional dance competition I was hoping to sweep.

He seemed to be buying it. That's the thing about nice people who think of themselves as holy warriors on a sacred mission: it's so easy to convince them that God put you in their path to make it easier on them. It's like they're so entitled that they can't see the ends of their own noses anymore. Relaxing a little, he leaned back toward me, face smoothing toward something like neutrality. "What would you want for the location of the Manhattan Nest?"

"Five thousand," I said. "Inflation, you know." I waved a hand. "Double it and I'll tell you how many dragons are down there and how to disable the defenses."

"I think we could come to an agreement," he said, with a smile. "But I'm afraid I don't have that kind of money with me. We detained one of your . . . cousins . . . in this park earlier today, and I was assigned to watch for more, just in case."

"Well, then, it's both of our lucky day," I chirped. "Do you want to walk with me to the bank?"

Dragons don't really do wire transfers or virtual money. The questions of whether or not they legally exist aside—a surprising number have social security numbers and full citizenship, having come over with the colonists during the days of the *Mayflower* and vicious American expansionism. An equally surprising number don't. Because they're reproducing parthenogenically, it's not uncommon to meet whole groups of dragons who can pass themselves off as identical twins. A lot of them don't see the point in paperwork. And none of that matters, because to a species that cares about money because it can be converted into gold, numbers on a screen aren't "real" enough.

The only dragons I've ever met who understood bank balances as a form of wealth have been in Los Angeles, where they're more likely to have jobs with health insurance and direct deposit, and where the Nest is managed by a laidly worm named Osana, whose biological drive to acquire gold is less severe.

The man shook his head, very slightly. "No," he said. "I have a better idea."

Mistake one: he didn't verify that I was actually a dragon—or dragon princess, as he probably still thought about them—before we left the park. I could have been anyone. I could have been a rogue cryptozoologist with a bone to pick, who saw tricking him into taking me back to his base as a way to deal with some of my well-placed aggressions.

Mistake two: he didn't frisk me, either before we left the park or after we entered the deserted, echoing concourse of the Manhattan Mall. He just assumed that I wasn't a danger to him, and let me walk alongside in my fully-armed glory.

The shopping center must have been beautiful when it was thriving, a monument to modern commerce and innovation. Now it felt like walking through the world's biggest Spirit Halloween Store in waiting, empty storefronts and closed metal grates on all sides. The man, who had yet to introduce himself, led me straight down the center of the mall toward the JCPenney's, which was as empty as most of the stores around it, a gaping maw leading to a cavern full of naked mannikins and abandoned store fixtures.

Most of the metal grating in front of the dead department store had been pulled down like all the rest, but one of the three pieces that made up the barrier was raised by about five feet, leaving a gap a fully grown adult could easily duck through. I pretended not to notice. It would have been easy to miss—it blended well with everything around it, and with so many stores gated off, it only made sense for the eye to fill in the gaps.

"This way," said my escort, and gestured for me to follow him into the abandoned department store.

I paused to ask myself what a dragon who was desperate enough to sell out her Nest would do at this point, following a sworn enemy of her species into an off-site location, and stopped walking. "Nuh-uh," I said. "Out here, if I scream, maybe someone comes. In there? I scream, no one shows up, you take me apart so you can brag to all your Covenant buddies about how much you murdered me. I'm not taking another step without compensation."

"Are you fucking serious?" he snarled, and for a moment, he wasn't the calculatedly neutral lookout who'd been lucky enough to snag a dragon without the common sense to stay clear. He was a warrior for God whose placid, accommodating target was suddenly pushing back, and he didn't like it.

I took a step backwards, away from him. "I don't like the way you're talking to me," I said, putting a quiver into my voice. "Maybe this is a bad idea."

He sighed in obvious, unconcealed frustration and pulled out his wallet, producing three crisp hundred-dollar bills. "Here," he said imperiously, shoving them at me. "An advance. You'll get the rest of your money once my superiors have heard what you have to say."

I took the money and shoved it into the pocket of my yoga pants, pretending not to notice that he had just changed the deal from paying me for information to paying me for information if his superiors liked it. It didn't matter. He'd never been planning to pay me anyway. A single helpful dragon wasn't enough of an asset to bother cultivating like that.

No, if he had a coherent plan, it involved chaining me to something and removing parts of my body with bolt cutters until they were absolutely sure I'd told them everything I knew. I just hoped that the fact he'd taken the bait so quickly meant they weren't done interrogating Madison. They had no reason to be gentle with her—or with me, as long as they thought I wasn't human. Zealots are nasty like that.

I walked beside him into the gutted JCPenney's. He paused once we were inside, turning to pull the grate down and snap the deadbolt into place. How cute. I wasn't supposed to get out of here alive. I mean, I'd known that, but I hadn't expected him to be quite so blatant about it. He would never have been able to cut it in the competitive field of serial killing, that was damn sure.

The escalators were still running, whether or not the mall's ownership knew that, and he led me over to one of them, the two of us heading together up to the top floor of the department store—the one without a view of the street or the rest of the mall. I scanned my surroundings, forcing my expression to stay neutral, as if nothing about this smelled bad to me in the slightest. Nope, nothing unusual here. Just a nice man leading an innocent little lamb off to her death.

I was so going to enjoy breaking this fucker's fingers.

At the top of the escalator, a section of the store had been cordoned off with tarps. He pulled one aside, and led me into what looked like a generic tech-company call center, complete with makeshift cubicles. Most of them were empty, but a few were occupied by workers in clothing just as far from appropriate business casual as his own. I kept looking around myself, trying to project an air of "distracted innocent with no idea what's about to happen to her." Inwardly, I was punching the air, almost giddy with delight.

This was the headquarters we'd been looking for this whole time. Who could have known it would be as easy as walking up and turning myself in? Of course, it probably helped that they'd lost a lot of agents when Grandma and Grandpa were in town, and while they'd been replacing them as quickly as they could, the replacements were the less-experienced kind, people who'd finished their training but might never have seen a field mission before. Looking around, I counted six Covenant agents, not including my escort, and no sign of Madi. No blood, either, which I chose to take as a good sign.

Not like I had many others.

One of the men stood and walked cautiously toward us, hand hovering over his hip in what was all too clearly the preparation for drawing a weapon. I wanted to smack him for that level of amateurish broadcasting, and probably would have, if it hadn't been working in my favor.

"Who's this?" he asked, and at least showed the sense not to use his companion's name.

"Alicia," said the first man. "She approached me in the park. She's looking to sell information about the local dragon Nest."

"Is that so?" The second man gave me an assessing look. "We already have one adult. Why do we need another? You were supposed to be watching for those juveniles you lost earlier."

Creep number one scowled briefly. "We didn't realize they were with her," he said. "And information given under duress is always harder to trust than information given freely."

"Is that so?" Number two looked at me. "You're offering to give us information that can be used against your own kind?"

"My own kind? Puh-leeze. They're not my 'own kind.' They're a bunch of cheap, petty b—"

"All right," he said, interrupting me. "I just need to be sure." He looked to number one. "What did you promise it?"

So even when we were pretending that I was an ally, not an asset, I didn't warrant a gender? Romance languages gender *tables*. I narrowed my eyes slightly, deciding that my current persona allowed me that much. "Uh, five *thousand* dollars, cash," I said. "And I don't say a word until I get it, got it?"

Number two frowned briefly, leading me to wonder whether my little pantomime was going to be cut short by the need to defend myself. Then he nodded, and said, "Get it from petty cash. I'll entertain our . . . guest."

Number one scuttled off. I frowned a little at number two. "What do you mean, 'you already have one'?" I asked. "Did you already buy this information?"

"That's none of your concern," he said. "What I need from you is the location of the central Nest. We know it exists. We know you have a male there, and we know he can't be moved. That means we'll have to go to him. We *very* much want to meet him."

His smile was too wide, and showed too many teeth. Even the most naïve dragon wouldn't have been able to look at that and believe in the purity of his intentions. That was a smile that wanted to finish what its ancestors started. That was the smile a species saw before its own extinction.

I swallowed, hard, and it wasn't entirely a put-on. "I'm not sure I should tell you that. Who is it that you have?"

"Think about the money," he cajoled. "The lovely, lovely money. So much money. Don't you want the money?"

"I do, but . . ."

"But nothing," he said, more sharply. "You came here to sell information, and I'm offering to buy. You don't want to back out on an agreement, do you?"

Dragons don't share the bogeyman obsession with contracts. He was testing me. I looked him dead in the eye, sniffed, and asked, "What do you take me for, bogey trash? We don't have a contract, but I want my cash."

He smiled again, more naturally this time. "Ah, good. I was starting to worry that our location had leaked enough to attract grifters."

Grifters, no. Enemies, yes. "Who do you have here?"

"You're not going to let that go, are you?"

"No, I'm not."

He sighed. "It says its name is 'Madison.' We caught it in the park earlier today. But you know that, don't you?"

"Heard Madi'd gone up for breakfast and not come back," I said, rolling my shoulders in a shrug. "I knew where she was going, and I hoped she'd run into you. Just because it meant I was on the right track. I've been trying to find you all week."

"Why?"

"Like I said. I have information, you have cash, it's a match made in heaven." I let myself look just a little nervous. "Where's Madi, though? Is she selling you the same thing?"

"Madi doesn't trust us. Doesn't want us to meet the family."

"That's sad." I paused, then perked up, like I'd just had an amazing idea. "I know! Why don't I talk to her? I'm sure she'd understand once I explained things to her."

He paused, then asked warily, "Things like what, exactly?"

"Like those nasty old control freaks down in the Nest don't know what's best for the rest of us. Like the world is changing, and we need to change with it. Like you have money." I smiled a predatory smile, trusting him to misinterpret its edges. "Money fixes a lot of problems."

He paused, looking around, and I could virtually see him do the math that got him what he wanted and kept his cash in his coffers. "Of course," he said smoothly. "Follow me."

He turned to lead me deeper into the cubicle maze, and I did, watching carefully as the people we passed got out of their seats and followed us. Counting him and the man from the park, there were six agents in the building. Normally, those would have been unsettling odds. With the element of surprise more on my side than theirs and the amount of anger I was currently carrying, that was fine.

He led me to a janitor's closet with a closed door, the man from the park waiting just outside. I blinked guilelessly. "I thought you were going to the petty cash," I said, trying to sound more surprised than suspicious.

"I have your money," he said, and held up a bundle of hundreds. "I figured you'd wind up here, one way or the other, so this seemed expedient. I assume we're taking it inside to join the other one?"

"Yes," said the second man. He didn't blink as I snatched the money from the first man, riffling through it before I shoved it into my pocket. He was probably assuming they could just take it off me once they killed me. American money launders well. The blood probably wouldn't even stain.

"Excellent," said the first man, and unlocked the closet door.

The light was on inside, fluorescent and unwavering, which made it all the easier to see the woman tied to the chair propped at the back of the closet. Her head was hanging, but I could see her black eyes and swollen lips, and the bloodied tips of her fingers. I didn't have to feign revulsion as I looked at the men around me and asked, "What the hell is *this*?"

"What you asked for," said man one, and placed his hands on my shoulders, shoving me forward into the closet—or trying to, anyway. A shove only works if the person doing the shoving puts enough force into it, and he wasn't expecting me to have my feet braced. I slammed my head backward, delighting in the crunch as the back of my skull met his nose. His nose lost that little encounter, giving way. He let go of me, staggering back with a wet cry of dismay. I was already turning, pulling the gun out of my waistband with my right hand and one of my throwing knives with my left. I'm not truly ambidextrous, but my teacher insisted that I be able to throw with both hands before he'd declare me competent to carry knives in the field. He said it would save my life one day.

By the time I finished my turn, one of the four agents who'd followed man two and me from the cubicle maze had her own gun out and raised, preparing to fire. I flung the knife without hesitation, turning it into part of my ongoing motion, and it caught her in the center of the throat, causing her to stagger back and drop the gun. That particular hit might not be fatal, but it would definitely keep her out my hair for a little while. I shifted my focus to the other five, the four uninjured and the one with the nose gushing blood down his face and front.

"You were trying to trick me," I said, primly. "You were going to lock me in this closet, kill us both, and take back my money. That's not nice."

"You're not a dragon at all," said man two. "Are you?"

"I never actually said I was. Just that I had information on the location of the Nest. You know what else I have? A gun, and a damn good reason to be mad at you people. You know what I don't have? A code against killing. So thanks for giving me something to do today."

Man two tried to slam the closet door. I met it with a mule kick, slamming it back out and into the wall, then shot two more of the agents as they reached for their guns. The one with the knife in her throat was on the floor now, making an unpleasant gurgling sound. Huh. Guess that was a kill shot after all. That left three more, including man two, who was scowling at me.

"Price," he accused.

"Pissed," I countered. "You people—you *people*—we didn't ask you to come here. We didn't ask you to purge our city. And now my husband is *dead*. Because you couldn't stay away when you weren't wanted."

"We have a mission—" he began, and stopped when I spun and shot one of his agents who'd been trying to sneak up on me.

"I want you out of this city," I snapped, returning my attention to him. "All of you. The trouble is, I can't *send* that message, can I? If I let you live, you go mewling to the Covenant for more resources. If I kill you, no one knows I want you gone. If I write 'get out of my city' on the walls in your blood, we wind up with the FBI getting involved, and no one wants that. Not you, not me, not the Covenant. How many agents do you have left?"

"Hundreds," he said. "You'll never stop us all. We will cleanse—"

I shot his last uninjured agent, leaving only him and man one on their feet.

"Tick-tock," I said. "How many?"

He took a breath, shaky and unsteady, and said, "Seventeen. Including the two of us. Please. We haven't hurt you. We could work something out. Be reason—"

I reasonably put a bullet between his eyes.

"That was for Dominic," I said, and shot the last of them before I moved to untie Madison. "Hey, Madi. Can you stand? Do you think you'll be able to walk?"

She made a pained sound and didn't say anything. I looked at her bruised mouth, the way she was pressing her lips together, and tried not to think about what her teeth might look like.

"I killed them too fast," I said.

She nodded vigorously, even as she let me help her out of her seat. She still had shoes, and they seemed to have concentrated their abuses on her face and fingers. Half her nails were gone. I reached out to catch her before she could fall, stabilizing her.

"We have to get though the mall to get back down to subway level," I said. "People may stare, but this is New York. As long as you don't look like you're in distress, they're going to assume I'm taking care of you. Can you make it that far?"

She nodded, fire in her eyes.

"Great," I said. "Just give me a little while to loot the place, and we can go." I helped her out of the closet and past the bodies, pausing only to retrieve my knife from the corpse on the floor, and together we made our way out to the little cubicle maze, where I scrounged up a backpack and began grabbing anything that looked like it might be useful. Laptops, ledgers, a locked cashbox that Madi snatched out of my hands and hugged like a teddy bear, a few additional weapons, they all went into the bag, although I had to take the cash-box from Madi first. If we hit a metal detector, we were fucked.

No one else came in while we were searching for things we could steal. If we were lucky, the returning Covenant agents would take this as a botched robbery and not pin any of the blame on the local cryptids. If not, I had a number now. Fifteen field agents remaining. I could take that many of them out.

And maybe if I did, I'd be able to convince myself that Dominic wasn't mad at me for failing to save him. Maybe I could sleep at night.

Madi's arm slung around my shoulders, I started helping her out of the department store and back into the mall. Opening the grate was no trouble, although the creak when I rolled it up made a few people turn to look at us. Otherwise, no one paid attention as we made our way out to the street and across to the park, where Alicia came flying through a flock of pigeons, causing one of those explosions, and wrapped her arms around a wincing Madi.

"We need to get her to St. Giles's," I said. "Can you lead the way?"

Alicia nodded rapidly, and then, after a quick glance at Madi's bloody hands, gestured for us to follow her back across the street to the escalator. It wasn't a happy ending—I'd just killed six people, and Dominic was still dead—but it was a step in the right direction, and the dragons were safe, for now. Plus, Candice was going to be pretty pleased when I handed her five thousand dollars of the Covenant's money.

Maybe that could be enough for the moment. Maybe I could find a way to keep on breathing after all.

The elevator doors opened. I took a deep breath and held it, stepping into the little metal box to begin my descent back into the dark, where the monsters lived. Where I was increasingly sure that I belonged.

Price Family Field Guide to the Cryptids of North America Updated and Expanded Edition

Aeslin mice (Apodemus sapiens). Sapient, rodent-like cryptids which present as near-identical to non-cryptid field mice. Aeslin mice crave religion, and will attach themselves to "divine figures" selected virtually at random when a new colony is created. They possess perfect recall; each colony maintains a detailed oral history going back to its inception. Origins unknown.

Basilisk (Procompsognathus basilisk). Venomous, feathered saurians approximately the size of a large chicken. This would be bad enough, but thanks to a quirk of evolution, the gaze of a basilisk causes petrification, turning living flesh to stone. Basilisks are not native to North America, but were imported as game animals. By idiots.

Bogeyman (Vestiarium sapiens). The thing in your closet is probably a very pleasant individual who simply has issues with direct sunlight. Probably. Bogeymen are close relatives of the human race; they just happen to be almost purely nocturnal, with excellent night vision, and a fondness for enclosed spaces. They rarely grab the ankles of small children, unless it's funny.

Chupacabra (Chupacabra sapiens). True to folklore, chupacabra are blood-suckers, with stomachs that do not handle solids well. They are also therianthrope shapeshifters, capable of transforming themselves into human form, which explains why they have never been captured. When cornered, most chupacabra will assume their bipedal shape in self-defense. A surprising number of chupacabra are involved in ballroom dance.

Dragon (Draconem sapiens). Dragons are essentially winged, fire-breathing dinosaurs the size of Greyhound buses. At least, the males are. The females are attractive humanoids who can blend seamlessly into a crowd of supermodels, and outnumber the males twenty to one. Females are capable of parthenogenic reproduction and can sustain their population for centuries without outside help. All dragons, male and female, require gold to live, and collect it constantly.

Ghoul (Herophilus sapiens). The ghoul is an obligate carnivore, incapable of digesting any but the simplest vegetable solids, and prefers humans because of their wide selection of dietary nutrients. Most ghouls are carrion eaters. Ghouls can be easily identified by their teeth, which will be shed and replaced repeatedly over the course of a lifetime.

Hidebehind (Aphanes apokryphos). We don't really know much about the hidebehinds: no one's ever seen them. They're excellent illusionists, and we think they're bipeds, which means they're probably mammals. Probably.

Huldra (Hulder sapiens). While the Huldrafolk are technically divided into three distinct subspecies, the most is known about *Hulder sapiens skogsfrun*, the Huldra of the trees. These hollow-backed hematophages can pass for human when they have to, but prefer to avoid humanity, living in secluded villages throughout Scandinavia. Individual Huldra can live for hundreds of years when left to their own devices. They aren't innately friendly, but aren't hostile unless threatened.

Jackalope (Parcervus antelope). Essentially large jackrabbits with antelope antlers, the jackalope is a staple of the American West, and stuffed examples can be found in junk shops and kitschy restaurants all across the country. Most of the taxidermy is fake. Some, however, is not. The jackalope was once extremely common, and has been shot, stuffed, and harried to near-extinction. They're relatively harmless, and they taste great.

Johrlac (Johrlac psychidolos). Colloquially known as "cuckoos," the Johrlac are telepathic ambush predators. They appear human, but are internally very different, being cold-blooded and possessing a decentralized circulatory system. This quirk of biology means they can be shot repeatedly in the chest without being killed. Extremely dangerous. All Johrlac are interested in mathematics, sometimes to the point of obsession. Origins unknown; possibly insectile in nature.

Laidly worm (Draconem laidly). Very little is known about these close relatives of the dragons. They present similar but presumably not identical sexual dimorphism; no currently living males have been located.

Lamia (Python lamia). Semi-hominid cryptids with the upper bodies of humans and the lower bodies of snakes. Lamia are members of order Synapsedia, the mammal-like reptiles, and are considered responsible for many of the "great snake" sightings of legend. The sightings not attributed to actual great snakes, that is.

Lesser gorgon (Gorgos euryale). One of three known subspecies of gorgon, the lesser gorgon's gaze causes short-term paralysis followed by death in anything under five pounds. The bite of the snakes atop their heads will cause paralysis followed by death in anything smaller than an elephant if not treated with the appropriate antivenin. Lesser gorgons tend to be very polite, especially to people who like snakes.

Lilu (Lilu sapiens). Due to the striking dissimilarity of their abilities, male and female Lilu are often treated as two individual species: incubi and succubi. Incubi are empathic; succubi are persuasive telepaths. Both exude strong pheromones inspiring feelings of attraction and lust in the opposite sex. This can be a problem for incubi like our cousin Artie, who mostly wants to be left alone, or succubi like our cousin Elsie, who gets very tired of men hitting on her while she's trying to flirt with their girlfriends.

Madhura (Homo madhurata). Humanoid cryptids with an affinity for sugar in all forms. Vegetarian. Their presence slows the decay of organic matter, and is usually viewed as lucky by everyone except the local dentist. Madhura are very family-oriented, and are rarely found living on their own. Originally from the Indian subcontinent.

Manananggal (Tanggal geminus). If the manananggal is proof of anything, it is that Nature abhors a logical classification system. We're reasonably sure the manananggal are mammals; everything else is anyone's guess. They're hermaphroditic and capable of splitting their upper and lower bodies, although they are a single entity, and killing the lower half kills the upper half as well. They prefer fetal tissue, or the flesh of newborn infants. They are also venomous, as we have recently discovered. Do not engage if you can help it.

Oread (Nymphae silica). Humanoid cryptids with the approximate skin density of granite. Their actual biological composition is unknown, as no one has ever been able to successfully dissect one. Oreads are extremely strong, and can be dangerous when angered. They seem to have evolved independently across the globe; their common name is from the Greek.

Sasquatch (Gigantopithecus sesquac). These massive native denizens of North America have learned to embrace depilatories and mail-order shoe catalogs. A surprising number make their living as Bigfoot hunters (Bigfeet and Sasquatches are close relatives, and enjoy tormenting each other). They are predominantly vegetarian, and enjoy Canadian television.

Tanuki (Nyctereutes sapiens). Therianthrope shapeshifters from Japan, the tanuki are critically endangered due to the efforts of the Covenant. Despite this, they remain friendly, helpful people, with a naturally gregarious nature which makes it virtually impossible for them to avoid human settlements. Tanuki possess three primary forms—human, raccoon dog, and big-ass scary monster. Pray you never see the third form of the tanuki.

Ukupani (Ukupani sapiens). Aquatic therianthropes native to the warm waters of the Pacific Islands, the Ukupani were believed for centuries to be an all-male species, until Thomas Price sat down with several local fishermen and determined that the abnormally large great white sharks that were often found near Ukupani males were, in actuality, Ukupani females. Female Ukupani can't shapeshift, but can eat people. Happily. They are as intelligent as their shapeshifting mates, because smart sharks is exactly what the ocean needed.

Wadjet (Naja wadjet). Once worshipped as gods, the male wadjet resembles an enormous cobra, capable of reaching seventeen feet in length when fully mature, while the female wadjet resembles an attractive human female. Wadjet pair-bond young, and must spend extended amounts of time together before puberty in order to become immune to one another's venom and be able to successfully mate as adults.

Waheela (Waheela sapiens). Therianthrope shapeshifters from the upper portion of North America, the waheela are a solitary race, usually claiming large swaths of territory and defending it to the death from others of their species. Waheela mating season is best described with the term "bloodbath." Waheela transform into something that looks like a dire bear on steroids. They're usually not hostile, but it's best not to push it.

Yong (Draconem alta aqua). The so-called "Korean dragon" shares many qualities with their European relatives. The species demonstrates extreme sexual dimorphism; the males are great serpents, some easily exceeding eighty feet in length, with no wings, but possessing powerful forelimbs with which to catch and keep their prey. The females, meanwhile, appear to be attractive human women of Korean descent, capable of blending easily into a human population. Unlike European dragons, their health is dependent on quartz rather than gold, making it somewhat easier for them to form and maintain their Nests (called "Clutches").

PLAYLIST:

"If I Die Young" . . . . The Band Perry
"Opening Up" . . . . *Waitress*
"Labour" . . . . Paris Paloma
"Bones of a Lifetime" . . . . Eddie From Ohio
"Sweet Valium High" . . . . Charlotte Sometimes
"Fire" . . . . Delta Rae
"Shovel and Bone" . . . . *Alleluia! The Devil's Carnival*
"Ghost in You" . . . . Counting Crows
"Song Beneath the Song" . . . . Maria Taylor
"I Hate Everyone" . . . . Get Set Go
"Dirty Work" . . . . Halestorm
"Long Day's Waiting" . . . . Chris Conway
"This Is Why We Fight" . . . . The Decemberists
"The Owl" . . . . Rexway
"The Bones of You" . . . . Elbow
"Splatter Splatter" . . . . Moxy Früvous
"The Babysitter's Here" . . . . Dar Williams
"Chords" . . . . The Amazing Devil
"Gone to America" . . . . Steeleye Span
"Movie Kisses" . . . . Thea Gilmore
"End of the Dream" . . . . Evanescence
"If I Die Young, Part 2" . . . . Kimberly Perry

ACKNOWLEDGMENTS:

When I first proposed Mary as our next narrator—something that made a lot of sense, when you consider her relationships to the rest of the family, and her unique position as the person who knows them all, always has, and always will—there was some concern that she might be too similar to Rose, who narrates the Ghost Roads books and is also very, very dead. But Mary had a story to tell, and her place in the family needed to be firmed up and illustrated, and honestly, I'm so glad that I stuck with her. She's a hell of a lot of fun as a narrator, and I hope you've enjoyed this time with her just as much as I have.

I remain a resident of Seattle, and remain steadfast in my determination to stay put for as long as humanly possible. I like where I live, I like my house and my social circle and my cats and my stuff. So I think I'm good. As I write this, we're still in the middle of a global pandemic, and that makes me even less likely to roam. I hope you're all okay with the decision not to include Covid-19 in the InCryptid setting. There was just no logical way to make it work, and unlike the real world, fictional realities do need to hang together narratively. Even ones as ridiculous as this.

It's late 2023 as I'm writing this, and there have been the usual round of changes on my part, as well as more travel than I necessarily wanted to go in for. Another handful of conventions, a trip to Disney World to keep a decade-long promise to one of my dearest small humans, and lots of time in the swamp. Lots and lots and *lots* of time in the swamp.

It's gratitude time! First and foremost, thanks must be offered to my agent, Diana Fox, who remains my staunchest advocate, and utterly willing to ride into battle for my sake, championing me and this series with endless poise, grace, and vicious firmness. I appreciate her more than words can say.

Thanks to Chris Mangum, who maintains the code for my website, while Tara O'Shea, who manages the graphics. The words are all on me, which is why the site is so often out of date. Something's gotta give, and it's usually going to be me! Thanks to Terri Ash, who has joined the team as my new personal assistant—if you email through the website I just mentioned, she's the one who'll send your mail on to me. She's essential, and I am very glad she's here.

Thanks to the team at DAW, and to our new team at Astra, which includes my new editor, Navah Wolfe.

Cat update (I know you all live for these): Thomas is a fine senior gentleman now, and while he has a touch of arthritis, his sweaters help to keep him warm, and I've set up cat stairs all over the house so he can still come and go as he pleases. Megara remains roughly as intelligent as bread mold, and is very happy as she is—this is not a cat burdened by the weight of a prodigious intellect! Elsie is healthy, fine, and very opinionated, and would like me to stop writing this and pet her. Tinkerbell is a snotty little diva who knows exactly how pretty she is, and Verity would like to speak to the manager. Of life. (If that all seems familiar, it's because it is. The cats are stable, which is wonderful.)

A new cat has joined our clowder. Kelpie, who is a Maine Coon descended from the same bloodline as my lamented Alice, is a caliby girl, and an absolute joy in all ways.

And now, gratitude in earnest. Thank you to everyone who reads, reviews, and helps to keep this series going; to Kate, for picking up the phone when I call her in a panic; to Phil, who knows what he did; to Shawn, for being the best brother a girl could possibly want; to Chris Mangum, for being here even when it's inconvenient; to Wing Mui, for keeping me socializing outside my head; to Manda Cherry, for a heated car seat and a wonderful friendship; to Crystal Fraiser, for regular friendship and grilled cheese; and to my dearest Amy McNally, for everything. Thanks to the members of all four of my current ongoing D&D games. And to you: thank you, so much, for reading.

Any errors in this book are my own. The errors that aren't here are the ones that all these people helped me fix. I appreciate it so much.

Let's go home.